The new Zebra Regency Romance logo that you see on the cover is a photograph of an actual regency "tuzzy-muzzy." The fashionable regency lady often wore a tuzzy-muzzy tied with a satin or velvet riband around her wrist to carry a fragrant nosegay. Usually made of gold or silver, tuzzy-muzzies varied in design from the elegantly simple to the exquisitely ornate. The Zebra Regency Romance tuzzy-muzzy is made of alabaster with a silver filigree edging.

"SABRINA! WHAT A THING TO SAY! . . .

Get you foxed? Never!" Jareth grinned. "Just a bit on the go, perhaps? I do want you to enjoy the evening, and personally, I find champagne *very* relaxing." His expression sobering, he said abruptly, "Now we're alone, we must talk. Yesterday you agreed to stay on in London for a while. I don't want you to leave England at all."

Sabrina's heart constricted. "Jareth, you're talking nonsense, you know. I must go back some day. And it's all arranged that I should marry Stefan."

"Do you love Stefan? Do you *really* want to marry him?"

"N-no. But what has that to say to anything? Don't you remember, we talked about this when we first met, and we agreed that people of our station in life don't marry for love."

"I didn't agree to anything of the sort," Jareth said harshly. He stood up, pulling Sabrina out of her chair and into his arms. He crushed his mouth to hers in a kiss that went on and on. . . .

THE BEST OF REGENCY ROMANCES

AN IMPROPER COMPANION   (2691, $3.95)
by Karla Hocker
At the closing of Miss Venable's Seminary for Young Ladies school, mistress Kate Elliott welcomed the invitation to be Liza Ashcroft's chaperone for the Season at Bath. Little did she know that Miss Ashcroft's father, the handsome widower Damien Ashcroft would also enter her life. And not as a passive bystander or dutiful dad.

WAGER ON LOVE   (2693, $2.95)
by Prudence Martin
Only a rogue like Nicholas Ruxart would choose a bride on the basis of a careless wager. And only a rakehell like Nicholas would then fall in love with his betrothed's grey-eyed sister! The cynical viscount had always thought one blushing miss would suit as well as another, but the unattainable Jane Sommers soon proved him wrong.

LOVE AND FOLLY   (2715, $3.95)
by Sheila Simonson
To the dismay of her more sensible twin Margaret, Lady Jean proceeded to fall hopelessly in love with the silver-tongued, seditious poet, Owen Davies—and catapult her entire family into social ruin . . . Margaret was used to gentlemen falling in love with vivacious Jean rather than with her—even the handsome Johnny Dyott whom she secretly adored. And when Jean's foolishness led her into the arms of the notorious Owen Davies, Margaret knew she could count on Dyott to avert scandal. What she didn't know, however was that her sweet sensibility was exerting a charm all its own.

Available wherever paperbacks are sold, or order direct from the Publisher. Send cover price plus 50¢ per copy for mailing and handling to Zebra Books, Dept. 3221, 475 Park Avenue South, New York, N.Y. 10016. Residents of New York, New Jersey and Pennsylvania must include sales tax. DO NOT SEND CASH.

Romantic Masquerade

Lois Stewart

ZEBRA BOOKS
KENSINGTON PUBLISHING CORP.

For Ann, Judy and Joyce.
Thanks.

ZEBRA BOOKS

are published by

Kensington Publishing Corp.
475 Park Avenue South
New York, NY 10016

First printing: November, 1990

Printed in the United States of America

Prologue

Lord Jareth Tremayne stirred into wakefulness. He could feel an object like a sharp stone digging into the small of his back and something with the texture of pumice rubbing the skin off his face. He opened his eyes to meet the interested gaze of an enormous and friendly mongrel dog.

With a startled exclamation, Jareth heaved himself into a sitting position, only to grab at his head as an excruciating pain nearly lifted off the top of his skull. Lord, he must have been castaway last night; he could just remember emptying the second — or was it the third? — bottle of red Madeira with old Jack Wyndham and beginning on a bottle of Strip-Me-Naked.

As his hand strayed to the exquisitely tender swelling behind his ear, he glanced down at himself and observed with a start the dried blood staining the folds of his immaculate cravat and the lapels of his elegant tight-waisted tan coat. Getting foxed was one thing, but he looked and felt as if he'd been in a mill and had gotten the worst of it. Now that he put his mind to it, he could dredge up a vague memory of driving his curricle along a narrow, dark country lane smack into the midst of a running gun battle between the excisemen and what appeared to be a gang of smugglers. That must have been when somebody hit him over the head.

Squinting against the first rays of the rising sun, he gazed around him, fighting back a stab of panic when he could not immediately identify his whereabouts. He was sitting beside a pond in the middle of a grassy open space surrounded by the straggling buildings of a small village that had not yet roused itself to face the new day. Jareth emitted a cackle of amusement that caused another crescendo of pain to crash through his skull. It was Fairlea, of course. For a moment he had failed to recognize his family's ancestral village. But then, he hadn't been near the place for ten years, not until yesterday, when he'd driven down from London for his nephew's funeral. Jareth closed his eyes against the unwelcome memory. . . .

. . . The service was already over. As he came into Fairlea, Jareth could see the last of the mourners trailing into the churchyard behind the small coffin. Reining in his team, he sat in his curricle beside the stone wall bordering the churchyard, watching as the vicar began the graveside service. In the crowd of mourners, he could easily make out his brother Lionel's tall, black-clad form.

Abruptly, Jareth flicked his reins, putting his horses into motion. From his perch behind the driver's seat, his tiger inquired doubtfully, "Ain't yer goin' ter yer nevvy's fun'ral, m'lord?"

"No. That dead little boy won't miss me. Nobody will," Jareth muttered, half under his breath. It was true. He could see now that it had been a mistake to come down here for the burial of little Daniel, a child he'd scarcely known and whose pathetically short life had ended at the age of seven from a sudden bout of fever. Certainly Jareth's presence at the funeral would not

6

be welcomed by Daniel's father. Lionel Tremayne, Seventh Marquess of Winwood, had not spoken to his younger brother for years. Jareth's arrival would be regarded as an intrusion rather than a mark of respect for the dead.

"Yer never setting off fer London wif'out a change o' horses, m'lord," blurted the tiger when Jareth took the road out of the village.

"We'll stay the night at the inn here. But for now, we're going to Winwood Park. It's only two miles from Fairlea."

Later, rounding the last curve of the long driveway leading to Winwood Park, Jareth felt an illogical pang of surprise. He hadn't visited the Tremayne family seat for many years, not since his father's death, and somehow he had expected the place to look different. But the house hadn't changed; it still stood, serenely beautiful in the flowing lines of its elegant Italianate proportions, fronted by a two-story Palladian portico.

Not allowing himself the moment's thought that might have caused him to reconsider this visit, Jareth jumped down from the curricle, handing the reins to the tiger. The butler who opened the door was new to the Tremayne employ. He didn't recognize Jareth, conducting him silently up the magnificent double mahogany staircase to the drawing room on the first floor.

Christabel hadn't changed, either. Swathed in black crepe, she sat in a chair by the window, apart from the women of the neighborhood who had gathered to make their sympathy calls. Despite the lines of grief marking her delicate features, she looked more beautiful than ever. With her silver-gilt hair, milky skin, and incredible violet eyes, she had always reminded Jareth of some exquisite Dresden figurine.

The violet eyes widened in shock when she caught sight of him. "Jareth," she faltered, "is it really you?"

Hesitating for a brief moment, she rose, putting down her prayer book. Muttering a few words of excuse to her guests, she took Jareth's arm, leading him out of the drawing room and down the corridor into the library. She turned then, looking up at him with a hungry intensity, as if she were memorizing his features. "I never expected to see you today, but thank you for coming," she said softly. "My darling Daniel—" She paused, blinking away a film of tears. "You—you've seen Lionel?"

"No. I didn't go to the church. I wanted you to know how sorry I felt, but . . ." Jareth shrugged.

Christabel nodded in complete understanding. "It might be better this way." Looking away, she said, almost as if she were talking to herself, "We haven't talked for so long, not since—"

Not since the day you ended our betrothal and told me you were going to marry my brother, causing my life to collapse around me, Jareth finished silently. Studying her averted face, he was conscious of a slowly growing wave of astonishment. The breathtaking beauty was the same, and she was infinitely touching in her grief for her little son, but she could no longer pierce his heart with a glance, a word, the mere fact of her presence. Somewhere over the years, without realizing it, he'd exorcised the ghost of his passion for Lady Christabel Mannering. But before he could digest this startling new self-knowledge, a drawling, slightly slurred voice from the doorway said, "Well, this is an unexpected pleasure, my dear brother."

The Seventh Marquess of Winwood was only three years older than his younger brother, and closely resembled him. But Lionel's tall, rather burly figure lacked Jareth's lithe grace, and the touch of heaviness in his features caused him to miss by a hairsbreadth Jareth's classically austere good looks. Nor had Lionel ever possessed Jareth's gift for friendship, for drawing people

8

to him. Jareth had not been long out of infancy before he realized the extent of his older brother's jealousy and dislike.

Lionel advanced into the room, bringing with him a strong odor of liquor. Obviously he had been drinking since long before his son's funeral. He paused, looking at Jareth from head to toe with an exaggerated air of interest. Reaching out for the lapel of Jareth's coat, Lionel fingered it between thumb and forefinger, saying, "Weston, I presume, or perhaps Stultz. Or has the 'Corinthian of Corinthians' found himself a new tailor? If so, I predict the dandies will flock to the man in droves. Now that Brummell's been forced to flee the country, you've surely become the acknowledged leader of the *ton*."

Stepping back, Jareth said coolly, ignoring Lionel's mocking tone, "The coat's from Weston, matter of fact. God forbid that I should have any plans to succeed the Beau."

"Good. The best laid plans can go awry," sneered Lionel. "That includes your transparent ambition to become the Eighth Marquess of Winwood."

"Lionel!" gasped Christabel. "Think what you're saying—"

"I don't need to think. I know my brother's mind like the palm of my hand. Instead of staying decently away from my son's funeral, Jareth's come down here to crow over me, to make me squirm while he flaunts his position as heir apparent to the estate." Lionel jabbed a heavy finger into Jareth's chest. "Enjoy your new status while you can, little brother. You'll be out of the succession before you know it. Christabel and I intend to have a large family of Tremayne sons."

Tight-lipped, Jareth turned to Christabel, who had lapsed into horrified silence. "I'm sorry," he told her. "I shouldn't have come. I've only made things harder for

9

you. Good-bye, Christabel."

Lionel's gibing voice followed him to the door. "We'll send you an announcement as soon as Christabel is increasing."

Emerging from the great front portico of the house, Jareth heard a familiar voice call out. He looked out to see Jack Wyndham, a childhood crony and Eton schoolmate, who had settled into a placid country existence years before, on succeeding to his father's title.

"I say, Jareth, is that really you?" called Wyndham. "It's been a dog's age since you were in these parts. Come along to the Grange this evening, and we'll crack a bottle and catch up on your doings. I hear you've become a real out and outer, a Pink of the *ton*."

Forcing a smile, Jareth waved to his friend. "Delighted, Jack. I hope you've kept up your father's wine cellar!"

Good old Jack Wyndham, thought Jareth. He and Jack probably didn't have much in common any more, but any company tonight was preferable to his own black thoughts.

Chapter One

"Turn around, my dears." Reclining gracefully on a Grecian-style sofa, Fanny, Lady Latimer, inspected her stepdaughters with a languidly critical eye as they pirouetted before her. She looked with approval at eighteen-year-old Daphne Latimer's dress of delicate white muslin, edged at the hem with flounces of lace interspersed with tiny pink rosebuds. "My dear Daphne, you look quite charming. Madame Manet did very well with your first ball dress."

Daphne's small, regular features became suffused with color. "Thank you, Mama," she murmured with a shy smile.

Lady Latimer turned her gaze to Daphne's older sister, Sabrina Neville, who wore a simple, high-necked gown of dull gray bombazine, made with long, close-fitting sleeves. Concealing her hair completely, a bonnetlike cornet of black lace was tied primly under her chin.

Lady Latimer's expression became pained. "Sabrina, you're never going to wear that — that *thing* to a ball? It's scarcely modish enough for a farmer's wife to wear to church, or for a governess to take tea with the family.

11

Not to speak of that ghastly shade of gray. Since you've decided to go into second mourning—and about time, too, in my opinion; it's been over a year since Oliver died—why didn't you choose a pretty shade of mauve? And at the very least, you might have worn a bit of jewelry. Your godmother's diamond and ruby necklace, for example."

"Godmama's necklace is much too ornate for this gown," Sabrina told her stepmother matter-of-factly. *It's also paste,* she thought, *a cheap and clumsy copy, and your sharp eyes would detect the substitution immediately.*

"Well, perhaps," Fanny said grudgingly. She peered at Sabrina's lace cap. "What about that dowdy cornet, however? Must you wear it to a ball? It makes you look positively matronly."

"Well, but Mama, I *am* a matron." Sabrina's dark blue eyes held a glint of laughter.

"What flummery!" snapped Lady Latimer. She was a thin, dark-haired woman of great elegance, who looked younger than her years. Only the peevish line between her eyebrows hinted that she was almost forty. "You're a very young and pretty widow of twenty-one, Sabrina, not a faded middle-aged relic. You should be putting your best foot foremost, dressing attractively, with an eye to marrying again."

"I don't wish to be married, Mama." Sabrina's tone was respectful, but dismissive.

Lady Latimer's lips tightened. "You must do as you like, I suppose. You are, after all, your own mistress. At any rate, now that you've put off your blacks at last, it's good of you to offer to chaperon Daphne to this ball. Naturally, I would have been happy to do so myself, despite my poor health"—Fanny put a delicate white hand to her forehead, as if to relieve a painful pressure—"because, as her stepmother, I'm well aware that dear Daphne, for one, should be thinking of marriage."

Fanny shrugged. "Of course, it's highly unlikely that she would meet an eligible *parti* at a dull provincial assembly. Now, if we had taken a house in London for the season, as I wanted to do—"

"We couldn't afford to take a London house for three months, as you know very well, or to buy Daphne a grand London wardrobe," said Sabrina patiently.

"We wouldn't be talking of expense if our solicitor hadn't insisted that we sell the London town house," Fanny went on in martyred discontent. "I've always thought that Mr. Gibson showed very poor judgment at the time of your father's death. I can't imagine why my dear Sir John retained the man as the family solicitor for so many years. Mr. Gibson kept saying that we were on the verge of ruin, that we had to retrench here, or sell something there. A real tempest in a teapot. In truth, it only needed a touch of good management to put our affairs to rights."

"And Sabrina's little fortune that she inherited from Great-aunt Arabella," interjected Daphne quietly.

Looking discomfited, but only for a moment, Fanny rejoined, "Well, of course, Sabrina, it was kind of you to offer your money, even though your brother Adrian objected so strenuously, but why shouldn't you wish to help your family? However, I thought, and still think, that you shouldn't have pensioned off old Higgins in order to take over his duties as steward for the estate. In my day, a lady of quality would never have dreamed of doing such an unfeminine thing."

Sabrina pasted a smile of polite attention on her lips while she shut her ears to the complaints she had heard so often before. Her stepmother seemed unable to grasp the fact that the days of high living for the Latimer family were long gone.

A childless young widow, Fanny had married Sir John Latimer some five years previously. She was a woman of expensive tastes in clothes and jewelry and furniture, fond of entertaining lavishly both at home in Sussex and in London, and her adoring husband had indulged her every whim. At his death a little more than a year ago, it was discovered that Sir John had died penniless and deeply in debt. He had plunged heavily on the Stock Exchange and had made disastrous bets at the track. When, shortly afterwards, Sabrina had returned home following the death of her young husband in Vienna, she had found her twin brother, Adrian, on the point of selling the estate in order to pay off the staggering mortages that his father had taken out on the property. It was then that she had offered her small inheritance and it was used to liquidate the most pressing debts and allow Daphne and their stepmother to remain in the family home.

"And I do think, Sabrina — though, as you know, in general I never like to criticize — that you worry unnecessarily about money," Fanny concluded. "In fact, sometimes you sound just a bit — well, a bit miserly. Take the drawing-room furniture, for example, so shabby that I'm mortified to receive guests in the room."

"I'm sorry, Mama, but replacing the furniture is quite out of the question this year. I must make some long-delayed repairs on the outbuildings of the home farm, and Adrian just wrote to say that he needs several new horses —"

"Did I hear my name mentioned?"

"Adrian!" Daphne jumped up from her chair to rush to throw her arms around the neck of the tall young man standing in the doorway of the morning room. "Why didn't you let us know you were coming?"

"Oh, I got to feeling a bit homesick for the old place, and I thought I'd dash down for a few hours." Adrian held Daphne at arm's length. "Here, now, don't you look beautiful, Puss," he said with an admiring grin. "Where

14

are you off to? A ball at Eastbourne? Capital, I'll come along with you." His arm around Daphne, he came into the room, giving Sabrina a fond hug and greeting his stepmother with dutiful affection.

Sir Adrian Latimer strongly resembled his twin sister, Sabrina. Like her, he was tall, slender, and graceful, with the same dark blue eyes and a mane of tawny hair the color of ripened corn. Despite their strong resemblance, however, he seemed younger than Sabrina, lacking her air of calm maturity.

Fanny, who had always doted on her stepson, patted the sofa invitingly. "Come sit down and tell us all the London gossip, Adrian. We might as well be living at the ends of the earth for all the news that reaches us in Sussex."

"Oh, come, Mama, you're only fifty miles from London here," said Adrian, sitting down obediently beside Fanny. "As to gossip, well, the season's just begun, you know, and town is still a bit thin of company. Actually, there's really only one topic of conversation in London these days. Byron's gone. Left England a week ago. Forced out, according to the *on dit*, completely ostracized by society."

"But how could that be?" Daphne inquired, distressed. She was fond of reading wildly romantic novels in the Gothic style, and she adored the poems of Lord Byron. "I thought Lord Byron was so exceedingly popular, with people rushing to buy out his poems on the day of publication."

"Oh, I'd say it was the accumulation of scandal. His divorce, his relationship with his sister—"

"Adrian!"

Stopped short by his stepmother's swift intervention to spare Daphne's virginal ears the gamier aspects of her favorite poet, Adrian hastily switched to a lively account of his regimental experiences as a lieutenant in the First

Life Guards. During the previous year, Adrian had served with distinction in the Waterloo campaign.

"And we hear that the Prince Regent is busily redesigning our uniforms," he ended with a laugh. "We're to wear claret-colored overalls, and our helmets will be in the Roman style in white metal. Good thing Prinny doesn't intend to wear the uniform himself. He's gotten so fat that he'd look as queer as Dick's hatband on dress parade."

Neither Fanny nor Daphne appeared to find anything unusual in Adrian's manner, but Sabrina, who had always been closely attuned to her twin's moods, sensed an underlying tension beneath Adrian's smiling small talk. Something was amiss with him, something that had sent him tearing down to Sussex on this unexpected visit. She resigned herself to a private talk with him later in the evening.

Glancing at the clock on the mantel, Lady Latimer reminded her stepchildren that it was time to leave for the ball. She remarked to Adrian, "As I was telling Sabrina, I would have been happy to chaperon Daphne tonight, in spite of my delicate health, but you and Sabrina will fill my shoes beautifully. You young people go along and enjoy yourselves. I shan't mind in the least being left alone."

After Fanny had said good-night and left the room, Adrian said with a grin, "Mama would have us think she's been wasting away since she came into the family, but she's really as strong as a horse. She trots out her poor health whenever she doesn't want to do something that might inconvenience her."

Sabrina chuckled. "Yes, I daresay she'll spend the evening curled up in bed with a box of bonbons and one of those novels that she's always confiscating from Daphne."

"Probably *Castle Rackrent*," said Daphne, giggling.

"Yesterday I found a copy tucked under the seat of Mama's chaise longue." She paused, her amusement fading. "Mama means well, but I do wish she wouldn't keep after you about finding a second husband, Sabrina. Why can't she understand that you and Oliver had such a happy marriage that you can't bear to put anyone in his place?"

Busying herself with draping a black China lace scarf over her shoulders, Sabrina replied after a moment, "You forget that when Mama was young, love matches weren't at all the crack. In fact, they were considered quite common."

"Oh, I know," said Daphne disapprovingly. "Things aren't that much different today, really." She added wistfully, "I was only fourteen, but I remember thinking how beautiful and romantic your courtship was, Sabrina. When Oliver arrived in the county to visit his cousins before going off to his first posting in the foreign service, I don't suppose he had the least notion of getting married. Well, everyone kept saying he was a penniless younger son! But from the first moment that you met, it was plain that you were meant for each other. It would have been a—a *sacrilege* if either of you had married someone else!"

"What a romantic you are, Puss," said Adrian indulgently. "I must say, though, Sabrina, that it was a nine days' wonder in the county when you and Oliver dashed off to London to get married by special license. Never saw Papa enact such a Cheltenham tragedy. He wanted you to marry the Lydgate fellow, as I recall, the one who inherited his uncle's property."

"That's enough ancient history," Sabrina said with a somewhat forced laugh. She examined Adrian's well-cut dark blue coat and plain white waistcoat and then glanced at the tiny gold watch pinned to her bodice. "The coat and waistcoat will do, but you have just five

17

minutes to change into knee breeches and pumps before it's time to leave for the ball."

Dusk was falling as Sabrina and Daphne and Adrian entered their carriage in front of Latimer House, a rather heavy stone-built mansion situated near the famous "Seven Sisters" cliffs overlooking the English Channel. The house was sheltered by a copse of ash and willow trees from the sometimes merciless winds that blew over the South Downs. The mansion and the acres that surrounded it had been the property of the Latimer family for two centuries.

The carriage rolled along the winding driveway away from the house and across a stretch of undulating downland to Fairlea, a tiny hamlet of old flint-walled houses, a small late-Norman church and a village green adorned with a pond covered with water lilies. A short drive from Fairlea brought them to the seaside town of Eastbourne and the Lambe Inn, a half-timbered building dating back to medieval times. Situated at the head of the High Street, the inn was the site of the assembly ball.

Inside a large room that had been converted to a ballroom, Daphne was swept onto the floor by the first of a succession of eager partners. Sabrina settled herself in a chair on the sidelines near a group of gossiping turbanned dowagers, and Adrian remained with her, ignoring the plaintive stares from a number of partnerless young women and their hopeful mamas. After Sabrina had smilingly refused several requests to dance from old acquaintances, Adrian looked at her curiously, saying, "You used to love to dance, Sabrina."

"Oh, you know that balls are simply an excuse to allow girls to set their caps for a husband," she said lightly, "and I've no desire to enter the marriage mart."

"Not ever?"

"Not for the time being, at least."

Adrian reached over to press her hand. "I'm sorry, old girl. I didn't realize you still missed Oliver so much." He cleared his throat. "Sabrina, I didn't come down here just for the visit, much as I like seeing all of you. I must talk to you. I—the fact is, it's bellows to mend with me—"

"Later, Adrian. A public ball is no place for a serious discussion. We'll talk when we get home. Here comes Daphne. Don't let her see that you're upset."

Daphne came up to them on the arm of a thin-faced, gray-eyed young man of medium height, whose pleasant smile relieved his somewhat angular features from severity. He wore a blue frock coat with gold-laced buttonholes, a high white stock, and white breeches and stockings.

"Sabrina, Adrian, I want you to meet Captain Gordon Stanhope, a very old friend," exclaimed Daphne, her pretty face flushed with excitement. "We met several years ago when he used to visit his sister Betsy at Ravenhill Academy. You remember, Sabrina, that Betsy was my closest friend at school, even though she was several forms ahead of me."

"Mrs. Neville, Sir Adrian." Captain Stanhope made a correct bow. "My sister reminded me that Miss Latimer lived in the vicinity, but I certainly never expected to meet her at the very first social function I've attended since I arrived in port!"

"It's always a pleasure to meet a Navy man—" Adrian paused, staring at the captain's shoulders, which were bare of the silver epaulets designating naval rank.

The captain smiled. "I'm a revenue commander, Sir Adrian. Some years ago we were authorized to wear a naval uniform, but minus those pretty silver epaulets."

"Hold on," said Adrian, knitting his brow. "Didn't I hear something—yes, I have it now. The Admiralty is about to take over control of the revenue cruisers of the

Preventive Water Guard from the Board of Customs."

"Yes, the change went into effect last month."

"I understood that the Admiralty was appointing commanders from the ranks of the half-pay naval officers," Adrian observed. "Obviously I was wrong."

"No, not at all. New appointments to the cutter service will be from the Navy, but the Admiralty has decided to retain a number of revenue commanders from the old Customs service." Captain Stanhope smiled boyishly. "I'm one of the lucky ones. I don't quite know how I would have adjusted to being a landlubber. I've been a cutter commander for almost ten years. I never wanted to be anything else."

"Gordon's new cutter is being constructed at a shipyard in Newhaven," said Daphne eagerly, and Sabrina raised a mental eyebrow at her shy sister's easy use of the captain's Christian name. Gordon Stanhope must have been a frequent visitor to Ravenhill Academy. Daphne continued, with an important little air of knowledgeability, "The boat has a burthen of one hundred sixty tons, which of course makes it a cruiser of the first class, and it will carry sixteen 'smashers!' "

"Carriage guns. Six and eight pounders of the carronade type. Excellent guns for use against smugglers," explained the captain with an amused look at Daphne. As the orchestra struck up for a country dance, he put out his hand for Daphne's program. "There's a mistake here," he observed, looking closely at the card. "We must remedy that." He marked out the names of Daphne's partners, scrawling his own initials against the remaining dances. He extended his arm to Daphne, saying coolly, "This is mine, I believe?"

"Well!" Adrian whistled under his breath, watching his sister take her place in the set with the captain.

"Yes," said Sabrina with a sigh. "Like it or not, I'll be obliged to play Friday-faced duenna and tell Daphne that it just isn't done to dance more than two dances with the same man."

"Puss does seem taken with the fellow. Know anything about him?"

"I think I recall Daphne's telling me that her great friend Betsy Stanhope was the daughter of a yeoman farmer somewhere in the Weald."

"Oh." After a moment, Adrian said, only half in jest, "The good captain will soon be at sea, Sabrina. He won't have much time to dazzle impressionable young females."

But in Sabrina's opinion the damage had already been done. Daphne appeared to grow more starry-eyed as the evening wore on, and in the carriage returning from the ball, she could talk of nothing except Captain Stanhope. "The Admiralty holds yearly competitions for the greatest number of smugglers captured and turned over as seamen to the Royal Navy," she reported. "Two years ago Gordon won a prize of five hundred pounds for capturing fifteen smugglers. He says he hopes to win again with his new cutter. Oh, did I tell you, Sabrina? He'll be stationed at Newhaven when he takes over his new command, so I'm sure we'll be seeing a great deal of him. He asked for permission to call on Mama, by the way."

"I don't know if that's wise," said Sabrina after a pause. In the darkness of the carriage, she felt rather than saw the quick indignant turn of Daphne's head.

"And what does that mean, pray?" demanded Daphne.

"Only that I'm sure Mama will not wish you to encourage the acquaintance."

"Oh, and why not?"

"Daphne, Captain Stanhope is undoubtedly a fine young man, but his standing in society is simply not equal to yours. Didn't you once tell me that your friend

Betsy's father was a yeoman farmer?"

"I thought better of you, Sabrina," Daphne said coldly. "I didn't realize you were a snob, as high in the instep as Mama herself." She lapsed into an injured silence, from which she refused to be drawn until they arrived back at Latimer House. After the sleepy footman had admitted them and bolted the door, Daphne announced frigidly that she was tired and would retire to bed immediately.

"You did the right thing, Sabrina," Adrian murmured as he watched Daphne's rigid little figure ascending the staircase. "Better to point out Gordon Stanhope's ineligibility now before Daphne fixes her fancy on him." He cleared his throat. "You know I told you I wanted to speak to you on a personal matter—"

"I haven't forgotten, Adrian. Let's talk in the morning room. I'll even have a glass of claret with you. That punch they served at the ball was insipid."

As they neared the door of the morning room, Adrian checked his stride. "Did you hear that? Sounded like shots to me—somewhere near the home farm, I think. Been having much trouble with poachers lately?"

Sabrina, too, had heard what sounded like a fusillade of shots in the distance, and her nerves had tightened. She replied casually, "Yes, we had some poaching during the winter. There are a number of discharged soldiers and sailors in the area who haven't been able to find employment since Waterloo. I daresay it's only to be expected that some of them might turn to poaching. I'll speak to the gamekeeper in the morning."

After Adrian had seated himself opposite Sabrina, glass in hand, he seemed reluctant to come to the point. He sipped his claret appreciatively, saying, "Papa laid down an excellent cellar. This claret is as good as any I've tasted."

"Enjoy it," Sabrina remarked dryly. "When it's gone,

there won't be any more. It's one luxury we can certainly do without. I believe Papa paid fifteen guineas to the dozen for this lot. Another reason why he died deep in Dun territory."

Adrian looked acutely uncomfortable. "Sabrina, I don't believe I've ever told you how much I admire the way you've managed estate matters this past year. Old Higgins was past the job of steward, and as for me, even if I had sold out of the regiment, well, you know I never had any head for figures. Quite simply, you've towed us all out of the River Tick. That's why it's so hard for me to tell you —"

"Wait." Sabrina lifted her head, listening intently. The light knock was repeated. "Who could that be at this hour? The servants are all in bed. I'd best see who it is before the whole household is awakened."

Picking up a candle, she went into the entrance hall, followed by Adrian, and slid back the bolts. "Tom," she exclaimed in surprise. The soberly dressed young man standing in front of her was the son of their tenant on the home farm. He was breathing hard, as if he had been running. "Is something wrong, Tom? Your father, is he ill?"

Tom Cavitt cast a nervous glance at Adrian, standing behind Sabrina. "Could I talk ter ye, private like, ma'am?"

At the sight of the youth's desperately anxious face, Sabrina did not hesitate. "Adrian, would you excuse us?" After her mystified brother had rather reluctantly left the hall, she said, "Now, then, what is it?"

The words came tumbling out of Tom's mouth. "You know that cargo we dropped yesterday at the Sisters, ma'am? Well, we was bringing it up tonight when we was jumped by the excisemen, jist past the turnoff fer Latimer House. One o' the riding officers and maybe one dragoon was hit afore they managed ter get away."

"Hurt? Badly?" asked Sabrina tensely.

"Don't know, ma'am. Anyways, jist as we was getting underway again, along comes a swell in a curricle smack inter the middle o' the ponies, an' Nate, 'e hit this gent over the 'ead, and now Nate's saying we ought ter kill 'im. The rest o' the crew, we was trying ter talk the cap'n out o' it, but knowing there ain't no ways we could stop Nate, not if 'e was really to get the bit 'tween 'is teeth. I thinks to meself, I'll go fer Mrs. Neville. O' course, it may be too late," added Tom heavily. "P'raps the cap'n's already 'ad 'is way."

But before he finished speaking, Sabrina had put down her candle and was out the door, holding up her skirts and running as fast as she could down the driveway, with Tom pelting along behind her, panting for breath. When they reached the intersection with a narrow country lane, she paused, and then, still followed by Tom, started walking slowly and quietly toward a knot of men, who were arguing so vehemently among themselves that they failed to notice her approach until she was almost upon them.

"Hold on, it's Mrs. Neville," she called out quickly when one of the men suddenly became aware of her presence and reached automatically for the pistol in his belt.

"Ye 'ad ought ter be more careful, ma'am, creeping up on us like that," said the man reproachfully. "I might a shot ye, not knowing who ye was."

"It's all right, Zeke." Brushing past the man, Sabrina walked over to the figure lying unconscious in the middle of the circle formed by the crew of the smuggling cutter *Mary Anne*. She dropped to her knees beside the limp body, gazing in horror at the blood that covered the man's face. Fearfully she put out her hand to touch his head. Her delicately exploring fingers traced a large ugly bump forming behind the right ear, but she sighed in relief when she discovered that the laceration on the temple, though bleeding freely, was only a surface wound. Perhaps the man was only stunned.

She paused, staring down at the man's still face. In the waning moonlight filtering through the leaves of the trees, she could make out clearly his bold, handsome features, his eyes shaded by absurdly long black eyelashes. He was young, probably in his early thirties, and his slim but powerful-looking body was dressed impeccably in expensive, well-tailored clothes. There was also a strong odor of liquor about his person.

Slowly Sabrina rose, her eyes roaming around the ring of tense, weather-beaten faces to settle on the burly, hard-bitten man who faced her defiantly from his position slightly in front of his crew. Behind him and his men, a knot of ladened pack ponies moved restlessly beneath their heavy loads, and from a distance came the sound of waves crashing against the cliffs of the Sussex coast.

"So, Captain Peggoty, from what Tom tells me, I arrived in the nick of time to prevent a cold blooded murder," she said coldly.

Nate Peggoty turned his gaze from the tall, elegant young woman to Tom Cavitt, standing beside her. The youth shifted his feet uncomfortably beneath the captain's venomous stare.

"Young Tom, 'e hadn't ought to've come a whining ter ye," grunted Peggoty in his flat, assertive voice. " 'Twarn't no need ter bother ye, Mrs. Neville."

Sabrina's eyes flashed a sudden fire. "No need to bother me? When you've just had a run-in with the riding officers, in which at least one of them was killed or wounded? No need to bother me, when you were on the verge of murdering another man who happened to wander into the middle of your fight with the excisemen? The *Mary Anne* is my boat, Captain Peggoty. Everything about her, including the activities of her crew, concerns me."

"That 'un"—Peggoty flicked a look at the unconscious man—"that 'un saw me shoot the riding officer. Forbye 'e gives evidence agin me, Mrs. Neville, ye know as well as I do, I'm fer the nubbing cheat."

"You're borrowing trouble with your talk of hanging," exclaimed Sabrina impatiently. "This stranger couldn't have gotten more than a passing glimpse at you. It's a dark night, for one thing, and from the smell of gin about him, I'd say he was very drunk."

"Well, but e' ain't no stranger," Peggoty was saying, when he wheeled suddenly to his left, snatching the pistol from his belt. "Come out o' there," he barked into the thick undergrowth beneath the trees. He lowered his weapon as a tall slender figure emerged into the lane.

"Adrian! What are you doing here?" Sabrina exclaimed.

Her brother sounded aggrieved. "I should be asking you the same question. I saw you pelting down the driveway from the morning room window, and I had to discover what were you about, tearing around the countryside in the middle of the night with young Tom Cavitt. It was a leveler, let me tell you, when I found you"—his gaze swept the circle of silent men and the restless pack ponies—"when I found you mixed up in a rum go like this. These fellows look like smugglers to me." He strode toward her, and as the tense-faced group of men parted before him, he caught a glimpse of the unconscious figure at her feet. "My God, Sabrina," he gasped in a strangled voice, "that's Lord Jareth Tremayne."

"Lord Winwood's brother? The famous dandy, the friend of Beau Brummell and the Regent?" asked Sabrina, startled.

"That be wot I be trying ter tell ye, Mrs. Neville," put

26

in Peggoty. "This cove, 'e ain't no stranger. No, 'e 'asn't been in these parts fer many years now, but I rekernized Lord Jareth right away, an' I say, we can't take any chances that 'e may 'ave rekernized me or the other lads 'ere. I say, we gits rid o' 'im."

"An' *I* say, Cap'n, we can't do that," snapped the man named Zeke, in what was apparently a continuance of a long-running argument. "Ye ain't thought wot would 'appen if we killed a lord o' the realm."

"What's this? Peggoty wants to kill Lord Jareth?" inquired Adrian in a horrified undertone. "Why, in God's name?"

Sabrina explained in a low voice. "Peggoty and his men were surprised by the excisemen, and they shot a riding officer. Peggoty is afraid Lord Jareth recognized him and will testify against him." Raising her voice, she said brusquely, "Zeke is quite right. If anything were to happen to Lord Jareth, we'd have the militia swarming around here like a hive of angry bees. In any case, I won't allow any killing. There's been enough violence tonight. Zeke, sling Lord Jareth over the back of one of those ponies and deposit him in a place where he'll soon be found. The village green at Fairlea, for example."

Peggoty held up his hand. There was an air of controlled menace about the man as he said, "Zeke takes my orders, Mrs. Neville. I'm the captain o' this crew."

Sabrina stared him down imperiously. "Not for long, Peggoty, if you don't follow *my* orders." She motioned to Zeke. "Best get Lord Jareth away as soon as possible. You don't want him to come to his senses and get a close look at you."

Zeke hesitated momentarily, slanting a quick sideways glance at Peggoty, before moving to unload one of the ponies. Standing frozen in hard-breathing, malignant silence, Peggoty made no attempt to stop him. With the help of one of his mates, Zeke draped the inert

27

body of Lord Jareth across the pony and moved slowly off in the direction of Fairlea. Avoiding Peggoty's eyes, the rest of the crewmen began distributing the casks that Zeke had unloaded on the backs of the remaining long-suffering ponies.

Sabrina turned to Peggoty. "I suggest you get this consignment moving immediately, Captain," she said coolly. "There's always the possibility that the excisemen will return with reinforcements."

"I hope ye won't live ter regret this night, Mrs. Neville," Peggoty muttered.

"Is that a threat?" Sabrina snapped.

Peggoty returned her gaze without expression, except for the banked fires behind his eyes. After a moment he shrugged. "A threat? No. I'd jist like fer ye ter keep in mind that killing—or even wounding—an exciseman is a capital offense. Ye may 'ave started me—aye, an' the crew o' the *Mary Anne,* too—on the road to the gallows." He put a finger to his cap. "Good night, Mrs. Neville. Mr. Cavitt will be giving ye the reckoning from this voyage. Ye'll be making a 'andsome profit. Our cargo included a thousand ankers o' brandy."

As Sabrina, walking surprisingly fast considering that she was still wearing her fragile evening slippers, turned into the driveway of Latimer House, Adrian, pelting along behind her, finally recovered his voice. He had been listening in petrified silence to Sabrina's dialogue with Peggoty, so overwhelmed by what he was hearing that he had seemingly been struck dumb.

"Sabrina, I can't believe that you've gotten yourself mixed up with the smuggling trade," he spluttered at last. "How could you do such a low, disgraceful thing?"

"Then at least half the population of England must share my disgraceful proclivities," Sabrina retorted, not breaking stride. "They're drinking brandy, or smoking tobacco, or wearing silken gloves and shawls, all of which entered the country without a tuppence of duty being paid on them."

"Oh. Well, drinking an occasional glass of smuggled spirits, that's one thing. Everybody does that. But gentlemen—and especially ladies of quality!—don't soil their hands with the dirty business themselves. If you were to be caught out, your reputation would be ruined. You might even go to jail."

Whirling around so abruptly that Adrian nearly tripped over her in the darkness of the driveway, Sabrina said fiercely, "Before you say another word, let's understand each other. If it weren't for my smuggling profits, you'd have had to put Latimer House on the market long ago. My 'fortune,' as Daphne keeps calling it, scarcely made a dent in Papa's debts. There was nothing left to make the mortgage payments or to pay for the improvements on the property."

"But—my God, Sabrina! I had no idea—why didn't you tell me?"

Sabrina's fierceness evaporated. She resumed her walk down the driveway, saying, "Oh, I saw no reason for both of us to agonize over our plight. If all goes well, in about five years I'll have cleared enough to pay off the mortgages, with something left over for Daphne's portion and Mama's jointure. Papa hadn't even secured Mama's money, you know."

"How did you raise the wind to buy the boat?" asked a subdued Adrian as he trudged along beside her. "That must have cost you a yellow boy or two."

"Two thousand pounds," Sabrina replied tersely. They were approaching the house now, and she paused on the steps to face Adrian with a sudden gurgle of laughter. "I sold Godmama's jewels—the diamond and ruby necklace with the matching earrings and bracelet—to buy the boat. I always disliked the set, and now I'll never have to wear it!"

She pushed open the heavy entrance door. The candle she had put down when she answered Tom Cavitt's summons was only half-consumed. The tumultuous events of the evening certainly hadn't taken very long. Picking up the candle, she headed for the morning room. "We've had enough excitement for one night. Let's pour ourselves a fresh glass of wine and have our talk."

Moments later, setting down the decanter, Sabrina turned around with a filled glass in either hand to find her brother still standing in the doorway of the morning room, his young face a mask of misery.

"Oh, come, Adrian, don't look so lowering. The excisemen aren't going to catch up with me, and in any case I don't intend to be a smuggler all my life."

"Sabrina, I don't know how to tell you this." Adrian walked over to a chair and sank bonelessly into it, staring at his sister in despair. "I need ten thousand pounds. Immediately. It's a debt of honor."

Sabrina put down the glasses and sat down opposite him. The merriment had died out of her face. "Translate that for me. Are you talking about a gambling debt?"

"I — yes. Night before last I lost ten thousand pounds playing macao at White's."

"I see," said Sabrina bleakly. "I wasn't aware that you were a member of White's. In fact, I thought we'd agreed that you couldn't afford memberships in any of the better clubs."

"I'm not a member of White's. Captain Morgan took me there as his guest. I swear to you, I didn't have any intention of gambling when I went there — oh, I thought I might risk a pound or two at hazard, but nothing more. Then — I don't remember quite how it happened — I found myself playing macao. The stakes were horrendous, and my luck was quite out. I kept writing IOU after IOU, not realizing how much I was losing." Adrian looked up at Sabrina in desperation. "I must pay the debt, or be blackballed all over London. I came down here, hoping against hope that you might find the ten thousand for me, but after what happened tonight, I see that's impossible. There's nothing for it but to sell the estate. I'm sorry, it seems so unfair after all the sacrifices you've made for the family, but I don't see what else I can do. A debt of honor *must* be paid."

At his sister's quick, instinctive shake of her head, Adrian rushed on. "It's true, Sabrina. You *know* it's true. Papa always said, 'Don't play if you can't pay.' If he were here today, he'd tell me to pay this debt of honor even if it meant sacrificing everything I owned."

"And your family, too, presumably." Sabrina's voice, to her anxious brother, sounded as cold as ice. She lapsed into silence, her forehead creased with thought. "Who held the macao bank?" she asked at last. "Who has your IOU's?"

Adrian looked surprised. "Didn't I mention that? It was Lord Jareth Tremayne."

"What?" Sabrina stared at her brother, stupefied. "How could a man of Lord Jareth's reputation and experience allow a fledgling like you to gamble with him?"

"He couldn't very well stop me, now could he? I'm of age," flashed Adrian. "And gambling is how Tremayne makes his living, and a very good one, too, I'm told. But it doesn't matter. I must pay up. I'll go to the solicitor tomorrow and arrange to put the estate on the market."

"I can't stop you from doing this if you've made up your mind to do so," said Sabrina quietly. "However, I think you're overlooking one important fact: these are hard times. Since the end of the war, the bottom's fallen out of the wheat market, and bankers all over the country are calling in their loans."

Adrian's face fell. "I didn't know . . . Then what will we do?"

"I'm not sure. It's just possible I may be able to help,"

said Sabrina slowly. "Go back to London. Tell Lord Jareth you need more time. Tell him you'll pay your debt within the month. Then cross your fingers and hope for the best."

Chapter Two

Driving into the village of Fairlea next morning, shortly after sunrise, Adrian Latimer reined in his pair to avoid running over a man who was racing across the road toward the village green. Gazing after the man, Adrian watched him leaning down to extend a helping hand to a second man who sat slumped beside the pond on the green in the company of a large playful dog.

"My God," breathed Adrian in sudden sick apprehension. He'd forgotten Sabrina's instructions to the smugglers to dump the unconscious Lord Jareth in some public place where he would be found quickly. In the press of his own problems, in fact, Adrian had forgotten all about any possible injury to Tremayne. Jumping down from the curricle, Adrian tossed his reins to his tiger and ran over to Lord Jareth, who was on his feet but was leaning rather heavily against the arm of his good Samaritan, whom Adrian now recognized as the innkeeper of the Fairlea Arms.

The man was saying, "It gave me a turn, Lord Jareth, let me tell ye, when I looked out the winder a bit ago and saw yer lordship alayin' on the green. O' course, ye 'adn't come back ter the inn ter spend the night—not that it's any affair o' mine," he added hastily.

"Lord Jareth!" Adrian exclaimed as he came up. "I

was just passing by on my way to London—are you in difficulties? Can I be of any help?"

Carefully turning his head, Jareth looked at Adrian with bloodshot eyes. "Thank you—Sir Adrian Latimer, isn't it? I'm not sure that anyone can help. I ran into a pack of smugglers—I think they were smugglers—late last night while I was considerably worse for wear after a drinking session with my friend, Jack Wyndham. In the process I seem to have lost my curricle and team, not to speak of my tiger."

"There they are now, m'lord, I fancy," said the innkeeper, pointing to a diminutive figure who had entered the village from the opposite direction, slowly leading a pair of horses. "Leastwise, it looks like yer team an' yer tiger. Dunno about yer carriage."

"Damnation! If anything's happened to those horses . . . Not mine, of course, only job horses picked up at the last posting house, but still . . . A man feels a certain amount of responsibility." Apparently imbued with a sudden burst of energy, Jareth pushed aside the innkeeper's supporting arm and strode across the green, followed by both men.

"Well?" Jareth demanded as he came up to the tiger. "What's the damage, Tom?"

"The horses are fine, m'lord," the youthful tiger replied hastily. "A bit tired, like, that be all. But the curricle—" He tossed a guilty, defensive look at his employer. "Y'see, when they villains dragged ye out o' the curricle last night, the team bolted, and afore I could get them under control, we went off the road agin a tree. The off wheel, it's smashed, m'lord."

"Well, let's be grateful the damage is no worse. Where've you been all night, then?"

The tiger looked even more guilty. "I'm sorry, m'lord, but wot wif the excitement an' the strange roads an' all, I jist got lost. Wandered around, leading the team all

34

night, until I finally rekernized somefing familiar."

"Don't worry about it, Tom. You did your best." Jareth turned to the innkeeper. "Send out a wagon, please, landlord, to bring in the curricle. Tom will have to stay here while the repairs are being made. I must get back to town."

"I'd be most happy to take you to London in my curricle, Lord Jareth," Adrian said swiftly.

Jareth looked down at his bloodstained and disheveled clothes. "Kind of you, Latimer. I don't like to delay you, however. I'd need time to change into something more presentable, and a large pot of coffee wouldn't come amiss."

"No problem at all," Adrian assured him. "I'm quite at your disposal." He walked with Jareth across the road to the Fairlea Arms.

An hour later, in the private parlor of the inn, Adrian rose as Jareth entered the room, immaculately dressed in skintight pantaloons, shining Hessians, and an impeccably fitting coat in dark blue superfine from Weston's inspired fingers. His dark, strong-featured face was pale, and he avoided sudden movements of his head, but his hair was carefully arranged à la Brutus.

"Sorry to keep you waiting, Latimer. I'm without the sage counsel of my valet, and it took me nine tries to tie my damned cravat."

Adrian stared at the gleaming white perfection of Jareth's Osbaldeston knot, and immediately realized how amateurishly he had tied his own cravat. But then, he comforted himself, a lowly lieutenant in the Household Cavalry need not aspire to the elegance of an acknowledged leader of the *ton*.

Over steaming coffee and several slices of cold beef and ham, Jareth's physical indisposition seemed to improve, and he ate with good appetite. "I begin to feel more human," he observed. He frowned slightly. "My memory must be playing tricks on me, however. I could swear there was a woman connected with that smuggling business last night. I seem to remember hearing a female voice speaking with considerable authority."

Adrian put down his fork abruptly.

"You don't fancy the ham, Latimer?" asked Tremayne, wiping his mouth and setting down his napkin.

"Lord Jareth, I must speak to you," Adrian blurted. "It's about the money I owe you."

Jareth raised an inquiring eyebrow.

"The blunt I dropped in the macao game at White's the other night," Adrian explained, flushing as Jareth's expression seemed to suggest, very subtly, that gambling debts were not a proper subject of discussion at a gentleman's breakfast table. "The fact is, I'm pinched for the needful at present, but I want you to know that I'll have the ten thousand pounds for you in one month's time, if that's agreeable to you."

"But of course," said Jareth coolly, as if the matter were of no moment at all.

Adrian's flush deepened. "Thank you. That's settled, then." Rising, he said, "Shall we be on our way?" As he walked out of the inn with Lord Jareth, he repressed a pang of dismay at the thought that he would be cooped up in his curricle for almost five hours with a man who made him feel as gauche as a schoolboy.

Holding a tea tray, Lotte paused inside the door to stare in surprise at Sabrina, who was sitting in a wing chair beside the window. "You're awake early, *meine Frau,*" said the plump, matronly abigail who had accompanied Sabrina to England from Vienna.

"Yes, I didn't sleep well," Sabrina replied. "Put the tray on the table beside my chair, Lotte."

"You do look tired, *meine Frau.* Perhaps you stayed up

36

too late with Sir Adrian. The Herr left very early this morning, by the way, just as the sun was coming up. He seemed quite cheerful. Not like when he arrived last night."

There was definitely an inquisitive note in Lotte's voice. Far from feeling overwhelmed in a strange new country, she had taken to life in Sussex with relish, quickly assuming a proprietary interest in the Latimer family. She was especially fond of Adrian, and for several minutes after setting down the tea tray she lingered in a transparent attempt to find out the reason for his sudden visit.

Well might Adrian feel cheerful, thought Sabrina glumly as she sipped her tea. Last night she'd rashly promised to try to raise the ten thousand pounds he needed to pay his gambling debt. It wasn't that she was any the less angry at Adrian for losing the money. Actually, she could have forgiven almost any other peccadillo more readily. She loathed the very idea of gambling, though in this case she still felt strongly that an experienced rakehell like Jareth Tremayne shouldn't have allowed such a callow youth to sit in at his table. No, she'd promised to raise the money for Adrian because, in the long run, paying his debts was merely a matter of practical necessity. The future of the Latimer family fortunes depended on the retention of the ancestral family estate. Unfortunately, throughout a largely sleepless night, she'd been unable to think of a feasible way to raise the money that Adrian owed.

She set down her cup, getting up to pace the floor restlessly. Her eye wandered to the tiny portrait of her husband that sat in a position of honor on her writing table, and she paused to pick up the miniature. Often, during the past year, she'd been tempted to pack the portrait away to the back of a bureau drawer — any place where she wouldn't have to see it every day — but she knew she could never explain her action to her sister and her stepmother without revealing the sham of her marriage.

The Viennese artist had caught the outer Oliver exactly, Sabrina thought. His handsome boyish features, his laughing eyes, his look of devil-may-care enjoyment of life. But of the inner Oliver there was not a hint, not a suggestion, of the shallowness and the weakness that had destroyed him.

Sabrina sat down in the wing chair by the window, still holding the miniature. A slight, reluctant smile curved the corners of her lips. She and Oliver had been so breathlessly happy in the early days of their marriage, after they'd defied convention and the objections of both their families to rush off to London to be married by special licence. No matter that Sabrina had deprived herself of the opportunity for a London season, no matter that she and Oliver had had scarcely a feather to fly with, except for the income from her tiny fortune.

Sabrina couldn't remember exactly when she became aware that Oliver's fondness for gambling had become an obsession. During their first posting to Constantinople, he had gambled, both in clubs and in private homes, but then most people gambled socially, men and women alike. Sabrina hadn't thought much about Oliver's love for whist and hazard, though she did deplore his frequent losses. After all, she herself was a regular at the whist table, and she usually won more than she lost.

It was only when they were transferred to Vienna, where Oliver became First Secretary to the Ambassador, that she realized he couldn't leave the gambling alone, that it had become the most important thing in his life. He was also unlucky, falling deeper and deeper into debt, railing at Sabrina for refusing to sell her godmother's necklace and give him the proceeds, turning their small house into a virtual gambling den, where night after night he tried to win back his ever-growing losses. To give his house an even more convivial atmosphere, conducive to wagering large sums, he had even taught Sabrina the rudiments of faro, macao, and écarté, and insisted that she act each night as his hostess, often as dealer.

It was a member of the Austrian court, the Graf von Spenitz, who caught Oliver with a deck of marked cards and unveiled his cheating before his wife and a shocked roomful of people. Oliver denied the accusation, and, in a desperate move to redeem himself, challenged the Graf to a duel, during which the Austrian put a bullet into his head. After Oliver's death, the English Ambassador managed to hush up the reason for the duel, persuading those who knew about the cheating to be silent for the sake of the widow and the families of the young couple.

Sabrina shook her head against the hurtful memories. Rising, she replaced the miniature on the writing table, and then, struck by a sudden thought, she crossed the room to her bureau, where, after a moment's hesitation, she reached into the top drawer to withdraw a small painted and gilded box, wrapped in a handkerchief. Slowly she opened the box and took out a pack of playing cards. They were handsome, beautifully made cards, and the secret markings on their backs were skillful and practically undetectable. For the hundredth time, she asked herself why she hadn't destroyed the cards when she found them on the morning after the duel, still strewn across the table where the Graf von Spenitz had tossed them the moment he discovered Oliver's cheating.

It was an idle question. Of course she knew why she hadn't gotten rid of the cards. She'd kept them to remind her of the waste of Oliver's death and the folly of following her heart before her reason.

Oliver's handsome face and beguiling charm had

blinded her to his faults, and she'd rushed into a hasty marriage partly out of impulsive puppy love, and yes, if she were truthful, partly because her seventeen-year-old self had resented her new and interfering stepmother's presence at Latimer House. When she returned home, she'd been too proud to admit what a failure her marriage had been. She'd preserved Oliver's guilty secret, not only for his sake and that of his family but for her own. But she'd also determined to build a secure future for Adrian and Daphne, and after that for herself. Her future, she'd vowed, would include neither husband nor romance. She was not going to allow anybody — and especially not Lord Jareth — to interfere with her goal.

Sabrina took a last long look at the playing cards before replacing them in the box and wrapping them again in the handkerchief. She put the cards far back in the rear of the drawer and closed it with an air of finality. Now she knew what she had to do. When Lotte returned for the tray, Sabrina told her, "Bring me a portmanteau. And I'll want the dogcart in an hour."

Wandering into her sister's bedchamber later that morning, Daphne found Sabrina and Lotte busily transferring garments from the wardrobe to the portmanteau.

"Sabrina!" Daphne gasped. "Where are you going?"

"Eastbourne," replied Sabrina briefly.

"Eastbourne! But why . . . ?"

"I'm taking my clothes to Madame Manet to be refurbished into the latest mode. I think Mama is right. It's time for me to come out of mourning."

"Oh." Daphne looked thoughtful. After a moment, she observed, not without a trace of doubt, "I daresay Oliver wouldn't want you to stay in mourning forever."

"He would not," replied Sabrina firmly. "Oliver liked to see me in bright pretty colors."

"So he did." Daphne brightened. "Remember how

40

much he liked that pale green sprigged muslin you wore the first time you met him?"

"Yes. It was a beautiful frock."

"Sabrina—" Daphne hesitated, then plunged ahead. "I'd like to apologize for the way I acted last night. I didn't mean to be rude to you and Adrian. It's just—it was the way you talked about Gordon—about Captain Stanhope, as if he weren't good enough to associate with us, and it seemed so unfair."

Sabrina put her arm around Daphne. "I know. Life *is* unfair sometimes. I didn't mean to hurt your feelings either, Daphne. I liked your Captain Stanhope very much."

"But?"

"Let's not quarrel, Puss," said Sabrina gently.

"No, of course not." Daphne managed a smile. "I hope you have a good session with Madame Manet."

Lady Latimer trailed along after Sabrina into the hall. As the footman opened the door, Fanny peered disapprovingly out at the small two-wheeled vehicle waiting in front of the house in the charge of a groom. "Must you take the dogcart, Sabrina?" she asked. "You'll look a perfect guy, driving yourself and that huge portmanteau and those hat boxes into Eastbourne. Why not go in the carriage with Robin?"

"Robin has work to do on the estate today, Mama. I assure you, I'll look perfectly proper. Lotte is going with me, and you know what a dragon she is!"

"Well . . . It isn't as if you were driving in the city, I suppose. At least we won't be seeing you much longer in those clothes," Fanny observed, with a disapproving look at Sabrina's rather shapeless black bonnet and black pelisse. "I'm so glad you're finally taking my advice to come out of mourning."

41

How odd the difference a few years could make, thought Sabrina with a twinge of amusement as she climbed with Lotte into the dogcart and set off down the driveway. When she was seventeen, her stepmother's constant advice giving had driven her into rebellion. Today Fanny's strictures seemed mere pinpricks of irritation.

Before going on to Eastbourne, Sabrina made a detour to the home farm. As she halted the dogcart in the courtyard, young Tom Cavitt rushed over to help her down, and his father, Ezra, appeared in the doorway of the house.

"Please ter step inter the parlor, Mrs. Neville," announced Ezra, a spry, gray-haired man in early middle age, with a cheerful rubicund face. "P'raps you'll take a glass o' that there cowslip wine that ye fancied on yer last visit." He smiled at the abigail. "Lotte, I'm sure my wife has a bit o' something fer ye in the kitchen."

In the stiff, painfully neat parlor of the house, Sabrina made small talk about farm matters with Ezra and Tom while Mrs. Cavitt, plump and bustling, served her famous cowslip wine and biscuits. After his wife had left the room, Ezra turned to Sabrina, his face suddenly serious, and said heavily, "Ah, an' it were a bad business with the excisemen last night, Mrs. Neville."

Although Sabrina's identity as the owner of the *Mary Anne* was known to the crew, she had prudently enlisted Ezra Cavitt as the owner of record. He had always dealt with the day-to-day details of the smuggling operation, functioning as the intermediary between Sabrina and Captain Peggoty. Sabrina kept herself informed about the overall situation through her regular visits to the home farm, which occasioned no comment from her neighbors or the authorities.

"I was sorry ter hear that ye were drawn inter the trouble," Ezra continued. "I told young Tom he should've come ter me. 'Twarn't no place fer a lady."

"Tom did the right thing, Mr. Cavitt. I was closer than you were," Sabrina said quickly. "I came over as soon as I could this morning to ask if you've heard anything about the wounded excisemen."

"It's good news, ma'am. Tom, 'e jist returned from makin' inquiries in Newhaven. Tell Mrs. Neville, Tom."

A smile of relief on his face, Tom plunged into his account. "Neither one o' they excisemen were hurt bad, ma'am. They'll both be good as new."

"Thank God. What about Lord Jareth Tremayne?"

Tom's smile broadened. "Zeke deposited 'is lordship on the village green at Fairlea, like ye said. Jem Barrett — 'e's the landlord o' the Fairlea Arms — found Lord Jareth early this morning. Right as rain, except for an achin' 'ead, I'm told. What's more, Sir Adrian came along a bit later an' whisked 'is lordship off to London in 'is curricle."

Sabrina gave an involuntary chuckle. It served Adrian right, having to chat civilly with Jareth Tremayne during the long drive to London. She hoped her brother was exceedingly uncomfortable.

"So y'see, ma'am, ain't nothin' ter concern ye," Tom went on. "The excisemen, they 'aven't a notion who they was exchangin' shots with last night. Lord Jareth, 'e don't seem disposed ter ask any questions, neither. An' the cargo we brung in this time, it were a grand 'un. Our best ever. The usual brandy an' tea an' terbacco, o' course, and a good lot o' French gloves, an' some pretty China crepes an' silks."

"That's all very well, Tom," said his father, "but ye're forgetting one thing: Nate Peggoty." Ezra turned to Sabrina with a worried frown. "I wish ye 'adn't clashed with the cap'n, Mrs. Neville. Nate's a 'ard man, an' ye challenged him right in front o' 'is own crew. Made 'im look bad. Threatened ter take away 'is command. The thing is, Nate ain't ever agoin' ter ferget a slight like that."

"I couldn't let him kill Lord Jareth," said Sabrina sharply. "And I won't have a captain who considers smuggling profits more important than the life of a human being. I told Nate Peggoty from the beginning that he was to avoid all violence even if it meant losing a cargo."

"I know, an' o' course ye're in the right o' it, but—do ye know wot 'appened ter Nate's brother years ago? Dick Peggoty killed a revenuer wot tried ter board 'is sloop, an' somebody informed on 'im, an' poor Dick, 'e was 'anged."

"I hadn't heard about Peggoty's brother," Sabrina said slowly. "I see now why he kept talking about going to the gallows if he were recognized by Lord Jareth. He was thinking about what happened to his brother."

"That be it, ma'am."

"Well, all Nate Peggoty has to do in the future is to avoid shooting excisemen and threatening members of the most prominent family in the county, and he'll run no risk of being hanged," said Sabrina. She rose, straightening her bonnet. "I must be on my way to Eastbourne. Don't fret yourself," she told Ezra, who still looked concerned. "I don't see Nate Peggoty very often, but when I do, I'll try to keep our relations on an even keel."

Madame Manet's dress shop was located at the head of the High Street in Eastbourne, near the Lambe Inn. In the room back of her showroom, Madame walked about, carefully inspecting the garments that Lotte had taken out of the portmanteau and spread out on every available surface.

"Well, Madame Manet?" Sabrina inquired. "Can you remodel some of my gowns so that no one will suspect

44

I'm wearing last year's fashions? I wish I could commission you to make me a whole new wardrobe, but, as you've probably suspected, the Latimer family's not too plump in the pocket at the moment."

The dressmaker pursed her lips, saying, "You are fortunate, Madame Neville, that you were a resident of Vienna last year."

Sabrina laughed. "Really? Why do you say that?"

"Because the garments you brought back from Vienna were a year ahead of the fashions in England." Madame shook her head. "I remember so well when the English visitors started pouring into Paris after the Emperor was defeated — we couldn't believe our eyes, the English ladies looked so dowdy, so out of date."

She picked up one of the gowns, holding it up in front of her at full length. "It will be quite easy, in fact, to refurbish your clothes, Madame Neville. Take this crepe and net evening dress, for example: it already has the new gored skirt and wider sleeves. I will trim the hem of the skirt with a deep flounce of blonde lace, and place a row of satin cockle shells on the sleeves, and *voila!* You will be wearing a gown in the very latest mode. The same for your other dresses, *naturellement.* A knot of ribbon, a ruffle, a velvet rouleau, a tiny bouquet of flowers — that is all it will take." She peered at Sabrina over the top of her spectacles. "May I say respectfully that *anything* would be an improvement over what you are wearing?"

Sabrina laughed again. "My stepmother is in perfect agreement with you. When may I have my gowns back, madame?"

"A week. Ten days. I will let you know."

After one more stop at the millinery shop down the street, where Sabrina left off several of her high-crowned hats to be freshly trimmed, she turned the dog-cart out of the High Street and began driving back across the downs.

"I'm happy you'll be wearing pretty clothes again, *meine Frau*," Lotte observed. "You always looked so lovely in that white lace over blue satin frock. I remember you wore it to Fürst von Marlberg's ball." She darted a frankly curious sideways glance at Sabrina. "It was very sudden, *nicht wahr*, your decision to come out of mourning?"

"Oh, not so sudden. My year of mourning was up some time ago," replied Sabrina casually. She made a mental note to be on her guard against an incautious slip of the tongue that might give away prematurely her scheme to rescue Adrian.

As she came up the driveway of Latimer House, she was surprised to see a trim town chariot standing in front of the door. Leaving Lotte to take the dogcart around to the stables, Sabrina entered the house, saying to the footman who answered the door, "Who's our visitor, Robin?"

The footman — who was, in fact, in the straitened circumstances of the Latimer family, the whole of the male household staff — replied with an air of suppressed interest, "It's a Captain Stanhope, ma'am. Calling on Miss Daphne. A naval gentleman, I believe."

Oh, dear, thought Sabrina as she walked slowly down the hall to the parlor, stripping off her driving gloves as she went. She paused on the threshold of the room. A spot of bright color on either cheek, Daphne was saying in a high, tight voice, "It's such wonderful news, Captain, to hear that your sister Betsy is to be married. Perhaps she could come here for a wedding visit. Wouldn't that be exciting, Mama?"

Lady Latimer, who was sitting in such stiff majesty on the sofa that she might have been carved from solid wood, didn't open her mouth to reply to Daphne, merely inclining her head slightly.

Spotting her sister in the doorway, Daphne exclaimed in obvious relief, "Oh, Sabrina, I'm glad you're back. You remember Captain Stanhope, I'm sure."

Sabrina advanced into the room, extending her hand. "I do, indeed. I'm happy to see you again, Captain."

The relief in Gordon Stanhope's eyes matched the expression on Daphne's face. He bowed over Sabrina's hand, saying in a low tone, "Perhaps I should have waited to call, but I was so anxious to renew my acquaintance with Miss Latimer . . ." His voice trailed away as he shot a nervous glance at Fanny.

Sabrina took pity on him. "Daphne, perhaps Captain Stanhope would like to see the gardens."

"Well!" exclaimed Lady Latimer in outraged accents after her younger stepdaughter had disappeared with the revenue captain. "May I ask what you were thinking of, Sabrina? Sending Daphne off alone in the company of that man? The gall of him, coming here quite as if he considered himself an old friend of the family!"

"He *is* an old friend, after a manner of speaking," said Sabrina mildly. "Daphne's known his sister Betsy for many years."

"A yeoman farmer's daughter! A yeoman farmer's son!"

"For that matter, Mama, I understand that Mr. Stanhope is quite a prosperous yeoman farmer. And Adrian was telling me last night that revenue captains earn better than a hundred and fifty pounds a year. That's close to a senior naval officer's pay."

Fanny stared at Sabrina suspiciously. "And what, pray, has that to do with anything?" Her eyes widened. "Sabrina! Surely you're not thinking of this Stanhope person as a suitable *parti* for Daphne?"

"No. Daphne should marry in her own class. But Mama, you're rushing your fences. The man simply made a social call!"

"Yes, and then you sent Daphne out to be alone with him in the gardens," Fanny retorted. "Soon he'll be asking me for her hand."

"Time enough to worry about that if it happens. In any case, Captain Stanhope will be going to sea soon, and it's not likely that Daphne will see much of him. Mama, I'd like to talk about something. You remember Oliver's sister Maria?"

"Lady Yardley? Yes, of course. A sweet girl. Made a very good match. I believe you told me she was increasing."

"I stopped in the receiving office in the village on my way home from Eastbourne. There was a letter from Maria. Her confinement will be soon, and her husband's been sent off on some sort of diplomatic mission to Russia, and poor Maria's feeling unwell and lonely. She wants me to come stay with her in Kent for a few weeks. If you can spare me, I think I should go."

"That would be a Christian thing to do, Sabrina. You must go, naturally. We'll manage without you as best we can. I grudge no effort in such circumstances."

Later that evening, as Lotte was dressing Sabrina's hair for dinner, she muttered, *"Kein Brief."*

"What?" Sabrina met Lotte's eyes in the mirror. "No letter? Whatever do you mean, Lotte?"

"I mean that you are to the Lady Latimer telling fibs, *meine Frau*. We never stopped at the receiving office in Fairlea today. You got no letter from the sister of the Herr Neville." Lotte sniffed. "You're up to something, *hein?*"

Sabrina laughed, unresentful of the abigail's overly familiar words. In Vienna, it had taken Lotte only a short time to become almost a second mother to her. "I fear so, Lotte. After all the economy lectures I've preached to Mama, I couldn't very well tell her that I was gadding up to London!"

48

Chapter Three

Walking around the great carriage warehouse, Sabrina paused in front of a crane-necked phaeton, painted a brilliant yellow, with a high seat suspended far above ground level. It had two pairs of wheels of unequal size, the rear pair rising to a height of eight feet. "This will do nicely," she said with a satisfied nod.

The coachmaker scratched his head. He had already suffered a mild shock when the elegantly dressed young woman, obviously a member of the Quality, had arrived unescorted at his premises in Longacre, near Covent Garden. "That there 'igh flyer, t'aint prezackly a lady's carriage, ma' am," he said, staring dubiously at the vehicle. "I can't choose fer ye, natchurly, but if ye was ter ask me which one ter buy, I'd say a pony phaeton, with a footstep only a few inches above the ground, or even a gig—"

"No, I thank you for your advice, but I want the high flyer," said Sabrina firmly. "And I have no intention of buying. I wish to rent the phaeton—for one afternoon. Please send it around to my hotel before three o'clock tomorrow. I'm staying at the—"

"Rent the phaeton?" the coachmaker interrupted her, shocked. "Fer 'alf a day? Oh, I dunno as I could see me way clear ter doing that, ma'am—"

"Ten pounds."

The coachmaker's eyes widened.

Sabrina pressed her advantage. "It isn't as if the phaeton were new. Look at that scratch on the rear panel."

"Well . . ."

A little later, having concluded a rental bargain with Sabrina, the coachmaker, still looking somewhat befuddled, escorted his newest customer to a hackney cab. As the cab rolled briskly along Cranbourn Street, past Leicester Square and into the eastern stretches of Piccadilly with its higgledy-piggledy of shops and inns and great mansions, Sabrina reflected with considerable satisfaction that her plans were proceeding on schedule. Having caught the mail coach the night before in Newhaven, ostensibly on their way to visit Oliver's sister in Kent, she and Lotte had arrived in London early that morning, at the Swan with Two Necks Inn in Lad Lane. From there they had gone to the Pulteney Hotel in Piccadilly.

As she stepped out of the cab in front of the hotel and walked past the bowing footman, Sabrina felt a slight pang at what this muted luxury was costing her. The Pulteney was an expensive place to stay, partly because of the prominence it had received two years previously when the Czar of Russia and his sister had stayed there during the victory spring of 1814, partly because of the fame of its new-fangled water closets and its excellent kitchen and superlative French chef. However, climbing the stairs to the first floor, Sabrina consoled herself with the thought that she was not paying anything like the exorbitant two hundred pounds a week charged to the Czar and the Grand Duchess Catherine and their retinue.

Entering her modest suite, Sabrina found Lotte standing on the wrought-iron balcony, gazing across the road at the leafy expanses of the Green Park, where a herd of cows was grazing. "What's so fascinating about a few cows, Lotte?" Sabrina asked in amusement.

The abigail shook her head as she left the balcony. "Cows are cows, *meine Frau,* but you wouldn't expect to find them smack in the middle of London. Here's a message that came for you while you were out. I should say, for the Countess Dohenyi. Whoever *she* might be," Lotte added pointedly, handing Sabrina a folded slip of paper.

"Thank you," Sabrina replied calmly, refusing to take the abigail's bait. From her familiarity with the Latimer family situation, and especially with their finances, Lotte was well aware that only some extraordinary reason could have brought her mistress to London at the height of the Season. Lotte was becoming increasingly frustrated and out of sorts because, so far, no amount of hinting or coaxing had prevailed upon Sabrina to reveal what that reason was.

Sabrina opened the note. "It's from Adrian. He'll be here shortly."

Lotte's face brightened. "*Gut.* Perhaps the Herr can make some sense of what you're doing, which is certainly more than *I* can do."

But in this Adrian disappointed the abigail. When he burst into the suite a few minutes later, resplendent in his scarlet regimentals and plumed helmet, he wore a scowl of angry perplexity. "Now, see here, Sabrina, what are you up to? Why are you calling yourself the Countess Dohenyi? I never felt so out of countenance in my life, asking downstairs for my own sister under such an outlandish name! For that matter, what are you doing in London?"

Sabrina shot him a warning glance. "I've come to visit you, naturally. Do sit down, Adrian. Lotte, will you bring us a pot of tea and some of those little cakes that Sir Adrian likes so much?"

After the abigail had left the room, Adrian said impa-

51

tiently, "Out with it, Sabrina. Why are you masquerading as some kind of Italian aristocrat?"

"Not Italian. Hungarian."

Adrian threw up his hands. "So, Hungarian. It's still a dashed rum thing to do. What's wrong with being the Honorable Mrs. Oliver Neville?" He glared at her suspiciously. "You're up to something, Sabrina."

Sabrina laughed. "Mrs. Neville can't raise the wind for you. The Countess Dohenyi can—maybe."

Forgetting the vexing question of Sabrina's masquerade for the moment, Adrian leaned forward on the edge of his chair, saying eagerly, "I see what it is. Bless you, you've brought me the blunt. You said to wait a month, so I wasn't expecting anything so soon—"

"No, I'm sorry, I don't have the money. Not yet." Seeing her brother's face fall, Sabrina hastened to add, "Adrian, don't despair. I have every hope of getting the ten thousand pounds for you, but I'll need your help."

"*My* help?" Adrian stared at her, open-mouthed.

"Yes, I want you to tell me everything you know about Jareth Tremayne's daily routine."

Adrian leaped to his feet, his helmet toppling off his knee and clanging to the floor. "Sabrina, this is insane! I won't allow you to run the risk of losing your reputation by posing as some kind of shady foreign countess. And neither will I allow you to approach Lord Jareth in my behalf. I'd be the laughing stock of London if it should get out that my sister intervened with Lord Jareth to cancel a debt of honor. I'd have to resign my commission, leave London—"

"No, no, I haven't the faintest intention of asking Lord Jareth to forgive your debt," Sabrina said soothingly.

Keeping a wary eye on his sister, Adrian sank back into his chair. "So, what are you planning to do?"

"You'll have to trust me. Just tell me how Lord Jareth

spends his days."

Clearly, Adrian's apprehensions had not been dispelled. He sounded reluctant as he began to speak. "He's a real Go among the Goers, you know. Most afternoons, you'd probably find him at Manton's, cupping a wafer, or at Gentleman Jackson's rooms in Bond Street." At the mention of the great ex-champion of England, Adrian's eyes glowed. "Tremayne's a very handy man with his fives. I saw him go a round with Gentleman Jackson once. Lord Jareth's a pretty fighter for an amateur, excellent science and bottom, no shifting—"

"Adrian, keep to the point. I don't care a fig for pugilism. What else does Lord Jareth do to fill his days?"

"Well, at three o'clock he's usually at White's, of course. Used to join Brummell there every afternoon, before the Beau had to leave the country. Spends a good many of his evenings there, too."

"Yes, that's what I thought. He belongs to the club's inner circle, doesn't he? I daresay he sits in the famous bow window?"

"Yes, frequently. Along with Alvanley and Sefton and 'Ball' Hughes. Swells like that. Why?"

Sabrina shrugged. "I like to know as much as possible about an adversary."

Alarm reawakened on Adrian's face. "Sabrina—" He broke off as Lotte returned with the tea tray. To Sabrina's secret amusement, he seemed momentarily to forget about his troubles as he eyed the pastries and scones and tea cakes on the tray. Adrian was twenty-one, but he wasn't long past the days when his family had wondered if he had an insatiable omnivorous worm in his stomach.

As he wiped his mouth and reached out his cup for the last trickle of tea, Sabrina told him, "Listen carefully, Adrian. I don't want you to visit me again here at the hotel, and if we should by any chance meet in public, you must pretend not to recognize me."

Adrian put down his cup. "Sabrina, I don't like the sound of this," he burst out. "I feel as if someone's walking over my grave. I'd rather end up at point-non-plus than have you hurt in any way. Drop this mad idea, whatever it is. Give this Countess Dohenyi a decent death. Don't approach Lord Jareth."

"Nothing bad's going to happen," Sabrina assured him. "The worst possibility is that I won't be able to obtain the ten thousand pounds for you, but try to keep your thoughts hopeful. Now, when I have news, I'll contact you, but don't worry if you don't hear from me for some days, even as long as several weeks. Oh, one more thing. Do you know where Jareth Tremayne lives?"

"At the Albany, in Piccadilly. Used to be Melbourne House. Henry Holland converted the place into chambers for bachelors a few years back. Very elegant address." Adrian sounded almost as if he were reciting by rote. A fatalistic calm seemed to have descended on him. He kissed his sister at the door, tweaking her curls with a rueful grin. "You're a good girl, Sabrina, but I never could keep up with you. When we were born, I think you got all the brains for both of us."

Entering the front parlor of the Pulteney Hotel on the following afternoon, Sabrina could tell from the studiously averted though admiring glances directed at her by her female fellow guests that Madame Manet's remodeling of her wardrobe was a complete success. The round dress of peach-colored Jaconet muslin over a darker sarsnet slip was complemented perfectly by a matching spencer of white-striped lutestring and a large-brimmed Leghorn hat trimmed with four rouleaux of pale peach satin.

With Lotte by her side, Sabrina waited primly on a

settee in the parlor until one of the hotel servants, considerably out of breath, approached to murmur a brief phrase in her ear. "You're sure?" she questioned the lad. At his emphatic nod, she smiled. "Thank you, Seth. Here's something for your trouble. And please tell the stables to send around my phaeton at once."

A little later, mounting into the driver's seat of the high flyer in front of the hotel entrance, Sabrina reflected with glee that the bright yellow vehicle seemed to flaunt itself even more obnoxiously in broad daylight than it had in the warehouse. She and the phaeton could not fail to be noticed.

As they drove away from the hotel, Lotte looked down at the pavement perilously far below and gripped the side panel of the phaeton with white-knuckled hands, wailing, *"Gott im Himmel,* are you trying to kill the both of us?"

"Oh, Lotte, stop fussing. I'm perfectly capable of driving this phaeton without overturning it," Sabrina replied more confidently than she felt. She had driven many types of carriages from childhood, but now she was beginning to have a hollow feeling in the pit of her stomach as she discovered that it was one thing to handle the ribbons behind a gig or a pony cart or even a curricle along the quiet lanes of Sussex, and quite another to guide a crane-necked phaeton through the bustling traffic of Piccadilly.

"Everyone's staring at us," Lotte complained, still clutching desperately at the side panel. "I'm sure that London ladies don't drive carriages like this. I hate to think what your stepmother would say if she saw you."

Sabrina, too, hated to think about Lady Latimer's reaction to the high flyer, but fortunately Fanny would never find out about it. Meantime, judging by the frankly curious glances of fellow drivers and pedestrians, she was attracting precisely the sort of attention she

55

craved. She was feeling quite calm by the time she turned into St. James's Street.

Driving past the fashionable shops and hotels and clubs that lined the street, she slowed her team as she approached White's Club at Nos. 37 and 38. In front of the building she reined in her horses, lifting her head to gaze with innocent-appearing interest at the great bow window that had been constructed in the middle of the facade, with the original front door moved to its left.

Three men were sitting in the bow window, directing an occasional indifferent glance down at the passersby. One face — straight-browed, severely handsome — Sabrina recognized immediately, although, the last time she had seen it, the imperious dark eyes had been closed and the classically carved features had been drawn and haggard. She gazed directly into Jareth Tremayne's eyes for a long, deliberate moment, stifling an urge to giggle when she detected a glimmer of startled surprise on his impassive face.

Then, breaking eye contact, she put the team to a brisk trot. Lotte grabbed her sleeve. *"Donner und Blitzen!"* the abigail gasped. "It was bad enough, the way folk were gawking at us before. Here on this street, they're stopping dead in their tracks to stare at us, as if we each had two heads, or the horses were growing wings!"

Lotte was exaggerating, but not by much. The eyes of the dandies and the military men and the other gentlemen of means who were strolling along St. James's Street were glued on Sabrina. Although she didn't appear to belong to the ranks of the Fashionable Impures, she was flouting one of the most important rules governing the deportment of a lady of quality. No respectable female who valued her reputation would dare to show herself in St. James's Street in the middle of an afternoon. Sabrina knew that she couldn't have chosen a splashier way to introduce herself to Jareth Tremayne's attention. And, thanks to Seth, the obliging young hotel servant whom she had set to watch Lord Jareth's rooms at the Albany, she'd known exactly when and where to locate her quarry in the bow window of White's Club.

She turned into King Street and then left again. "You're imagining things, Lotte," she said lightly. "Those people aren't staring at us. It's the phaeton. Did you ever see such a bilious shade of yellow?"

"Don't try to bamboozle me," snorted the abigail, who had taken readily but not always accurately to Adrian's slangy idiom. "I saw what I saw. Are we going to drive around in this thing all day?"

"No, we're returning to the hotel now. Later we'll go to Hyde Park. Adrian says it's all the crack to be seen there in the late afternoon." As she drove on, Sabrina blessed her brother for his good-natured gossip about fashionable life in London. Never having enjoyed a London season herself, she would have to depend on what she remembered from Adrian's cheerful prattle about the *ton* to guide her in her pursuit of Jareth Tremayne.

Shortly after five o'clock, a hackney cab deposited Sabrina and Lotte at Hyde Park Corner, and soon they were walking sedately beside the Serpentine. Despite the more pressing concerns on her mind, Sabrina found that she was enjoying the colorful spectacle of fashionable London showing itself off. She admired the dashing horsemen on their superb mounts and the stylishly dressed ladies in their satin-lined carriages with powdered-haired footmen in gorgeous liveries. She also wondered briefly if it had been a mistake not to drive herself around the park in the yellow-painted high flyer. Most of the other pedestrians in the park appeared to be governesses with their schoolgirl charges or elderly respectable ladies. But no, this leisurely stroll had more possibilities than a drive in the phaeton, always provided that Lord Jareth Tremayne had decided to take the air in Hyde Park that afternoon.

Apparently he hadn't. Soon it was six o'clock by the tiny jewelled watch fastened to the bodice of Sabrina's spencer, and the parade of horsemen and vehicles and walkers had begun to thin out. She was about to retrace her steps toward Apsley House when she turned around at the sound of a carriage and promptly sprawled full-length on the grass beside the path.

"Liebchen! Was ist los? Are you hurt?" screeched Lotte, throwing herself down beside her mistress.

Sabrina said faintly, as she struggled to sit up, *"Ich weiss nicht . . ."*

"Let me help, ma'am."

A pair of strong arms reached down to lift her to her feet and to support her against a firmly muscled chest when she slumped against him with a cry of pain.

"Are you hurt, ma'am?"

"Es tut mir leid—" She paused, muttering with the faintest trace of an accent, "I must the English speak. I am sorry to trouble you, sir," she began again. "I fear I've twisted my ankle . . ." She lifted her head from his shoulder, her voice trailing away. As she looked into Jareth Tremayne's lean face, she could see a dancing flame ignite in his dark eyes, and she felt a quicksilver warmth enveloping her body. Her heart began to pound so hard that she moved away from him slightly, afraid that he might be able to detect her tumultuous pulse through the fine broadcloth of his single-breasted blue tail coat.

"You've been very kind, *mein Herr*—I mean sir," she concluded hastily, hoping that he wouldn't notice that her breathing was decidedly uneven. Not for one moment had she anticipated this man's sheer physical magnetism.

"Happy to be of service, ma'am, I assure you." The deep, resonant voice held a quiver of appreciative amusement. He seemed in no hurry at all to relinquish his hold around her waist. "If you've injured your ankle, perhaps I could be of further help?"

A cautionary thought crossed Sabrina's mind. Had she been totally transparent? Had Jareth Tremayne grasped that she was stalking him? Perhaps her drive past the bow window of White's Club had simply been too much. She pulled herself free from his supporting arm. "Thank you, but I couldn't possibly trouble you any further." She turned away from him, hobbling over to her hovering abigail.

"You can't walk on that ankle, *meine Frau*," Lotte clucked anxiously. "Wait here, and I'll go out to the gate and hail a hackney cab."

Lord Jareth came up to them. "No need for a cab, ma'am. I should be delighted to take you up in my curricle."

Sabrina shot him a quick glance. He sounded respectful, but beneath the formal correctness of his manner, she thought she could detect that fugitive glimmer of amusement. "Thank you, but—" She hesitated, her face registering an expression of demure confusion.

"But you don't know me," Jareth finished for her. "Pray allow me to remedy that situation." He swept off his high beaver hat and made a low bow. "May I introduce myself? My name is Tremayne. Lord Jareth Tremayne."

Sabrina hesitated for a moment, then flashed him a sunny smile, extending her hand. "How do you do, Lord Tremayne. I am the Countess Dohenyi."

Bowing over her hand, he said with a shade of apology, "Actually, it's not Lord Tremayne. Mine is a courtesy title only. It's Lord Jareth. Well, now that we're properly acquainted, may I rescue you from your predicament?"

Sabrina laughed. "Thank you, under the circumstances, I think it would be unexceptional for me to accept a ride back to the Pulteney Hotel."

"I'm honored, ma'am." He offered her his arm and walked her slowly over to the curricle. With Lotte's ample person wedged in beside them, the driver's seat of the vehicle was a tight fit.

Proving himself an excellent whip, Jareth expertly maneuvered the curricle around Hyde Park Corner and up the rise to Piccadilly. "You're a visitor to London, Countess?" he asked after a few moments.

"Yes, indeed. I've just come from Paris." At Lotte's quick gasp, Sabrina poked her elbow firmly into the abigail's ribs.

"Paris? But you're not French, surely?"

"Oh, no. I'm Viennese."

"Ah. I thought I recognized the accent. Will you be staying long in London?"

Sabrina knit her brow. "I don't really know," she replied with a show of openness. "I'd like to see more of the city, but—well, it's a little awkward for a female to go about unescorted, don't you agree? You see, I have no acquaintances here."

"You do now. I'd be most happy to escort you anywhere you care to go. London's a very interesting city."

Sabrina paused a moment before replying. "It wouldn't do, I fear," she said at last, allowing a hint of regret to creep into her voice. "You've been most kind, but—we don't really know each other, do we? I'm sure my uncle—" She broke off, biting her lip as if she had ventured onto dangerous ground. Leaning forward, she peered at the great stone gateway of the imposing mansion on their right. "That's Burlington House, is it not? I understand there's a beautiful curved colonnade in the forecourt."

Sabrina kept Jareth busy answering questions about the various buildings on their route until they arrived at the hotel. Handing her down from the curricle, he said, with the obvious intention of furthering their acquaintance, "I'll just help you into the hotel, Countess. Your ankle—"

Interrupting him, she said firmly, "Thank you, but I can manage by myself. Good-bye, Lord Tre—Lord Jareth. Thank you again for your assistance." As she turned to limp up the steps on Lotte's arm, she caught a glimpse of the baffled expression that had spread across Lord Jareth's face and suppressed a grin of enjoyment.

Lotte held her tongue until they arrived in their rooms, when she said accusingly, "Now, what's all this, *meine Frau?* I don't know how I kept silent when I heard you describing yourself as a Viennese. And that limp! You didn't twist your ankle at all. You just pretended to be injured so you could make the acquaintance of that gentleman, the same man who was sitting in the window of that building this afternoon."

"I never could fool you, could I?" Sabrina patted the abigail on her shoulder. "The fact is, Sir Adrian's made a cake of himself, and I'm trying to get him out of his scrape. Bear with me, Lotte, won't you? I'll tell you about it when I can."

"Well, if it's to help Herr Adrian . . ."

"Trust me. It will be all right." Sabrina yawned, taking off her hat. "I believe I'll wear the green *gros de Naples* at dinner tonight. I do hope the chef doesn't outdo himself again. I'll end this London visit as round as a butter vat."

As Sabrina was emerging from the hotel dining room later that evening, a hotel servant came up to her with a sealed note on a salver. Quickly skimming the few brief lines in the bold, slashing handwriting, Sabrina reached into her reticule, handing the servant a coin as she asked, "Where is the gentleman? In the front parlor? Thank you."

She walked down the corridor, remembering at the

last moment to walk with a faint limp as she entered the parlor. Jareth Tremayne was standing at the fireplace, leaning against the mantel. He straightened when she came into the room, his eyes kindling at the sight of her in the green gown and elegant fringed shawl of Lyons silk, with a wreath of tiny white roses in her tawny hair.

"Good evening, Lord Jareth," she said, remembering to tinge her voice with the charming echoes of Vienna. "Your note said that you had some property of mine?"

"I do. Here it is. You left your glove in my curricle this afternoon."

"Oh, is that where — I thought I might have lost it in the park," exclaimed Sabrina, lying smoothly. She had carefully dropped the glove on the floor of the curricle before getting out at the hotel. She took the fawn-colored leather glove from Jareth's hand and put it into her reticule. "Thank you. I'm sorry you were put to this trouble," she said with a slight, dignified inclination of her head, and turned to go.

"One moment, Countess. Would you care to attend the opera with me tomorrow evening? It's Catalani in *Semiramide*."

Sabrina twirled around, exclaiming delightedly, "Catalani? I adore her voice. I once heard her sing in Vienna." She cut herself short, saying primly, "It's kind of you to invite me, but I can't accept."

"Why not?" Jareth walked over to her, his easy confident smile indicating clearly that he regarded her refusal as the next move in a flirtatious chess game.

Sabrina took a quick breath. This was the critical point at which her plan could go awry before it was well started. She'd been walking a tightrope, snaring Jareth's interest and tantalizing him into an acquaintance by acting unconventionally, even a little scandalously. Now she must suggest to him that she was merely a naive and inexperienced girl, not a lightskirt ripe to fall into his bed.

"Why not attend the opera with you?" She looked at him reproachfully. "Because it wouldn't be proper. We haven't been formally introduced, and people might talk."

Raising an eyebrow, he observed coolly, "I daresay the people who saw you drive down St. James's Street today are already talking."

Widening her eyes at him, Sabrina exclaimed, "Oh, dear, my abigail had the right of it. She told me ladies don't drive phaetons in London. Was it so very bad of me?"

Jareth seemed somewhat taken aback. "Not the phaeton, no, though respectable females usually don't drive high flyers. However, ladies who value their reputations never appear unescorted on St. James's Street in the afternoon."

Sinking into a chair, the picture of woe, Sabrina stared down at the carpet. "I didn't know—then I've disgraced myself? Uncle Johann would be furious if he found out about it." She shook her head. "I should never have come here."

Darting a glance at Jareth out of the corner of her eye, she saw his expression change. He pulled up a chair and sat down beside her. "I can see you're distressed, ma'am," he said quietly. "Will you let me help? This Uncle Johann, for example. You sounded frightened when you spoke of him."

"Oh, no, not frightened," protested Sabrina. "That is, not exactly. He won't like what I'm doing, of course, but I didn't see why I shouldn't see a little of the world before—"

Jareth interrupted her. "My dear Countess, are you a runaway?" he asked bluntly.

"I—" Sabrina opened her mouth and closed it again. For a moment, she stared at him, a smile threatening to

63

curve the corners of her lips. "Yes, I am," she said at last. "I daresay that makes me seem very fast."

Jareth settled back against his chair, his eyes dancing. "It's not the usual thing, certainly. Do you care to tell me about it?"

"Well, now that you've guessed—" Sabrina turned to him as if she were relieved to be rid of a guilty secret. "You see, Uncle Johann became my guardian after my parents' death. After my husband died, Uncle brought me to Paris."

"You're a widow?" blurted Jareth.

"Yes, my husband was the Count Dohenyi, a Hungarian. A very rich Hungarian. I fancy that's why Uncle Johann wanted me to marry him, even though the count was an old man, really. We were quite poor."

"Did—were you married long? You seem very young."

"I'm twenty," replied Sabrina, blithely lopping a year off her age. "No, I wasn't married long at all. The poor count, he had a heart attack as we were walking out of the church, and he died that same day, leaving me a wealthy widow. So then Uncle Johann decided I should marry his son Stefan."

"To keep the money in the family, no doubt," said Jareth, a hard edge to his voice.

"Oh, of course. After all, Stefan and I had always been good friends, and with a wealthy wife he could expect to advance in his diplomatic career. He's First Secretary at the Paris embassy now."

"Which is why Uncle Johann brought you to Paris. And then you decided to run away to London."

"Yes." Sabrina sighed deeply. "I woke up one morning, and I got to thinking that I hadn't ever done one thing that hadn't been planned for me by someone else, and after I married Stefan it would be more of the same. So I had Lotte pack a bag for me and we sneaked out of the house and caught the diligence to Boulogne and the packet to Dover."

"Just like that?" Jareth broke into a chuckle.

"Yes, just like that."

He chuckled again. "How long will you stay in London?"

"Not more than a few weeks. I do love Uncle Johann, you know, and I don't want to worry him more than necessary. And besides," Sabrina added candidly, "this is a very expensive hotel and it's eating up my funds."

Jareth leaned across the space between them, extending his hand. "My offer stands. I'd love to show you London."

After a moment's hesitation, Sabrina put her hand in his. "Thank you. I know I'll enjoy it immensely. It will be a little like Cinderella, you know? When the ball is over, I'll have to return to Paris!"

Chapter Four

Sabrina smoothed the skirt of her open robe of white muslin sprigged with coral and thought with satisfaction that her dressmaker had accomplished wonders in updating the two-year-old gown. The filmy ruffles of mull muslin, laid on full, made the dress seem like new, and Madame Manet has used a scrap of leftover material to create a tiny spencer of coral-colored silk that put an elegant finishing touch to the costume. With a touch of surprise, Sabrina realized she was enjoying wearing pretty clothes again after so many months of hiding behind her widow's weeds.

Moving to her dressing table, she watched Lotte in the mirror as the abigail skillfully twisted her mistress's mass of tawny hair into a graceful twist at the top of her head. The corners of Lotte's mouth were curving downward, and she was unusually silent.

"Aren't you feeling well this morning, Lotte?"

"There's nothing wrong with my health, *meine Frau*."

"Well, something's amiss, that's plain enough."

"*That's* true, only it's nothing to do with me."

"Oh? What, then?"

"Now, don't you play the innocent with me," Lotte sniffed, jamming on Sabrina's head a deep-brimmed French bonnet trimmed with coral-colored satin ribbon and a large bunch of spring flowers. "You know you shouldn't be gallivanting about London with this Lord Jareth. You don't know anything about him. Why, he may be a man of loose morals. Even if he isn't, you could hardly blame him for attempting to take liberties with a female he hasn't been properly introduced to — especially a female who's posing as the Viennese widow of a Hungarian count!" She bit off her final words with considerable venom.

Sabrina said calmly, "But Lord Jareth really isn't a stranger. I know a great deal about him. He's one of the most talked-about men in London, and a member of a distinguished family in Sussex. A perfect gentleman, too. Look how helpful he was yesterday."

"When you pretended to sprain your ankle, *nicht wahr?* I remember it very well, *meine Frau,* and I also recall the expression on that man's face every time he looked at you. Like a hungry wolf." Lotte stepped back, her mouth set mulishly. "I think I should go along with you. *I'll* make sure this Lord Jareth keeps his place."

"Oh, don't be ridiculous, Lotte. Lord Jareth has no designs on my virtue." Sabrina paused. Was she so sure of the purity of Jareth's motives? True, he'd apparently been taken in by her masquerade as an unsophisticated foreign innocent who broke the rules of English society because she didn't know any better, but perhaps it wouldn't do any harm to reinforce the image he had of her?

"Oh, very well, Lotte, come along if you really think I need a chaperon," Sabrina grumbled. "I daresay Mama would agree with you. She keeps drumming into poor Daphne's head how careful a young lady must be of her reputation."

Lotte stared at Sabrina suspiciously. The victory had been entirely too easy. The abigail knew, better than most, how stubborn and self-confident her mistress could be. "H'mph," Lotte grunted, but said no more as she went to the wardrobe for her bonnet and shawl.

A little later, waiting with Lotte in the parlor of the Pulteney, Sabrina was chatting casually with the lady sitting next to her, a fellow resident of the hotel, when Lord Jareth entered the room, pausing in the doorway to raise his quizzing glass as he glanced carelessly around at the occupants of the parlor.

"My dear," Sabrina's new acquaintance twittered excitedly, "do you see that gentleman who just came in? I do believe he's the famous Lord Jareth Tremayne. He was pointed out to me once when I was driving in Hyde Park. He's the friend of the Regent, you know, and of Mr. Brummell, too. My son John calls him an 'out-and-outer, a Trojan.' John says everyone expects his lordship to replace the Beau as the leader of the *ton*. My, he *is* a handsome man, don't you agree?"

"Indeed," Sabrina said shortly. "Will you excuse me, please?" Rising, Sabrina crossed the room to Jareth. Out of the corner of her eye she caught the stunned expression on the face of the lady with whom she'd been chatting. Later, when she recovered from her surprise, the lady would no doubt delight in telling her son John that she'd talked to a friend of the famous Lord Jareth Tremayne.

"Good morning, Countess." Straightening from his bow, he looked down at her with an appreciative glint in his eyes. "Will you permit me to tell you how charming you look today? That color is very becoming."

"Thank you, Lord Tre—Lord Jareth." Sabrina made a deliberate effort to accentuate her slight Viennese accent. Lord Jareth was looking very elegant himself, she noted, in his biscuit-colored pantaloons and flawlessly fitting coat of dark gray and his modish blue and white striped waistcoat of twill jean.

"Shall we go?" Jareth glanced past her to Lotte, who

had come up to stand beside Sabrina with the air of a mastiff guarding a particularly choice bone. He looked at Sabrina inquiringly.

"Lotte insists on accompanying us," Sabrina said apologetically. Lowering her voice, she added, "I fear I must ask you to humor her. She's not just a servant, she's more like a foster mother, and she worries about my— my safety in this strange foreign city."

Jareth studied Sabrina thoughtfully. The expression on his lean, sharply planed face was unreadable, but she wondered with a shade of disquiet if those keen, rather cynical eyes were seeing right through her glib invention. However, he said merely, "Please believe I'm thinking only of your comfort. Have you considered that a curricle was designed to hold no more than two passengers?"

Sabrina beamed. "Oh, I'm sure we'll manage very well. Recall, we all fit into your carriage quite snugly yesterday."

He bowed again. "Then I'm quite at your disposal, naturally."

Snug was hardly the word for it, Sabrina thought some minutes later. It was one thing to crowd three people into a curricle to ride the short distance between Hyde Park and the Pulteney Hotel. It was quite another to endure such close quarters for a much longer drive. She ended by perching uneasily on a slim wedge in the center of the seat between Jareth and Lotte. More than once when she glanced sideways at Jareth she glimpsed a twitch in his cheek that betrayed his secret amusement. All he said, however, was, "Are you sure you aren't too crowded, ma'am?"

"Thank you, I'm quite comfortable," replied Sabrina, resisting the impulse to sit on Lotte's ample lap.

His strong hands controlling his powerful team with deceptive ease, Jareth swung the curricle into the tree-lined avenue of Constitution Hill. As they drove beside the walled gardens of Buckingham Palace, he asked, "Well, now, Countess, have you thought what sights you might like to see on our excursion this morning?"

"I understand the Emperor Napoleon's traveling carriage is on display at the Egyptian Hall. And what about Madame Tussaud's waxworks?"

"Mein Herr, could we go see the lunatics at Bedlam?" Lotte chimed in unexpectedly.

Jareth shot the abigail a faintly pained glance. "I've never considered the lunatics a suitable subject for a young gentlewoman's tender eyes," he said gently. "Madame Tussaud is, I believe, touring the provinces with her exhibition at present. As to Napoleon's carriage — do you have a pressing desire to see it today, Countess? Frankly, what I had in mind was to show you some of our grand London public buildings. But, of course, if you'd prefer to do something else —"

"Not at all," Sabrina exclaimed hastily. "I'm sure we'll enjoy what you've planned for us."

It seemed that Jareth fancied churches. A great many of them, scattered through central London. He led Sabrina and Lotte through St. Clement Danes, St. Mary-le-Strand, St. Paul's Cathedral, St. Margaret Pattens. In Westminster Abbey he insisted on showing them, not only the royal graves and memorials, but also all eleven chapels around the choir and the Cloister and the Chapter House for good measure.

After several hours of this ecclesiastical tour, Sabrina was beginning to eye Jareth with mounting suspicion, and Lotte, who was little used to walking, was showing signs of wilting. As Jareth ushered them under the lofty arches of the entrance to the Royal Academy in the Strand block of Somerset House, Lotte murmured plaintively, "Will there be much walking?"

"No, no, a short distance only; just through this vestibule here and into the salon," he assured her.

Which was true enough, after a fashion. No great amount of walking was necessary to see the hundreds of pictures on display, but the salon was crowded with art lovers, children, and assorted noisy dogs, making any movement difficult and impeding the view of the paintings, which had been hung haphazardly from floor to ceiling height. Lotte was soon reduced to a condition of numb endurance, hanging heavily on Sabrina's arm.

"Tell me, what do you think of this picture, Countess?" asked Jareth, when they had pressed through the crowd to stand in front of a lovely tranquil landscape depicting a rippling brook meandering past a countryman's cottage. He waited expectantly. Sabrina had the odd feeling that he was putting her to some kind of test.

"I like it," said Sabrina after a long moment's inspection. "It's beautiful but restful. And such a nice change from all those paintings of wild mountain chasms and assorted ruins."

A smile flashed across Jareth's face. "I hoped you'd say that. This picture was painted by Constable. He's not as appreciated now as he should be. Most people prefer those wild Italian mountain landscapes. For some reason I can't fathom, there's a passion nowadays for artificial ruins."

With a last admiring look at the painting, Jareth consulted the watch he plucked from the tiny pocket at his waistline, saying, "By Jove, it's not as late as I thought. We'll visit the Tower before we refresh ourselves with an ice at Gunther's." He smiled down at Lotte. "I think you'll enjoy the Tower," he said enthusiastically. "There's so much to see there — the Mint, the Armory, the Crown Jewels, the zoo. You'll like the zoo. They have lions, tigers, wolves, even hyenas. Fancy that: hyenas!"

Averting her eyes, Lotte muttered belligerently to herself in German.

"I'm so sorry, Lord Jareth," said Sabrina. "Lotte doesn't wish to go to the Tower. She's very tired. Too much walking, I think."

"But what about the hyenas? Do you have hyenas in Austria?"

"I have no idea," said Sabrina firmly. "I don't know anything about Hungarian hyenas, either. You've been very kind, Lord Jareth, showing us the sights, but I think we should return to the hotel now. Perhaps we could see the hyenas another day."

Jareth struck his hand to his forehead. "But of course. We'll start back at once. It was thoughtless of me not to realize Lotte was tiring." He took Lotte's arm as they walked out of the gallery to the street and helped her tenderly into the curricle. When they arrived at the Pulteney he put out his hand to assist her from the carriage and walked her into the foyer of the hotel. "Are you sure you can manage the stairs by yourself, Lotte?" he asked solicitously. "I'd be happy to assist you to the Countess's rooms."

"*Ja, danke, mein Herr,* I'll be fine now." Lotte's usually stolid face was wreathed in a smile of blissful appreciation at Jareth's attentions. She turned away to climb the staircase.

Sabrina murmured, "You didn't fool me for an instant, you know."

Jareth's handsome face was blank. "I beg your pardon?"

"Oh, come now, you must take me for a cloth-head." Sabrina made a mental note to avoid using slang terms that a Vienesse newcomer wouldn't be likely to know. She hoped Jareth hadn't noticed her slip. Hastily she went on: "You deliberately set out to bore Lotte to tears, and to run her off her legs, too."

"You mean Lotte wasn't interested in the churches or the paintings?" Jareth asked innocently. He pursed his lips. "Perhaps Lotte wouldn't have become so weary if we'd taken her to view the lunatics at Bedlam."

Biting her lip to keep from laughing, Sabrina scolded, "You were trying to discourage poor Lotte from accompanying us on our next excursion."

"I plead guilty at the bar," said Jareth, his eyes dancing. "Are you going to punish me, Countess?"

"You certainly deserve some punishment. It was a dreadful thing to do. Poor Lotte!"

He cocked his head. "So dreadful you've decided not to continue with our excursions?"

"Well . . . perhaps not that dreadful."

"You relieve my mind. Tonight, for example, I thought we might have supper at Vauxhall Gardens." He paused invitingly.

After a moment's consideration, Sabrina said demurely, "That sounds interesting."

"Splendid. Now, then, do you really think it's necessary in the future to take Lotte along with us for your protection? I'm not an ogre, you know. I don't bite."

Sabrina met his eyes, with the lurking laughter in their depths, and chuckled. "Certainly I wouldn't want to see Lotte worn to a nubbin from her exertions. And as far as transportation is concerned, you were right about the design of a curricle. It was never meant to hold more than two people!"

In the event, Sabrina was a passenger that evening, not in the curricle, but in Jareth's trim town carriage. "Did your dragon object very much to being left behind tonight?" Jareth asked as they drove across Westminster Bridge.

"No, I think Lotte was too tired to object. She also seems to have lost her fears that you're a ravening ogre."

Jareth laughed. "Your abigail has a discerning eye."

Dusk was falling as their coachman drove the carriage down a narrow lane to stop in front of the unprepossessing porched entrance to a small building abutting on the lane. As she and Jareth passed through the doorway into the gardens, Sabrina drew a sharp breath at the contrast between the drab darkness of the lane and what seemed like a fairyland ahead of her. The buildings and paths of the park were illuminated by the flickering gleam of thousands of lamps and colored transparencies festooned among the trees and shrubbery. To her left was a magnificently curving arcade and in the large open space to her right there was an ornate Gothic pavilion, surrounded by a large crowd of people, where an orchestra was playing one of Mr. Haydn's symphonies.

"It's beautiful, Lord Jareth," Sabrina murmured.

"Yes, darkness hides a multitude of sins. The park in broad daylight looks a bit shabby, I'm told. The place isn't what it was in its prime, back in the days when the Regent was adored as the young and beautiful Prince Florizel. However, I hope we'll have a very pleasant evening. Shall we walk for a bit before we have supper?"

Strolling along a graveled, tree-bordered walk with Jareth, her hand tucked into his arm, Sabrina soon lapsed into a dreamlike state comprised of drifting moonlight, the insidious fragrance of blossoming spring shrubs, the sparkle of lamps swaying gently in the soft breeze — and a growing physical awareness of the man who walked beside her. She sensed the sinewy strength of the arm beneath her fingers, and she caught the faint whiff of freshly laundered linen mingled with the indefinable enticing scent of a healthy and faultlessly groomed male.

"We haven't walked too far, Countess? You're not tired?"

"Oh, no. I feel light as air, almost as if I'm floating," Sabrina sighed. In the next moment she stumbled when she tripped on a large rock. Instantly Jareth put an arm around her waist to steady her, and she could feel a thousand electric sparks shooting through her bloodstream. Slipping from his hold, she said breathlessly, "Why are some of the paths so dark? Surely the management could spare a few extra lanterns to prevent folk from losing their way."

Catching her hand to tuck it under his arm again, Jareth paused in front of the entrance to one of the darkened paths. From its depths they could hear the sounds of scuffling bodies and smothered giggles. Jareth laughed, saying, "I fancy most people who use these paths *want* to lose their way. If you like, we could walk in there a short distance to prove my point."

"Oh, no," said Sabrina hastily. "I'll take your word for it."

"Then if you've had your fill of walking, shall we have supper? I'm feeling quite ravenous."

They ate in a private box decorated with paintings of nymphs cavorting in an idealized countryside. The box, one of many occupying alcoves around the perimeter of the main enclosure, faced the orchestra pavilion. An attentive waiter brought a bottle of champagne, and as Jareth reached over to fill Sabrina's glass he said, "What can I tempt you to eat? Some chicken? A bit of roast beef? A pastry or two and a slice of pineapple? One delicacy you must taste—the famous thin-sliced Vauxhall ham. And a glass of their Arrack punch too, of course."

After they'd ordered and the waiter returned with their food, Jareth asked, "Well? Does the ham live up to its reputation?"

Sabrina chewed a piece of the ham slowly. "Mm. It's quite good. And very thin."

"The management boasts that you can read a newspaper through a slice of their ham. One enterprising wagster a few years back decided to see if he could cover the entire surface of the gardens from one thinly sliced joint."

"And did he?"

Jareth paused in the act of lifting a forkful of roast beef to his mouth. "I really don't know," he said after a moment's thought. "It seems a rather caper-witted thing to do, in any event. A little like Brummell betting a crony that 'a certain person would die before another certain person.'"

"Were you that crony?"

Jareth raised an eyebrow.

Careful, Sabrina thought. I'm not supposed to know anything about the *ton*. "One of the ladies at the hotel mentioned you were a friend of Beau Brummell, so I wondered."

"It's true, I was a friend of the Beau, but I never make foolish bets," said Jareth coolly. "I always expect to win."

"Oh. Do you gamble a great deal, Lord Jareth?"

He poured himself a second glass of champagne. "I do. I regard it as a profession of sorts, and I do very well at it. Here in England, as you may not know, younger sons get short shrift with the family purse strings. We poor souls must earn our livelihoods as best we can. I earn mine at the tables."

Some of the magic evaporated from Sabrina's evening. She looked at her companion's smiling, assured face and thought, poor Adrian, he hadn't been a person to Jareth, only a source of income. She wondered if Jareth had paused for even one second to consider whether Adrian could afford to play for such high stakes. Reaching for a glass of Arrack punch, she drank half of it before she remembered that she had never cared for the taste of the potent mixture of rice, molasses, and coconut.

"You've turned very quiet, Countess," Jareth observed a little later.

Sabrina managed a smile. She couldn't afford to allow her feelings to interfere with her plans to rescue Adrian.

"I'm enjoying the music," she said brightly. "That young woman has a lovely voice."

Jareth turned his eyes toward the orchestra pavilion, where a pretty girl stood in one of the upper boxes singing a popular air. "Eliza Vestris," he nodded. "She'll go far, I think. All London is humming that song of hers, 'Cherry Ripe.' " Reaching across the table for Sabrina's hand, he held it in a loose grasp, saying, "We have more important matters to discuss."

"Indeed, Lord Jareth? What important matters?" The touch of his hand seemed to be conducting some kind of current between them that made her nerve ends dance on the surface of her skin.

"Well, this very formal way we've been addressing each other, for one thing. Won't you call me plain Jareth? And I'll call you . . ." He paused, looking foolish. "I can't believe I've been such a slow-top—I don't know your Christian name."

"It's Sabrina."

"Sabrina. Sabrina. It's beautiful, like you. Do I have your permission to use it?"

"Why not?" But she slipped her hand away from his, picking up her glass. "Could I have a little more champagne?"

Watching her over the rim of his glass, he said, "Tell me more about your Uncle Johann."

"Uncle Jo—" For a split second Sabrina panicked. Mention of her imaginary uncle had drawn a complete blank. She'd have to be on her guard in the future to remember all the details of the tale she'd invented. "What about Uncle Johann?"

"Well, do you expect him to come flying across the Channel, breathing fire and brimstone as he prepares to force you back to Paris?"

"N—no. Why should he?"

"You didn't leave a note telling him you were going to

London?"

Sabrina stared at him. "Why would I do anything as shatter-brained as that?"

Chuckling, Jareth replied, "Perhaps because you're a dutiful niece and you wouldn't wish to worry your old uncle?"

"Duty is one thing, and idiocy quite another," Sabrina shot back.

Jareth sank back in his seat, laughing so hard he could barely speak. Finally, he managed, "Dear Sabrina, I just wanted to be sure your loving uncle wouldn't arrive to snatch you away from me before I had a chance to know you better." He lifted the bottle of champagne, observing with a slight frown that it was empty, and motioned to a hovering waiter.

When their glasses had been replenished, Jareth inquired, "How long has your uncle been your guardian?"

"Oh . . . for many years. Since I was a small child." Sabrina realized she should have given more thought to her background story. For lack of preparation, she might give herself away with conflicting details. At the moment, however, her brain didn't seem to be functioning very well. She'd had one glass too many of champagne, that was it, and the Arrack punch, too, was adding its toll. And it didn't help that Jareth had moved his chair much closer to her. She found his nearness very distracting.

"Did you have anything to say about your marriage to a much older man?" Jareth asked.

"I—no. Why should I? It was Uncle Johann's duty to provide for me. Don't English parents arrange the marriages of their children?" Sabrina asked innocently.

"Oh, to some extent, I daresay. A match must be suitable, naturally. I think we allow for personal preferences, though."

"You mean a marriage for love? Uncle always said

such matches were bourgeois."

"I see." Jareth cleared his throat. "So you had no feelings for your husband? And what about this cousin your uncle now wants you to marry? Do you like him?"

"Why—I hardly knew my husband. We were never alone before the wedding, and then, as I told you, he collapsed as we were leaving the church. As for my cousin, he's always been like an older brother to me." As if she felt a sudden embarrassment, Sabrina lowered her eyes. "I don't think you should be asking me these questions, Lord Jareth," she said primly. *He's jealous,* she thought with a catch of excitement.

"I beg your pardon, Sabrina, it's just that . . ." Jareth moved his chair even closer. She could feel the hard muscles of his thigh through the gossamer thinness of her gown. "Haven't you ever wondered about love? Haven't you ever wanted this . . . ?" Slipping his arm around her, Jareth cupped her chin with his free hand. Slowly he lowered his head, brushing his lips against hers in fleeting mothlike kisses until her mouth opened beneath his lips like the petals of a flower and a quicksilver shiver of desire rippled through her body.

"Here, now, my good man, you're never going to keep this dressy bit of muslin to yourself, are you?" At the sound of the loud, jocular voice, Sabrina pulled herself away from Jareth, her face flaming.

The man standing in front of them was young and fashionably dressed, though the waistline of his coat was so pinched in that he resembled a pouter pigeon, and his starched shirt points were so high that he could move his head only with difficulty. A strong odor of gin wafted from his person.

Rising leisurely, Jareth surveyed the man through his quizzing glass. As the slow, deliberate moments dragged by, the stranger seemed gradually to shrink under that glacial stare. At last Jareth lowered the quizzing glass

79

and drawled in a voice tinged with polite surprise, "I believe you have the advantage of me, sir. Do I know you?"

His face reddening, the man said defensively, "No offense meant. The thing was, I saw the doxy was acting downright friendly with you, and I thought . . ."

In a fluid lunge, Jareth grabbed the stranger's cravat, twisting it sharply. "Neither I nor the *young lady* — particularly the young lady — have any desire to be friends with you. Do you think you can remember that?"

"Yes. Let go," gasped the man. Jareth released his iron clutch and the man staggered back, his eyes widening. "I know you. I saw you box once at Gentleman Jackson's. You're —"

"It's immaterial who I am, or who you think I am. Good night, sir." As the man stumbled off, Jareth sat down beside Sabrina in the box, his face grim. "I apologize for subjecting you to that. I should never have brought you to Vauxhall Gardens. Any riff or raff with the price of a ticket can come here. I should have known that some drunken cit would make a scene." He paused, looking at her with a twisted smile. "A scene that was mostly my fault. I shouldn't have kissed you in public, much as I enjoyed it. It simply whetted that loose fish's appetite for mischief. The fact is, Sabrina, it behooves a lady of quality like you to think twice before being escorted about town by a rogue like me. That damned cit won't be the last person to assume you're a lightskirt because you're seen alone in my company. Perhaps you'd be wiser to pack up your portmanteau and fly back to Paris and Uncle Johann!"

It would definitely be wiser — and safer — to fly back to Sussex and Latimer House, Sabrina mused. She'd known it was going to be difficult to maintain a precarious balance between unworldly innocence and ladylike allure. What she hadn't counted on was Jareth Tremayne's sheer physical appeal. She thought back to the first time Oliver had kissed her. Pleasant, tender, mildly exciting. Nothing like the incendiary flame that Jareth's lips had ignited. She couldn't allow it to mean anything. She'd managed to retrieve control of her life from the wreckage of her marriage to Oliver. She wasn't going to risk her independence a second time to the enslaving chains of love. From now on, she'd keep Jareth at arms' length.

"Well?" His voice broke through her musings. "Have you heeded my warning? One that I made very reluctantly, by the way! Will Uncle Johann be greeting his runaway niece in the near future?"

She smiled at him. "You promised to show me London. I haven't seen it yet."

"Be it on your own head, then. You can't say I didn't try," said Jareth lightly. His fingers gave him away. Wrapped like a vice around the stem of his wine glass, they relaxed instantly at Sabrina's decision to stay in London.

When Sabrina returned to her rooms in the Pulteney that evening, she found Lotte peacefully asleep in a chair in the sitting room.

"Wake up, Lotte. See for yourself that Lord Jareth has returned me safely in one piece."

Slowly blinking herself awake, Lotte muttered, "I never had any doubts about the Herr after he treated me so kindly this afternoon. He's a fine gentleman, *meine Frau.* You're in no danger from him."

Perhaps not, thought Sabrina. *Perhaps the danger is in myself.*

Chapter Five

The next morning, Lotte seemed only mildly disturbed when she was told she wouldn't be accompanying Sabrina on her outing with Jareth, although the abigail couldn't refrain from saying, "Mind, I still don't think it looks proper for you to gad about alone in the Herr's company, even if he is such a fine gentleman. Mark my words, it'll be billows to mend with us if the Lady Latimer finds out what you're up to."

"Bellows, Lotte. Bellows to mend," replied Sabrina with a gurgle of laughter. "If you're going to quote Adrian's slang, please do it accurately. And don't worry about me. I plan to be very discreet."

Lotte put up no further objections, but Sabrina suspected the abigail's retreat from her notions of strict propriety was due only partly to her softened attitude toward Jareth. Her change of heart probably owed even more to the narrow dimensions of his curricle seat and her strong aversion to exercise.

In the days that followed, Sabrina occasionally wondered when or if Jareth gave a thought to the other concerns in his life. He was constantly in her company, in a succession of lovely, bright days and balmy evenings. Later she was to recall the delightful weather with nostalgia when it became evident that the year 1816 had produced the worst weather in living memory, except for that brief shining stretch in the month of May.

Under Jareth's expert guidance, Sabrina began to explore London. They joined the crowds in the cramped temporary wooden shed at Montague House to admire the Parthenon marbles that Lord Elgin had recently brought back from Greece. They visited the Royal Exchange with its piazza where the colorfully dressed traders from many nations cheerfully haggled and concluded bargains with each other. They even enjoyed the hospitality of one of the big London breweries, where they were treated to a large steak broiled on a shovel and washed down with a pint of the proprietor's "best entire." Sabrina happily informed Jareth the beer was nearly as good as the Viennese version.

In the evenings when they didn't drive into the countryside to dine at a quiet inn, they went to the theater. They shivered through Edmund Kean's performance as Shylock at Drury Lane, watched respectfully as John Kemble thundered his way through *Coriolanus* at Covent Garden, and thrilled to Elizabeth Billington's beautiful voice at the Royal Italian Opera House.

"You know, Sabrina, I feel more at home here than I do at the patent theaters," murmured Jareth one evening as they sat in a box at the Sadler's Wells theater, nestled among the poplar trees on the outskirts of the hilltop village of Islington. "I must have low tastes, I suppose, but I *like* pantomime and farce and acrobats and acts like that Red Indian Chief down there throwing his tomahawk—you won't see anything like *that* at Covent Garden these days!"

Sabrina tried to imagine the stately actor-manager John Kemble taking part in the Indian war dance that had just been performed on the stage below her, and began to laugh so hard that tears came to her eyes.

Poking her in the ribs, Jareth whispered reprovingly,

83

"Shush, you'll disturb the lad's concentration."

Holding her breath, Sabrina glued her eyes on the little boy—ten years old, at the most—who was walking a tightrope from the stage to the upper gallery, holding a sparkling pinwheel in either hand and treading the rope as lightly as if he were strolling along the Strand. When the child had walked safely down again, she slowly expelled her breath, belatedly realizing she'd been clutching Jareth's arm in an agony of suspense. He turned his face toward her, his arm tensing under her touch, and she could sense rather than see in the semidarkness of the box the tiny flicker of flame at the back of his eyes.

Withdrawing her hand, she edged her chair slightly away from him. During these past few days—was it really almost two weeks since she'd contrived to meet Jareth in Hyde Park?—she'd done her best to evade physical contact with him, except for the unavoidable support of his strong slender fingers when he helped her in or out of his carriage. To her relief, he hadn't attempted to kiss her again since their evening at Vauxhall Gardens, but she was constantly aware of the controlled sensual tension beneath his smiling mask. More than ever she was grateful for her invented alter ego, the virginal Viennese widow. Sabrina was convinced that the Countess Dohenyi's untouched virtue was largely responsible for Jareth's remarkable restraint.

She turned her attention to the stage, where the curtain was rising on the evening's main diversion, a musical play or "burletta" based on *A Midsummer's Night Dream*. Covent Garden and Drury Lane were the only theaters licenced under royal patent to perform legitimate drama, but the lesser theaters had gradually succeeded in winning the right to stage prose plays, provided the production contained at least five songs in every act.

The Titania of tonight's performance was a handsome young woman with long curling blond hair streaming from beneath the garland of flowers that crowned her head. Her acting ability left something to be desired, but her clear voice rang out sweetly when she sang, "What angel wakes me from my flowery bed?" Gradually, however, it dawned on Sabrina that Titania—Sabrina consulted her program and discovered the singer's name was Maria Castanelli—was playing directly to Jareth. Frequently moving out of position on the stage to look up at his box, she delivered her songs and spoke her dialogue as if he were the only person in the audience. Sabrina couldn't observe any reaction on his face. He appeared to be watching the play with a bland enjoyment. By the third act everyone in the theater was quite aware of what Maria was doing, and her last song was disrupted by a loud, raucous noise. Turning a questioning eye toward Jareth, Sabrina found him convulsed with silent laughter.

"It's a catcall," he gasped when he could catch his breath. "A nasty little wind instrument that disgruntled theater customers use to inform actors their performances have been found wanting."

Seemingly unperturbed, Maria finished her song and later sauntered on stage for a curtain call to tepid applause. Smiling brightly, she ignored a second unpleasant blast from the catcall. Then, sinking to the floor in a graceful curtsey, she kissed both hands to Jareth, who looked back at her with a wooden face. As she was leaving the stage a young man entered the box and handed Jareth a folded note.

Hastily scanning the note, he sat in silence for several moments, thoughtfully pursing his lips. At last he said, "Will you excuse me for a moment? I won't be long, I promise."

"Don't hurry on my account," she said coolly, turning her eyes to the masked man in the parti-colored Harlequin costume who had just bounded onto the stage. "I'm looking forward to seeing this man Ellar's act. Didn't you tell me he may rival the great Grimaldi?"

"Indeed. I'm sure you'll pass your time most enjoyably until I return," Jareth said noncommittally.

After he left, Sabrina tried to watch the closing pantomime, but not even the Harlequin's final soaring leap through a window could hold her attention. Perversely, her mind kept wandering to Jareth and what she presumed was his visit to the greenroom to see Maria Castanelli. It must have been crystal clear to everyone in the theater that the actress hadn't picked Jareth out of the audience by blind chance. They had to be old acquaintances, *very* old and close acquaintances. For a moment Sabrina felt an illogical flash of resentment. How dare Jareth bring her to Sadler's Wells to watch his doxy throwing out lures to him! She'd have thought he had better taste, or at least more consideration for her feelings.

Almost immediately she abandoned her anger. Probably Jareth couldn't have anticipated Maria's blatantly obvious behavior. In any case, his private life was none of Sabrina's affair. And within a few days, say a week at most, she'd be leaving London, her mission accomplished, and the chances were good that she'd never see him again. By the time Jareth returned to the box, as the actors were taking their final curtain calls, Sabrina had recovered her composure. Her glance skimmed over the scratch on his cheek and the disheveled state of his expertly tied cravat, but all she said was, "You missed a brilliant performance."

He shrugged. "Another time, perhaps." Picking up her jewel-hued silk scarf, he draped it around her shoulders. "Shall we go?"

They walked across the rustic bridge spanning the little stream that ran beside the theater and stepped into their waiting carriage. As the town chariot swung into the New Road, Jareth broke what was fast becoming an awkward silence. "A little tetchy with me, Sabrina?"

"Why, no. Should I be?"

"Don't play games, Countess."

Sabrina heard the note of suppressed amusement in Jareth's voice and had a sudden urge to hit him. "I wasn't aware I was playing games," she said icily.

Her blood ran cold when he said with a note of surprise, "Do you realize you seem to lose some of your accent when you're angry? I wonder why that is?"

Sabrina tried to read his expression in the dim light from the carriage lamps and failed. She forced herself into a playfulness she didn't feel. "If I speak better English when I'm angry, perhaps I should lose my temper more often!"

"You admit it, then? You *were* angry?"

"Yes," she snapped, before she could stop herself. "I like to be treated with common courtesy. If you wanted to see your actress friend, why did you bring me along?"

"I'll be happy to explain what happened if you'll let me. Will you?"

"I—there's no need . . . Yes."

"Well, then, I didn't have the faintest desire to see Maria tonight—incidentally, her real name is Emma Stokes. It's all the crack these days in the theater to have an Italian name. She wasn't supposed to play Titania in this performance. There was an illness in the cast. After she made a cake of herself by overplaying so outrageously to me, I thought it was only fair to tell her—that is to say, I went to the greenroom to—oh, damnation, Sabrina, I don't know how else to say it without appearing loose in the shaft. I told Maria I was cutting the acquaintance."

Jareth had begun his account with his usual languid poise. He ended by sounding so harried, so uncharacteristically unsure of himself, so *young*, that Sabrina was immediately reminded of Adrian, and her fit of pique melted away. "The young lady didn't take your news very kindly, I gather," she observed, a ripple of amusement in her voice.

She could feel Jareth stiffen beside her in the half-darkness, and for a moment she expected a glacial retort. It had probably been a long time since someone had ventured to make fun of him. Then he began to laugh. "Don't tell me you noticed this scratch on my face and the damage to my cravat. My valet will have a fit of the vapors when he sees Maria's handiwork. His reputation will be in tatters. He prides himself on the impression I give to the world."

"His reputation may be quite safe. Perhaps nobody in the *ton* was present in the theater tonight."

"One can always hope." After a brief pause, Jareth said, "I'm sorry if I embarrassed you, Sabrina."

"Not at all. I enjoyed the evening very much, Jareth."

"I, too."

They rode in companionable silence for a while. Once Jareth groped for her hand, then apparently thought better of it. When they were making the turn into the Edgeware Road he said, "Have you given any thought to what you'd like to do tomorrow?"

"No. You always seem to come up with something interesting. There is one thing, though: I'm beginning to feel a little guilty for absorbing so much of your time. Surely you must have business matters that need attending to occasionally?"

"Nothing as important as you." The remark seemed to come out of his mouth involuntarily, shocking him into a momentary stillness. He cleared his throat. "Sabrina, a friend has asked me to dinner tomorrow night. Will you come with me?"

Sabrina felt petrified. This was the first time he'd invited her to meet his friends. In a way, it was flattering. It proved that he'd put her in a class apart from the little actress at Sadler's Wells. It was also dangerous. Until now, being in his company only in public places, she'd felt comfortable, unafraid that she might be unmasked. Since she had never had a London Season, and had been out of the country for several years, she was a stranger to the *ton*, and they to her. But anything might happen in a small private gathering of people close to Jareth. There she'd have to be constantly mindful of her fictitious identity among a group of people who would certainly not be as blindly well-disposed to her as Jareth was. One slip of the tongue could give her away.

"Will you come with me, Sabrina? Lady Melbourne is a very dear and old friend, though she's not very well these days. She's Lady Caroline Lamb's mama-in-law, as you may know. I think you'd find her and her guests interesting. I know they'd like you."

That settled it. The mention of Lady Melbourne, next to Lady Holland perhaps the most prominent hostess in London, sent a chill through Sabrina's veins. Who could say whom she might encounter in the house of a woman who'd entertained all the great and near great in England? It was even remotely possible, she supposed, that someone she knew from among the county gentry in her own small corner of Sussex could be among the guests.

"Thank you, Jareth, but I must decline your invitation," she said firmly. "I didn't come to London to socialize. I came to see the sights."

"You've seen most of them," Jareth grumbled. "Soon I'll run out of inspiration."

"I doubt that. You're very resourceful. I daresay you'll easily produce enough interesting attractions to fill my remaining days here. After all, I shan't be here much longer, you know."

"I'm only too well aware of that—Sabrina, don't pitch gammon to me. It's obvious you don't want to go with me to Melbourne House, and I'd like to know the reason why."

Sabrina bit her lip in frustration. Strong-willed, accustomed to having his own way—particularly with adoring females—Jareth wouldn't accept refusal easily. She tried again. "I think you're forgetting I'm a stranger and a foreigner here, Jareth. I'd feel so out of place, not knowing anybody. . . ."

"Nonsense, you'd soon feel at home. It won't be a grand soiree, I assure you, just a small dinner party for some of Lady Melbourne's close friends. The Regent may even appear at some time during the evening, if that's any inducement."

"The Regent!" Sabrina allowed her voice to squeak with alarm. "I couldn't go to a place where I might meet the Regent. I don't have anything to wear! I came away from Paris with exactly three gowns suitable for evening occasions, and you must be weary of seeing all of them. None of them is grand enough for royalty!"

"Sabrina, don't be a peahen. Your frocks are beautiful, and you always look suitably dressed. Besides, it's Lombard Street to a China orange that Prinny would consider you the most beautiful woman in the room if you were wearing only your chemise—" He cut himself short, falling into a fit of coughing. "Sorry. Didn't mean to be indelicate," he muttered.

Sabrina suppressed a laugh. "Stop throwing the hatchet at me, Jareth," she said severely. "It's all very well for *you* to say that my gowns are becoming. *I* know I can't go to Melbourne House looking like a country cousin. I'm persuaded you wouldn't wish to see me embarrassed among all those elegantly gowned ladies."

Unexpectedly Jareth gave in. "I don't wish to see you do anything you don't want to do, Sabrina."

She stared at him suspiciously, but his expression was unreadable in the gloom of the carriage. He chattered away on inconsequential topics until they arrived at the Pulteney.

On the following afternoon, however, she discovered he hadn't given up the fight; although, when she met him in the parlor of the hotel to begin their daily excursion, it was apparent he'd been *in* a fight. He sported a large dark bruise on his cheekbone.

"What happened to you, Jareth?"

"My sparring partner tipped me a settler this morning," Jareth said cheerfully. "My own fault. I'm shockingly rusty. I haven't been spending enough time in Gentleman Jackson's salon." He cocked his head at her, grinning. "Of late, the Fancy has taken second place in my life to another interest."

"Then perhaps you'd better pay less attention to that interest and more to your pugilism," Sabrina teased. "I'd as lief not be held responsible for your injuries."

After he handed her into his curricle in front of the hotel, he turned his team northeast on Piccadilly rather than southwest in the direction of Hyde Park.

"I thought we were going to Kensington Palace," Sabrina remarked in surprise.

"You won't mind if I take care of an important errand first? We can go to the Palace later."

Sabrina eyed him curiously. It was the first time he'd given a private matter precedence over one of their outings. And his face wore an expression that seemed to combine gleeful anticipation with a touch of guilt. He looked, in fact, like a small boy who had just taken successful aim at his schoolmaster with a slingshot.

In Cranbourn Street, a short distance from Leicester Square, Jareth halted the carriage in front of a shop whose sign proclaimed, "Madame Simone, Modiste."

"Here we are, then." Tossing his reins to his tiger,

Jareth left the driver's seat and held up his hand to help Sabrina from the carriage.

She remained in her seat, looking from Jareth to the shop window, which displayed several beplumed bonnets in the latest mode. "If your important errand is with the modiste, you won't need my assistance," she said coldly. "Doubtless my taste would differ from any other lady's."

"Oh, the devil, Sabrina, I'm not interested in any other lady. I came here to buy you a gown to wear to Melbourne House tonight."

Momentarily Sabrina fell out of character, completely forgetting her pose as the unconventional Countess Dohenyi. She glared at Jareth in outrage. "Buy me a gown? You forget yourself, sir. You may purchase as many garments as you please for one of your fancy pieces, but not for me, I thank you!"

"Do you realize how lovely you are when you're angry?" Jareth countered. "And how much your English improves?"

Sabrina swallowed hard. Had she betrayed herself? But Jareth apparently had lost interest in her disappearing Viennese accent. He reached up to take one of her gloved hands, holding it firmly when she tried to snatch it away.

"Why can't I give you a gown?" he asked softly. "You never objected when I brought you a bouquet of flowers, or a packet of sugarplums from Gunther's. Why is this so different? You told me yourself that the Pulteney was very expensive, and I suspect you're not very plump in the pocket. Please, Sabrina. Let me buy you a beautiful gown and go with me to Melbourne House."

Confused and embarrassed, Sabrina glanced around her. Jareth's young tiger was standing at the horses' heads, so studiously ignoring their conversation that it was clear he wasn't missing a word, but there was no one else near them on the street. Well, what harm could it do, really, she thought. A new gown, a visit to Lady Melbourne, they were small things. Giving in to Jareth's wishes might even forward her plans. Her campaign had been based from the beginning on pleasing him, captivating him, lulling him into compliance until the decisive moment when she could strike for the kill.

Madame Simone was a large, amply endowed lady whose sharp black eyes fairly glistened when Jareth walked into her shop with a lady on his arm. *"C'est merveilleux* to see you again, Milor' Tremayne. How may I help you? A frock for *la petite,* perhaps? A bonnet, a muff, a fan? I can show you some beautiful shawls, also, just arrived from Paris."

Sabrina stifled an urge to laugh. She might as well have been invisible, for all the attention she was receiving from Madame Simone. It was quite clear whose preferences the dressmaker thought important. Jareth was obviously an old and valued customer.

Looking at Madame through his quizzing glass, Jareth said with a forbidding stiffness, "My *sister* would like to see some gowns. Of course, if you have nothing you consider suitable, we could go elsewhere."

The dressmaker's manner underwent an instant change. She curtsied deeply to Sabrina. *"Bein entendu,* Madame Tremayne, what did you have in mind? Something for the evening? A carriage dress?"

"It's the Countess Dohenyi, not Madame Tremayne," said Sabrina, trying to keep a straight face. "I need something very special for an evening affair."

"Ah." Madame Simone studied Sabrina's figure carefully. "Wait one moment, *s'il vous plaît."* The dressmaker returned with a dress draped carefully over her arm. It was made of gossamer net over a deep blue silk petticoat, trimmed with rows of delicate lace flounces caught up with tiny bouquets of roses and bluebells. "It is perfect for you, Madame, *non?* The petticoat and the little posies, they match your eyes exactly."

"Madame is right, Sabrina. It *is* your gown. Why don't you try it on?" said Jareth.

Sabrina did so and was lost. She knew she had never worn a dress that became her so well. And it fit perfectly. She didn't ask the price. It was undoubtedly more than she and Daphne and their stepmother had spent on their wardrobes for the entire year.

"Send the gown to the Countess Dohenyi's suite at the Pulteney Hotel before six this evening," Jareth instructed the dressmaker.

"*Mais oui.*" Madame Simone hesitated. "The bill, Milor'? Shall I send it to the Pulteney also?"

Jareth looked down his nose at her. "Certainly not. Put it on my account."

As she and Jareth stepped out of the shop to the street, Sabrina looked up at him, saying with a rather strained smile, "I shouldn't have allowed you to do that, Jareth. When I think of what Uncle Johann would say if he knew! I feel a bit like a kept woman." She was back in character as the Countess, but her remarks more nearly reflected her own sense of regret. She thought ahead to what she intended to do to Jareth, and suddenly her acceptance of his expensive gift made her feel little better than a common tart.

"What fustian," said Jareth roughly. "I can't abide these Friday-faced rules of conduct. Why shouldn't I be able to give you a gift?"

You know as well as I do why you shouldn't, Sabrina was about to say, when she looked over Jareth's shoulder into the eyes of a tall young man dressed in a double-breasted scarlet coatee and blue overalls, and a black and gold helmet with a black horsehair crest upon his tawny locks. As if he'd been turned into a pillar of salt, the young man stood rooted to the pavement, staring at Sabrina and Jareth in open-mouthed shock. Then an expression of outraged displeasure crossed his face, and he opened his mouth to speak. Sabrina's heart sank. *Oh, Adrian, don't be a ninnyhammer. Watch your tongue or you'll have us both at a stand.*

Jareth's eyes followed Sabrina's gaze. "Ah—Latimer, isn't it? Good day, sir."

The sound of Jareth's decisive voice caused Adrian to blink and to gulp back whatever he'd intended to say. A sudden bright color flooding his face, he mumbled, "Er . . . good afternoon, Lord Jareth."

Somewhat reluctantly, Jareth added, "Countess, may I present Lieutenant Sir Adrian Latimer? Our families are by way of being neighbors in Sussex. Latimer, this is the Countess Dohenyi."

Sabrina nodded her head slightly. "You are in the English army, Sir Latimer?"

Adrian appeared to choke. After he subdued a fit of coughing he said, "Actually, I'm in the Household Cavalry, ma'am . . . First Life Guards." At this point he seemed to have recovered his poise. Looking straight into her eyes, he said, "And you, ma'am? You're from foreign parts? Would I be wrong to guess Italy?"

One for your side, Adrian. Drawing herself up as if she'd heard something unpleasant, Sabrina said haughtily, "You would be very wrong, Sir Latimer. I am Austrian."

"I beg your pardon." Adrian bowed. There was a steely note in his voice as he said, "Charmed to meet you, Countess. I hope you enjoy your visit to London. The shopping here"—his glance flicked to the shop behind them—"the shopping here in the city is said to be very fine."

After Adrian had gone off in the direction of Leicester Square, Sabrina breathed a sigh of inward relief. "Your friend Sir Latimer seemed a very nice young man," she remarked to Jareth. "So handsome, too, in those beautiful regimentals. I do think a gentleman appears to such advantage in a uniform. I daresay Sir Latimer is considered—how do you say it in English?—a great catch by all the young ladies and their mamas?"

Casting a rather unfriendly look at Adrian's departing back, Jareth said testily, "It's not 'Sir Latimer.' You call him Sir Adrian, or Lieutenant Latimer. And no, to the best of my knowledge, he's not being pursued by eligible females."

"Oh? Why not? Such a fine-looking man. And so aristocratic." Sabrina paused. She added doubtfully, "But perhaps Sir Lat—Sir Adrian's title is like yours, Jareth, not real?"

"Oh, his baronetcy's real enough. He's not a frippery courtesy lord, like me," replied a goaded Jareth. "However, I'd advise against setting your cap for him. I understand he's under the hatches, deep in Dun territory. Certainly the young fool is the most inept gambler I've ever met—" He broke off. "Well, that's neither here nor there. Look, Sabrina, must we talk about this fellow Latimer?"

"No, of course not," said Sabrina quietly. "Tell me more about Lady Melbourne."

That evening, as Jareth handed her down from the carriage in front of the classic Ionic portico of the elegantly simple mansion near the Horse Guards, Sabrina could feel the butterflies fluttering wildly in her stomach. They walked past the bowing footman at the door into a graceful circular vestibule lit by a lantern in its shallow dome and followed another liveried servant into a spacious drawing room. It seemed to be thronged with people. "I thought you said this was to be a small party," she whispered in a panic.

"It *is* a small party. When Lady M. hosts a really big

soiree she has people clinging to the chandeliers. You can't breathe in the crush. You look beautiful, Sabrina. Not a woman here can touch you."

His murmured compliment soothed the butterflies a little, and soon she became absorbed in the personalities she met as she walked slowly through the room on Jareth's arm, being introduced to one person, chatting briefly, then moving on to another.

"Aha, the mystery is explained!" A pleasant-faced man dressed in the height of fashion pounced on Jareth, patting him jovially on the shoulder. "Now I understand why we ain't been seeing you at White's, you sly dog." He addressed a frankly admiring glance at Sabrina. "Don't be selfish, Tremayne. Make me known to the lady."

"Pay this fellow no mind, Sabrina. He never did have any manners. Countess Dohenyi, my friend Lord Alvanley."

As he grasped her hand, Alvanley looked at her even more keenly. "But I know you. You're the lady who drove that yaller phaeton up St. James's Street. I was sitting in the bow window at White's that day. It was a bang-up set-out, and you handled the ribbons like a first-rate fiddler."

"Horrors, Lord Alvanley, pray don't mention that dreadful yellow phaeton," Sabrina exclaimed, laughing. "Lord Jareth tells me I committed an unforgivable sin in driving it on St. James's Street, though I find that very difficult to understand. In Vienna, you see, one street is like any other street."

"Ah, Vienna. One of my favorite cities. We must have a tête-à-tête about it one day soon. Where are you staying?"

"That, Alvanley, is none of your affair. I don't allow poaching in my territory," said Jareth firmly. He turned his back on his grinning friend, drawing Sabrina along with him to present her to the poet Tom Moore, who

97

told her with a sunny smile that she would shortly hear him singing for his supper. He also introduced Sabrina to the young and handsome Countess Lieven, wife of the Russian ambassador, who seemed underwhelmed to meet another pretty woman, and to the rakehell Irish peer, "King" Allen.

By degrees, Jareth edged Sabrina to the far side of the drawing room, where an obese elderly woman sat in an armchair holding her court.

"Lady Melbourne, may I present the Countess Dohenyi?"

Penetrating dark eyes in the ruddled old face shot a keen glance at Sabrina. "Leave me for a bit. I want a few words with the little gal," she said peremptorily to the people around her, and when they had scattered obediently she patted the chair beside her, telling Sabrina, "Sit down, child. Jareth, we don't need you. Bring the countess some punch."

After Jareth left, Lady Melbourne grinned widely, saying, "One of the pleasures of growing old, m'dear, is the privilege of being rude. So, then, you're the foreign widow who's caught Jareth Tremayne's eye. Ah, yes," she nodded. "I don't get around much these days, but I hear things. I know he's been seen all over London in the company of a strikingly pretty woman. He's been mighty chary about sharing you with his friends, however. I wonder why?"

Sabrina realized the palms of her hands were damp. She had to fight back a sense of panic in the presence of this lady. Lady Melbourne now bore little physical resemblance to the vibrantly beautiful woman who had long queened it over London society and who was reputed to have fathered each of her six children by a different lover, but the mind and the personality were still formidable.

"Jareth Tremayne's a great favorite of mine," her ladyship went on. "I've often thought, if I'd been just a little younger . . ." Her eyes sparkled wickedly, and Sabrina remembered that Lord Byron had professed to find her more interesting than his mistress, Lady Melbourne's wayward daughter-in-law, Lady Caroline Lamb.

"Tell me about yourself," Lady Melbourne continued. "You're no green girl, you won't take it amiss if I ask you how you caught Jareth's fancy. Oh, he's forever dangling after some female or other, but for years now he's been far too downy to be trapped by any of 'em. Can't blame the man, after the drubbing he took from that dreadful Mannering chit. Christabel, I think her name was. Don't suppose he's told you about her. Well? You're from Vienna, is that right?"

This was a new development, Sabrina told herself. Who was this Mannering woman? Did Jareth have a broken heart somewhere in his past? She shook off the thought, concentrating on satisfying Lady Melbourne's curiosity with as little information as possible. She said merely that, as a young widow visiting Paris, she had taken it into her head on the spur of the moment to come to London. Lord Jareth was being immensely kind to show her the sights.

When she had finished, the older woman studied her thoughtfully. "So, you came here quite on your own, with only your abigail to accompany you? Odd. Your family didn't object?"

Hearing the amused note of skepticism in Lady Melbourne's voice, Sabrina shifted uncomfortably. She hadn't mentioned Uncle Johann and his desire to marry her off to his son the diplomat, on the theory that the more mystery in her background the better. Should she bring up the old gentleman now? Uncle Johann might add the note of verisimilitude that Lady Melbourne seemed to find lacking.

"Never mind," her ladyship said abruptly when Sabrina hesitated. "I've always said that no man is safe with another's secrets, and no woman with her own." She patted Sabrina's hand. "I think you're a good gal, m'dear. Make Jareth happy. I like the scamp." Jareth returned just then with several glasses of punch, and Lady Melbourne tapped him on the arm with her fan, saying, "Be off with you now, see that the countess amuses herself. And don't forget to bring her to tea one day next week."

"Did you have a nice chat with Lady M?" Jareth inquired as they moved away.

"Yes, but I think she's a witch. She sees right through you." Sabrina took a quick gulp of punch to recover her poise. She knew quite well what Lady Melbourne had said to her without the use of words. *I don't believe a word you're saying, my girl, but I know you're a lady of quality and I won't give you away.* A variant, probably, on what Sabrina took to be Lady Melbourne's own philosophy: a married woman of position may do as she likes provided she's discreet.

Jareth laughed. "You aren't the first person to say something like that about Lady M. She's as shrewd as she can hold together."

Having escaped from her unnerving session with her hostess, Sabrina relaxed and began to enjoy the evening. After the drab, bleak months in Sussex, when she'd been forced to expend all her time and all her energies in the effort to keep her family financially afloat, it felt exhilarating to be beautifully dressed at an elegant function in the company of a handsome man who admired her and of his friends who were equally admiring. She ate Lady Melbourne's lavish dinner with good appetite and listened entranced to little Tom Moore's singing, and didn't turn a hair at the end of the evening when the Prince Regent dropped in on his old friend Lady Melbourne for one of his informal visits.

The enormously obese man who stood in the doorway

chatting with the horde of hangers-on who immediately surrounded him, was no longer the handsome prince who had caused such heartthrobs in his youth, but he still had an eye for the ladies. Within minutes of his arrival he was standing in front of Sabrina, being introduced by Jareth, and bowing his famous graceful bow — albeit with the aid of a cane — and smiling the practiced smile that still had the capacity to charm.

"So you're from Vienna, my dear Countess. Tell me, are all the Austrian ladies as lovely as you?"

"None of them receive such graceful compliments, sir, I can tell you that," said Sabrina demurely.

The Regent's smile broadened. He liked a woman who knew how to flirt. "How long will we have the pleasure of your company in London?"

"I must be leaving soon, alas."

"Not so soon, I trust, that you'll be unable to visit me at Carlton House. Tremayne, I'm having a little musical evening Tuesday week. I'd be delighted to have you and the countess among my guests." He paused, striking his forehead with a pudgy hand. "Bless my soul, Countess, I'm forgetting I came here with a gentleman who would be most interested to meet you — Prince Paul Esterházy, the Austrian ambassador. A Hungarian, I believe. You'll have much to talk about." He turned his head to look out over the room, as if searching for the ambassador.

At that moment Sabrina gave a great gasp and clutched at Jareth's sleeve. "I don't feel well," she muttered. "It's so warm in here. . . ."

Minutes later, sitting back against the softly upholstered squabs in Jareth's carriage as they drove out of the courtyard of Melbourne House, Sabrina said faintly, "I'm so sorry to spoil your evening. Just take me to the Pulteney, then return to Melbourne House to be with your friends."

"I'll do nothing of the kind," said Jareth roughly. "What matters is your health. Are you feeling better?"

"Oh, yes, much better. There's nothing wrong with me. It's as I told you, it was so very warm in the drawing room."

Actually Sabrina's legs still felt weak. It had been such a narrow escape. Over a year previously, in the early stages of the Congress of Vienna, she'd been introduced to Prince Paul Esterházy at a ball in Schönbrunn Palace. Possibly — very probably — he might not have recalled that meeting. She was the wife of a very junior English diplomat, after all, and the ballroom had swarmed with royalty and important personages bearing the most exalted titles in Europe, but Sabrina hadn't dared to take the chance that she might be recognized. Her fainting spell might not have been a strikingly original solution to her problem, but it had served its purpose. It had rescued her from Lady Melbourne's drawing room and the sharp eyes of the Hungarian diplomat.

She shivered beneath the silky folds of her shawl, not from the cold — the spring night was balmy — but from the realization that time was running short. The longer she allowed this charade to continue, the greater her chances of being exposed. As soon as possible, now, she must finish spinning her web around Jareth Tremayne and complete the task that had brought her to London.

Chapter Six

The Thames in midmorning was like a broad highway, crowded with the white and brown sails of wherries and barges busily plying the river in both directions. The pleasure boat bobbing in the water at the foot of the landing stairs at Westminster Bridge looked frivolous, out of place, with its soft carpeting and brightly colored awnings, but Sabrina gazed at it in delight. "Jareth, what a wonderful surprise. Ever since I came to London I've longed to sail along the river."

"Well, this won't be a sailing excursion, exactly," Jareth smiled, motioning to the crew of rowers on the aft deck, "though I hope you'll enjoy it nonetheless." He took her arm, helping her down the landing stairs and into a comfortable chair in the forward section of the boat. Soon they were gliding past the tree-lined terraces of Westminster Hall and the low willowed shore at Milbank. A soft-footed young man in a plain dark coat brought them steaming cups of tea. "Any difficulties with Gunther's, Harris?" Jareth inquired, glancing past his valet to the large hamper reposing on the deck.

"None, my lord. Everything is just as you ordered. The lobster looks especially fine."

"What luxury," Sabrina sighed, sipping her tea and then setting down her cup on the small table next to her chair while she tightened the ties of her bonnet against the freshening breeze. "I've never had lunch on a boat before."

"Nor will you today. We'll make a landing on the shore for a picnic," Jareth grinned. He lowered his voice to add, "I thought we should have a little privacy." Reaching out to tuck a wind-blown tawny curl beneath her bonnet, he gazed at her searchingly. "You look very well this morning, Sabrina. After you fainted last night, I was afraid you might not feel up to coming out with me today."

"I told you there was no need to worry about me. I've always been excessively healthy. I didn't know what came over me, but even if I had still felt ill this morning, this marvelous bracing air would have cured me."

Sabrina leaned back in her chair, watching the lovely scenery unwind past the boat. Over there were the grounds of the Royal Hospital at Chelsea, and soon after that Fulham's Bishop's Palace and its extensive market gardens came into view, followed by the sight of the stately villas lining a stretch of the river near Chiswick.

"Here we are," Jareth announced, as the boat slid into a landing stage on a gently sloping grassy shore. He jumped onto the landing, extending his hand to Sabrina. The valet, Harris, followed with the heavy food hamper from Gunther's, and several of the rowers carried a table and two chairs to a level place beneath a large tree. In minutes Harris had draped the table with a snowy cloth and set it with fine china and gleaming cutlery. Opening a bottle of champagne with a quiet dexterity, he placed it on the table in a silver bucket filled with ice.

Jareth nodded to the valet. "That will be all for the moment. Go along with you now. Find an anchorage a bit downstream where the crew can have a rest. You brought some food for the men?"

"Yes, my lord. Bread and cheese and beer."

"Very good. Come back for us in two hours."

After the boat had disappeared downstream, Jareth delved into the hamper. "Let's see what Gunther's has for us. Splendid! Their specialty, Perigord pie, one of my passions. Some fine-looking Westphalian ham. Truffles. Apricot tart—did you know my friend Alvanley has a fresh apricot tart on his sideboard every day of the year?"

"And what, pray, is that?" Sabrina inquired, gazing at the next offering with a raised eyebrow.

"Reindeer tongues from Lapland. A great delicacy, I'm told."

"Some of the ham, please. And the lobster," said Sabrina hastily.

Everything Sabrina put in her mouth tasted like ambrosia, though she would have been hard put after the meal to say exactly what she ate. The food simply seemed perfect, part of a perfect setting, as they sat beneath the rustling branches of the tree, caressed by a vagrant breeze off the river where the sunlight danced on the surface of the rippling water. The brush of Jareth's fingers against her hand when he poured her a glass of champagne was as light as the wings of a butterfly, but Sabrina was aware of his touch in every fiber of her being. And when the comfortable silences lengthened and they were speaking more with their eyes than their lips, she knew with a quick stirring of alarm that they'd been alone in this magical sylvan place for too long.

"More champagne? Your glass is empty," said Jareth, pouring the wine without looking at what he was doing, while his eyes remained locked on her face.

Sabrina wrenched her eyes away. "You've poured more champagne on the tablecloth than you've put in my glass," she pointed out with a laugh. "It's of no consequence. You don't want to get me foxed in the middle of the day."

"It might be interesting," he murmured.

She searched her mind for a less dangerous topic. "I've just realized, Jareth, that I know very little about you," she began with an air of ingenuous surprise. "I've told you all about Uncle Johann and Cousin Stefan and my—my late husband. But all you've said about yourself is that you were the younger son of a lord and you come from . . ." She wrinkled her brow. "You come from the same place as that handsome young officer we met the other day."

The expression of dreamy, flirtatious tenderness faded from Jareth's face. He shifted in his chair, averting his eyes. "There's nothing very engrossing about me, I fear," he said shortly. "I have one brother, the present Marquess of Winwood. He lives with his wife at Winwood Park, our family seat in Sussex."

"Do you have other family?"

"No. Lionel's my only close relative. He and his wife Christabel had a son who died recently. They have no other children." The clipped finality in his voice said plainly that the subject was closed.

Sabrina studied Jareth's face surreptitiously. His mood had changed markedly. Why didn't he want to discuss his family? Possibly, she thought sympathetically, he'd had an especially close relationship with the little boy who died. It suddenly struck her as somewhat odd that she knew very little about the Tremaynes personally, even though they were the most prominent family in the county. Well, perhaps it wasn't so odd. Being at least ten years younger than Jareth and his brother, she had never met either of them while she was growing up. She'd gathered from Adrian—and yes, from something Nate Peggoty, the captain of her smuggling boat, had said—that Jareth had rarely visited in Sussex in recent years, although there'd been no suggestion that his absences had been caused by family difficulties. Now, however, his mention of his sister-in-law's name jogged her memory. What had Lady Melbourne said last night about a Christabel Mannering? Not that it was any of Sabrina's affair. Better, in fact, if she didn't pursue it. She knew she should be edging away from intimacy with Jareth. It would be easier for her peace of mind to do what she had to do if she could prevent herself from becoming too personally involved.

To her dismay, she heard herself saying, "Are you and your brother estranged?"

Jareth's lips clamped together stubbornly. For a moment Sabrina thought he would ignore her question. Then he said reluctantly, "We don't get along well, no."

There. Let well enough alone. She said quickly, "Forgive me, Jareth. I didn't mean to pry."

He must have heard something in her tone—a note of hurt or rejection—that she herself didn't realize was there. He took her hand, saying hurriedly, "And I didn't mean to be sharp with you, Sabrina. Oh, the deuce, there's no reason you shouldn't know—Lionel and I have been at odds since I was in my cradle. For some reason he's always resented me, God knows why. I was never a threat to him. As the elder son he was going to inherit everything, the title, the estate, without lifting a finger, but I never objected to that. It was his right. What he *didn't* have the right to do was to steal Christabel away from me when he knew how desperately I loved her—" He broke off, flushing a dull red. "Sorry," he muttered. "You certainly don't want to hear about my callow heart-stirrings."

"Please don't apologize. I quite understand why you wouldn't wish to discuss a lady you care about," said Sabrina, unable to keep the stiffness out of her tone. What did it matter if Jareth had once loved his brother's wife?

"Care about?" Jareth stared at her in astonishment.

"Lord, Sabrina, you've got it all wrong. I don't care a fig for Christabel now. Back then, though—eight, nine years ago . . ."

The dam having burst, Jareth's words seemed to pour out of his mouth involuntarily. Sabrina had the impression he'd forgotten she was there. Listening, half unwillingly, she could picture a very young Jareth—boyish, inexperienced, unsure of himself, not yet the polished leader of fashion and man about town—as he met and fell rapturously, tumultuously in love with a golden-haired beauty who possessed every perfection of face and form and character. Sabrina guessed that Christabel hadn't been quite real to him. She was more a princesslike figure from a fairy tale who deigned to accept him as her Prince Charming, who pledged him her troth in secret, until she could pluck the courage to inform her mother that she wanted to marry a younger son without a feather to fly with. Then came the night at Almack's, when Jareth, all unsuspecting, introduced his older brother to his love, and someone else—possibly the gossipy Lady Jersey—had whispered into Christabel's delicate little ear that Lionel Tremayne would enjoy an income of forty thousand pounds a year when he succeeded his invalid father as Marquess of Winwood.

"She said she'd made a mistake," Jareth said in a low, monotonous voice, still as if speaking to himself. "She said she'd been too young to know her own mind when she promised to marry me—we'd both been too young—and now that she'd met Lionel she realized she'd been more in love with love than with me. She wished me well, she hoped I'd find someone to love as much as she loved my brother. If I could have believed her—but I *knew* she didn't love Lionel, it was the money and the position she wanted, the things her mother had been scheming to get for her since she was born." He hugged his arms tightly to his chest, protecting himself

108

from the onslaught of a remembered pain. "At first I felt a little like dying. Then I thought of enlisting in the dragoons as a common trooper. Finally I managed to grow a hide stout enough to keep the world at bay, the female part of it, at any rate. . . ."

As Jareth fell into abstracted silence, gazing out over the river where the late afternoon sun was burnishing the waves into gold, Sabrina's heart ached for his younger self and the torment he'd endured at the hands of his golden sister-in-law. Then her feelings of pity were succeeded by the disquieting thought that she and Jareth were both survivors in the wars of love, both of them determined not to be wounded again. She hadn't allowed for this. It might be that he'd be too wary for her and her schemes.

"I'm sorry, Jareth," she said softly.

"What?" He turned back to her, his eyes bemused for a moment, then gradually clearing. Suddenly he smiled ruefully. "Did I really tell you all that foolishness about Christabel? I've kept it locked up tight inside myself all these years, shivering at the thought that somebody would discover I was such a gull. And now I've told you . . ." He shook his head. Glancing downstream, he pulled out his watch. "There's the boat," he said, sounding almost relieved. "Harris is dead on time."

After the valet had packed up the remains of their feast and they were settled again in their comfortable chairs on the forward deck, Jareth said, "You're in no hurry to return, are you? Let's continue upriver for a bit, past Kew and Richmond and Teddington to Hampton Court for a look at the palace."

"I'm in no hurry at all. It's been a lovely day, Jareth. I almost wish it could go on forever."

"I can't arrange that, I'm afraid, but see here, we could drive back to Richmond tonight, if you're not weary of Surrey by that time, and have supper at the

Star and Garter Inn on the Hill."

The sun was just setting that evening when Jareth's carriage deposited them on the very summit of Richmond Hill. Standing beside Jareth on the garden terrace of the inn, Sabrina breathed a sigh of delight as she gazed southwest at the lovely vista of the Thames Valley, with its woodlands and tender green meadows and the undulating blue ribbon of the river.

"Joshua Reynolds used to live in the house across the road from the inn," Jareth told her. "He painted this same scene many times."

When they left the terrace to enter the dining room of the inn, it was apparent to Sabrina that Jareth was a frequent and highly esteemed customer. They were ushered to the most desirable table, where a drove of vigilant servants vied to anticipate their every wish.

"It's a good thing we came here in the middle of the week," Jareth remarked after he had approved the wine and the first course had arrived. "The place is beginning to be quite popular, even a bit crowded on Sundays, when many Londoners come out here to dine and escape the commotion of the city." He lifted his glass to sip his claret and added casually, "The hotel's recently been enlarged to accommodate overnight guests."

Sabrina looked at him sharply. Was he testing the waters with his last remark? Before the evening was over would he suggest staying the night? In his next breath, however, he said prosaically, "Very fine salmon, don't you think? The goose is good, too. Fattened just enough."

"Yes, it's excellent," Sabrina agreed, though her mind wasn't on the goose. She hadn't been able to put her finger on it, but there was a subtle difference about Jareth this evening. In most respects he was his usual self. Urbane, charming, attentive, a shade arrogant. But there was something . . . Yes, that was it, she thought. Even when he was at his most outgoing, she'd always sensed a shell of reserve that he'd erected to shield his most private feelings, a kind of mental No Trespassing sign. Tonight that invisible barrier was no longer in place. He seemed relaxed, cheerful, open. Younger.

Her thoughts began circling each other. His innermost defenses had been breached this afternoon when he told her about Christabel's betrayal. She'd half-expected him to regret confiding in her, to feel so embarrassed about revealing his slavish adoration of a woman who had jilted him that he would reerect his barriers higher than ever. Exactly the opposite seemed to have happened, and the development made her uneasy. She wanted Jareth interested, attracted, captivated—but she didn't want him too close.

"You're eating like a bird," he said, breaking into her thoughts. "I hoped you'd like the food. The Star and Garter kitchen is one of my favorites."

"The food's delicious," she hastened to assure him. "The problem is that I haven't fully recovered from our picnic feast this afternoon."

Jareth laughed. "I must tell my valet how much you appreciated his selections. Harris prides himself on his knowledge of cuisine. Shall we take a turn in the gardens before we start back to the city?"

They stood for a few moments on the terrace, tracing the winding course of the Thames below them from the jeweled ribbon of lights marking the hamlets and farmhouses along its banks. "It's even lovelier than the view in daylight," Sabrina murmured.

"It's beautiful in all seasons. Wait till the end of summer, when the leaves begin to turn."

"But I won't be here then," Sabrina exclaimed in surprise. "You know I'll be returning to Paris soon."

He turned abruptly to face her. In the shifting gleam of the swinging lanterns that dimly illuminated the velvety darkness of the gardens, she couldn't make out his features clearly, but she could hear the note of urgency in his voice.

"Sabrina, I've been wanting to talk to you — why must you set a date to go back to Paris? Why can't you stay on for a while?"

"Oh, I couldn't do that, Jareth," Sabrina said quickly. "Uncle Johann —"

"The devil take Uncle Johann!" Jareth exploded. "You're allowing him to take over your entire life. It isn't as if you were still a child, without means, needing his protection. You're a grown woman now, independently wealthy from what you tell me. You're your own mistress. Stay in England, Sabrina. Let's enjoy each other's company for a while longer."

"I'd like to stay on for a bit, but I really can't treat Uncle Johann so inconsiderately," she replied with a touch of reproach. "He and Stefan are the only family I have. Then, too, my funds won't last forever."

"If that's all — look, there's no need to concern yourself about money. If you're a little pinched for the needful, I can raise the wind for you." He hesitated. "I know it's too soon to speak of it, too soon for you to make such a decision, but later . . ." His voice deepened, and he reached out to trail his fingers gently, caressingly, across her cheek. "Later you might want to remain here permanently."

Sabrina's face flamed in the darkness, and she felt a treacherous undertow dragging her deeper into dangerous waters. "Please don't say any more," she said breathlessly, backing away from him.

"Sabrina —"

"No, please, Jareth, I think we should return to London now." She knew she sounded disjointed and confused, like some socially inexperienced miss fresh out of the schoolroom. It was the impression she wanted to create, but it also accurately reflected her own inner turmoil.

"It's all right, Sabrina," Jareth said soothingly. "I didn't mean to upset you. We can talk about this another time. I'll order the carriage."

During the drive back to London, Sabrina chattered inanely about the meal they had just eaten, about the beauty of the scenery along the Thames, about anything neutral and safe that came into her mind, and Jareth, sitting relaxed on his side of the carriage, made no attempt to steer the conversation into more intimate channels. After he had escorted her into the vestibule of the Pulteney, he merely said a quiet good-night, telling her he would be back the following afternoon to escort her to Runnymede.

Sabrina spent a sleepless night. Her conscience had been aroused to vigorous life. Before she had actually met him, she'd had no difficulty justifying to herself her plot to manipulate Jareth in order to extricate Adrian from his predicament. It had all seemed so black and white. Jareth had taken callous advantage of her young brother and he deserved to be punished. An eye for an eye, a tooth for a tooth. Now that she knew Jareth as a flesh and blood man, not a faceless antagonist, however, she found herself wavering. Granted, he shouldn't have allowed a feckless youth like Adrian to gamble with him, but almost certainly he hadn't done it with deliberate malice. And shouldn't Adrian have assumed a greater responsibility for his own actions? In any case, did Jareth's offense compare with the injury she was about to do to him?

Originally she'd intended only to entice Jareth into a harmless flirtation — harmless to both of them. She hadn't known about his thwarted love affair with Christabel, which had apparently left such deep scars that for years he'd refused to become seriously emotionally involved with another woman. Tonight, though, it had been obvious that he was falling deeply in love with her. If she carried through her plan, vanishing afterwards as suddenly and mysteriously as she'd first appeared on the scene, wouldn't she risk shattering his life again, even more completely this time?

Arriving very early at the Pulteney the following morning, Adrian said grumpily to Lotte when she answered his knock, "I daresay my sister is still abed, but you'll have to rouse her. I'll be late reporting for duty as it is."

Opening the door wider, Lotte waved him into the sitting room without saying a word. As his sister emerged from her bedchamber, Adrian exclaimed belligerently, "I know you told me not to come here unless you sent for me, Sabrina, but dash it, this is important. I came by yesterday, and the day before that, too, as Lotte must have told you, but you're never here, you're always gadding about somewhere with Tremayne, and that brings me to what I want to talk to you about: what on earth was in your mind, allowing Lord Jareth to buy you gowns or heaven knows what other fripperies? And don't try to deny it, I *saw* you coming out of that dressmaker's shop in Cranbourn Street. I vow, it was all I could do to remember that you were still pursuing that idiot scheme of posing as an Italian—no, I beg your pardon," Adrian added with exaggerated courtesy, "that you were posing as an *Hungarian* countess, and I wasn't supposed to know you. Next thing you know, you'll have Tremayne thinking you're some kind of high flyer or even worse—"

Adrian broke off as he noted Sabrina's wan face and subdued expression. "Well, now, I've no wish to upset you," he said uncomfortably. "Mind, I still can't stomach this masquerade, but . . . Oh, the devil, I should have relied on your good sense. You always had more of that than I did! Doubtless it had already occurred to you that you might have seemed indiscreet." Glancing at the clock on the mantel, he added, "I'll be off, then. Prinny is inspecting us today."

"Adrian, please stay a moment. I have something to tell you."

"I can give you five minutes," Adrian replied cheerfully. With his usual carefree attitude toward life, he seemed to have dismissed from his mind his worries about Sabrina's potentially scandalous behavior. He sat down in an armchair, eyeing the tea tray on the side table. "Lotte, is there any tea left in that pot?" As the abigail handed him his cup he looked at Sabrina with a faintly expectant grin, saying, "I like a good gossip as much as the next one, but I daresay I've already heard your news. That is, if it's about Tremayne."

"What about Lord Jareth?" Sabrina asked, her eyes narrowing.

"The latest *on dit* sweeping the town is that Tremayne ruined Viscount Castlewood night before last in a whist game at White's." At Sabrina's blank expression, Adrian crowed in triumph. "So you hadn't heard. The story goes that Castlewood had been losing heavily to Tremayne all night and tried to recoup by wagering his entire estate in Devon. He lost. According to one estimate I heard, Castlewood's income from his properties was twenty thousand a year."

"What stupidity!" exclaimed Sabrina scornfully. "Does the Viscount have a family?"

"A widowed mother and a younger sister, I believe. I fear they'll be under the hatches now, poor things. Especially since . . ." Adrian frowned. "I can't swear it's true, mind, but last night in the mess Captain Carstairs told me he'd heard a rumor that Castlewood had shot himself to death." He stared at Sabrina, who had turned a pasty white. "Good God, what's the matter with you? You didn't know Castlewood, did you?"

"No. No. It — it seems such a dreadful waste, that's all. Adrian, you should go. You'll be late for duty."

As Adrian rose, reaching for his helmet, he said, "What was it you wanted to talk to me about?"

"Oh . . . nothing important. It can wait until I see you again. I'll send word when I have your money. It won't be long now."

Giving his sister a hasty hug, Adrian walked to the door, pausing to look curiously at the row of strapped portmanteaux ranged next to the door. "Going somewhere, Sabrina?"

"No."

Adrian looked askance at the clipped monosyllable but left without asking any further questions. After Lotte had closed the door behind him, she motioned to the portmanteaux. "Did I hear you right, *meine Frau?* We are not traveling today?"

"No," said Sabrina shortly. "Unpack the luggage."

Shortly after noon on that same day, a knock sounded on the door of Sabrina's suite. Taking the note from the hotel servant, Lotte hesitated, staring at the door of the inner room, which had been firmly closed against her since early morning. Finally, her lips clamped together determinedly, Lotte strode to the door of the bedchamber and wrenched it open. "A message for you, *meine Frau.*"

Seated in a chair by the window, an unopened book in her lap, Sabrina looked up at Lotte with a vacant stare. In a moment her eyes cleared and she extended her hand for the note. Its few brief scrawled lines read, "Dear Sabrina, did I get the time wrong? I've been waiting in the parlor for half an hour. I hope you haven't decided against coming out with me today."

After a long pause, Sabrina muttered, "Send word downstairs to Lord Jareth that I'll join him in twenty minutes." She rose, going to the wardrobe to take out a walking dress of pale green muslin. Hastily pulling it on, she sat down at the dressing table, brushing a discreet film of color on her face to hide her pale cheeks and piling her hair on the crown of her head in a careless knot that slipped loose immediately and had to be repaired by Lotte's skillful fingers. Donning her pelisse and bonnet Sabrina started down the stairs to the hotel parlor, forcing each reluctant step.

This morning at the crack of dawn she had awakened a surprised Lotte with an order to pack her belongings. During the long night Sabrina had realized she couldn't bring herself to carry out her scheme against Jareth. She'd faced the fact that her decision to leave London with her plans unfulfilled meant the probable sale of the Latimer estate in order to pay Adrian's gambling debt to Jareth, unless she could persuade her brother to swallow his pride and ask Jareth for an extension of payment on the debt. And that seemed an unlikely occurrence, considering the perversely illogical masculine code of honor by which both men conducted their lives.

Sabrina had been prepared to give Adrian the disappointing news when he arrived at the hotel this morning. The news of Lord Castlewood's ruin at Jareth's hands had changed her mind. The story had sickened her. It had caused her to relive the unhappy years of her marriage to Oliver, whose enslavement to gambling had caused his own death and nearly wrecked Sabrina's life. Now this unknown Lord Castlewood had come to the same miserable end, leaving his family destitute and bereaved. Sabrina couldn't forgive Jareth for his part in the tragedy. Why hadn't he exercised a tiny amount of human compassion? Why hadn't he sensed he was pushing Castlewood beyond the limits of his endurance? Would he have cared? With a creeping horror, Sabrina had speculated that Adrian, had he continued to gamble, might have suffered the same fate as Castlewood.

Pausing on the threshold of the parlor, Sabrina pasted a lighthearted smile on her lips as she looked around the room for Jareth. "I'm so sorry to have kept you waiting," she told him when he came up to her. "I overslept and Lotte wouldn't awaken me. You know she's like a mother hen with her chick. She thinks you keep me out too late!"

Jareth chuckled at her smooth lie. "Lotte's the best of chaperons," he joked in turn. "Concerned, but conveniently never there!"

In the curricle, as Jareth headed the team west toward the tollgate at Hyde Park Corner, he said tentatively, "When I didn't find you waiting for me in the parlor today, I thought you might be annoyed with me."

"Really?" Sabrina opened her eyes wide. "Why would you think that?"

"Well . . . I pressed you last night to extend your stay."

"Oh, that." Sabrina dismissed the subject with a smile. "I daresay I fell into a panic for a bit, thinking how angry—and yes, how concerned, too—Uncle Johann would be if I stayed much longer. But do you know, Jareth, I think you were right. There's no reason why I shouldn't remain in London, at least for a short while longer."

"You relieve my mind to no end," Jareth grinned. "We can discuss later just how much longer your stay will be."

For the most part he seemed his usual self during their leisurely drive along the Western Road toward Exeter, but Sabrina soon detected the fine lines of strain beside his mouth. And several times she had to repeat a remark

118

when he lapsed into a moment or two of introspective silence.

"Now it's my turn," she observed after one of his pauses. "Are you annoyed with me, Jareth?"

He jerked his head to stare at her in astonishment. "Good God, no, Sabrina."

"Oh. You seem troubled."

He hunched his shoulders, as if to ward off her comment. Then he said with an undertone of reluctance, "Perhaps I'm a shade blue-deviled. I heard this morning about the death of—of an acquaintance."

So, Sabrina thought, he does care, at least a little. Though not enough to stop his destructive gambling, probably. Aloud she said, "An acquaintance, not a close friend? Then I don't understand—but perhaps you were fond of him, even though you didn't know him well?"

"Actually, he was almost a stranger to me. But when you sit with a man for five hours at a whist table—a young man who appears to be in perfect health—it's a shock to hear he's killed himself." Jareth's lips tightened. "He left a mother and sister in straitened circumstances. I've been trying to think of a way to settle some money on them without making it seem like charity."

"Poor ladies. I hope you can help them. I'm sure you will," Sabrina murmured sympathetically, but her mind was racing. She could use this opening. She need only bide her time.

Crossing the Thames by the bridge at Staines, they spent a pleasant half-hour strolling through the meadows at Runnymede, enjoying the lovely stretch of the river, fringed with graceful willow trees and sprinkled with waterlilies, and arguing amicably about the exact place where King John had signed the Magna Carta. Afterwards they stopped for lunch at the King's Head in nearby Egham.

Over a plate of cold salmon, Sabrina began her campaign with an innocently inquisitive question. "You told me you were playing cards with your young friend the night before he died, and I remember your once mentioning that you supported yourself by gambling. Do you gamble often, Jareth?"

Cocking an amused eyebrow, he said, "I hope you won't consider me a monster of depravity, but yes, I'm at White's almost every night."

"Not recently, surely? You've taken *me* somewhere every night for almost two full weeks." She tossed him a reproachful glance. "Jareth! Do you go straight to the tables after bringing me back to the Pulteney?"

He laughed outright. "Guilty as charged."

"But when do you sleep?"

"My dear, sleep is a matter of total indifference to a gambler."

Making a face at him, she remarked, "Uncle Johann doesn't approve of ladies playing cards. He says it's unbecoming in a female."

"Lord, Sabrina, don't let him come to London, then. He'd die of shock. Most English ladies of the highest rank are avid gamblers. The duchess of Devonshire was once so heavily in debt because of her gambling losses that she tried to obtain a loan from the French Minister of Finance."

"Well, that's doing it a little too brown, of course, but it does sound very exciting," said Sabrina enviously. "Jareth, why don't you take me to White's one evening so I can see how you go on?"

Spluttering, Jareth put down the glass of wine from which he had just taken a sip and wiped his lips with his napkin. "Are you mad, Sabrina? I can't take you to a gentleman's club."

"Where do females gamble, then, if gentlemen don't allow them into their clubs?"

"Ladies of quality play in private homes. The—the

other kind goes to hells."

"Could we go to one of these hells?"

Jareth choked on a second sip of wine. "Don't pitch that gammon to me, my girl. You must know I couldn't let you risk your reputation by going to one of those low haunts."

"But didn't you also tell me once—how did you put it?—that some people might assume I'm a lightskirt because I'm seen alone in your company?"

"That's different."

"Why is it different?" Sabrina leaned across the table to place her hand over Jareth's. "Please take me to a hell," she coaxed. "What harm could it do? I'm a stranger in town, so I'm in no danger of losing my reputation. How can people gossip about me if they don't know who I am?"

"You're not a complete stranger," Jareth shot back. "You met several of my friends at Lady Melbourne's house."

"Well, the ladies I met there looked so proper, I'm sure they'd never dream of going to a hell. And I'd say our chances of encountering one of your men friends is very small. *They'll* all be patronizing respectable clubs like White's and Brooke's."

"Sabrina, be reasonable."

"No, *you* be reasonable. You haven't given me a single convincing reason why it would be so horrendous for me to go to a hell. I'm only asking for a few minutes, Jareth, for a mere *peek*. If you refuse to take me, you know, I could always go by myself."

He glared at her. "The devil of it is, you're fully capable of doing such an outrageous thing." He threw up his hands. "Very well. I know I'm going to regret this, but I'll take you to a gambling hell tonight—the newest and most inconspicuous one I can find. We'll stay exactly one half-hour, and I pray we don't meet anyone we know."

* * *

Jareth's town chariot stopped that evening in front of a tall, narrow house in a street off Pall Mall. Helping her down from the carriage, he said hopefully, "You can still change your mind. I don't want to sound like a sermonizing parson, Sabrina, but I'd be remiss if I didn't tell you again that you shouldn't be here."

"You promised, Jareth."

He shrugged his shoulders in defeat. "So be it, then."

As she walked up the steps of the gaming house, Sabrina braced herself to enter a den of iniquity. Certainly her first impression did nothing to dampen her preconceived idea. At Jareth's knock, a peephole opened in the door. A voice belonging to the eye that was staring out at them from the peephole asked Jareth, "Be ye a member, Guv?"

"No. What's the subscription? A pound? Here you are. The name's Tremayne."

As they entered the hall, the doorkeeper, a muscular man with a battered face and misshapen ears, murmured, "I be 'appy ter see ye again, m'lord. The best o' luck ter ye."

For a moment Jareth looked blank. Then he exclaimed, "By Jove, it's Nat Poston, isn't it? I saw you fight the Game Chicken."

"Exactly so, m'lord. An' I seen *ye* go two rounds wi' Gentleman Jackson oncet. Ye peel werry well. A pretty fighter indeed fer an amachoor."

"Thank you, Poston. That's high praise from an expert." Nodding to the ex-pugilist, Jareth turned away, taking Sabrina's arm. They walked down a softly lit, thickly carpeted corridor and into a large, well-appointed drawing room crowded with patrons gathered around the gaming tables in the center of the room.

"I expected something much more squalid," she murmured, eyeing the elegant chandeliers and the handsome furniture.

"No, they don't stint furnishing these places. They want to attract the swells." Jareth paused on the threshold, his head turning slowly as he looked closely at the occupants of the room. "Good. I don't see a soul I know," he muttered. "Well, now that we're here against my better judgment, Sabrina, what shall we do first? My game is hazard. Shall we have a look?"

As they pressed through the crowd, Sabrina slowly realized that the clientele of the gaming house represented a mix of people. A sprinkling of elegant dandies leavened a more ordinary group of citizens, ranging from soberly dressed men with the look of prosperous merchants to seedy-looking individuals in threadbare clothes. The women present were elaborately overdressed, their faces thick with paint. Whatever its aspirations to appeal to the *ton*, this place had a raffish air.

Sabrina stood slightly behind Jareth as he took his place at the hazard table. She wasn't familiar with the game. Though Oliver had turned their Vienna home into a quasi-professional gambling club, he'd stopped short at installing a hazard table.

"Will you have the dice, sir?" one of the croupiers inquired.

Jareth nodded, handing the croupier a wad of banknotes in exchange for counters that he placed in a bowl provided for the purpose. Placing several of the counters on the green baize surface of the table in front of him, he announced, "Seven's the main," and threw the dice.

"The caster nicks the eleven," said the croupier, pushing a number of counters toward Jareth, using a small rake.

"Seven's the main again," said Jareth, leaving his winnings on the table. This time he threw a four.

"The chance is four. Odds against the caster two to one," intoned the croupier.

The dice came up six, then eight. On the third throw Jareth had his four. The croupier pushed over another pile of counters. "Let it ride," Jareth said coolly, and threw a seven. A little murmur came from the knot of men gathered around the table as the mound of counters grew. Gazing thoughtfully at his winnings, Jareth withdrew all but a handful of counters before he picked up the dice again. "Main of seven." He threw a two and a one.

"Deuce-ace," said the impassive-faced croupier, raking in Jareth's bet and pushing the dice toward him.

Jareth shook his head. "I'm done. Cash me in."

"How much did you win?" Sabrina said in a low voice as she walked away from the table with Jareth.

"A thousand, give or take several pounds."

A thousand, thought Sabrina. A tenth of the total sum that's causing Adrian such anguish, and Jareth had won it effortlessly in a minute or two at the hazard table. She felt a surge of disgust. Gambling was such a dirty business. It made her feel dirty to be forced to use it in her attempt to save Adrian's future, but it was the only weapon she had.

"Why did you stop playing?" she inquired with a spurious air of interest. "You made only one unlucky throw, and you lost only a few counters."

"That, my dear innocent, is the secret of my success. I can sense when my luck's turning. The dice didn't feel right after I threw the deuce-ace. I make it a point never to pursue the Goddess of Fortune when she frowns on me."

"Do you always win, Jareth?"

"Practically always. I can't afford to lose if I'm to keep up my way of life. Have you seen enough of this establishment?"

"Not yet. What's that game over there?"

"That's a faro bank."

With Jareth growing increasingly impatient, Sabrina made a brief tour of the gaming house, standing for a few minutes beside the tables set up for whist and piquet, watching the play at the faro bank, lingering for a longer period at the macao table, where she told Jareth, "This game looks interesting. I'd like to play a little."

"Not on your life," he snapped.

"But Jareth—"

He took her arm in a hard grip, forcing her slowly but unobtrusively toward the door of the room. "I agreed to take you here, more fool I, but I'd be an even bigger fool if I let you gamble," he said under his breath. "I've given you enough rope, Sabrina. Now it's time to leave."

Pretending to sulk, Sabrina allowed Jareth to march her into the hallway and past the guardian pugilist at the door.

"I never thought you'd be such a spoilsport," she grumbled, after they entered the carriage waiting in front of the house. "You're a prude, Jareth."

"Call me what you like, but you should be grateful I came to my senses," Jareth retorted. "If we'd met even one person in that hell who was known to me, the fat would have been in the fire."

"Oh, you're exaggerating, as usual. I don't see any great moral perversity in playing a hand of macao," Sabrina protested. "It looks like such a simple game, too. I daresay I might have won a tidy sum."

Jareth began to laugh. "More likely you'd have been fleeced royally. You don't learn to be a winner at any game after watching the play for a few minutes. I'll tell you what, Sabrina. If you really want to learn how to play macao, I'll teach you. Come to my rooms for supper tomorrow night. After we dine, I'll give you a gaming lesson."

Piqued, repiqued, slammed, and capotted, Sabrina thought exultantly, quite unconsciously using the language of the game of piquet that she knew so well. Now the game was hers. Jareth had handed it to her on a platter. "I'd love to learn how to play macao," she replied warmly. "That is, if you don't think it would be improper for a lady to go alone to a gentleman's rooms?"

After a moment of blank silence, Jareth chuckled. "Touché, my girl," he said appreciatively.

Chapter Seven

"Es ist sehr schön, meine Frau," Lotte exclaimed, watching Sabrina turn to look at her reflection in the cheval glass from all angles. "It's so beautiful a gown. The heavenly blue color and those tiny bouquets of bluebells and that rouleau of silk and pearls at the neckline and the sleeves — *wunderbar!*"

She wanted to be beautiful tonight for her assignation with Jareth, and it was fitting she should wear the lovely gown he'd bought for her, thought Sabrina as she sat down at the dressing table. It was also an irony that only she could appreciate, employing an expensive gift that he'd given her as part of the arsenal she was using against him.

"Don't keep wiggling your head, *meine Frau,*" Lotte complained. "How do you expect me to do your hair properly if you won't sit still? Why are you so fidgety tonight?"

Sabrina looked at her reflection in the mirror; her dark blue eyes were brilliant with a nervous excitement, and her cheeks had a bright tinge of color that owed nothing to the rouge pot. She must get hold of herself.

"There," said Lotte approvingly as she planted a tiny jeweled comb in the smooth coil at the crown of Sabrina's head. "Perfect. Where will you go tonight with the Herr, looking so splendid?"

Sabrina was spared the necessity of lying—for Lotte would have violently disapproved of a cozy dinner for two in Jareth's rooms—when the abigail, cocking her head at the sound of a knock on the outer door of the suite, left the bedchamber to answer the door.

Rising quickly, Sabrina went to the wardrobe, taking down one of her hatboxes. Delving into it, she removed a small object and spread apart the linen handkerchief in which it was wrapped. Slowly she opened the painted and gilded wooden box, and for a long moment she stared down at Oliver's playing cards, the ones he'd used on that fatal night in Vienna when the Graf von Spenitz had caught him cheating and had challenged him to a duel. Such pretty, useless things, to cost a man his life. Her lips tightening, she closed the box and slipped it, minus its linen wrapping, into her reticule.

Hearing the murmured sound of voices in the next room, Sabrina picked up her shawl and reticule and walked into the sitting room. To her mild surprise she found Jareth there, talking to Lotte. Until now, he'd been scrupulously careful to avoid the faintest appearance of impropriety when he called on her, waiting for her to join him in the parlor of the hotel instead of coming to her suite.

"I'm much too early," he said, looking faintly embarrassed. "I was looking forward to tonight so much . . ." He cleared his throat. "Rather than cool my heels in the parlor, I thought I'd come up and see if by any chance you were ready to go. I've been having a fine chat with Lotte—although we still don't agree on the wisdom of going to view the lunatics at Bedlam," he added teasingly.

Lotte beamed with pleasure at the attention Jareth was showing her. Gazing approvingly at his black coat, black pantaloons buttoned tight to his ankles, and impeccable white marcella waistcoat, she said to Sabrina, "I was telling the Herr it must be a grand affair you two are attending tonight. You both look all the crackers, as the Herr Adr—"

"'All the crack,' Lotte," Sabrina interrupted. Her voice sharpened. "I've told you before, you mustn't use English slang incorrectly. People will laugh at you." She noted with a pang the hurt expression on Lotte's face at the reprimand. Probably no harm would have resulted if the abigail had mentioned Adrian's name in Jareth's hearing, but Sabrina had been unwilling to take the chance that Jareth would connect her with her brother. Adrian's Christian name was too uncommon for comfort.

Flashing a puzzled glance at Sabrina, Jareth patted Lotte's shoulder, saying warmly, "Never you mind what your mistress says. I know a compliment when I hear one!"

Instantly Sabrina gave Lotte a brief hug, saying, "I'm sorry. You speak better English than I speak German. My accent is hopeless!" Out of the corner of her eye she could see Jareth's quick little nod of approval, and she knew she'd bridged the awkward gap. Tonight of all nights she couldn't afford to be removed from the pedestal of his good opinion.

Later, as they walked down the stairs, Jareth said lightly, "I was glad to find I'm still in Lotte's good graces."

"Oh, you've definitely made a conquest," Sabrina assured him.

"I'm happy to hear that. I need every advantage I can get," he replied, flashing her a sidelong impish grin.

Jareth's rooms were a short carriage drive away from the Pulteney on Piccadilly. He lived in the Albany, which had begun its life over thirty years before as the original Melbourne House. Lady Melbourne and her husband had traded their mansion to the duke of York in exchange for his house in Whitehall. A few years previously the duke had sold the mansion, which had been converted into chambers for bachelors, with a large block added on either side of the gardens.

As Jareth handed Sabrina down from the carriage at the entrance to the Albany, it was still quite light in the long spring twilight, and he murmured, "We'll go in by the servants' stairs, I think. A bit less risky."

"Still guarding my reputation, Jareth?"

"I'll remind you that these are bachelor chambers," he said calmly. "Female visitors, aside from fancy pieces, are usually mothers or sisters, and everyone knows I have neither."

In Jareth's rooms, handsomely furnished with a quiet good taste, a small fire glowed in the sitting-room fireplace against the chill of the evening, and Harris, Jareth's valet, welcomed them to a table set with crisp white linen, shining silver, and a bowl of flowers.

Sabrina gazed with delight at the large rose-colored double blossoms surrounded by glossy green leaves. "What lovely camellias."

"They're from Lady Melbourne. When I told her I wanted to present you with a bouquet, she ordered her gardener to raid her greenhouses."

"Did you tell her I was dining alone with you in your chambers?"

"Certainly not. You must think me a perfect flat," Jareth replied, his eyes twinkling. "Although, provided we didn't call attention to our indiscreet conduct, I'll warrant Lady M. would have given us her blessing. She took a great liking to you the other night."

"She's very fond of you, Jareth. In fact, she hinted

130

that if you two had been closer together in age . . ."

Jareth laughed. "Lady M. was bamboozling you. I can assure you she had, and still has, her own interests!" He took Sabrina's shawl, handing it to his valet, and pulled out a chair at the table. "Please sit down, or Harris will fall into a fit of the dismals at our neglect of his dinner."

Pouring their wine, Jareth lifted his glass, murmuring, "To a memorable evening. You look so beautiful tonight, Sabrina."

"It's your gown," she laughed. "Even the plainest woman would look beautiful in it."

"And you'd look ravishing in the plainest gown."

Moving so quietly and unobtrusively that Sabrina was scarcely aware of his presence, the soft-footed Harris served a turbot with lobster sauce, a boiled fowl, turtle and roast duck with asparagus and peas, a gooseberry and currant pie, a soft pudding, and a mound of hothouse fruits washed down with burgundy, Madeira and champagne. As he began clearing the table an hour later, a glimmer of disappointment crossed the servant's impassive face at the sight of so much untouched food.

"Your dinner was delicious, Harris," Sabrina hastened to tell him. "However, you provided enough food for an army."

Jareth emptied a bottle of champagne by refilling Sabrina's glass. "Bring us another bottle, Harris—no, make that two—and then you can leave."

After the valet's departure, Sabrina lifted her glass, gazing at Jareth over the rim. "Much more of this and you'll have me castaway," she joked. "Or is that what you had in mind?"

"Sabrina! What a thing to say! Get you foxed? Never!" Jareth grinned. "Just a bit on the go, perhaps? I do want you to enjoy the evening, and personally, I find champagne *very* relaxing." His expression sobering, he said abruptly, "Now we're alone, we must talk. Yesterday you agreed to stay on in London for a while. I don't know how long a stay you had in mind, but a few days, a few weeks—that's not enough, Sabrina. I don't want you to leave England at all."

Sabrina's heart constricted. She'd hoped she could do what she had to do tonight without breaching the fragile wall of restraint that until now had prevented any acknowledgment of the strong current of emotion flowing between them. "Jareth, you're talking nonsense, you know. I must go back someday, to Paris first of all, and later to Vienna."

"Why must you go back? Does your uncle have any authority over you? Don't you control your own fortune?"

"Yes, but Uncle Johann has always managed my affairs . . . and it's all arranged that I should marry Stefan."

"Again, why? Do you love Stefan? Do *you* really want to marry him?"

"N-no. But what has that to say to anything? Don't you remember, we talked about this when we first met, and we agreed that people of our station in life don't marry for love."

"I didn't agree to anything of the sort," Jareth said harshly. "All I know is that I've been in hell these past few days, imagining the future without you." He stood up, pulling Sabrina out of her chair and into his arms. Drawing a deep shuddering breath at the sudden hard pressure of his tautly muscled body against her soft flesh, he crushed his mouth to hers in a bruising kiss that went on and on, robbing both of them of breath, until he had forced her lips apart so that he could explore the honeyed sweetness within. An explosion of desire rocked Sabrina's body and she strained against him, feeling the unfamiliar devouring urge to be possessed completely by this man who held her entire being enthralled in the power of his conquering masculinity.

Gradually his fierce embrace relaxed, and he lifted his head to look down at her, his eyes still dazed with passion. "My darling Sabrina, I wasn't sure until this moment — you feel the same as I do, don't you? I love you. *I love you.*" He laughed shakily. "It feels so strange, saying that. I haven't said it to anyone since . . ." His arms tightened around her. "It feels strange, yes, and frightening and wonderful, to surrender myself to you without reservations. Sabrina, tell me that you love me. You've already told me with your lips and with your body, but I need to hear it."

"Yes, oh yes, Jareth, I love you," said Sabrina softly as she looked into his eyes, the words slipping from her mouth without her volition, as if she were held enslaved by the shimmering threads of a sensual enchantment.

With a groan, he locked his mouth to hers in a savage kiss that hurt as it turned her bones to jelly, pulling her ruthlessly closer to him in the quickening of his arousal. The alarm bells sounded in Sabrina's head. She couldn't let Jareth love her. Nothing but disaster could result. She doubled her hands into fists, digging them into his chest, trying to push herself away from him. "Jareth, please, let me go, we can't do this," she muttered, moving her head frantically back and forth in an effort to free her mouth from his demanding lips.

Slowly his hold slackened and his eyes cleared. "I'm sorry, love. I was rushing my fences," he said with a wry smile. "I keep forgetting you're not really a widow, that you've never actually —" He broke off, reddening. "And now I'm sounding like a callow yokel, instead of someone who's been on the town for years."

Slipping his arm loosely around her waist, he led Sabrina to a settee in front of the fireplace and sat down with her, cuddling her against his shoulder. "We must make plans," he began eagerly. "The first thing you should do is write to your uncle. Tell him you're not returning to his household. Tell him you're going to marry an Englishman. I hope he'll want to come to London for our wedding, even offer to give you away. Your cousin Stefan, too, is more than welcome! Which reminds me, while you're waiting for your uncle's reply and preparing for the wedding, you shouldn't be staying at a hotel. I'm sure Lady Melbourne would be delighted to have you stay with her. I'll go see Lady M. first thing tomorrow morning. You should also have your uncle instruct your bankers to transfer your funds—what's the matter? What did I say?"

Sabrina had been sitting in stunned silence, her thoughts in such a chaotic jumble she hadn't been able to piece together a coherent sentence. How could she have permitted this to happen? She'd known Jareth was becoming increasingly emotionally involved, she'd certainly been aware of her own treacherous responses to his touch, to his mere presence. But she'd promised herself that, whatever else came of her escapade, she was going to make sure he emerged from it with his heart intact, suffering no greater injury than a blow to his male ego. Now he'd declared his love for her and proposed marriage. Even worse, she'd admitted to him and to herself that she was head over heels in love with him.

"What did I say to upset you, Sabrina?" Jareth repeated, his face troubled. "Was it my suggestion that you stay with Lady Melbourne? Do as you like about that, naturally. My only thought was that it might cause gossip if I married you straight out of the Pulteney Hotel! Or was it my remark about your bankers?"

He took both her hands, forcing her to look at him. "Sabrina, you must know I'm no gazetted fortune hunter. I don't care if you have a penny to your name. Let your uncle keep control of your fortune, or divide your income with him, or let him keep it all, if it would make you feel better. I don't want your money. I want you."

The damage was done, Sabrina thought drearily. All she could do now was to go on with her scheme so that Adrian, at least, would benefit from it. She pulled her lips into a smile, allowing a tremulous note to creep into her voice as she said, "I'm not upset, Jareth. It's just—it's all so new to me. I can't really take it in. I came to London a few days ago to see the sights, and now you're talking of marriage! We're going so fast it's making my head spin."

"My darling, I'm so sorry, I've been rushing you," Jareth said remorsefully. "We'll do whatever you want, whenever you want to do it, but Sabrina"—his grip on her hands tightened into a painful vise—"Sabrina, you meant it when you said you loved me? You're not going to leave me?"

Sabrina stared back into the dark eyes fixed so anxiously upon her and lied. "Of course I won't leave, but—Jareth, I can't decide anything tonight. I must have a little time to think. You understand, don't you?"

The tension left his face. "Take as much time as you like, love, provided you stay with me." He bent his head to brush her lips in a gentle kiss. "Now, then," he said cheerfully, "shall we have our card-playing lesson? That's how I lured you up to my lair!"

He brought a small folding mahogany card table from a corner of the room and set it in front of the fireplace, drawing up two chairs. From a drawer in an elaborately carved secretary he produced a pack of

135

playing cards and a box of counters. "First things first," he smiled, retrieving a bottle of champagne and their glasses from the dining table. After he poured the wine he sat down at the card table, motioning Sabrina to the other chair.

"Macao's a variation of vingt-et-un, of course," he observed, shuffling the cards, "except that players are dealt only one card, and the object of the game is to make a nine, not twenty-one. Aces count one, court cards and ten's don't count. Ordinarily I'd deal out the cards until one of us received an ace to become the first dealer. Since this is only a practice session, I'll deal. Here's a stack of counters for you. Make a bet before I deal."

Pretending to deliberate, Sabrina cautiously pushed two counters in front of her.

"Go on, plunge as hard as you like," Jareth said in amusement. "We're not playing for real money. When you lose all your counters I'll replenish your supply from this box." He dealt them each a card face down.

"Oh? What makes you think I'll lose?" Sabrina said pertly.

"My love, it's a foregone conclusion. You're playing with me, remember?"

"Ah, yes, the king of the gaming tables," Sabrina scoffed. She lifted a corner of her card to peer at it, then looked up at Jareth inquiringly.

"If your card is a seven, eight or nine, you have a natural," he explained. "If I can't match or better you, I pay you the amount of your wager for a seven, twice that for an eight, and triple the amount for a nine."

"It's an eight."

He took a quick look at his card. Solemnly he handed her four counters. "The deal passes to you. Give each of us one card down. That's it. Do you have a natural? No, neither do I. Now we draw. Recall that

136

the object of the game is nine. If you have anything except an ace, two, or three, or a court card, I'd advise against taking another card."

Holding a six, Sabrina made a show of deep thought before saying, "I stand."

He turned up his card, showing a five. When she turned up her six, he complained, "Beginner's luck, it never fails. It's a good thing we aren't playing for real money." He pushed a pile of counters in front of her. "More champagne?" he asked, holding up the bottle.

"Not for me. I want to keep my head clear so I can beat you."

"Then I must do the honors. We can't let this priceless liquid turn flat. What would Harris say? He assured me he bought the finest, most expensive champagne in Gunther's cellars." Sipping his wine, Jareth reached across the table to imprison Sabrina's hand. "If truth be told, I don't need strong drink to intoxicate me," he said huskily. "All I need is you."

Sabrina swallowed hard against the lump in her throat. He looked so young and adoring as he gazed at her with his heart in his eyes. Could she really go on with this? Then Adrian's face came into her mind, followed by Oliver's, and behind him another face, unfamiliar, blurred and wavery in its crimson outline — the young gambler Castlewood after he blew his brains out. Repressing a shudder, she said archly, "Compliments are all very well, my lord, but you promised to show me how to play macao."

During the next half-hour, Sabrina pretended to absorb the essentials of a game at which she had long been an excellent player. As it happened, she received unusually good cards and the luck was running against Jareth. Looking from the pile of counters in front of her to his small stack, she crowed, "There, I told you I could win at macao. If you hadn't prevented me from playing a bit at that gambling hell, think how much I might have won!"

"My dear girl, the Captain Sharps would have made mincemeat of you in two minutes if I'd allowed you to play," retorted Jareth.

"I nearly forgot," Sabrina said abruptly. She delved into her reticule, taking out the gilded box containing the playing cards. "I found these today when Lotte and I went shopping in Oxford Street. Aren't they pretty? The shopkeeper said they were made in Austria. I thought we might use them tonight. Who knows, they might bring me luck."

"You don't need any luck," he told her in mock chagrin. "By all means, let's use your cards. They might bring *me* luck!"

"And why don't we play for real money?" Sabrina inquired, with the air of one who has suddenly thought of a novel idea. "It would make the game so much more interesting. Now that I've learned to play so well, the odds in your favor aren't nearly as great." She tossed him a saucy smile. "I'd like to win a handsome sum from you, Jareth. London is such an expensive city, and my pockets—what's that expression you English use?—my pockets will soon be to let!"

"Sabrina, I've told you, there's no reason for you to worry about money," he said in quick concern. "What's mine is yours."

Shaking her head, she said seriously, "Perhaps I'm being prudish, but I really can't accept money from you until—until, well, you know," she floundered. "Until after we're married," she finished in a rush.

"But meanwhile, you don't object to relieving me of my blunt at the gaming table, is that it?" Jareth replied, laughing. "Very well, we'll play for real stakes. Let's see—we have red, yellow, and blue counters. Shall we say a penny for the red, a shilling for the yellow and a pound for the blue?"

"Jareth, you're making fun of me. Those are childish stakes. Why not five pounds for the red, fifty for the yellow, and a hundred for the blue?"

The smile slowly died out of Jareth's eyes. "My God, Sabrina, I know professional gamblers who play for lesser stakes than that. What if you lose — no, *when* you lose. How are you going to pay me back?"

Sabrina tossed her head. "Why do you assume I'll lose?" she asked coolly. "If I do, I'll apply to my bankers through Uncle Johann."

Opening his mouth, Jareth clamped his lips shut again against an obviously angry retort. After a moment he said dryly, "Don't say I didn't warn you, my love."

The markings on the cards Oliver had once used to such larcenous effect were undetectable except to the keenest eye. In the dim light, Sabrina was sure Jareth wouldn't notice. Oliver had been playing macao the night before he died, using a special deck in which only the seven's, eight's and nine's were marked, making detection that much more difficult. The dealer using such a deck could not, of course, win every hand, but the odds were overwhelmingly in his favor. Sabrina also had another weapon. During the period in Vienna when she'd acted as hostess to Oliver's gaming friends, she'd learned to deal "seconds" — to slip a card from beneath the top card so skillfully and swiftly that the move was virtually invisible. It had been purely a parlor pastime. It had never occurred to her to cheat her guests, and she'd been unaware that Oliver was using marked cards.

Half an hour into their game, after a hand in which Sabrina had boldly staked five blue counters to win fifteen hundred pounds on a natural nine, Jareth looked incredulously at the stack of counters in front of her.

"I've never known a rank amateur to have such luck," he muttered, his speech slightly slurred. He'd finished the bottle of champagne and was well into a second, and he'd shown increasing signs of testiness as Sabrina, beginning her play with a feigned timidity, had made her bets larger and larger. "You must have thirty or forty blue counters in front of you," he grumbled.

Sabrina knew that she had exactly forty-five blue counters, and her remaining yellow and red markers totaled a shade over five hundred pounds. She shuffled the cards, surreptitiously noting that the top card was marked, and drew a deep breath. Now or never. Shaking her head, she said sympathetically, "Your luck really has been wretched, Jareth. I feel a little guilty, winning so much . . ." Suddenly she pushed her pile of counters into the middle of the table. "There! I'll give you a chance to make up your losses on one hand!"

Jareth looked rather blearily at his tiny stack of counters. "That's handsome of you, Sabrina, but if you should win I'd have to give you an IOU."

"Oh, don't concern yourself about that," Sabrina replied airily. "I know you're good for any sum." Holding the cards with her fingers curled around them, she dexterously dealt Jareth the second card in the deck and herself the top card. She knew she had given herself a natural of seven, eight, or nine. There were exactly eleven chances out of fifty-one that the second card that she had dealt to Jareth had also been a natural. The odds were enormously in her favor, but . . . She peered across the table at Jareth's card and her stomach squeezed into a excruciatingly painful knot. The second was also a marked card. Was his card higher than hers?

"Well, Sabrina, I do believe the tides of fortune are running my way at last," Jareth said gleefully. He flipped his card, showing an eight.

Slowly Sabrina extended her hand, her fingers trembling as she grasped her card and turned it over. "I fear your natural isn't quite high enough, Jareth."

He stared at the nine of diamonds, even reaching out to touch the card, as if to verify it was actually there. Then he leaned back in his chair, looking at Sabrina with a crooked smile. "You're my prize pupil, my love. I must remember in the future to keep my teaching talents under a basket."

"I was very fortunate."

"Oh, I think your triumph went a little beyond beginner's luck," he said dryly.

Sabrina glanced at him quickly, wondering if his remark had a double meaning, but he merely seemed tired and more than a little intoxicated. Picking up the cards, she put them back in their ornate painted box.

Rousing himself, Jareth began arranging the counters in neat piles, separating them by colors. "I make it five thousand one hundred pounds. Doubled, naturally. A very nice evening's work, even by my standards." He hesitated, looking at her with an uncertain smile. "Just to set matters straight, you weren't funning, were you, Sabrina? We *were* playing for real money?"

Sabrina opened her eyes wide in surprise. "Why, yes. Of course, if you think the stakes were too high, or if I won too much—"

"Not at all," he said curtly. "I'll write you an IOU at once."

"Oh, don't do that. Give me a bank draft. It will be less trouble for you. And make it out for an even ten thousand. I don't want to seem greedy."

A curtain came down over his eyes, leaving them expressionless. "As you like, naturally." He rose, walking over to the secretary. In a moment he returned with the bank draft. Handing it to her as she sat at the card table, he said coolly, in the same tone he might have used in discussing the weather with an acquaintance, "I trust you'll enjoy spending this. You can buy a large number of new frocks with ten thousand pounds."

She knew the emotions that must be roiling beneath that controlled exterior. He was confused, he was angry, he was hurt. Perhaps he was even feeling the beginnings of suspicion, and she couldn't afford that. Pretending to study the bank draft, she giggled, saying, "It's hard to believe this bit of paper is actually worth so much money. When we started playing for real stakes, I thought how wonderful it would be if I could win a few pounds from an expert gambler like you. And now see what I've done!" She looked up at him, smiling provocatively. "Buy new frocks for myself? Never! I'll buy something for you, Jareth. How much do horses cost?"

His carefully blank mask dissolved, and he pulled her out of her chair and into his arms. His eyes brimming with laughter, he exclaimed, "Sabrina, you wretch, you beautiful ninnyhammer! I should wring your neck. Do you realize that *no one* has ever taken as much as ten thousand pounds from me in one sitting?" He shook her playfully. "The least you can do is to salve my ego a bit. Confess, now. It wasn't your skill that beat me, it was a confounded run of luck!"

Sabrina grinned, waving the bank draft in front of his nose. "Whatever it was, I'm going to keep *this!*" The clock on the mantel chimed softly, and she exclaimed in alarm, "Good God, Jareth, look at the time. It's one in the morning. We must be going. You don't want Lotte revising her good opinion of the Herr, do you?"

"Perish the thought." Jareth rolled his eyes. "She might forbid the banns." He crossed to the bellrope beside the fireplace to ring for his valet and order the carriage.

Later, as Jareth's town chariot approached the Green Park and the Pulteney Hotel, he was saying, "So it's settled then, I'll go see Lady Melbourne in the morning, and you'll write to your uncle immediately and—my love, what is it?"

Sabrina had sat abruptly upright, freeing herself from his encircling arm. "Jareth, I love you," she whispered, staring into his face in the dim light of the street lamps, as if she were memorizing his features.

"And I worship you, love—" He broke off as she threw her arms around his neck, kissing him passionately, desperately, straining against him when her touch ignited an answering flame in his body.

The carriage stopped, and neither of them noticed until the door opened and the coachman reached in to pull down the steps. Jareth tore himself away from Sabrina, muttering a strangled curse when he became aware that they were the object of attention from an interested urchin, much too young to be abroad at that hour, and several passing gentleman who had been imbibing too freely of Blue Ruin.

"Now I've compromised you well and truly in full view of the public," he murmured. "It's a good thing you've already promised to marry me."

"I don't care if all London sees us," Sabrina said tensely. She leaned over to kiss him again, her mouth hard and demanding against his lips. "Good-bye, Jareth. Don't bother to come inside with me."

"Of course I'm coming—Sabrina, wait."

But she was already out of the carriage and halfway up the steps of the hotel. His forehead furrowed in a puzzled frown, Jareth checked his instinctive move to follow her and stood watching as she disappeared through the door of the Pulteney.

Chapter Eight

When Lotte answered his knock, Adrian pushed past her into the sitting room of Sabrina's hotel suite. "By all that's holy, Lotte, what's wrong with my sister?" he demanded. "Her note said I should come immediately, it was urgent, but I could hardly read her handwriting, it was so scrawled—" He stared at the portmanteaux and bandboxes stacked in the center of the room, and at Lotte's plain dark bonnet and cloak. "Has something happened? Where *is* Sabrina?"

Lotte shook her head. "I don't know, *mein Herr*, and that's the truth of it," she said miserably. "When I brought her tea this morning, she was already awake. In fact, I don't think she'd slept at all, she looked *schrecklich*—dreadful. She'd packed all her belongings, every last thing we'd brought with us, and she was sitting in a chair in her bonnet and pelisse, watching the clock on the mantel. She wouldn't answer my questions, wouldn't say a word, just stared at the clock until it struck half after seven. Then she bounded up from her chair, telling me to be ready to leave for Sussex the moment she returned, and bolted out the door. *Mein Herr*, I'm troubled about the mistress. She's not herself. There's something very wrong."

"She must have sent off the hotel servant with her

message to me as she was leaving the hotel," Adrian muttered. He looked at the clock. "It's after nine," he said uneasily. "Where could she be? Lotte, haven't you any idea where she went, or why she's suddenly decided to leave London? Does it have anything to do with getting my mon—that is to say, is she leaving on my account?"

Lotte shook her head again. They waited in apprehensive silence as the minutes dragged by. The clock was striking the half-hour when Sabrina walked into the room. Her face was drawn and pale, with dark circles under her eyes.

"You're here, Adrian. Good." Her voice sounded dull.

"In heaven's name, Sabrina, where have you been? Lotte and I were half out of our minds worrying about you."

She shrugged. "It's no great mystery. I was visiting the offices of Ransom, Morland, and Company, the bankers in Pall Mall." Reaching into her reticule, she handed him a packet of notes. "Here you are. Ten thousand pounds in one hundred pound notes. Pay your debt of honor, Adrian, and don't ever gamble again. Another time I won't be able to help you."

Adrian turned the packet of notes over in his hands, his expression a mixture of relief and bewilderment. "It's wonderful, Sabrina. Thank you." He paused, looking uncomfortable. "Who—where did you get the money?"

"Don't ask," she snapped.

His gaze sharpened. "I know you've been seeing Lord Jareth—Sabrina, you promised me you wouldn't ask him to forgive the debt." He shook his head. "No, of course you didn't do that. There'd have been no need for any money to change hands in that case. Was it a loan, then, from these bankers of which you spoke?" When Sabrina didn't reply immediately, he squared his shoulders, saying earnestly, "I daresay I haven't the right to force your confidences, but I *do* think I should know the source of this money. I fully intend to pay you back, and if the money was a loan I must know the terms and the interest rate—"

"You needn't worry about repayment," Sabrina interrupted him. "The money wasn't a loan. I earned it."

"Earned it? Ten thousand pounds?" Adrian inquired incredulously. "How —?"

"Yes, earned it. It was at the sacrifice of my self-respect, but I earned it," Sabrina burst out. She broke off, biting her lip. "Adrian, please take the money and go. Lotte and I are leaving London immediately. You're holding us up with all this chatter. Go *now*, Adrian," she added, her voice breaking, as he showed signs of wanting to argue with her.

"If that's what you want me to do," Adrian said quietly. Placing his arm over her shoulders he gave her a brief hug. "Thank you, Sabrina. You've saved me from the cents-per-cent or worse, and I'll be forever grateful. Good-bye. I'll be down to see you and Mama and Daphne soon."

As Adrian went down the stairs he passed two of the hotel porters coming up.

"You've sent for a cab?" Sabrina asked one of the porters when he and his companion entered the sitting room and started to load themselves down with the luggage.

"Yes, ma'am. It be at the door now."

"Excellent. Take the luggage down at once. I'm in a great hurry."

After their bags had been brought to the entrance of the hotel and while they were being loaded onto the roof of the waiting hackney cab, Sabrina gave a quick glance around her, noting that one of the porters was in earshot. Raising her voice, she gave her instructions to the driver of the hackney: "Take us to the Bull and Mouth Inn in St. Martins-le-Grand."

146

As the cab moved away in the direction of Pall Mall and the Strand, Lotte said hesitantly, "We *are* going home to Latimer House, *meine Frau?*"

It took Sabrina several moments to come back from the grim, withdrawn mood into which she seemed to have retreated. Staring at the abigail, she said shortly, "Yes, of course. Where else would we be going?"

"Well . . . it was only that we arrived in London at the Swan with Two Necks Inn. Perhaps you plan to travel on another coach line?"

"No, we're returning to Sussex the same way we came. First I have an errand at the Bull and Mouth."

"Oh." Lotte still looked puzzled. She tried again. "The mails, *meine Frau*, they all leave in the evening, *ja?* And the day coach to Newhaven—won't it have left already? It's long past nine o'clock."

"We'll wait at the Swan with Two Necks for the evening mail."

"But—you look so tired, *meine Frau*. Mightn't it be more comfortable for you to spend the day in your suite at the hotel instead of waiting at the inn for the departure of the mail coach? Or we could travel by post chaise. Then we could leave at our convenience."

"It wouldn't have been safe to stay at the hotel for a moment longer than necessary. And I can't afford to travel by post chaise," Sabrina said impatiently. After a brief pause she blurted, "In any case, a chaise would be too easy to trace."

"Not safe to stay at the hotel? Trace a post chaise? *Meine Frau*, I don't understand this craziness. What's wrong with you?"

Sabrina slumped back against the squabs, closing her eyes. "Nothing. Everything. I think I've sold my soul to the devil."

Lotte exclaimed in quick concern, "Don't say things like that, *Lieblinge—*"

"I don't want to talk about it, Lotte." The weary finality in Sabrina's tone silenced the abigail.

In the courtyard of the Bull and Mouth, Sabrina left Lotte sitting in the hackney while she made her way to the stables. An ostler came up to her, touching a grimy forefinger to his forehead. "Kin I 'elp ye, ma'am?" he asked, obviously finding a lady of quality distinctly out of place in these surroundings.

Sabrina looked at the man closely. He had an honest, open face, and he seemed intelligent. She opened her reticule, taking out a five pound note. "I need a favor," she told him. "A gentleman may come to the inn inquiring about me. He's young, handsome, fashionably dressed, and he'll be driving a pair of magnificent matched bays. If he does come here, I want you to tell him that a lady of my description, accompanied by an abigail and with large quantities of luggage, hired a post chaise and left the Bull and Mouth at eleven o'clock this morning."

The ostler nodded thoughtfully, eyeing the five pound note dangling between her fingers. "This 'ere cove, 'e'll likely want ter know where ye were 'eading?" he inquired after a pause.

"Yes. Tell him you thought you heard me instruct the postilions to take me to Dover."

The ostler nodded again. "Ye kin count on me, ma'am. I'd be 'appy ter obleege ye."

"Thank you." With another long look, which he met unflinchingly, Sabrina handed the ostler his money and returned to the hackney cab. "The Swan with Two Necks in Lad Lane," she told the driver.

Jareth was a late riser, not because he was particularly slothful, but because he seldom left the gaming tables at White's to retire to his bed until the night was winding down. This morning was no exception. At about the same moment that Sabrina and Lotte were dismissing their cab in front of the Swan with Two Necks Inn, he sat up in bed, yawning and stretching, wincing at the sudden sharp throbbing in his head. Would he never learn? Champagne in more than small quantities always left him with a monster of a headache the following morning, and last night he'd downed the better part of two bottles. Sabrina had drunk no more than a glass.

Sabrina. The image of her beautiful vibrant face made him forget the pain of his headache. A blissful smile curved his lips. She was his now. He didn't have to worry anymore about when she'd leave London, or whether Uncle Johann would succeed in forcing her to the altar with his odious son Stefan.

"Your tea, my lord. Would you care for your breakfast now?"

Jareth looked up with a start. He'd been so lost in his thoughts he hadn't heard his valet enter the bedchamber. "By Jove, yes, Harris. I'll have breakfast immediately. I've a million things to do today." Gulping down a cup of scalding tea, he got out of bed, shrugging his arms into his dressing gown as he walked into the sitting room.

He was well into a large plate of ham and poached eggs, washed down with a tankard of beer that seemed to be rapidly curing his aching head, when Harris, who had been quietly tidying the room, brought him the ornate Viennese playing card.

"I found this on the floor near the fireplace, my lord."

Glancing at the card, Jareth set it down on the table, saying carelessly, "Thank you. I'll see it gets returned to its owner." He paused, his forkful of ham halfway to his mouth, as he observed the valet's expression, usually so discreetly self-effacing, now tinged with curiosity. "What is it, Harris?"

The valet hesitated. "This card, my lord. It's not one of ours, of course, but—perhaps you'd care to have a closer look at it."

His eyes narrowing, Jareth picked up the card. The nine of Diamonds. Sabrina had taken ten thousand pounds from him last night with this card. He still found it almost impossible to comprehend her incredible beginner's streak of luck. Turning the card over, he examined it closely. In the bright spring sunlight streaming in through the windows he could plainly see the minute marking on the back of the card. Last night, castaway on champagne as he'd been, and in the dim light of the candles, he hadn't noticed the almost invisible marking. And naturally, it hadn't occurred to him to be on the alert for cheating when he was playing cards with the woman he loved.

He drew a deep breath. Cheating. How could he even think of using that word in connection with Sabrina? There must be some other explanation for this marked card. Wait. She'd told him that she bought the deck of cards yesterday in Bond Street. Could the deck have been tampered with at the shop? But if so, why . . . ? And if Sabrina hadn't taken advantage of this marking—and doubtless those on the other cards of the deck—how had she managed to win all that money from him?

There was only one way to find out. Throwing down his napkin, he shot up from the table, tearing off his dressing gown as he headed for his bedchamber. "Have the curricle brought around. I'm leaving in ten minutes," he exclaimed over his shoulder.

"Ten minutes, my lord?" Harris sounded horrified. "I don't think we can complete our toilet in ten minutes. If we don't get your cravat right the first time around—"

"To hell with my cravat."

The valet blenched.

150

A scant half an hour later, Jareth strode into the Pulteney Hotel and up the staircase to Sabrina's suite, where he found a group of maidservants busily sweeping and dusting and changing linens, but no Sabrina and no Lotte. "Do you expect the countess back soon?" he inquired. "Perhaps she's at breakfast?"

"She's gone, sir. From the hotel, I mean. Left here round about ten o' the clock this morning," replied one of the maids.

Suppressing a curse, Jareth inquired impatiently, "Where did she go?"

"Beggin' yer pardon, sir, I dunno. One o' the porters who brought down the lady's luggage, 'e might tell ye."

Minutes later, driving away from the Pulteney, Jareth thought dully that he was almost certainly going on a fool's errand to the offices of his bankers. The porter at the hotel, pocketing the silver crown proffered to him, had recalled with little prompting that the countess had ordered the hackney driver to go to the Bull and Mouth. No, the lady hadn't left any message for Lord Jareth. No, she hadn't left a forwarding address. So now Jareth knew that Sabrina in all probability had already left London. Only an idiot would believe she hadn't cashed his bank draft before quitting the city.

At the banking premises of Ransom, Morland and Company, Jareth was told by a polite underling that a young lady had indeed appeared at the bank as soon as it opened for business, and they had, of course, cashed Lord Jareth's draft for her immediately. Would there be something amiss?

Climbing back into his curricle, Jareth pushed his horses at such a spanking pace that he narrowly avoided colliding with a brewer's dray, causing even his imperturbable tiger to utter a stifled exclamation of alarm. Jareth didn't hear it. He continued to drive oblivious to his speed, avoiding any further near-accidents by virtue of superb reflex actions combined with perfect physical coordination and complete mastery over his animals. His heart ached as if it were being crushed in an iron vise, but his emotional hurt was rapidly being consumed in a wave of burning anger and resentment at his own stupidity.

How could he have been such a gull? The famous Jareth Tremayne, Dandy of Dandies, Pink of the *ton,* an out-and-outer, a trump, a Trojan, up to every rig and row in town. And he'd been completely bubbled by a slip of a tawny-haired adventuress. Looking back on his relationship with Sabrina, he could see that she had stalked him every inch of the way. She'd first caught his attention by driving down St. James's Street, eyeing him impudently as he sat in the bow window. Then she'd waylaid him in Hyde Park on the pretense that her ankle was twisted, and had further ensnared him with her touching tales of her widowed life under the genial tyranny of her Uncle Johann.

The telltale signs of Sabrina's duplicity had been everywhere, and he'd been too besotted to notice them. That accent, for instance. The bewitching Viennese accent that had been nothing but pure fakery. Why hadn't he become suspicious of her when anger or carelessness caused the charming accent to slip? Why hadn't he questioned her convenient fainting spell when Prinny had wanted to introduce her to the Hungarian diplomat, Prince Paul Esterházy, at Lady Melbourne's house? The prince had probably been one of her earlier victims, and she was afraid he'd denounce her for a scheming trollop!

Jareth's thoughts continued to revolve chaotically. Uncle Johann! The Viennese uncle probably didn't exist, or, if he did, he was her protector, not a relative. He was as much a figment of Sabrina's imagination as her pose of unconventional innocence. She'd played him like a trout on a casting line, his brain turning into mush like that of a lovesick schoolboy as he slipped deeper under her spell, until the carefully prepared moment when she'd taken a fortune from him with a pack of marked cards. He was sure it wasn't the first time. This woman was a practiced gambler who had often used her physical allure to prevent her hapless quarry from suspecting her cheating ways. And to think he'd refrained from making love to her for fear of soiling her virginity. How she must have laughed at him for that.

Jareth swallowed against the bitter taste of bile in his mouth. Sabrina had overshot herself this time. No matter how long it took, no matter how much it cost, he was going to make her pay.

At the Bull and Mouth Inn he headed for the stables, where he caught the eye of one of the ostlers.

"A lady who hired a post chaise this morning?" the man said doubtfully in response to Jareth's question. "We have so many customers who travel post, do y'see—"

"You'd remember this lady if you'd ever seen her," Jareth interrupted. "She's tall and quite beautiful, and she has hair the color of ripe corn. She'd have been alone, except for her maid."

"Ah, *that* lady." The ostler nodded wisely. The pound note Jareth extended to him vanished into his pocket. "Indeed, sir. She 'ired a chaise and four ter go ter Dover, not three hours agone."

He'd thought as much, Jareth reflected, as he returned to his curricle and put the team in motion. However, it had been as well to check. Most travelers bound for France went by way of Dover, heading for Calais or Boulogne, but it was also possible to sail from a number of other ports. He had, of course, been convinced that Sabrina would head for the Continent by the first available transportation. It was imperative to catch up with her at Dover, or to intercept her shortly after she crossed the Channel. With a long enough lead — several days would do it — she would arrive in Paris far ahead of him and almost certainly be out of his reach, making any pursuit useless.

Jareth made the journey to Dover in just under ten hours, faster than the time of the crack mail coaches, by driving his horses to the limit of their speed and endurance. The countryside flashed by in a blur: New Cross, Blackheath, Gad's Hill, Rochester, the Medway flats, Canterbury, then on to Barham and Dover, where he stepped down on stiff legs in front of the King's Head at one o'clock in the morning. Sabrina wasn't there, had never been there. Nor, when he drove to the other first-class inn in Dover, the Ship, did he find any trace of her. However, neither the Ship nor the King's Head had any vacancies. As full of juice as Sabrina was with his ten thousand pounds in her pocket, it was probable that she'd been forced to lodge in one of the ramshackle inns kept by retired sailors, as he himself would be obliged to do to obtain a bed for what remained of the night. He'd check the other hotels in the morning, before the packet sailed.

Four days later Jareth was back in London, frustrated and weary. He'd found no trace of Sabrina in any of the Dover inns. Had she misstated her destination to the ostler at the Bull and Mouth in order to confuse her trail? She must have sailed from another port. In an interminable, exhausting drive, he'd proceeded to investigate hotels in Folkestone, Brighton, Newhaven, Southampton, and Gravesend, to no avail. Sabrina had vanished. Perhaps she'd dismissed the chaise and postilions from the Bull and Mouth at some intermediate point, going to ground in the countryside to wait for her trail to grow cold before she left England. It was probably useless even to check with the postilions from the Bull and Mouth. Too much time had elapsed.

On his drive into the city he considered looking into a last possibility that Sabrina had caught a French trader at a London dock, but immediately abandoned the idea. Again, too much time had elapsed. Not once had it occurred to him that his beautiful Viennese adventuress had traveled dog cheap by humble stagecoach.

When he walked into his lodgings at the Albany his valet greeted him with heartfelt relief. "My lord, I was beginning to be concerned about you. It's been four, no, five days since I heard from you—" He broke off with an expression of horror as he took a second look at his master. Jareth's exquisite coat and pantaloons were grubby and unpressed, the once masterfully tied Trône d'Amour knot in his cravat was a sad parody of itself and there was a definite growth of stubble on the patrician chin.

"If your lordship were to allow me to make a suggestion," the valet said in an aggrieved voice as he removed Jareth's coat, giving it a look of loathing, as if it had suddenly become contaminated, "might it not be helpful in the future if I were to accompany your lordship on your journeys out of town? It's especially worrying when I don't know where you are, or how long you'll be away. And it can't add to your lordship's consequence, or mine, for you to be seen in a state like this—"

Jareth transfixed the valet with a cold stare. "I pay you a generous stipend to take care of my wardrobe, Harris. And occasionally, only occasionally, I allow you to help me when I tie my cravat, if I'm in a particularly good mood. Otherwise I can manage my life quite nicely without your assistance. Please remember that."

The valet stepped back with a bow. "Certainly, my lord," he replied woodenly.

Hunching his shoulders, Jareth drew a long breath and expelled it. With a smile that contained little mirth, he said, "Sorry, Harris. If I'm blue-deviled, there's no need to make you suffer for it. Draw me a bath now, there's a good fellow, and lay out something suitable to wear to White's."

"Very good, my lord. Before you bathe, you might wish to read a letter that came for you."

"I'll take care of my correspondence when I return from the club," said Jareth impatiently, turning on his heel to head for the bedchamber.

"Yes, my lord. This letter, however, it's from Winwood Park, my lord."

Jareth paused in his tracks. What could Lionel possibly want? He stretched out his hand. "Very well, I'll read it now."

The letter wasn't from Lionel, though. "My dear Jareth," read Christabel's tiny, perfect handwriting, "I must see you. I fear something dreadful may happen here. I don't know where to turn. I can't put anything down in writing; I must talk to you in person. Please come down to Sussex as soon as you possibly can. Your devoted sister-in-law, Christabel."

Jareth frowned. Christabel must be mad to expect him to go to Winwood Park. His last meeting with his brother had been decidedly unpleasant. And yet . . . Christabel must have been desperate to write to him. Did he have the right to ignore her plea for help?

Strolling into White's later that evening, Jareth was outwardly his usual self, impeccably dressed, every waving lock in place, his features schooled into an expression of cool impassivity. Intercepting him on the threshold of the card room, Lord Alvanley said with a genial clap on the shoulder, "I say, Tremayne, where've you been of late? I missed you at Prinny's soiree last night. I thought he'd invited you to bring your charming

156

countess."

"The countess has returned to the Continent," Jareth replied, shrugging.

"Ah, that explains your disappearance," Lord Alvanley laughed. "Been wearing the willow, have you?"

Jareth lifted an eyebrow. "My dear Alvanley, when is the last time you noticed me wearing the willow? The countess and I enjoyed a lovely amorous interlude, and now it's over. Care to join me in a game of hazard?"

The tone was light, even mocking, but Alvanley caught the glint of steel in Jareth's eyes and said hastily, "I'm with you. I feel lucky tonight."

At three in the morning, after some six hours of play, Jareth ended his game of hazard with a profit of over twenty thousand pounds and moved to the whist table, where he followed the same style of play, alternately winning and losing and winning again, and reacting to each win or loss with the same cold indifference. He also continued to drink, downing bottle after bottle of claret, which for many hours appeared to have not the slightest effect on either his speech or his card playing.

Lord Alvanley, who had left White's on Thursday morning at the time Jareth began playing whist, returned to the club on Friday afternoon. Casually glancing into the card room, he spotted Jareth at a whist table and beckoned to a hovering servant. "How long has Lord Jareth been playing whist?"

The servant rolled his eyes. "As best I kin tell, m'lord, 'e's bin asitting at that table fer better than a full day, since early yestiday morning."

"Winning or losing, would you say?"

"More winning than losing, ye kin lay yer last megg on that, m'lord."

"Drinking heavily?"

"Well—'e's been dipping rather deep, that I *will* say, m'lord."

Sighing, Alvanley walked to the whist table, where Jareth and his partner had just scored a bumper, consisting of two triples and a rubber score of two. The opponent to Jareth's left rose, pushing back his chair. "That finishes me, Tremayne. You'll have the family home if I keep playing. I never saw such a confounded run of luck in my life." The man's partner nodded, saying, "My sentiments exactly."

"As you please, gentlemen." Jareth looked up, appearing to have trouble focusing his eyes. "Hello, Alvanley," he mumbled. "Will you sit in? We'll find a fourth." His face was gray and haggard, and Alvanley could hear a telltale slur in his voice.

"Not this time. Jareth, I must talk to you," Alvanley said urgently. "Need your advice. Matter of the heart," he added, lowering his tone to a confidential murmur.

Jareth blinked his eyes. "I'm jus' the man for you, old fellow. Know all about . . . all about . . ." Slowly dragging himself to his feet, he took a step toward Alvanley, only to collapse in a limp heap on the floor.

"Do you feel as dreadful as you look?" inquired Lady Melbourne, an amused smile lighting her dark eyes as she stared up at Jareth's pasty skin and the dark eyes that seemed to have retreated deep inside their sockets.

Leaning down to kiss the hand she extended to him, he pulled up a chair next to her and sat down. "I've felt healthier," he admitted wryly. "I try not to move my head too quickly. It might fall off. Did you want to see me about anything in particular?"

"Do I need a reason for you to come to see me?"

"No, but you don't usually send for me."

"Perhaps I wanted to see if the leopard had changed its spots," Lady Melbourne said calmly. "Someone told me you just spent forty-eight hours at White's without once

158

leaving the gaming tables. Is it true?"

"As near as makes no difference. Is your 'someone' named Alvanley?"

"I never reveal the names of my informants." She gazed at him thoughtfully. "Jareth, I would have sworn you were a sensible man. A little drinking, a little gambling, a little wenching—nothing in excess. What's happened to change you?"

A muscle twitched in his cheek. "Perhaps I'm weary of being a pillar of rectitude. Perhaps I feel it's time to sow my wild oats. I am, of course, not accountable to anyone," he said pointedly.

Lady Melbourne laughed. "Don't think to fob me off by being so toplofty, my lad. I know you too well for that." Casually she added, "You didn't bring that charming Viennese gal to have tea with me. How is she?"

"Well, I trust. She returned to the Continent several days ago."

"I'm sorry to hear that. I'd looked forward to improving our acquaintance. Will she be visiting London again?"

"I have no idea." Jareth looked Lady Melbourne squarely in the eyes. "What the countess does in future is of no interest to me."

"I see. Perhaps that's why she left England, then," Lady Melbourne said pensively. "I had the impression that she was quite fond of you."

"That was a take-in, Lady M. Sabrina isn't capable of affection for anyone except herself," Jareth snarled. He paused, an expression of almost comic chagrin crossing his face as he realized what he had said and the interpretation Lady Melbourne would undoubtedly give it.

She looked at him in silence for several moments. Then, reaching over to give him a gentle pat on his knee, she said, "I think you're wrong, you know. The countess isn't like the other one, that yaller-haired sister-in-law of yours, I could swear to it. But there, that's enough from an interfering old women. Are you planning to go to Epsom for the Derby?"

Sometime later, as he left Melbourne House, Jareth wondered grimly if his emotions were as transparently obvious to everyone as they were to Lady Melbourne and Lord Alvanley. He writhed inwardly at the prospect of being the butt of the *ton*'s ribald amusement. Not that anyone in London knew his Hungarian countess was an unscrupulous adventuress rather than a decorous widow, and he was confident that neither Lady M. nor Alvanley would spread any gossip about him and Sabrina. However, he'd made the mistake of introducing her to his friends at that gathering at Melbourne House, where no one could have missed seeing the heart he was wearing on his sleeve. If he were to be asked about Sabrina or her sudden disappearance from the London scene, he wasn't sure that he could conceal his feelings. Damn Sabrina! Why couldn't she simply have found a clever way to entrap him into a card game with her marked deck? Then only his pride would have been hurt. Why had it been necessary to make him fall in love with her?

During the drive back to his rooms in the Albany, his temper failed to improve. When he entered the sitting room he stopped short on the threshold, giving the occupant of the wing chair by the fireplace an unfriendly stare. "You'll have to excuse me, Latimer," he said curtly. "I had a late night last night, and I'm not up to seeing anyone today."

Flushing a dull red, Adrian rose. "I don't wish to intrude, naturally, Lord Jareth," he said stiffly. "However, I've tried repeatedly to see you during this past week and you've always been out — and I really do have an important matter to discuss with you. I persuaded your valet to allow me to wait here until you returned today."

"Sir Adrian has left numerous messages for you, my lord," murmured Harris. "You'll find them with the rest of your correspondence in your secretary."

Out of sorts though he was, something in Adrian's mortified young face caused Jareth to throw up his hands and say grudgingly, "Very well, then, Latimer. What's this important matter that can't wait?"

Adrian reached into his box pouch. "It's quite simple, Lord Jareth. I want to pay you the ten thousand pounds I lost to you at macao a month ago. You were kind enough to grant me thirty days' grace, for which I thank you. Here is your money."

Accepting the thick packet of notes, Jareth gazed at the money indifferently. "Thank you, Latimer. A piece of friendly advice — if you plan to continue playing macao, study the game."

"I appreciate the advice, but I won't be doing any gambling in the future," said Adrian ruefully. "I promised my sister —" He broke off, saying with a rather strained smile, "The fact is, I'm the head of my family now, and I can't afford to drop my blunt at the tables."

A warning bell rang somewhere deep in Jareth's consciousness. He looked hard at Adrian, studying the tall graceful figure, the classically handsome features, the dark blue eyes and the mane of tawny hair. "I haven't spent much time in Sussex in recent years, so I'm afraid I don't know many of the county families, the younger members especially," he said casually. "You have a sister? And is your mother still living?"

"I have a stepmother," Adrian mumbled, avoiding Jareth's eyes. "And I have two sisters." He put on the helmet he'd been holding in the crook of his arm. "I won't keep you, Lord Jareth. Thank you for your patience in waiting for your money. Good-bye, sir."

Jareth made no move to detain Adrian, who departed so hastily that he nearly bowled over Harris at the door.

It wasn't necessary to detain Adrian. A few judicious inquiries at the Horse Guards about the Latimer family would tell Jareth anything he cared to know. Actually, he had no need to make those inquiries. He already knew, with a deep-down certitude, that one of Adrian's sisters was named Sabrina.

It couldn't be sheer coincidence. A week ago Sabrina had won ten thousand pounds from him. Ten thousand, two hundred pounds, to be precise. He could hear her voice saying, "Make out your bank draft for an even ten thousand. I don't want to seem greedy." Today Adrian Latimer had paid him exactly ten thousand pounds, which *could* have been coincidental, except that Jareth had suddenly realized, when Adrian mentioned his sister, that the youngster was a mirror image of Sabrina, a taller masculine version of Jareth's enchanting Hungarian countess.

Chapter Nine

As Sabrina entered the morning room, Lady Latimer glanced up from her letter, her eyes narrowing as she looked at her stepdaughter's gown of dark gray muslin and her prim cornet of black cambric. Fanny herself was bandbox perfection in a morning dress of delicately sprigged rose-colored muslin, with the merest wisp of a white lace cap on her carefully arranged dark hair.

"My dear Sabrina, I thought it was understood that you were permanently out of mourning."

Sitting down opposite her stepmother, Sabrina picked up a two-day-old copy of the *Morning Chronicle*. "I feel comfortable in these clothes, Mama," she said quietly, "and what does it matter what I wear in the house?"

"What does it matter—?" At this gross heresy words failed Lady Latimer, who could not conceive of an occasion when a lady would not be concerned about her appearance.

Daphne bounced into the room. "There you are, Sabrina. I missed you at breakfast. I wanted you to tell me all about your visit to your sister-in-law, but you were a slugabed this morning," she teased. "It's hardly to be wondered at, of course. You arrived home so late yesterday, and you looked so tired. Why on earth didn't you write us you were leaving Lady Yardley's house? We would have sent the carriage to meet you in Newhaven."

"I left Yardley Place on the spur of the moment. One of Maria's cousins arrived unexpectedly to keep her company, so I wasn't needed any longer," Sabrina prevaricated quickly. "I know I should have written to tell you I was coming, but that would have meant staying in Kent an extra day or two, and I was anxious to be home. I'm sure estate matters have piled up while I was gone."

"And how is Lady Yardley?" inquired Fanny. "It must have been very comforting for her to have dear Oliver's wife with her in her moment of trial."

Assuring Fanny that Maria was doing very well, Sabrina felt a sudden chill as she reflected how quickly the story she'd told to cover her trip to London would have been unmasked if her sister-in-law had chanced to write to her at Latimer House during her absence. Fortunately, Maria hated to write letters. The secret of Sabrina's whereabouts for the past several weeks was safe.

"Come, Sabrina, now that you're rested and feeling more the thing, do tell Mama and me all your news," said Daphne, pulling up a chair.

"I don't have any," laughed Sabrina. "Maria and I had a very quiet time during my visit. Don't forget, she's only a month or six weeks from her laying-in."

"Well, then, I must tell you that Daphne and I have some news that will interest you, even though we've been rusticating dully at home while you've been flitting about the countryside," said Lady Latimer with an air of importance tinged with the discontent that surfaced so often in her conversation. "We have a new neighbor. Appleton House has been sold at last."

"I'm glad to hear it. The house has been vacant for far too long. Have you met the new owner?"

"Indeed, yes. He's Lady Marston's brother, a retired Navy captain. When Daphne and I took tea with Lady Marston last week she introduced us to Captain Ranger.

164

Now that he's retired from the Navy, he wants to put down roots, he told us. He was delighted to find a suitable property near his sister." Fanny added in a carefully casual tone, "The Rangers are a very good family. Not titled, but of fine old stock."

"Does he have a large family?"

"He's a widower, Sabrina. A young, childless widower," said Lady Latimer impressively. "I should say he's not yet forty. Comfortably fixed, too. Lady Marston says he inherited a goodly sum from his late wife's estate, and he also was awarded a large amount of prize money during the war. But you'll soon see for yourself how pleasant and personable he is. Lady Marston has invited me and Daphne to dinner two days hence. I'm sure she'll want to include you in her invitation, once she knows you've come home."

Sabrina suppressed a sigh. The matchmaking gleam in her stepmother's eye was quite unmistakable. Fanny would make sure that an invitation to Sabrina from Lady Marston would be forthcoming. In an attempt to steer the discussion away from Captain Ranger's perfections, Sabrina asked Daphne, "So what have you been up to while I was gone, Puss?"

Daphne's pert face lighted up. "The most wonderful thing has happened! Betsy Stanhope, my dearest friend at Ravenhill Academy, has come to Newhaven to visit her brother." Blushing slightly, and looking away from Lady Latimer, Daphne continued, "I daresay you remember meeting Betsy's brother, Gordon — Captain Stanhope — before you went off to visit Lady Yardley."

"Oh, yes, I remember the captain well." Sabrina flicked a glance at Fanny, who looked distinctly uncordial at this mention of the young revenue captain whose friendship she so strongly disapproved for Daphne. "How long will Miss Stanhope be visiting in the area?"

"Until Gordon completes fitting out his new cutter.

That will be in about a week, perhaps a few days more than that." Daphne swallowed hard, a sudden desolate note audible in her voice. She went on with a forced cheerfulness, "Betsy wanted to spend as much time as possible with Gordon before he goes to sea. She won't have many opportunities to see him in the future, since she'll be getting married soon and going off to live with her husband in Antigua." Turning to Fanny, Daphne said, "May I have the carriage this afternoon, Mama? I promised Betsy I'd visit her today."

"You may not," Fanny snapped. "If Miss Stanhope wishes to see you, she can come to Latimer House."

Biting her lip, blinking against the tears welling into her eyes, Daphne choked, "You're being cruel and unjust, Mama." She jumped up from her chair and rushed from the room.

"Well!" exclaimed an outraged Lady Latimer.

"Don't you think you might have been a little severe?" Sabrina inquired.

Fanny bridled. "Are you implying that I don't have the right to watch over Daphne's interests?"

"Certainly not. You're Daphne's guardian. But are you really safeguarding her interests? I know you don't approve of Gordon Stanhope as a possible husband for her. I agree with you—I think she can look higher than the son of a yeoman farmer. However, if you persist in your antagonism, you may find that you're only stiffening Daphne's determination to continue the friendship. Both the captain and his sister will soon be leaving the area, so what's the harm in allowing Daphne to visit Miss Stanhope? What justification, really, do you have in forbidding it? Daphne and Betsy Stanhope were intimate friends all during their years at Ravenhill Academy."

"I'm bearing that in mind. I haven't asked Daphne to deny the friendship, and Miss Stanhope's station in life is just high enough so that it would be improper of me to refuse to receive her at Latimer House. But I *cannot* in good conscience allow Daphne to go to Newhaven to visit her. The girl's brother is fitting out his boat there, and you know as well as I do, Sabrina, that Daphne would be spending all her time in Gordon Stanhope's pocket while his loving sister carefully looked the other way, or even left the pair alone to do God knows what! *Now* tell me, pray, that I'm being cruel to my stepdaughter!"

"Don't talk fustian, Mama," said Sabrina lightly. "I know quite well how fond you are of Daphne. However, I might remind you it's easier to catch flies with honey than with vinegar! How would it be if I were to accompany Daphne on a visit to Miss Stanhope? I promise you I'd be a vigilant chaperon."

"Well . . . I'll think about it," replied Lady Latimer grudgingly. "I must say, I hardly look forward to the prospect of seeing Daphne fall into a fit of the dismals! Perhaps one day next week you might take her to Newhaven, but only for a brief visit, mind, and only to the house where Miss Stanhope has lodgings. Would you believe it, Captain Stanhope has actually invited Daphne to the boatyard for a tour of his cutter! Now I ask you, is that any place for a young woman of quality?" She looked up as a housemaid entered the room.

"Mr. Cavitt wants to see me at the home farm," said Sabrina after reading the brief note the housemaid had given her.

"I've never understood why you consider it necessary to conduct your business with Mr. Cavitt at the home farm," Fanny interrupted. "When old Higgins was steward, I'm sure Ezra Cavitt went to see *him*. After all, Sabrina, you have a position to maintain. You may have assumed Higgins's duties—against my better judgment, as I've so often told you—but you shouldn't forget you're the daughter of the house."

Sabrina had a sudden vision of Fanny's reaction if she were informed that her stepdaughter transacted estate business away from the house in order to conceal the fact that Ezra Cavitt not only managed the home farm but acted as Sabrina's agent in a smuggling venture.

"You look so tired, Sabrina. Your color isn't good either," said Lady Latimer, peering at her closely. "You must have worn yourself out caring for Lady Yardley. Do tell Mr. Cavitt to come see you here."

"Oh, Ezra likes to show me about the premises, you know, and his wife's day would be blighted if I didn't sample her cowslip wine," said Sabrina cheerfully. "And I'm feeling very well. In fact, I need some fresh air and exercise. You're quite right, I was cooped up inside Maria's house far too long. Actually, I think I'll walk to the home farm instead of taking the dogcart."

Escaping from the house with a feeling of relief, Sabrina didn't immediately start off toward the home farm and her interview with Ezra Cavitt. She wanted, needed, to be alone. Last night she'd avoided talking to Fanny and Daphne by pleading fatigue. Lady Latimer's sharp eyes had already discerned that Sabrina wasn't herself, and doubtless Daphne, too, would soon guess that something was troubling her older sister.

Roaming aimlessly about the grounds, Sabrina walked through the walled kitchen garden and into the orchard behind it, breathing in the soft scent of the apple blossoms and searching for violets and wild phlox and cowslips along the banks of the lively little brook that edged the orchard. A little later, still walking slowly, she followed the well-trodden path to the cliffside through turf starred with late spring wildflowers, pausing to check for birds' nests in the spinney where she and Adrian had so often played hide-and-seek. She stood for a while at the edge of the cliff, listening to the murmuring of the waves far below, looking off to her left to the sheer heights of the Seven Sisters.

Reluctantly leaving the cliffside, she retraced her steps to the house and walked down the driveway to the lane leading to the main road. It was so good to be back at Latimer House, she reflected as she walked along the lane, lifting her head to sniff the fragrance of the first dog roses in the tangle of bushes arching out from the hedgerows. She loved every familiar corner of the old place, to which she'd fled as a haven of refuge after the shambles of her marriage to Oliver. The estate would remain in the family now, for Adrian and his children and his children's children, and she hoped she would always have some connection with it, but she'd paid a fearful price to make that possible.

Had it been worth it? To ensure that Adrian would retain the ownership of Latimer House, she'd lied and cheated and denied her most intimate feelings. She'd also lost any chance of happiness with a man she might have loved. An ironic smile curved her lips. After Oliver died, she'd vowed never to put her heart at risk again. Her resolve had lasted only until she looked into Jareth Tremayne's dark eyes and felt the magic of his touch. What was done was done, and she would never see Jareth again, never tremble to the compelling ardor of his lips against hers, but she would always wonder if she could have done things differently.

What if she had simply told the truth? What was so sacrosanct about that absurd male code of honor that dictated paying a gambling debt ahead of any other obligation? She could have avoided all the lies, all the foolish masquerades, all the heartbreak, if only she'd gone to Jareth and asked him to forgive Adrian's debt, or at least to give her brother a long period of grace in which to find the money. But she hadn't done it, and now she'd have to live with her folly.

At the brief bark of a welcoming dog, she looked around her in surprise, having been so locked into her dark thoughts that she'd failed to realize she'd walked the short mile to the home farm. As she entered the courtyard, Tom Cavitt emerged from the stables, a welcoming smile on his cheerful, open young face.

"Good day ter ye, Mrs. Neville," he called. "Father said as ye was acoming ter see us."

"Good afternoon, Tom. I wasn't sure you'd be here. I thought you might be at sea."

"The *Mary Anne* dropped anchor in Newhaven last night. Glad I was ter see home port again, too. We had some fearsome weather in the Channel. All ter the good fer our purposes, o' course. Rain an' high winds make it harder fer the revenooers ter find us."

"Was it a successful run?"

Tom grinned. "Wait till ye 'ear, Mrs. Neville. 'Ave a look at this, fer starters." He pulled from his pocket a large square of brightly patterned silk. " 'Gays,' they calls 'em. Pretty, ain't they? We got ten gross o' the things. Took hardly no space in the hold, and Nate, 'e thinks they'll sell fast like." He glanced up at the sky, which had darkened considerably since Sabrina had left Latimer House. Several drops of rain splattered on his face. "Looks like the end o' our fair weather. Father 'oped we'd 'ave a bit more sunshine, ter 'elp the crops along, after our bad spring. Best ye come in, Mrs. Neville, afore ye gets wet."

As Tom ushered Sabrina into the neat front parlor, Ezra Cavitt rose to greet her, his ruddy face expressing his pleasure at seeing her. "I was happy ter 'ear ye was back, Mrs. Neville. We've missed ye."

"I wasn't gone a month, Mr. Cavitt," Sabrina laughed. "However, it's nice to be missed. I'm glad to be back." She paused as a solid, thickset figure rose from a chair in the corner. "Captain Peggoty," she said in surprise. "I didn't realize you'd be here." She didn't allow her unspoken criticism to surface, although it had always been understood that the captain of her smuggling cutter would keep his contacts with her at a minimum in order to prevent gossip from linking her to the ownership of the boat.

"I needed ter talk wi' ye, ma'am," Peggoty grunted, his hooded eyes expressionless in his square-cut face, bronzed to a leathery darkness from sun and wind.

Before there could be any discussion of the most recent voyage of the *Mary Anne*, the customary solemn ritual had to be observed. Plump Mrs. Cavitt produced her cowslip wine and delicious little cakes, beaming at the praise Sabrina bestowed on them, while Ezra made his polite social inquiries.

"Miss Daphne, she was atelling me ye was visiting Mr. Oliver's sister," Ezra observed. "Increasing, the good lady is, Miss Daphne said. And 'ow did the crops look in Kent?" His placid comments continued until his wife left the room with one final respectful bob of her head to Sabrina.

After the door closed behind Mrs. Cavitt, Sabrina said pleasantly to Nate Peggoty, "Tom tells me you had a good run this time."

The cutter captain reached into his pocket, handing her a rather grimy bit of paper on which he'd laboriously scrawled a series of figures. "Ye kin see fer yerself, Mrs. Neville," he said complacently. "One hundred an' ten half-ankers o' brandy, one hundred an' fifty half-ankers o' Geneva, fifty-five bags o' tea, nineteen bags o' terbacco — that's bettern' three hundred pound o' manufactured terbacco. And," he finished impressively, "five hundred bottle o' the best port. They tell me the big London wine merchants git five shillings the bottle fer port, sellin' ter the swells."

"This is wonderful, Captain Peggoty," said Sabrina,

looking up from her study of the rough invoice. "We'll all make a fine profit from this voyage. What was it you wanted to talk to me about?"

"Well, now, there's several things."

Peggoty moved his chair closer to Sabrina and leaned toward her with a confidential air that made her want to increase the distance between them. She'd always felt vaguely uncomfortable in the presence of this rough man, sensing the capacity for brutality beneath his hard-bitten impassivity, sensing, too, the lurking antipathy toward her and others of her class that was concealed by his careful politeness. However, despite her personal distaste for the man, she was convinced he had the necessary seaman's skills and the iron nerve to command her smuggling boat.

"First off, Mrs. Neville, I think ye should consider investing in a Geneva factory in France. I've known some who've done that, and very successfully too. Owning the source o' supply likely would moren' double yer profits in Strip-Me-Naked."

Sabrina frowned. Smuggling in gin was one thing. Making her own was quite another. Presumably, though, her responsibility for making the dandies and the members of the urban lower classes drunk on Geneva would be the same whether or not she owned the factory. "I'll give it some thought," she said after a moment. "Was there anything else?"

"Aye, I'm thinking about changing our method o' delivery. Wi' yer approval, I reckon we should stop landing our cargo on the shore. Instead we'll try 'sowin' the crop.' " At Sabrina's puzzled expression, Peggoty added, "We'll sink the tubs o' spirits offshore, attaching 'em ter a recovery line marked by a buoy. Then, when the coast is clear, we'll recover the goods wi' 'creeping irons'—grappling hooks."

"That sounds sensible. You'd be much less likely to be

detected while you were landing the goods. I agree," said Sabrina. "If that's all, then . . ."

"Begging yer pardon, that ain't all. Last month, ye may remember, the Admiralty took control o' all the revenue cutters from the Board o' Customs. That'll mean more danger fer us in the trade. Most o' the revenue cutters will be commanded by ex-Navy officers. Ye won't catch *them* staying in port in bad weather, or turning away from a fight if they be out-gunned. Nay, Mrs. Neville, we must change wi' the times. I want more guns fer the *Mary Anne*, ter put us on more even terms wi' the revenooers. We got four two-pounders an' a brace o' nine-pounders now. I'd say we need at least eight more guns, an' they should be carronades, very effective at short range, as ye might know. An' I shouldn't object ter having a pair or two o' swivel guns, neither."

Sabrina stared at Peggoty. "Good God, Captain, you want to turn my boat into an arsenal. Look, you've sailed the *Mary Anne* for just on a year now, and during that time, to the best of my knowledge, you haven't needed to fire a shot to defend yourself. Why should the future be any different?"

Lifting his chin, Peggoty stared back at Sabrina. "I told ye, this 'ere new revenue service will be quite another kettle o' fish," he said heavily. "When I'm attacked—an' attacked I'll be, mark my words—I want ter be able ter fight back."

Rising, Sabrina settled her bonnet securely on her head and picked up her reticule, saying, "It's quite out of the question. There will be no additional guns for the *Mary Anne*. What's more, my original orders stand: rather than risk injury either to your men or the crew of an exciseman, you're to be prepared to lose your cargo."

"Lose my 'ide is more likely," Peggoty said sourly. "Mrs. Neville, be reasonable, do. It ain't simply a question o' losing the cargo. If we're caught by the excisemen wi' contraband on board, we go to jail or worse. It's true, there's new ways o' concealing cargo — inside hollow bulkheads, false bows, double bottoms, the like — but that would mean a big expense o' refitting an' a long stretch when we couldn't go to sea. Or we could try another new trick: fasten our casks in line on a warp wi' sinkers attached and throw 'em overboard when we sighted a revenue cutter. But then we couldn't begin to handle the volume o' spirits we've been bringing in, an' there goes yer profits — an' ours. In any case, there'd be no guarantee we wouldn't be caught out on *something* if we was ter let the revenooers board us like we was lambs fer the slaughter. Nay, Mrs. Neville. I'm not willing ter risk rotting in jail fer the rest o' my life, or ter go ter the nubbing cheat like my brother Dick, all fer the lack o' a little gumption ter fire a gun."

"And *I'm* not willing to risk the life of any man, whether he be one of my crewmen or a revenue seaman," Sabrina snapped. "Find out how much it would cost to install false bulkheads, and look into other methods of concealing cargo, but until we're able to make those changes I forbid you to shoot at a revenue cutter."

Not a ripple of emotion crossed Peggoty's saturnine face, but Sabrina caught a flash of anger in the hooded eyes. "I dunno as I could sail the *Mary Anne* wi' me 'ands tied like that."

"That's up to you. If you can't comply with my orders perhaps you should consider giving up your command. Fine seaman though you are, it wouldn't be impossible to replace you."

Confronting Sabrina in malignant silence as the seconds ticked by, Peggoty finally grunted, "It's yer boat, Mrs. Neville. Reckon I'll do as ye say." He turned, leaving the room without another word.

Waiting until the door had closed after him, Ezra said anxiously, "Was that wise, Mrs. Neville? As I tried ter tell ye afore, ye didn't ought ter run afoul o' a man like Nate. I'm fearful 'e'll do ye a mischief."

"I have to live with myself, Mr. Cavitt," said Sabrina quietly. "I couldn't bear to spend money that had blood on it. I meant what I said. If Captain Peggoty won't follow my orders, I'll replace him." She smiled at young Tom, whose forehead was furrowed in a worried frown. "I wouldn't hesitate to give you the command, Tom. I probably should have done so in the beginning."

"Don't speak like that," Tom exclaimed in quick alarm. "If Nate was to 'ave an inkling I was out fer 'is command . . . Besides, ma'am, 'e's the best seaman in these parts, bar none."

"I suppose he is. Very well, we'll let matters stand for the time being. Keep me posted, Tom."

It had been raining fairly heavily during Sabrina's meeting with Nate Peggoty and the Cavitts, but only an occasional drop was falling when she stepped out of the farmhouse, and she refused Tom's offer to drive her home. As she trudged along the muddy road her thoughts were bleak. The scene with Peggoty had been unavoidable, even if it had stirred up the latent hostility the cutter captain had always felt toward her. Nate didn't like taking orders from anyone, let alone a woman, and a member of the gentry to boot. However, Sabrina had considered it essential to make Peggoty realize she would brook no violation of her orders against violence. She shivered at the thought of being responsible for the death or injury of another human being. Please God she would be able to get out of the smuggling game before very long.

When she reached Latimer House she hurried into her bedchamber to change her slippers, wet and filthy from the mud of the roadway. Daphne poked her head around the door, exclaiming, "Merciful heavens, Sabrina, why didn't you wear your pattens? You'll catch your death if you get your feet wet like that. What will Lotte say?"

"She'll tell me I should have worn my pattens," Sabrina retorted.

Daphne grinned, settling into a comfortable position on the bed as she watched her sister place her bonnet and pelisse in the wardrobe.

"Remember how furious it used to make Mama when she'd find me curled up on your bed, talking to you while you dressed to go out?" Daphne inquired. She added wistfully, "I've missed you these past few weeks. I've no one to talk to. Mama is always lecturing me."

"She means it for the best," Sabrina replied mildly, sitting down in an armchair near the bed.

"Oh, I know. . . . Sabrina, what is so dreadfully wrong about wanting to visit my friend Betsy?"

Sabrina gazed at Daphne's pretty, discontented-looking face, smothering a sigh. "Nothing's wrong. Mama has no objection to your seeing Betsy Stanhope. You know quite well why she doesn't want you to go to Newhaven, however."

"She doesn't want me to see Gordon. It's so unfair. You'd think Gordon was a — a felon, instead of a man who's about to risk his life apprehending criminals!"

"Daphne, has Captain Stanhope proposed marriage to you?" Sabrina asked bluntly.

"N-no, of course not." Daphne's face flooded with color. "We're *friends!*"

"I'm glad to hear that. Friends is what you should remain."

"Sabrina, I don't understand you at all. What if someone had talked to you like that when you first met Oliver?" Daphne burst out.

"The cases aren't really alike, you know," Sabrina said gently. "Oliver and I belonged to the same social class. Supposing you and Captain Stanhope were to become

176

more than 'friends.' Supposing you were to marry. You'd find yourself cut off from your own kind, because, unfair though it may seem, the gentry and yeoman farmers just don't mingle socially." Leaning forward to clasp Daphne's hand, she added, "Don't be angry with Mama and me, Puss. All either of us wants is for you to be happy."

Daphne pulled her hand away and slid down from the bed. "I'd like to believe that," she said distantly. "Somehow, I can't."

Sabrina drew a deep breath as she watched her sister flounce out of the room. Something would have to be done about Daphne. A match with an ineligible man like Gordon Stanhope was out of the question, but Sabrina remembered all too well her own headstrong romanticism at the same age, when Oliver had seemed the only man in the world for her. Sweetly reasonable arguments about Gordon's ineligibility would have no effect on Daphne's starry-eyed yearnings, and Fanny didn't seem to realize that her open, constant opposition was having the opposite effect to what she intended. She must be persuaded to allow Daphne to visit Betsy in Newhaven. The visit would take the edge off Daphne's rebellion, at least for the time being, and after that . . . Both Stanhopes would be gone in a few days, and Daphne was very young. Wishful thinking it might be, but it was entirely possible that she'd become interested in someone else during Gordon Stanhope's absences at sea.

"Sabrina, it's almost time to leave for Merryton Court. Oh, splendid, you're nearly ready." Lady Latimer entered the bedchamber, nodding approvingly as she observed Lotte adding the final touches to Sabrina's hair.

177

As Sabrina had surmised, Lady Latimer had lost no time in applying to Lady Marston for permission to include her older stepdaughter in the invitation to dinner at Merryton Court. It was so blatant an exercise in matchmaking that Sabrina had initially decided not to accept the invitation. She knew that Fanny's sole interest in having her attend the dinner was to introduce her to Lady Marston's retired Navy captain brother, and the last thing in the world Sabrina wanted at this time was to meet a prospective suitor, or, indeed, a new man of any size, shape, or age. Rather than provoke Fanny into a tantrum, however, or, even worse, a long silent bout of sulking, Sabrina had pretended to be pleased with the invitation. If this Captain Ranger were to show signs of interest in her, which wasn't at all certain, Sabrina considered that she was quite capable of discouraging his advances.

"That pale yellow silk is very becoming," said Fanny, examining Sabrina's gown with the expertise of a connoisseur. "It's one of the dresses Madame Manet refurbished for you, isn't it?" Her eye caught a glimmer of blue from the open door of the wardrobe, and she walked over to look at it. Spreading out the gossamer net skirt of the gown over its deep blue silk petticoat, she exclaimed, "How lovely! Those tiny bouquets of roses and bluebells are exquisite. I don't believe I've ever seen this dress before. Is it new? It looks like the latest fashion from Paris."

Flashing Sabrina a quick glance, Lotte hastily moved away from the dressing table and began tidying the room, her lips clamped tightly together. Since their return from town, it had been a trial for the talkative abigail to keep silent about Sabrina's activities during the weeks she was absent from Latimer House.

Mentally cursing her stepmother's observant eye, Sabrina said coolly, "The gown's new to me, Mama. My

178

sister-in-law wanted me to have it. Maria'd bought it before she realized she was increasing, and she thought someone ought to get some wear out of it."

"Indeed. Lady Yardley has a nice sense of style." Fanny studied the gown, her eyes narrowing. "Why don't you wear the dress tonight, Sabrina? Capt—no one at the dinner will be able to take his eyes off you!"

Sabrina swallowed a lump in her throat. Wear the gown Jareth had given her? She could remember every moment of the last occasion she'd worn it, at the dinner in Jareth's rooms at the Albany. She had only to close her eyes to evoke the sound of his voice, the look in his eyes, the touch of his hands, in those last moments before she'd gone beyond the bounds of forgiveness by cheating him out of a small fortune with Oliver's marked cards.

"Oh, I'd rather not," she managed to say. "I couldn't refuse to accept the dress for fear of hurting Maria's feelings, but I don't think it suits me. A little too ornate for my taste." She rose, reaching for the fringed shawl of Lyons silk Lotte was holding out to her. "Shall we go?"

Merryton Court was not the ancient family seat of the Marston family. It had been purchased some five years previously by Benjamin Marston, a factory owner from the Midlands who had made a vast fortune during the war and had been named viscount for his contributions to the war effort.

During the drive to Merryton Court, Daphne had been very quiet. As she walked with Fanny and Sabrina into the drawing room, Daphne muttered to her sister, "I daresay any hostess in our social class would be delighted to welcome Gordon into her drawing room if he were as wealthy as Lord Marston!"

Casting a quick sideways look at Daphne's resentful expression, Sabrina was thankful that no one else had heard her sister's comment. Unfortunately Daphne wasn't too far off the mark. An elderly wealthy man could climb the social ladder very nearly as far as he cared to go, and in the next generation few would remember his children's origins. Even Fanny, for all her snobbery about the Latimer family ancestry and her own, would view Gordon Stanhope in a different light if he possessed a handsome fortune.

Try not to think about unpleasant things tonight, Daphne," Sabrina murmured. "We'll talk again tomorrow." She looked up to greet her hostess. Amanda, Lady Marston, came swooping down on her guest as if she were overjoyed to see a long-lost bosom friend, although they had actually met for the first time after Sabrina's return from Vienna and had seen each other rarely since then. Her ladyship's plump face with its rather bulging eyes was beaming as she exclaimed, "Mrs. Neville, how nice to have you back with us again." With a rather perfunctory nod to Fanny and Daphne, she took Sabrina's arm to lead her across the drawing room, continuing to chatter as they went. "Lady Latimer was telling me you'd rushed off to Kent to care for your sister-in-law. The poor lady is well, I trust?" At the far side of the room Lady Marston paused in front of a tall man who was chatting with the Reverend Ralph Varrick, vicar of the parish church in Fairlea. The clergymen greeted Sabrina warmly. "So you've returned to us, my dear. My wife will be happy to hear it." He motioned to his companion. "Mrs. Neville, may I present Captain Ranger?"

Lady Marston's brother took Sabrina's hand in a close clasp, looking keenly down at her out of sharp blue eyes set in a pleasant, weatherbeaten face. He appeared to be between thirty-five and forty years of age. "I feel as if I already know you, Mrs. Neville, from what my sister has told me about you," Captain Ranger said, smiling.

Before Sabrina quite realized what was happening, she was seated in a cozy, out-of-the-way corner of the

180

drawing room beside the captain, who clearly was determined to monopolize her attention. She felt bewildered, at a loss to explain Lady Marston's sudden interest in her, much less the captain's seeming eagerness to improve their acquaintanceship. Sabrina had assumed that Fanny's matchmaking was entirely one-sided, not a joint effort with Lady Marston! If their hostess wanted to introduce her brother to the local females, why single out a penniless widow?

It didn't take long to solve the little mystery. Though charming and well-bred, Ivo Ranger apparently pursued his social goals with the same tenacity that must have characterized his performance as the commander of a blockading ship with the Channel fleet during the long war with Napoleon. At the beginning of their conversation Sabrina asked, "Do you have any regrets about leaving the Navy, Captain?" His prompt reply revealed his frame of mind quite clearly.

"No, I've had enough of the sea, Mrs. Neville. I've had my fill of cramped quarters, weevils in the ship's biscuits, and cold wet watches in the middle of the night. I've bought myself a snug little property—perhaps you know it? Appleton House?—and I plan to settle down to the life of a country gentleman."

"I hope you'll be happy here," said Sabrina, smiling. "I'm prejudiced. I'd rather live in Sussex than anywhere else in the world."

"Oh, I'm quite satisfied with Sussex. I like living in Appleton House, and I'm happy to be near my sister and her husband. There's only one thing lacking. I have no wife."

Sabrina felt a slight shock. She wasn't used to such directness. "My stepmother told me you were a widower, Captain. I'm very sorry."

"No need to be," Captain Ranger said coolly. "My wife died long ago. Margaret was sweet and gentle and very young. We were happy, but now that I'm older I want a different kind of wife. A more mature woman, a stronger woman who's had some experience of life. She needn't have a large dowry. I'm well provided for the future." His eyes twinkled. "However, I shouldn't at all object to marrying a paragon who was also ravishingly beautiful."

There was no doubt about it. Captain Ranger's gaze was frankly admiring. Under other circumstances, Sabrina reflected, she might have been intrigued by his unconventional bluntness. He was certainly an attractive man. Now, however, the memory of a pair of laughing dark eyes and an irresistible quirkish smile intruded between her and Captain Ranger, and all she felt was a sense of apprehension. The captain might prove to be as persistent in his attentions to her as had been his devotion to duty during the relentless naval blockade that had caused Napoleon's downfall.

"I daresay paragons are in short supply," she said with a noncommittal smile. "I haven't noticed any in the vicinity!"

"Oh, but I'm a patient man," the captain replied, smiling. He glanced at the door of the drawing room, where the butler had just appeared to announce dinner. "My sister tells me we're to sit together, so we can continue our discussion at the table." He whistled softly. "Amanda's cup runneth over. She invited Lord and Lady Winwood for dinner, but she wasn't at all sure they would come."

Her eyes following the captain's gaze to the two newcomers who were talking to Lady Marston at the door, Sabrina's heart turned over. For a fraction of a second she might have been looking at Jareth. The height and the powerful figure were the same, and the well-shaped dark head and the incisive aquiline features, but the Marquess's frame was developing a slight paunch and his face was marked by lines of dissipation.

"Amanda informed me that Lord and Lady Winwood rarely accept invitations from the lesser county families," Captain Ranger murmured to Sabrina. "My sister will dine off this triumph all year! Do you know the Winwoods well?"

"No. The Latimers are among the 'lesser county families.' We don't travel in such rarified circles." Sabrina stared almost painfully at the silver-gilt hair and exquisitely beautiful face of the black-clad figure who stood beside the Marquess. Christabel. Jareth's young, lost love.

At dinner Sabrina had to force herself to concentrate on Captain Ranger's low-voiced conversation as her eyes kept straying to the other end of the table, where Lady Winwood sat at Lord Marston's right hand. Later, when the ladies left the men to drink their port, there seemed to be a giant magnet drawing Sabrina to a chair beside Christabel in the drawing room.

"I don't believe we've met," said Lady Winwood with a dazzling smile when Sabrina came up to her. "Poor Lady Marston didn't have the opportunity to introduce us to anyone. Lionel and I were almost late for dinner." Up close, Christabel's fragile loveliness was even more overpowering, enhanced by the wispy black silk of deepest mourning. No wonder Jareth had plunged into a life of determined bachelorhood when he'd lost her.

"I'm Sabrina Neville, Lady Winwood. Before I was married I was a Latimer."

"I'm so sorry, Mrs. Neville. I'm afraid I don't know the local families as well as I should," said Christabel with a pretty show of sincerity. "I'm from Yorkshire, myself. My husband — well, Lionel doesn't really like to socialize very much. Is your husband here tonight?"

"I'm a widow. My husband died in Vienna a year ago."

"Oh." Christabel's wonderful violet eyes filmed with tears. "Perhaps you may have heard—I lost my little son recently. Tell me, does the hurt ever go away?"

"Eventually. I don't think we humans could survive for very long at that initial level of grief," Sabrina said gently, feeling like a hypocrite. By the time Oliver died she'd ceased to love him, regretting only the useless tragedy of his death. Whatever Christabel's faults, though, whatever cruelties she'd practiced on Jareth, no one could doubt her attachment to her son.

"I think there must be a bond between people who have lost a loved one," said Christabel wistfully. "Perhaps you'd care to visit me at Winwood Park, Mrs. Neville?"

Sabrina's sense of black humor rippled to life. She tried to imagine the expression on Jareth's face if he chanced to find her hobnobbing with the woman who had jilted him all those years ago.

The men of the party now joined the ladies in the drawing room. Ivo Ranger made for Sabrina like a homing pigeon, finding them a secluded corner in which to enjoy their coffee. "Are you usually home in the afternoons, Mrs. Neville?"

"Most days, yes. I live a very quiet life. I've only recently left off my blacks, you see."

Sabrina's distinct lack of enthusiasm and her reference to her bereavement passed over Captain Ranger like water off a duck's back. "If you'll allow me, I'd like to ask Lady Latimer for permission to call," he was saying, when they were interrupted by a loud voice.

"Here you are, Ranger. What a rum go, monopolizing the prettiest girl in the room." His speech slurred, unsteady on his feet from the effects of too much port, the Marquess of Winwood reached down for Sabrina's hand and pulled her to her feet.

"How d'you do, m'dear. I'm Winwood. What might your name be?"

Easing her hand away from the Marquess's damp grasp and stepping back slightly to avoid a blast of wine-soaked breath, Sabrina curtsied. "How do you do, Lord Winwood. I'm Sabrina Neville."

She wondered if Christabel had ever regretted throwing over Jareth Tremayne in order to become a wealthy marchioness.

Chapter Ten

"We're ready to go, Mama. Is there anything Daphne and I might do for you in Newhaven?"

Lady Latimer looked up from her embroidery to stare stony-faced at her stepdaughters as they stood, dressed in bonnets and pelisses, at the door of the morning room. "I can't imagine *anything* that would interest me in Newhaven," she sniffed. "Tell me, pray, why are you leaving so early? I thought you were paying an afternoon visit to Miss Stanhope."

"I wanted to spend as much time as possible with Betsy," Daphne replied, a shade self-consciously. "Recall, I shan't have many more opportunities to see her. Sabrina, shall we go?"

"One moment, please. I have something to discuss with your sister," said Fanny.

"Yes, what is it, Mama?" said Sabrina patiently. It was several days since she'd wrung permission from her stepmother for Daphne to visit Betsy Stanhope, but apparently Fanny was still far from resigned to it.

Fanny picked up a letter from the table beside her. "This note came a few minutes ago. Lady Marston has invited us for tea tomorrow afternoon at Merryton Court."

"How kind," said Sabrina. "Will you thank her for me,

and make my excuses? I must spend the whole day tomorrow doing the accounts."

"I'll do nothing of the kind," retorted Fanny. "I wouldn't offend Lady Marston for the world. You can do your precious accounts some other time."

"I daresay I could, but I don't choose to."

"Yes, and I know why!" A wave of angry color suffused Lady Latimer's face. "You suspect that Captain Ranger will be taking tea with Lady Marston, and you don't wish to see him. Don't deny it, Sabrina! The captain has called here twice since you met him at Lady Marston's dinner party, and both times you've managed to avoid him. Yesterday I swear I could hardly look him in the eyes when you sent word you had the headache. And the day before that you had the maidservant tell him you weren't in the house when the entire household knew full well you were up in your bedchamber. Now, far be it from me to interfere in your life—you're a grown woman, no longer under my care—but I wonder what you can be thinking of, Sabrina. Here's a presentable man—young, personable, well-off—who seems to be taken with you, and you're doing your best to send him to the right-about before he's so much as made you an offer!"

"Perhaps that's the point," said Sabrina quietly. "I don't wish Captain Ranger to make me an offer. I think it would be kinder to make my feelings known to him before he does so, if indeed that's what he has in mind, rather than to embarrass him with a refusal."

Fanny threw up her hands. "I don't understand you. Don't you want your own establishment? Adrian will marry some day, you know, and Latimer House will have a new mistress. Do you think either of us will enjoy continuing to live here under those circumstances? For myself"—the familiar note of martyrdom crept into her voice—"for myself there's no alternative, but you, Sabrina, wouldn't you like to have a home and family of your own? If you won't think of yourself, think of dear Daphne. If you were married to a man of substance, you might take a house in London and give her the Season I wasn't able to make possible for her!"

"Mama, please," interjected Daphne reproachfully. "I don't *need* a London Season, especially if it would mean a great sacrifice on Sabrina's part. I'm sure Captain Ranger is a very worthy man, but I'm also sure Sabrina isn't ready to . . . to love again, and I think you must accept that."

"And what has love to say to anything?" snapped Fanny. She looked past Sabrina and Daphne in the doorway to the maidservant who was hovering behind them. "Yes, what is it, Rosie?"

"Are you at home, my lady? A Captain Ranger is calling. The same gentleman who was here yesterday."

"Ah." Fanny sighed with satisfaction. "Tell the captain that Mrs. Neville and Miss Daphne and I will be with him in the drawing room in a moment."

After the maidservant had gone, Sabrina said coldly, "You've put me in an embarrassing position, Mama. I told you Daphne and I were about to leave for Newhaven."

Lady Latimer tossed her head. "It won't hurt you to delay your trip for a few minutes. It's a matter of common courtesy."

Pressing her lips together against an unwise retort, Sabrina shrugged. "For a few minutes only, then."

Ivo Ranger rose from his chair as the ladies entered the drawing room. "Lady Latimer, it's kind of you to receive me. I fear I'm becoming a nuisance!" To Sabrina he said, "I felt I had to call to inquire about your health, Mrs. Neville. Your headache is better, I trust?"

"Much better, thank you." Gazing into Ivo Ranger's keen blue eyes, Sabrina realized with a flick of annoyance that even if he suspected her headache was fictitious it wouldn't affect his behavior in the slightest. It would take more than an excuse or two to put him off his determination to pursue her acquaintanceship.

"I fear my visit is inopportune, Mrs. Neville," he observed, glancing at her bonnet and pelisse. "I noticed one of your grooms bringing a dogcart to your front entrance. Perhaps you and Miss Latimer were about to go somewhere?"

"Oh, Sabrina and Daphne are in no great hurry, Captain Ranger," Fanny assured him hastily. "They were merely planning to visit a young friend of Daphne in Newhaven. Do sit down."

Daphne caught her breath, but before she could say anything Captain Ranger said smoothly, "The sky is somewhat overcast. You ladies would be most uncomfortable in the dogcart if it rained. I'd be delighted to take you to Newhaven in my carriage."

"Oh, we couldn't impose on you," exclaimed Sabrina. At the same time Fanny was saying with a pleased smile, "Why, how kind of you, Captain!"

"That's settled, then," said Ivo Ranger.

The leisurely five-mile excursion to Newhaven took under an hour, and Sabrina was forced to admit to herself that the captain's carriage was a more comfortable vehicle than the dogcart, and that Ivo Ranger was a pleasant escort, putting Daphne at her ease at once by asking polite questions about her friends the Stanhopes. Entering the town they passed the ancient Norman Church of St. Michael and drove along the harbor, where Sabrina caught a glimpse of her boat, the *Mary Anne,* at anchor. Betsy Stanhope's lodgings were in a respectable private residence near the dignified old Bridge Hotel.

Betsy was a sweet-faced, rather plain young woman who appeared to be several years older than Daphne.

She greeted her guests in the parlor of the house with a shy cordiality, expressing delight at meeting Sabrina for the first time and accepting without confusion the unexpected arrival of Captain Ranger.

While Daphne chatted with the captain, Betsy spoke confidingly to Sabrina. "I'm treasuring every moment of this visit," she said. "I'll be living so far away from everyone after I'm married. It will be years, probably, before I see Daphne or my brother again." She paused, glancing hesitantly at Sabrina. "I'd hoped that Daphne might come to my wedding and we'd see a bit more of each other before I left England . . ."

Sabrina thought it highly unlikely that Fanny would allow Daphne to be contaminated by a social occasion at a yeoman farmer's house, but forbore to comment.

Glancing at the watch pinned to her bodice, Betsy said apologetically, "Luncheon will be a trifle late, I fear. My brother must have been delayed."

Of course. Poor Fanny. She'd been perfectly right to suspect that Daphne would find a means of seeing Gordon Stanhope during this visit to his sister. Every aspect of the day had probably been carefully orchestrated. When Gordon arrived a few minutes later another of Fanny's fears was realized.

"I understand we're both seamen, Captain Stanhope," said a smiling Ivo Ranger when they were introduced. "Miss Latimer has been telling me you're in the process of fitting out a new revenue cutter. As a former Navy man I'd be very interested to see something of what you're doing."

"As a matter of fact, I'd planned to invite our guests to visit the cutter after luncheon," Gordon beamed. Coming over to Sabrina, he said, "Would you object to such a visit, Mrs. Neville?"

The hopeful, coaxing expression on his thin face, redeemed from plainness by the speaking pair of lively

190

gray eyes, melted any resolve Sabrina might have had to act as an overly strict chaperon. What harm could there be in visiting the cutter? What Fanny didn't know couldn't hurt her! "Daphne and I would be delighted to see your boat, Captain Stanhope."

He lowered his voice to a murmur. "I can't thank you enough for coming here with Daphne. My sister hasn't felt entirely comfortable visiting her at Latimer House." He smiled ruefully. "For that matter, neither have I! Lady Latimer has made it quite clear she disapproves of both of us."

"It's nothing personal," Sabrina exclaimed. She cut herself short, biting her lip.

Gordon said quietly, "Oh, I know quite well what it is, Mrs. Neville. It's a matter of ancestors."

Sabrina looked away. What reply could she give to such transparent honesty?

After a brief lunch, served by a rather flustered landlady and a gangling kitchen maid, Gordon offered to drive Daphne to the boatyard in his hired gig. "So Betsy and Mrs. Neville and the captain won't be crowded in the carriage," he explained with a straight face.

At the harbor, strolling with the rest of the party along the dock toward the boatyard, Sabrina noted with a slight unease that Nate Peggoty, moving with his characteristic rolling seaman's gait, was walking in her direction. When he came abreast of her he touched his cap perfunctorily and she responded with the barest nod, preparing to pass him. She tensed when the cutter captain paused in front of her. "I be surprised ter see ye here, Mrs. Neville. I don't expect ye've come ter inspect the *Mary Anne*," he muttered, his familiar malevolent grin curving his mouth.

Glancing quickly ahead of her, Sabrina was relieved to see that Betsy and Captain Ranger were beyond earshot. "I've come to visit the boatyard," she replied with a cold stare. "A friend is fitting out his new revenue cutter."

Snickering, Peggoty said softly, "I wonder now what yer friend the revenooer would say if 'e knew 'e was showing off his ship ter a smuggler? Ye'll have ter give me a full report on this new cutter. I 'ear tell it be a grand 'un."

Sabrina stared at Peggoty for a moment without speaking. The man's malicious insolence was getting out of bounds. He'd obviously accosted her here in public, though no one was supposed to know they were even acquainted, to give vent to the venom she'd aroused at their last meeting, when she'd threatened to take away his command. "I don't know anything about boats," she said curtly. "That's your job." With another nod, she swept past him.

The boatyard was a bustle of activity as the workmen swarmed over Gordon's cutter. Remembering Captain Ranger's declaration that he'd been happy to leave the Navy, Sabrina had difficulty keeping her face straight when the inspection of the ship turned into an intense dialogue between two sailors who seemed to forget that anyone else was present. Daphne actually showed signs of pouting.

"I hear these revenue cutters are the fastest vessels afloat," Ivo Ranger remarked as he stood on the deck of the *Vigilant*, his keen glance raking over every inch of the ship. "That extralong running bowsprit allows you to vastly increase the sail area, of course. What do you carry? A gaff sail, double square top sails, a jib sail?"

"Yes, all of those plus a flying jib. And, as I'm sure you've noticed, the cutter has massive running backstays, in order to take the strain of these enormous sails."

Captain Ranger nodded appreciatively. "Clinker built, too, I see. Makes for a stronger hull. What armaments will you be carrying?"

"Sixteen smashers," said Gordon proudly. "Six and eight pounders. Swivel guns, too, naturally."

Ivo Ranger held out his hand. "Well, Captain Stanhope, I'm convinced you're commanding a vessel that will give you the advantage over any smuggler you might encounter. Good hunting to you and the crew of the *Vigilant!*"

"Thank you." Gordon grinned, returning the hand clasp. "Perhaps you'd like to sign on for a voyage?"

As she listened to the two men exchanging their bantering comments, it crossed Sabrina's mind for the first time to question Lady Latimer's fears that Daphne's continuing friendship with Gordon Stanhope would lead to marriage and a mésalliance her sister would almost certainly come to regret. Would a match between the two necessarily be a mésalliance? The revenue captain was a strong man, already a success in his chosen profession, and self-confident. Today he'd betrayed not the faintest sign of unease in associating with a man whose social status was decidedly superior to his own. His sister, too, was a lady who could hold her own in any gathering. Why shouldn't Daphne be allowed to choose her own way to happiness?

Sabrina sighed. She was being a romantic herself. First love was so exciting and enticing, especially when one was eighteen, but it bore little relation to reality. Her marriage to Oliver was certainly proof of that! In the years to come, the rosy illusions of romance would inevitably fade, and Daphne would resent being trapped in a bourgeois social circle, separated from the friends and places she'd known all her life.

Sabrina's musings were interrupted when Betsy, casting a quick glance at Daphne's vague expression of discontent as Gordon and Ivo Ranger continued their discussion of naval matters, said to her brother, her eyes twinkling, "I'm sure you and the captain could talk about boats all afternoon, Gordon, but Daphne and I and Mrs. Neville are hungry and thirsty. We'd like our tea, please. Mrs. Dorrance has promised us strawberries and clotted cream."

Gordon laughed. "I wouldn't dream of asking my guests to choose between the *Vigilant* and one of our landlady's luscious teas. Come, Daphne, if you don't distrust my ability to handle the ribbons, I'll drive you back to the lodging house."

"Well!" said Sabrina an hour later, after she and Betsy and Captain Ranger had run out of conversational topics and had allowed a second pot of tea to grow cold while they waited for Gordon and Daphne to return. "Can it be that Captain Stanhope finds it more difficult to navigate on land than on the sea?"

"I expect they forgot the time," Betsy said rather nervously. "It's a lovely day for a drive."

"Oh, indeed, but not, I submit, when one is expected to tea," replied Sabrina dryly.

Captain Ranger looked mildly censorious. "I would have thought Captain Stanhope—but there, Mrs. Neville, if you're concerned about your sister, perhaps I ought to go in search of them." He returned to the parlor of the house several minutes later with Daphne and Gordon in tow. "I found our lost sheep just turning into the street," he announced cheerfully.

"I'm sorry, Mrs. Neville," Gordon muttered in an aside to Sabrina. "The time just slipped away. Daphne and I got to talking, and—well, you know I'll be going to sea soon."

As might have been expected, Daphne looked both apprehensive and faintly guilty, but there was also a suppressed air of excitement about her that puzzled Sabrina. As they walked to the carriage for the return trip to Latimer House, Daphne murmured, "I know I shouldn't have gone off with Gordon alone like that.

Mama would be so furious. Are you—are you going to tell her?"

"Of course not," Sabrina replied in a low voice. "When did I ever tell tales on you? I must say, though, I wish you hadn't done the very thing that Mama warned you about: spend half the day in Gordon Stanhope's pocket! It really wasn't very discreet of you. I think Captain Ranger may have been a little scandalized."

Daphne's fair skin colored at Sabrina's mild reproach. "And *I* think it's none of his affair," she whispered fiercely. "Yours either, Sabrina. I have enough trouble with Mama!"

Sabrina hunched her shoulders resignedly. Thank God the Stanhopes would be gone in a few days. Gordon would, of course, be sailing in and out of Newhaven for the time being, but there would be practically no opportunity for him to see Daphne, and there was some hope in the old adage, "Out of sight, out of mind."

Daphne flounced into the carriage, taking little part in the conversation on the return drive, though Captain Ranger did his best to draw her out. "I really envy your friend Stanhope. Seeing that splendid cutter almost made me decide to go back to sea again," he was saying jocularly to her when the carriage drove into the village of Fairlea.

"Captain Ranger, would you mind stopping briefly?" said Sabrina suddenly. "I promised to buy my abigail some thread while I was out today."

"Not at all. I have an errand myself with the landlord of the inn. Miss Latimer?"

"I'll stay in the carriage, thank you," said Daphne distantly.

It took Sabrina only a few minutes to buy Lotte's thread in the tiny shop near the village green. As she stepped out of the shop, she paused to glance at the curricle and pair being driven into the village from the direction of the Lewes road, followed by a post chaise whose roof was crowded with luggage. She stiffened at sight of the familiar curricle, a chilling wave of fear washing over her, paralyzing her limbs momentarily. Then, unable to think coherently, she wheeled abruptly, heading for Ivo Ranger's waiting carriage.

A sinewy hand grasped her arm. "Not so fast, Mrs. Neville. We have matters to discuss."

Sabrina lifted her head to gaze into Jareth's dark eyes, which were blazing with a murderous rage. She gaped at him. "You called me Mrs. Neville. How did you — ?"

The pressure of his fingers increased painfully. "What did you take me for, some beef-witted Johnny Raw?" he gritted. "Oh, you covered your tracks like a flash boman prig — and I don't have to translate *that* for you, do I, my fine Viennese imposter? When I think how often I had to explain our English slang to a dewy-eyed foreign innocent!" He shook his head with an expression of self-loathing. "But that's neither here nor there. You tricked me into thinking you were heading for the Continent, so I chased you to every port in southern England. You miscalculated only once. Didn't it occur to you that I might become suspicious when you disappeared with my ten thousand pounds and shortly afterward your twin brother arrived at my lodgings to pay me that exact amount? Didn't it occur to you I might suddenly realize how much Adrian Latimer resembled you?"

Drawing a ragged breath, Sabrina tried to calm her treacherous heart. Even in this bitterly hostile mood, Jareth still had the power to send her pulses pounding at his least touch. "You've every right to be angry, Jareth," she began, striving to keep her voice steady. "I know I shouldn't have deceived you about my identity. I did it to save Adrian's pride. I didn't want him to know I'd won the money to pay his debt from the very man who held his vouchers. If I hurt you, disappointed you, I'm sorry, and I know we can't be friends again. But at least you have your money. Can't we leave it at that?" She attempted to free her arm from his grasp. "Please let me go. We don't have anything more to say to each other."

"Don't pitch that gammon to me," Jareth retorted savagely. "Nothing more to say to each other? Look, I admit I was a fool to let myself get entangled in your poisonous web, I was a fool to play cards for high stakes while I was foxed to the ears, but I'm not totally stupid. When I find a marked card on my sitting-room floor after a losing game of macao, I have to conclude that my opponent cheated me!"

Sabrina felt as if the earth had opened up to swallow her. She'd hoped to disguise her trail so thoroughly that Jareth wouldn't be able to track her down. She'd even snatched some small comfort from the thought that, supposing he did manage to find her eventually, she would have lost nothing that she hadn't already lost. She'd long since forfeited his love and trust by disappearing without a word of good-bye. The one danger that hadn't occurred to her was the possibility that Jareth would discover she'd cheated him with marked cards.

"What? No more excuses? No more lies?" Jareth gibed at her as she remained sunk in stupefied silence. "For once in your life, my charming imposter, have you been struck dumb?"

"Jareth, we can't talk here," Sabrina burst out. She tried to wrench her arm from his hold. "Later, when you're not so angry—"

His grip intensified, his fingers biting into her flesh. "We'll talk now," he said between his teeth. "I've tracked you across half of England for the opportunity to have this little chat with you."

"If I might be of any assistance, Mrs. Neville, I'm quite at your disposal," came a calm voice behind them.

As Jareth swerved to confront Ivo Ranger, Sabrina unobtrusively pulled her arm free. Before Jareth could voice a furious challenge to the other man, she said shakily, "Thank you, Captain Ranger, but I'm in no need of help. This—this gentleman and I were merely having a discussion. I'll join you and my sister in a moment."

Searching Sabrina's face in a long, solemn look, the Navy captain stepped back, bowing slightly. "As you wish. I'll be at the carriage if you should want me."

Jareth swung back to face Sabrina. During the brief interval with Ivo Ranger he'd managed to bring his anger under control, but she could see the banked fires behind his eyes. "Well, well, what a resourceful woman you are, Sabrina," he drawled. "In just over a week you've brought another lover up to scratch. You captured him under your own name, too. What a shame. He might have been so much easier to captivate if you'd posed as a Viennese widow of an Hungarian count."

The scathing contempt in Jareth's voice shattered the mood of abject guilt that had been weighing down on Sabrina, leaving her with the feeling that she deserved every bitter word of condemnation that he cared to hurl against her. Suddenly her natural sturdy independence took over, and she felt a burning urge to strike back at him. "It would have been futile to pose as an Hungarian countess with Captain Ranger," she said coldly. "He's far too intelligent to be taken in by a false accent and an air of demure innocence."

Jareth turned white to the lips. "You—you make Harriet Wilson and the rest of the Fashionable Impures look like schoolgirls," he choked. "At least they're honest. They give fair value for the price. They don't cheat."

"No doubt you're speaking from a vast experience of demireps and fancy pieces," Sabrina snapped. "Good day, Lord Jareth. You'll forgive me if I hope that we don't see each other again."

"Sabrina, I haven't finished with you—"

"Oh, I think you have," Sabrina said, tilting her chin. "Unless you plan to use brute force, and then I think my friend Captain Ranger might have something to say about that."

He checked a quick motion to grab her arm again and prevent her from leaving. He spoke quietly, but with an undercurrent of grim malice that made her shudder. "Go, then, but don't delude yourself that you've heard the last of me. I've got a score to settle with you, and I won't rest until I do it."

Several moments later, as he was handing her into the carriage, Ivo Ranger murmured, "Are you all right, Mrs. Neville?"

"Certainly," Sabrina replied, lifting her eyebrow. "Why shouldn't I be?"

"Sabrina, who was that man you were talking to?" Daphne inquired. "You seemed to know him very well, but I don't believe I've ever seen him before."

"Nobody important. Just someone I used to know."

Chapter Eleven

"Sabrina! I could swear you'd turned deaf! I've asked you the same question twice now without the courtesy of an answer."

Lady Latimer's exasperated voice roused Sabrina from her brooding thoughts. She glanced out the window of the carriage, faintly surprised to observe in the deepening twilight that they were already passing through the village of Fairlea on their way to Alfriston. She hugged her shawl closer around her shoulders against the dank chill of the June night. It had rained heavily through most of the day.

"I'm sorry, Mama. What was it you were saying?"

"I merely asked you for news of your sister-in-law. Lotte informed my abigail that you had a letter from Yardley Place this afternoon."

"Yes, the letter was from Maria's cousin. Maria had a son three days ago. I wish now I'd stayed on in Kent a little longer, since the baby came early," Sabrina added without turning a hair. She'd told the story of her imaginary visit so often that now it almost seemed to her that she *had* spent several weeks at Yardley Place.

"I'm glad to hear everything turned out well. I would have thought, naturally, that you'd inform me immediately about Lady Yardley's successful laying-in." Fanny's tone sharpened. "I must say, neither you nor Daphne has been very talkative these past two days — since you returned from Newhaven, as a matter of fact. Did something happen there that you haven't told me?"

"Of course not, Mama," Daphne said quickly.

It was almost true, Sabrina reflected. On their return from Newhaven, Captain Ranger had accepted an invitation from Fanny to stay on for an early supper, and during the course of the meal he had cheerfully described their day to Lady Latimer, including, to Daphne's horror, a mention of Gordon's presence at luncheon and their tour of the new revenue cutter. However, Fanny had listened to the account with unexpected calm. She seemed to feel that Ivo Ranger's participation in the activities had somehow sanitized them. Moreover, Ivo had tactfully omitted any reference to Daphne's hour-long disappearance with Gordon.

"I was pleased to hear that Captain Ranger will be attending the assembly at Alfriston tonight," Fanny went on in a tone of great satisfaction. "As you're both aware, I don't in general have a high opinion of these provincial affairs. However, when the Lord Lieutenant of the county sponsors a celebration in honor of the anniversary of the battle of Waterloo, one can hardly grudge the effort required to attend it. I think it displays great civic responsibility on Lord Winwood's part, don't you? By the way, I so enjoyed seeing Lord and Lady Winwood at Lady Marston's house the other evening. I met Lady Winwood a number of times in London when she was first married, but in recent years she and her husband haven't mingled much in county society. What a beautiful creature she is, to be sure, and how brave of her to attend public functions when she's suffered such a recent bereavement."

As so often happened when Fanny began one of her monologues, Sabrina was able to listen to her with only a part of her attention. Her mind, as it had been for the past two days, was fixed on Jareth. By now she was largely over the shock of seeing him so unexpectedly, and she'd buried, finally and forever, a fugitive hope that somewhere, sometime, she and Jareth might come together again. He hated her now. He had good reason to feel that way, of course, and yet . . . There was a sore spot in her heart when she recalled how swiftly and overwhelmingly he'd condemned her. During those halcyon weeks they'd spent together in London she'd have thought he'd learned to know her better. He should have sensed that she wasn't merely a venal adventuress, that there must have been an overwhelming reason for her to act as she had.

She stirred restlessly in her seat. Why think about what might have been? More to the point, she should be deciding how to deal with Jareth's threat to "settle their score." What could he have in mind? She hadn't done anything illegal by posing as an Hungarian countess. And she had only the vaguest notion of what the law might say about cheating with cards, but, strictly speaking, Jareth wasn't out of pocket a shilling as a result of their card game. Adrian had already returned to him the money she'd won.

Nevertheless, she kept remembering the black anger in his voice when he made his threat. On the day following their meeting in Fairlea she'd started nervously at every knock at the door, half-expecting him to storm into Latimer House, but he hadn't come. A sensible man, albeit an angry one, he must have been aware that she would have refused to see him, and he could hardly have forced open the door of her bedchamber!

She'd also been apprehensive about attending this ball tonight at the Star Inn, until she reflected that Jareth almost certainly wouldn't be there. He probably wasn't even aware that the event was taking place. If he should learn of it, he might assume that he could track Sabrina down by going there, but in that case it was highly unlikely he would run the risk of encountering the Marquess and Marchioness of Winwood, who would be the official hosts of the ball. The enmity between Jareth and Lionel ran too deep. She knew that Jareth had virtually exiled himself from Sussex for many years to avoid any contact with his brother. And finally, even supposing Jareth did come to the ball, it would be difficult for him to confront her personally in the midst of such a large crowd of people.

Sabrina was still reassuring herself that she had nothing to be nervous about when the carriage entered the outskirts of Alfriston, an old market town on the banks of the River Cuckmere. To the side of the little village green, near the ancient market cross and a tall chestnut tree, stood the Star Inn, its sturdy timbered facade dating from medieval times when it had been a hostelry maintained by the monks of Battle Abbey. The large red lion at a corner of the building had once been the figurehead of a seventeenth-century Dutch ship.

When Sabrina and Fanny and Daphne entered the large ballroom at the rear of the building, they found the room already nearly full. "Daphne, did you know those two were going to be here?" demanded Fanny in an angry whisper as she stared at Gordon Stanhope and his sister, who were standing near the door.

"Yes, I did, Mama," Daphne replied, coloring. She continued with an uncharacteristic show of defiance,

"Gordon and Betsy told me two days ago they planned to attend the ball. This isn't a private party, you know. It's a public celebration of the Battle of Waterloo. They have as much right to be here as we do."

Lady Latimer looked pained. After a moment she sniffed, "I'm not going to make a public scene about this, my dear. I trust I have too much breeding for that. I'm also going to test *your* breeding. You are not to spend the entire evening dancing with Captain Stanhope, is that clear?"

"Yes, Mama," said Daphne meekly, but before she turned to greet the Stanhopes, Sabrina caught the gleam of triumph in her eye.

Fanny received Gordon and his sister with decided coolness, but her stony expression softened slightly when Betsy told her, "I'd like to take this opportunity to say good-bye, Lady Latimer. I'm leaving Newhaven tomorrow. Gordon, of course, is sailing on Monday."

"I wish you a safe and pleasant journey home, Miss Stanhope. And to you, Captain, a successful voyage," Fanny said graciously. Watching Daphne go off with the brother and sister, she displayed an uncharacteristic resignation. "I can't believe our good fortune," she murmured to Sabrina. "Imagine, soon we won't have to worry about either one of that precious pair, and perhaps dear Daphne can settle down to think of something more important. And I never thought I'd be happy to see Miss Stanhope, but I daresay her presence here tonight will prevent the tongues from wagging quite as hard as they might otherwise!"

Fanny's good temper was restored completely when Ivo Ranger strolled up to them. "I'd hoped to arrive before you'd promised all your dances," he told Sabrina with the air of calm assurance that always put her teeth slightly on edge. "May I have the first waltz and the first country dance? And as many others as

Lady Latimer will permit," he added, his eyes twinkling.

"Oh, I have nothing to say about that, Captain Ranger," Fanny said archly. "Sabrina is quite her own mistress, you know."

"Your stepmother is a most understanding woman," said Ranger with a smile as he led Sabrina out for the first waltz.

"I must tell Fanny how much you admire her," Sabrina laughed. She enjoyed dancing with Ivo Ranger. He waltzed as competently as he must have commanded his ship during the Channel blockade. Having won Fanny's tacit approval to dance as many dances with Sabrina as he liked, however, he was rapidly becoming a problem she would have to deal with sooner rather than later. His single-minded pursuit was beginning to remind her of an inexorable tide washing in on her private shoreline. Walking off the dance floor with him after the waltz ended, she was debating the best way to dampen his ardor when she found herself staring into Jareth Tremayne's eyes. He was standing against the wall, his arms crossed over his chest, looking every inch the Corinthian of Corinthians. Every lock of black hair was carefully in place, his cravat was a dazzling perfection of starched white linen, and his black coat and pantaloons were molded to his lithe body with a creaseless fit that proclaimed the magic hand of Weston.

As she met Jareth's dark implacable gaze, Sabrina was seized by a sudden mindless panic. She murmured to Ranger, "I feel a trifle faint. If you could find a quiet corner . . ."

"Certainly. I'm sure one of the private parlors must be free."

Seated in the snug parlor, whose occupants had been ousted by Ivo Ranger's ruthless competence, Sabrina waited for him to return with a restorative glass of port. Now that she'd had a moment to recover she felt ashamed of her cowardice. If Jareth had come to this ball at the Star Inn to confront her, she couldn't evade him indefinitely, and there was no reason why she should. She was no weak-kneed, lily-livered female. She was certainly capable of giving him a thorough-going setdown.

When Ivo Ranger came back with a tray containing two glasses of port, she smiled her thanks, sipping her wine slowly. "I feel perfectly well now, Captain," she said several minutes later, putting her glass down. "I think we should get back to the ball. You said something about a country dance, I believe?"

He put out his hand. "Could you indulge me for a moment, Mrs. Neville? I have something rather important to say."

Sabrina felt a quick stirring of alarm. "Perhaps a ball isn't quite the place for an important discussion?" she temporized.

"Now is as a good a time as any. I've never been one to shirk an engagement, not in the Navy and not in my private life," he replied bluntly. "Mrs. Neville—Sabrina—I don't think my intentions can have been in doubt from the first moment we met. I'm asking you to marry me."

Even though she'd guessed what he was going to say, Sabrina was shocked by Ranger's proposal. "Captain, this is absurd. We've known each other only a few days, a week at most—"

"At our time of life a lengthy courtship isn't necessary. Both of us are past the stage of romantic first love. As I told you, I want to settle down to the life of a country gentleman with an attractive, capable wife of good family who will give me a houseful of children. You're more than attractive, and I know you've

206

been managing your brother's estate, and very well too, for at least a year. So, assuming a young widow like yourself would prefer her own establishment, I should say we're exceptionally well-suited. I see little point in delaying our decision merely for the sake of convention." He paused. "That's assuming also that you don't dislike me personally."

"I like you very well," Sabrina said hastily. "My difficulty, however, is that I don't wish to be married to anyone."

Ranger considered this. "If you were a very recent widow—but no, my sister tells me your husband died well over a year ago. Perhaps—please believe I've no wish to be intrusive—you have an interest in someone else?"

"I do not." Sabrina knew her denial sounded overly loud and vehement.

The captain looked at her thoughtfully. His intent expression changed into a slow smile. "Then, with your permission, I'll make a strategic retreat and come back to fight another day."

As his gaze followed Sabrina out of the ballroom, Jareth checked an instinctive move to go after her. He could wait. She would have to return to the ball at some point in the evening. He'd guessed that she would be present at this important county social occasion, and his guess had been right. Breathing deeply, he cursed the wave of hungry longing that had swept over him at his first glimpse of her across the room. Why, when he knew exactly who she was and what deviltry she was capable of, did she still have the power to move his senses? In the pale green silk gown he'd seen her wear so often in London, with her tawny curls lustrous in the candlelight and those deeply blue eyes sparkling as she smiled up at her companion—the same man who'd been escorting her in Fairlea several days before—she looked as exquisitely beautiful as he remembered her. And she was also as deceitful and as avaricious as he remembered, he reminded himself.

He moved his shoulders impatiently. Sabrina wasn't his sole reason for coming to the Star Inn tonight to attend a function that normally he would have avoided like the Black Death. After his sickening clash with Lionel at little Daniel's funeral, he'd made up his mind never to put himself again in a situation where he might meet his brother. But Christabel's letter had sounded desperate. He hadn't been able to ignore her plea to come down to Sussex to meet with her. Now that he was here, however, it had dawned on him that such a meeting would be difficult to arrange. He couldn't visit her at Winwood Park without Lionel's knowledge, and any attempt to meet her secretly would probably be a disaster. His best opportunity to talk to Christabel might well be in the midst of a large public gathering like the anniversary ball at the Star Inn.

He looked up at a sudden flurry of activity at the door of the ballroom. The official patrons of the ball had arrived. Unnoticed in the crowd, Jareth watched as Lionel and Christabel were surrounded by acquaintances. Waiting until Lionel was engaged in conversation with an official-looking gentleman who was probably one of the organizers of the ball, Jareth edged his way through the throng to Christabel's side just as the music struck up again. "This is my dance, I believe," he murmured in her ear.

Flashing him a look of startled surprise, Christabel glanced nervously at her husband, still deep in conversation and unaware of Jareth's presence. Then, with only an instant of hesitation, she placed her hand on

208

Jareth's arm with fingers that trembled, and in a moment they had melted into the crowd of waltzers on the dance floor.

"Jareth, you must be mad," she muttered. "I've been waiting and waiting to hear from you, I've been almost out of my mind with worry, and here you suddenly appear before me at a public ball! We can't talk here. Lionel has probably spotted us already. Why didn't you send me a message you'd arrived in Sussex?"

Jareth looked down at the lovely face beneath the tiny black cap of mourning crepe that contrasted so exquisitely with the silver-gilt hair and the incredible violet eyes, and once again realized that Christabel had lost the power to make his heartbeat quicken. So much, at least, Sabrina had done for him, he thought savagely. She'd made it impossible for him to respond to the echoes of his lovesick youth, just as she'd shattered any possibility that one day he might learn to trust another woman.

"If you're thinking of a secluded meeting anywhere in the vicinity, think again," he told Christabel calmly, as they swung gracefully around the dance floor. "The wife of the Lord Lieutenant of the county is far too well-known to go unnoticed. Sooner or later Lionel would hear about it. This is our only chance, Christabel. Lionel can't very well accuse us of a secret rendezvous in the middle of a ballroom!" Jareth lifted his head, discovering his brother's eyes fixed on him across the floor. "Lionel's seen us. Pray that this is a long waltz. You have until the music stops to tell me what's troubling you."

Christabel gasped, her delicate features suddenly looking pinched. "I can't, there's not enough time . . ." She swallowed hard. "Jareth, I think Lionel's going mad. He drinks constantly, from the time he awakens

209

in the morning until late at night. He's half-seas over right now. He almost fell on his face getting out of the carriage. I nearly died of embarrassment."

"Lionel's usually a trifle under par," said Jareth with a touch of impatience. "Is this what you wanted to tell me, that Lionel's drinking more than he used to?"

"No, no, that's only part of it," Christabel said urgently. "Lionel can't seem to get over Daniel's death—though when my dear little boy was alive his father barely noticed him," she added with a corrosive bitterness. "Lionel talks about you constantly; he's obsessed with the idea that you're his heir. Sometimes I think he believes you were in some way responsible for my child's death. I told you he isn't rational. He keeps saying he'd rather see you dead than the next Marquess of Winwood. Jareth, I know the drinking is responsible for much of what he says, but he sounds more violent, more unbalanced, with each passing day. I'm afraid he may go over the edge soon. I'm terrified he might try to kill you."

"Christabel, has Lionel used violence on you?" Jareth demanded.

She bit her lip, while a wave of color suffused her face. "He—he slapped me once when I tried to argue him out of his absurd fancies. It was the gin that was responsible. I'm sure he wouldn't hurt me. It's you I'm concerned about."

"Don't be. When I leave Sussex this time, I won't be back. Lionel and I aren't likely to meet again in the near future. If we should meet, if he should come up to London, I can deal with him. I always could, you know. That's one reason he's always disliked me." As the strains of the waltz died away and the dancers began leaving the floor, Jareth released his arm from around her waist, swinging to face her as he said quickly, "Try not to worry, Christabel. I'm convinced it's the combination of grief and too much wine and Geneva that's making Lionel act this way. The passing of time will help. What would help most, you know, is another child."

Christabel's expression changed. "Nothing would please me more," she said under her breath. Lifting her chin she added with a rather difficult smile, "Thank you for coming down. I'm sure you're right about Lionel. I wish now I hadn't troubled you. I think I was a bit overwrought. Good-bye. Please don't bother to see me off the floor. I see a friend I wish to speak to."

Jareth stared after the slender black-clad figure, moving with the incomparable grace that had once enchanted him. He felt vaguely dissatisfied. Christabel had been genuinely distraught, and apparently he had given her little comfort. What had she expected of him? Was there really any danger that Lionel was "going over the edge?"

He seemed sane enough when he accosted Jareth a moment later. Angry, yes, and belligerent, and quite drunk, but Lionel was frequently all of those things. "What brings you here, little brother?" he sneered. "What interest could the leader of the *ton* have in a provincial celebration of Waterloo?"

"I have business in the area," said Jareth curtly. "And I believe the ball is open to the public." He nodded to Lionel, turning to leave.

"One moment," grunted Lionel, grabbing Jareth's arm. "I'm sponsoring this affair, and by God, you're not welcome here. Why don't you leave before I order someone to throw you out?"

Jareth reached for Lionel's hand, removing it from his arm and holding it in an iron grip that nearly made the bones crack. "Try it, Lionel," he gritted between his teeth. "Try throwing me out. It'll be bellows to mend for you and anyone else who takes me on. I'll go when I'm ready, not before. Is that understood?" He released Lionel's hand as he spoke and stood waiting, his eyes wary, his weight evenly balanced on both feet, his hands clenched loosely in front of him.

The aggressiveness faded from Lionel's face. Swaying slightly, he moved back a few inches. "No one doubts your prowess as an amateur pugilist," he blustered. "Fortunately, I have more regard for my guests than to subject them to the spectacle of my brother milling down assorted opponents. Just remember this, however. You're to stay away from my wife. You've danced your last dance with Christabel."

"*I* won't do anything to embarrass Christabel," Jareth said evenly. His watchful eye sighted Sabrina reentering the ballroom with her tall companion. "Let's agree to stay out of each other's way for the rest of the evening, shall we, Lionel?" He swung on his heel, heading for Sabrina, who stood on the far side of the room with her escort, talking to a fair-haired young girl and a man in a blue coat reminiscent of a naval uniform.

On the other side of the room, Sabrina was saying lightly to Gordon Stanhope, "I trust Daphne has told you that our stepmother firmly believes a young lady may dance no more than two dances with the same gentleman without embarking on the primrose path of dalliance."

"Sabrina!" Daphne protested, blushing hotly. "What a thing to say."

The young revenue captain didn't turn a hair. "Daphne and I are behaving with the utmost propriety," he said solemnly. "We've danced one waltz, and we're about to stand up together in the country dance that's forming. After that we'll sit out the remaining dances under the dragon eye of our chaperon. Now,

Lady Latimer may consider my sister a trifle young for that kind of responsibility, but Betsy has assured me that she'll remain awake on every suit."

Gazing into the limpid innocence of Gordon's eyes, Sabrina couldn't resist a chuckle. She liked a man with a sense of humor. She liked Gordon Stanhope. If only he weren't the son of a yeoman farmer, or if only he'd inherited a handsome fortune from an uncle in the British East India Company . . . "Be off with you," she said indulgently. "Enjoy the country dance."

As they watched Daphne and Gordon scamper off, Ivo Ranger extended his hand, saying, "Shall we join the set too?"

Before she could reply, a voice from behind her said, "Good evening, Mrs. Neville. I hope I'm not too late to claim one of your dances."

Taking a deep breath, Sabrina turned to face Jareth. "Good evening. This dance is taken, I'm afraid. Oh—I don't think you two have met. Lord Jareth Tremayne, Captain Ranger."

A spark of instant mutual dislike crackled through the air. "I believe we have met, in a manner of speaking," Ivo Ranger remarked with a long measuring look at Jareth. "How do you do, sir. Tremayne, did you say? Are you by any chance related to the Marquess of Winwood?"

"After a fashion. I'm his brother," replied Jareth aloofly. "Mrs. Neville, I believe there is a waltz following the country dance. May I have the pleasure?"

His voice was pleasant, courteous, but Sabrina could hear the iron-hard undertone. Jareth wasn't going to give up. It would be better to have the encounter over and done with. She inclined her head. "You may have the next waltz."

As they moved off to take their places in the set, Ranger murmured, "I don't wish to intrude, but are

213

you sure you really wish to dance with that man? The other day, in Fairlea, you seemed somewhat distressed when you were speaking to him."

"You're quite mistaken, Captain. Lord Jareth doesn't distress me. He merely bores me. However, he's an old acquaintance, and I daresay it won't hurt me to suffer through one dance with him."

She wished she felt as self-assured as she sounded, she reflected, as she went through the figures of the country dance with half her mind on the intricate steps and the other half on Jareth Tremayne. What did he want from her, other than the opportunity to give her another tongue-lashing?

She soon found out. He came up to her to claim his dance, outwardly polite and attentive, and as he slipped his arm around her waist at the first lilting strains of a waltz to which they'd often danced in London, her treacherous senses responded to his firm clasp and she could feel the familiar curlings of desire that his slightest touch had always aroused in her. But the darkly obsidian eyes that bored into hers lacked the faintest trace of warmth.

Without any preliminaries he said abruptly, "Do you remember my telling you once that I earned my living as a gambler? Well, I'm quite successful at my chosen profession. It enables me to live in expensive lodgings, to drive decent horseflesh, to dress like a gentleman, to keep up my memberships in my clubs. Naturally, I don't always win. Losing is one thing, part of the game. So I pay my gaming debts, but I can't afford to give away my blunt. Not as much as ten thousand pounds, at any rate. I came here tonight to ask you when you intend to return the money you owe me."

Sabrina missed a step as her temper began to rise. "I cheated you, yes, but you know full well I never intended to keep my winnings," she snapped. "You already have your money. You told me yourself that Adrian returned it to you. You can stop playing this cat and mouse game with me. I don't owe you anything."

He smiled thinly. "No, Mrs. Neville, that was my own money your brother gave me. The ten thousand pounds you bilked from me with your marked cards. What I'm referring to is *Sir Adrian's* money. The ten thousand pounds he lost to me at macao. I gave him a month's grace in which to find the money to pay his debt of honor and the month is now up. I want my ten thousand pounds."

Sabrina felt an hysterical desire to laugh. Jareth was quite right. Adrian *did* still owe him ten thousand pounds. If only she hadn't cheated and had won the money from Jareth legitimately—and the odds were even she could have done so, because she considered herself as good a player as he was—then Adrian wouldn't owe him a shilling. Not that Jareth would be any the less angry if she hadn't used those marked cards. It wasn't the money that mattered to him. What had embittered and enraged him was the betrayal of his love, and for that he wanted his pound of flesh.

"There's nothing more to be said, then," she said coldly. "Of course you must have your money. How can we arrange it? Would you accept so much per year until the debt is paid? With interest, naturally."

"No. I'm not a moneylender. I want cash."

Sabrina felt the stirrings of panic. Now she was penned into the same corner from which she'd tried so desperately to escape with her scheme to cheat Jareth out of his own money. Her family and her home were at risk again.

"Adrian and I don't have that much money," she said, striving not to let her emotions show. Not for anything would she swallow her pride and allow herself to appeal to Jareth's softer instincts. "We can only realize that large a sum by selling our estate," she went on. "That will take time. Since you're not a landowner yourself, perhaps you aren't aware of adverse conditions in agriculture since the end of the war. The price of corn, for example, has tumbled from a hundred and twenty shillings a quarter in 1813 to fifty-three shillings this spring. Tenant rentals are down, banks are calling in their loans. It won't be as easy to dispose of property as it was a few years ago."

"That's not acceptable either, Mrs. Neville. I don't choose to wait for my money."

The note of brutal indifference in his voice caused her poise to crack. "What is it you want from me, then?" she exclaimed fiercely. "I can't produce money out of a hat like some magician. And stop calling me Mrs. Neville. My name is Sabrina, as you very well know."

"You have so many names. Countess Dohenyi, for instance. One really doesn't know what to call you," said Jareth silkily. "Fancy piece, perhaps? Lightskirt? Ladybird?"

The music stopped just then, and Sabrina jerked away from him, her face burning angrily. His fingers bit into her arm, forcing her to stay by his side. "Unless you want to provoke an embarrassing public scene, *Mrs. Neville*, you'll hear me out."

Letting her arm go limp, Sabrina allowed Jareth to guide her through the crowd of dancers coming off the floor, out of the door of the ballroom and into the card room opening off the corridor. The room was half-filled with card players, most of them elderly, only a few of whom lifted their heads from their cards when Jareth and Sabrina entered the room.

"Well?" Sabrina demanded, swinging around to face

216

Jareth. "I'm listening."

"I have a proposition to make. How does this sound to you? We'll play one game of macao here and now. Sorry, no marked cards. If you win, I'll cancel your brother's debt. If I win . . ." He paused, a cruelly anticipatory smile curving his lips. "If I win, I'll still cancel the debt, but there'll be a forfeit."

"And that is?" Sabrina's mouth felt dry. Curse Jareth, he was enjoying every moment of this.

"If I win, you'll agree to spend a night with me. A significant part of a night," Jareth added meaningfully. "In other words, I'm not suggesting a repeat of those prim evenings in London when I escorted you to your door with no expectations of reward for wining and dining you."

A knife turned in Sabrina's heart. She couldn't remember feeling such pain. "I'll see you in hell before I share your bed!" she flashed. "I've offered to repay your money by selling off Latimer House. Take it or leave it." Once more she tried to break the hold of those iron fingers, glancing around her to observe with relief that none of the card players was showing any interest in her intense but low-voiced confrontation with Jareth.

"Think again, my dear. The alternative to sharing my bed might appear even more unpleasant to you. You'll play that game of macao with me, or I'll spread it all over London that you and your brother are a pair of Captain Sharps."

The knife turned even deeper in her heart. Jareth's charge of cheating would ruin Adrian's Army career, humiliate her stepmother, blast Daphne's chances of making a good marriage, ostracize the entire family from county society. She couldn't let that happen. Squaring her shoulders, she met Jareth's gaze with a cool dignity. "You leave me no choice. I accept your terms. I'll remind you, though, that you may find you're not the master gambler you think you are, just as you've already proved you're no gentleman, despite your reputation as the 'Corinthian of Corinthians'!"

A muscle twitched in Jareth's cheek, but that was the only indication he gave that her barb had struck home. "I applaud your decision, Mrs. Neville. I think my proposition is a fair one. We're both gamblers, after all." He motioned to a vacant table. "Now is as good a time as any, don't you think?"

Sabrina's legs felt so hollow she was glad to sink into a chair at the table. She watched Jareth in numb silence as he picked up a deck of cards and dealt them slowly, one by one, until he received an ace.

"My deal," he said, shuffling the deck. "One game only, is that understood?"

"Perfectly," she replied icily. He dealt each of them a card, face down. She pried up the corner of her card. A six. He eyed her questioningly. "I don't have a natural. Do you?" When she shook her head, he gave them each another card. Hers was a two.

"Will you draw a card?" Jareth asked.

"I'll stand," she replied with a dry mouth. The odds were with her. An eight ought to win.

Coolly Jareth turned his two cards face up. He had a 4 and a 3. He tossed her a measuring glance across the table. Had he noticed the almost imperceptible tightening of her fingers that she hadn't been able to control? "Seven is a good hand, but I think you have me beat," he said calmly. "I'll draw." Slowly he dealt himself a card down, equally slowly he peered at it without turning it up.

Sabrina's heart pounded. Jareth's dark face was expressionless. Only a two could defeat her. He'd had three chances out of forty-eight to draw another two. Whether or not he'd done it, whether he'd won or lost, he was deliberately prolonging her agony of suspense.

Finally he turned up the card. It was a two.

"You've won, Lord Jareth," said Sabrina, proud that she was able to keep the nervous tremor out of her voice.

Leaning back in his chair, he watched her with a hint of amused malice in his eyes. "I'm an excellent macao player when I'm not facing an opponent who uses marked cards. Well, Mrs. Neville? Shall we settle the details of our wager?"

"As you wish."

"Excellent. Tomorrow night, say at ten o'clock, I'll be waiting in my carriage for you at the end of the driveway leading to Latimer House. I'll reserve rooms at the Bridge Hotel in Newhaven. Are you known there? No? Even if you were acquainted there, it would have been a simple matter for you to disguise your identity with a veil. You see, I'm trying to keep our rendezvous as discreet as possible. I'll engage to have you back at the end of your driveway well before the sun is up, or anyone in your household is awake."

"Is that all?"

"Quite. Oh, one more thing. Wear that lovely dress I bought for you in London."

"You're a monster. I hate you." The words burst out of Sabrina's mouth before she could stop them.

Jareth laughed. "You surprise me, my dear. Why are you so upset at my arrangements? You stand to lose only a piece of your virtue, and I'm sure you don't pride yourself on *that!*"

Her face flaming, Sabrina leaped to her feet, taking a step toward Jareth with her hand lifted to strike at him.

A quiet voice stopped her in mid-stride. "Are you in need of assistance, Mrs. Neville?"

She whirled on Ivo Ranger with mixed emotions of

relief and chagrin. He gave off an aura of stolid reassurance as he stood there beside her, staring challengingly at Jareth, who rose to face him with the light of battle in his eyes.

Sabrina took Jareth's arm, saying playfully, "La, Captain Ranger, you have a lively imagination. Lord Jareth and I are such old friends, we say what we like to each other. Fancy your thinking we were quarreling!"

The ex-Navy captain's gaze went from Sabrina's flushed face to Jareth's tense dark features. "I'm afraid I've been quite dense, Mrs. Neville," Ivo Ranger said quietly. "You and Lord Jareth are obviously *very* old friends. Forgive me for intruding."

Chapter Twelve

"Daphne, will you have another cake?" Lady Latimer's gracious smile faded as Daphne, apparently startled by her stepmother's voice, spilled the contents of her teacup over the skirt of her light-colored muslin gown.

"What on earth has come over you, my dear?" Fanny inquired with an irritated frown, as Daphne jumped up from her chair, mopping ineffectually at her dress with a handkerchief. "Teatime should be a pleasant interval, a time when family members can come together to discuss their day. You've scarcely said a word since you sat down, and your mind is a thousand miles away."

"I'm quite all right, Mama," said Daphne hastily. "May I be excused? I'll just go up and change my gown."

As Daphne left the room, Fanny shifted her accusing gaze. "You, too, Sabrina. One would have thought you'd been struck dumb, also. Do you know what ails that child?"

Rousing herself to reply dutifully to her stepmother, Sabrina murmured, "Perhaps Daphne's a little tired after the ball last night."

Sabrina had been so wrapped in her own thoughts all day that she hadn't paid much attention to what was going on around her. It struck her now, looking back on Daphne's arrival at the tea table, that her sister had appeared unusually subdued, but with an underlying edge of nervous excitability.

"Nonsense," said Fanny. "At Daphne's age I danced until dawn every night during the Season and felt fresh as a daisy the next day. No, I daresay she's mooning after that Captain Stanhope. Thank heaven that man is going to sea!" She poured herself another cup of tea, and, as she stirred the milk and sugar into it, continued in a tone of satisfaction, "I will say, however, that Captain Stanhope conducted himself with decorum at the ball. No more than two dances with Daphne, and I was keeping close watch!"

Fanny's conversation rarely required a direct answer, merely an attentive expression on the part of her listener, and Sabrina's thoughts once more veered to the problem that had been filling her mind since her encounter with Jareth at the Star Inn the previous evening.

In one sense she was almost grateful to Jareth for issuing his brutal ultimatum, which had killed any emotion she'd ever felt for him except anger. Now at least she was free of those tormenting "if only's" and "what might have been's," and there was certainly no need to feel guilty any longer about her masquerade as the Countess Dohenyi. She'd agreed to sleep with Jareth tonight, and after that she'd never have to see or think about him again. But all through a sleepless night and a day that had dragged by interminably she'd been wondering if she could steel herself to go through with her bargain. It wasn't pride that was standing in her way. As she'd proved in the past, she was prepared to go to almost any lengths to preserve the Latimer estate for Adrian and Daphne and yes, Fanny. But the idea of selling her body for gain, as a payment to Jareth for keeping silent about her cheating, filled her with revulsion. She'd be no better than any Fashionable Impure with her box at the Opera, or the

222

painted drabs haunting the stews of Covent Garden.

Could she really pay that kind of price for her family's welfare? It was late afternoon now. She had until ten o'clock this evening to make up her mind. Would Jareth really make good his threat to expose her if she failed to meet him tonight at the end of the driveway?

"Well, my dear, that was a very quick change," Fanny remarked in faint surprise as Daphne, wearing a fresh dress, hurried into the morning room, short of breath and with her hair slightly disarrayed.

A moment later, hard on Daphne's heels, a maidservant appeared in the doorway. "A gentleman is calling, my lady. A Captain Stanhope."

Lady Latimer tossed Daphne a glance of deep reproof. "So that's why you rushed to change your dress. I must say, it was very sly of you to arrange this visit without telling me about it beforehand. I don't like this kind of behavior at all, Daphne." She drew a deep breath. "Tell Captain Stanhope that Miss Latimer is not at home," she informed the maidservant.

"Begging your pardon, my lady, the gentleman wishes to see *you.*"

"Me!" Fanny paused in astonishment. Then she said coldly, "Tell the captain I'm not receiving visitors today."

"Mama! You can't be so rude. You *must* see Gordon," Daphne burst out.

Fanny's face turned a dull red. Words failed her for several moments. "Ask Captain Stanhope to come in," she said at last, straightening her back to an alarming stiffness.

When Gordon entered the morning room shortly afterwards, he looked unusually solemn. Bowing, he lost no time getting to the reason for his visit, saying to Fanny, "Thank you for seeing me, Lady Latimer. I'm going to sea very soon, but before I go I want to ask you for permission to marry Daphne."

"I see." Fanny turned her head to address Daphne. "This offer comes as no surprise to you, I presume."

"No, Mama." Daphne was very pale, and her hands were clenched tightly together, but she returned Fanny's gaze without flinching. "Gordon asked me to marry him last night at the ball. We agreed that he would come to Latimer House today to make a formal offer for my hand."

"You'll want to know my prospects, Lady Latimer," said Gordon quietly. "I'm well able to support a wife. My pay compares very favorably with that of senior naval officers, and I've been fortunate in the amount of seizure money I've received over the years. I have twenty thousand pounds in the Funds. When my father dies—which I hope, naturally, will be far-in the future—I'll inherit his farm. I don't think you need fear that Daphne will ever want for anything."

"Your income is not at issue, Captain Stanhope. Your background is. I couldn't give my consent to this marriage if you had twice twenty thousand pounds in the Funds. Please believe I have no wish to offend you, but you must realize that your social station is far inferior to that of my stepdaughter. A marriage between you is impossible."

Watching the scene quietly, unable to intervene without muddying the waters, Sabrina admired Stanhope's self-control. He was obviously making a determined effort to keep his temper. "I consider myself quite respectable," he replied with a quiet dignity. "If Daphne doesn't feel she would disgrace herself by marrying me, I see no reason why my 'social station' should concern you."

"Your remark confirms the truth of what I've been trying to tell you, that you don't know how to act like a gentleman," said Fanny sharply. "I take my responsibilities as Daphne's guardian very seriously indeed. I would be remiss in my duty to my dead husband if I didn't safeguard his daughter from a gross mésalliance with a nobody."

"Mama! What a cruel thing to say," Daphne exclaimed, her eyes brimming with tears. She rushed to Stanhope's side, clasping his arm with both hands. "Gordon says I don't need your consent to be married," she said defiantly to Fanny. "He says that females can make a legal marriage contract at twelve years of age."

Lady Latimer's lip curled. "That may be, but I fancy you wouldn't relish giving up all the trappings of a proper wedding. If you marry Captain Stanhope without my consent, it won't be from Latimer House, with the vicar officiating and all your relatives and your friends from the county in attendance. Think about it, Daphne. Would you want to start your married life as the target of gossip and innuendo?"

His face turning grim, Gordon placed his hand protectively over Daphne's, saying, "I told you it might be like this, love. Don't cry, please. I promise you, it will all come right in the end, but I don't think there's much point in talking anymore now."

"Indeed there isn't," Fanny snapped. "You would oblige me, Captain Stanhope, by leaving my house immediately."

Gently disengaging himself from Daphne's clinging hold, the revenue captain said softly, "Good-bye, love. Just for now." Bowing formally to Fanny, he left the room.

Daphne collapsed into a chair in a storm of hysterical tears. Sabrina went to her quickly, putting an arm around the heaving shoulders. "Try to get hold of yourself, Daphne. This crying will wear you out. Look, let me help you to your bedchamber. Lotte will bring you something to make you feel better."

"Yes, do that, Sabrina," said Fanny in relief. She looked faintly guilty. "Daphne will feel much more the thing if she lies down."

Later, after Daphne had swallowed Lotte's soothing tisane, she managed to stop crying. Staring at Sabrina out of eyes that were red-rimmed and swollen, she said drearily, "Go ahead and get it over with. Tell me how improper it was to accept Gordon's suit when I knew very well Mama wouldn't approve."

Sabrina roused from a long, thoughtful, bittersweet silence. "I've no intention of telling you anything of the kind. I think Mama is wrong. If you want to marry Captain Stanhope I won't stand in your way any longer. You can count on my presence at your wedding. I daresay Adrian will come too."

"Sabrina!" gasped Daphne. "What made you change your mind? I thought you agreed with Mama about Gordon."

"I like Gordon," Sabrina said simply. "He's a strong man. I think he'll cherish you and keep you from harm all the days of your life. And you love him."

Starry-eyed, Daphne jumped off her bed to envelop Sabrina in a joyful hug. "Thank you, thank you. When folk see that you and Adrian are supporting me there'll be no possibility of scandal." She lifted her head, saying shyly, "It's because of Oliver, isn't it? You've always known that real love is more important than money or rank. You want me to be as happy as you were with Oliver."

Sabrina ruffled Daphne's fair hair affectionately. "Yes, Puss. It was because of Oliver."

And Oliver really was partly responsible for her change of mind, Sabrina reflected as she left Daphne and went to her own bedchamber, but not in the way her sister imagined. Sabrina's marriage to Oliver had failed for precisely the same reasons that Daphne's would succeed. It wasn't love that had been lacking in Sabrina's marriage; it was selflessness and strength of character. If

Oliver had put his wife first, if he had tried to conquer his gambling habit, if, once his cheating was discovered, he'd faced the consequences with gallantry, Sabrina might have retained her love for him. At the very least she would have tried to save the marriage. With Gordon, Daphne would always come first, and his strength would never fail her. Those qualities would go a long way to make up for the snubs and social ostracism that Daphne might encounter if she married outside her class.

Gordon Stanhope would doubtless be amazed to learn that his offer for Daphne's hand had helped his future sister-in-law to make up her mind about another important matter, Sabrina thought wryly as she entered her bedchamber. She'd decided to keep her rendezvous with Jareth. Despite the revulsion she still felt for a loveless mating, it was the only way she could ensure a future for Daphne and Adrian. Oh, she didn't believe for a moment that Gordon's feelings for Daphne would change if her brother and sister were publicly disgraced, but Sabrina wasn't willing to take any chances. Adrian, of course, would have neither military career nor estate if he were branded a cheat.

"And how is the *Fräulein* Daphne?" inquired Lotte, whom Sabrina found waiting for her in the bedchamber.

"Much better. Your tisane always does wonders."

"There was some trouble with the Lady Latimer, I hear."

Was it ever possible to keep family secrets from servants? Sabrina wondered. Certainly not from Lotte, whose inquisitive mind combined the instincts of a bloodhound with the relentlessness of the Inquisition.

"Don't gossip with the other servants about Miss Daphne's affairs, Lotte. If you're *very* discreet, I just may have some important news for you soon."

"The sailor, what a handsome man, *nicht wahr?*" Lotte

227

said, rolling her eyes.

Sabrina sighed. Lotte was incorrigible. She was also fanatically loyal. Feeling suddenly very tired, Sabrina sank into a chair. "Lotte, I need your help. *And* your discretion."

"Zu befehl, meine Frau." Lotte's plump face reflected the note of strain she heard in Sabrina's voice.

"I want you to tell my stepmother that I'm indisposed with a headache and won't be down to dinner. I've gone to bed with the draperies pulled shut and I don't want *anything,* not even a cup of tea or a piece of toast, least of all a visit from Lady Latimer or Miss Daphne. Do you understand that, Lotte? No one is to come into this room, under any circumstances."

Her eyes narrowing speculatively, Lotte looked at Sabrina. *"Ja,* you don't wish to be disturbed. Or is that you won't be here, and you don't wish the Lady Latimer to know that? Where are you going, *meine Frau?"*

"I can't tell you. I'll be leaving the house shortly after 9:30 — on foot, so you won't have to notify the stables — and I'll be back before dawn. I don't want anyone to know I'm gone. And be sure the rear door of the house is left unlocked so I can get back in."

"You're not going off alone in the middle of the night," Lotte declared. "I'll go with you."

"No. I need someone here to guard the gate. You'll remain in this room until I get back. Oh, and Lotte, I'll be wearing that dress I bought in London, the one with the blue silk petticoat and the bouquets of roses and bluebells."

Suddenly Lotte became very still. When she finally spoke, her remarks at first sounded irrelevant. "Cook was telling me a few days ago that the Marquess of Winwood's brother is staying at the Fairlea Arms. Seems he's been away for so long that most folk didn't recognize him! Do you know the Herr, *meine Frau?"*

"Yes. So do you, Lotte. You met Lord Jareth Tremayne in London." Sabrina's lips clamped shut with the
stubborn expression that told Lotte no other information would be forthcoming.

After Lotte had cautiously scouted the corridor leading past the kitchens, Sabrina slipped out of the back
entrance of Latimer House, walking swiftly but quietly
beside the darkened windows of the drawing room.
Fanny and Daphne would be taking their coffee in the
morning room on the other side of the house. It had
been another of those rainy days that were making this
summer a purgatory for farmers, and a slight drizzle
was still falling. It was difficult to make out objects in the
gloom, for which Sabrina was grateful. On a fine
evening it would still have been quite light at this hour,
and she would have run more risk of being seen when
she left the house. At midsummer in these northern lati-
tudes, the long twilights seemed to linger onto the
fringes of midnight.

Over her filmy blue gown Sabrina was wearing a long
dark hooded cloak that protected her from the rain and
made her nearly invisible as she entered the winding
driveway leading from the house to its junction with the
little cross-country lane. In the adjacent shrubbery she
could hear the rustling noises made by nocturnal animals, and once a small form, indistinct in the gathering
darkness, scurried across the road in front of her. She
wasn't alarmed. She'd been walking along this drive, unafraid, in all weathers and at all times of the day and
night since her earliest childhood. There was nothing
here that could harm her. As she approached the junction with the lane, however, her steps slowed. She came
to a stop. She could still change her mind, she thought,
her body making an involuntary half-turn in the direc-

tion of Latimer House. Then, drawing a deep, difficult breath, she began walking again, rounding the last curve of the driveway. A carriage stood in the lane, its lamps illuminating the tall figure in the beaver hat and the long, many-caped driving coat who was pacing impatiently back and forth beside the vehicle.

Jareth paused as Sabrina came into view. "You're late," he accused her, taking out his watch. "Well, almost late," he added grudgingly after he looked at the timepiece. Before Sabrina realized what he was doing, he took a quick step toward her, tearing open her cloak.

"Are you mad?" Sabrina gasped. She snatched her cloak away from his grasp, wrapping it securely around her. "Were you perhaps planning to rape me in the middle of the road?" she inquired with a scornful toss of her head.

"No, I've never found it necessary to rape anyone, and I also prefer a little privacy in my seductions," he replied coolly. "I was checking to make sure you were wearing the gown from Madame Simone's shop."

"Oh, and would you have sent me back to Latimer House to change my gown if I weren't wearing Madame Simone's creation?" Sabrina asked witheringly.

"No, but if you were wearing the dress I'd have some indication that you were prepared the observe the terms of our bargain." After a brief pause he said with an ironic smile, "I wasn't at all sure you'd come tonight. I should have known your instinct for self-preservation would be stronger than your dislike for me. Stronger certainly than any missish regard for convention or morals!"

Jareth meant his gibe to hurt, but it was having the opposite effect. He was making it so easy for her to hate him that she could submerge every other feeling in a blazing anger and contempt. Surrendering to him tonight would be only a temporary defeat. Someday, somehow, she'd find a way to pay him back for attempting to grind her pride and self-respect into the dust.

She lifted her chin, staring him down. "If you've no further comments to give me about my character, perhaps we might start our journey to Newhaven, Lord Jareth? I confess I'd like to finish with this—this little escapade as soon as possible. I have better and more interesting things to do with my time."

"You—" Jareth checked a quick, furious move toward her. Throwing open the door of the carriage, he put down the steps and turned to her with a theatrical, over-elaborate bow. "Your wish is my command, Mrs. Neville."

During the drive of five miles to Newhaven, Jareth lounged back against the squabs, his hat tilted lazily over his eyes, making an occasional desultory comment about the weather, to which she replied in monosyllables or not at all. Gradually he ceased talking, keeping so silent he might have been drowsing, or he may have intended to express his indifference to her presence, but Sabrina could sense the coiled tension in him when an occasional jolting movement of the carriage caused his leg to brush against hers. Each time it occurred she edged away, pressing herself against the opposite side of the carriage. It appalled her that the slightest physical contact with Jareth could sear her flesh through several layers of clothing, sending waves of tingling desire coursing through her veins. Why did she have such feelings for a man who despised her, who wanted to use her body as an instrument of revenge, a man whom she hated as she had never hated anyone in all her short life?

She tried to block out of her mind the reason for this nocturnal journey, clinging to each passing second as a postponement of her reckoning with Jareth. But, although she knew the leisurely drive was taking no more than its usual forty-five minutes, the time seemed to fly. Before she could compose her thoughts, the carriage stopped in front of the Bridge Hotel in Newhaven.

Jareth got out as soon as the coachman opened the door and let down the steps. He stood waiting on the pavement, extending his hand to help her down. Pulling the hood of her cloak more closely around her face, Sabrina stepped down, pushing his hand aside contemptuously. Shrugging, he motioned to the door of the hotel, where a servant stood waiting, obviously on the alert for their arrival. Sabrina kept her head down as they walked through the entrance. There was little chance that she would be recognized, since she had never stayed at the hotel and had only rarely visited the town, but she was glad the servant could see very little of her face beneath the enveloping hood.

"This way, m'lord," the man said to Jareth, bowing. "Your servant arrived some time ago."

The rooms Jareth had reserved on the second floor consisted of a cozy sitting room with a fire blazing on the hearth, opening into what Sabrina presumed was an adjoining bedchamber. Harris, Jareth's valet, stood next to a table near the fireplace, the table having been set with snowy linen, crystal, and silver. His wooden features registering a fleeting moment of surprise as Sabrina put back her hood, Harris bowed, murmuring, "Good evening, Countess."

Sabrina threw Jareth a quick, questioning glance. He'd told his valet to arrange a late supper for a lady, but it seemed he hadn't mentioned the lady's name. Harris recognized her as the Countess Dohenyi—and she would have wagered a considerable sum that the valet had never expected to see his master's vanished Viennese inamorata again—but Jareth hadn't revealed her real name. Was it a mark of kindly discretion on Jareth's part, a conscious effort to keep her from scandal, or had he simply regarded her identity as none of Harris's business? She almost wished it were the latter. She had no wish to be grateful to Jareth for anything.

"May I take your cloak?" Jareth said politely. As he slipped the garment off her shoulders, his long slender fingers lingered on her bare flesh in an unmistakably deliberate gesture of possession. So much for her conjecture that he might have retained some measure of consideration for her feelings. He smiled thinly when she moved abruptly away from him. Handing the cloak to the attentive valet, he pulled one of the two chairs away from the table, saying, "Please sit down. I'm sure Harris has ordered one of his usual superb meals for us."

Sitting opposite her, Jareth reached for an already opened bottle of champagne, filling both their glasses. "This is the vintage you seemed to enjoy so much in London. I reminded Harris to order several bottles," he remarked with a spurious solicitude. He lifted his glass. "To a renewal of the pleasures of our last evening together."

Sabrina gulped down several mouthfuls of the wine, hoping to get rid of a curious feeling of lightheadedness, as if her heart was pumping too much blood through her body. She made a furious resolve not to give Jareth the satisfaction of knowing his barbs were striking home. She redoubled her determination a few minutes later when she looked at the elaborate supper that Harris was placing on the table. Turbot with lobster sauce, a boiled fowl, turtle and roast duck with asparagus and peas . . . Exactly the same meal which had been served in Jareth's rooms at the Albany on the last evening they had spent together in London. He'd determined to make this experience as painful as possible. So be it. She could play the game as well as he.

Extending her glass, she said coolly, "May I have a little more wine? You're quite right, it's one of my favorites." She flicked a glance over the table. "The food looks delicious. Harris has outdone himself again."

As long as the valet remained in the room, replenishing the wine, bringing in the dessert course, clearing the table when it became obvious that his master and the lady were doing little more than moving the food around their plates, Jareth confined his conversation to impersonal topics. After Harris had gone, however, having drawn the cork of a third bottle of champagne, Jareth's manner changed abruptly. He leaned back in his chair, one hand on the table clasping the stem of the wine glass he had just refilled, while his dark eyes raked her person with a bold familiarity.

"When I started tracking you down with the help of my contacts at the Horse Guards, my dear Sabrina—there, aren't you pleased we're back on a first-name basis again?—I was relieved to learn your real-life story was almost as interesting as that Hungarian fairy tale you invented to ensnare me. It convinced me that our future relations would be as titillating as our initial acquaintance. So you really are a widow. Not Hungarian, more's the pity, but you did spend several years in Vienna. About that, at least, you weren't lying."

"So you've added spying to your other accomplishments. It doesn't surprise me."

"I merely wanted to be sure I wasn't suspecting Sir Adrian unjustly," Jareth said blandly. "If I'd discovered that his two sisters were blameless females who, firstly, were named Amanda and Esmerelda or something equally innocuous, who, secondly, didn't resemble him in the least, and who, thirdly, had never ventured beyond the borders of Sussex, I might have concluded that his payment of ten thousand pounds was a coincidence. But what did I find when I inquired at the Horse Guards? His twin sister, Sabrina—a ravishing creature with corn gold hair, according to one of my informants—had been the toast of Vienna while she was married to her late husband, a secretary in the British

234

diplomatic service."

The note of mocking amusement faded from his voice. Bracing himself on his elbows, he leaned across the table until their faces were nearly touching. "Did you really think you could carry off this masquerade, Sabrina?" he asked harshly. "Did you really think I wouldn't move heaven and earth to catch up with you? If you wanted the ten thousand pounds so badly, why couldn't you simply have asked me for it? It would have been kinder than tearing out my—" He swallowed hard, his mouth working, and sat back in his chair.

The tension crackling between them resembled the electric impulses that fill the air before a storm breaks. Sabrina had to force out the words that fell into the silence like tinkling ice. "I'm afraid I never gave the matter much thought. You see, I really didn't care about your feelings one way or the other."

The long slender hand tightened around the wine glass until the fragile stem broke. "We've been fencing long enough," he said roughly. "It's time to pay the piper, Sabrina."

Pushing back his chair, he rose, circling the table until he stood behind her. Slowly, purposefully, his fingers caressed the satiny flesh of her shoulders and throat, skimming tentatively, tantalizingly over the low-cut bodice of her gown. She tried desperately to hold herself rigid and unresponsive beneath the scorching touch of those knowing hands on her sensitive skin, but despite herself her pulse quickened into a raging tumult and she could feel a growing aching fullness in her breasts.

He bent his head to bury his face in the tawny mass of her hair, murmuring with a catch in his breath, "You smell like flowers; you intoxicate me. You make me forget everything except how much I need you." With a sudden lithe movement he pulled her out of the chair and swept her into his arms, crushing her against him in a savage embrace, bruising her lips in a scalding kiss that sent ripples of fiery yearning surging through her entire body. Lifting his head, his smoldering dark eyes bored deep into hers as he muttered thickly, "I know you don't love me, Sabrina, but you like this. You want me as much as I want you." His arms tightened until she could feel the proof of his arousal. "What a fool I was not to realize in London that I could have had you for the taking. You're a flesh and blood woman, not some counterfeit virgin."

Sabrina gasped as the rough hurting words shattered the thrall of passion that had made her oblivious to everything except Jareth's consuming sexuality. She began struggling to release herself, pushing desperately against him, her arms flailing his head and shoulders in blows that failed to loosen his iron embrace.

"What's the point of this, Sabrina?" he muttered. "You're only prolonging the inevitable. We made a bargain. You accepted the terms of that bargain by coming here tonight."

"And now I'm nullifying the bargain," she panted, still fighting to free herself. "I thought I could sleep with you for Adrian's sake, but I can't go through with it. The very thought of your hands . . . the very thought of it makes my skin crawl. I'd rather sleep with the devil. Or a—a street sweeper. Anything is preferable to sharing a bed with a loose fish like you, Lord Jareth."

The color drained from his face. His arms loosened their grip so abruptly that she lost her balance and staggered back against the table.

"I told you earlier in the evening that rape wasn't among my vices," he said in a clipped voice devoid of emotion. "Nor is sheer altruism among my virtues. You're quite free to cancel our agreement, naturally, but that leaves unsettled the question of my ten thousand pounds. I'll give you one week to produce it. After that

. . ." He shrugged.

"After that you'll throw mud over Adrian's name and mine in all your London clubs," Sabrina said contemptuously. "Well, I can't raise ten thousand pounds in seven days, so do your worst." Snatching up her cloak, she threw it around her shoulders and ran to the door of the sitting room. Wrenching it open, she turned to exclaim, "Good night, Lord Jareth. No, good-bye. One good thing, at least, will come out of all this. I won't have to see you or speak to you or have anything to do with you ever again." Slamming the door behind her she raced down the stairs, pulling her hood closer around her face as she went.

It was well past midnight, and she encountered only one drowsy servant in the vestibule before she shot out of the door of the hotel, keeping up her breakneck pace until she had crossed the drawbridge over the River Ouse. Then she slowed her steps to relieve the pressure in her lungs as she struck out for Latimer House. The night was dark and windy with a steady frigid rain that soon began to penetrate her thick cloak. At this rate she'd be a sodden mess before she reached home. She didn't care. All that mattered was that she had gotten away from Jareth and his cruelty. Her heart felt numb now, but she knew it would only be a matter of time before she started hurting.

In a few minutes she caught the sound of wheels and horses' hooves behind her, and soon the road was illumined by the lamps of the approaching vehicle. The carriage stopped beside her and Jareth threw open the door and stepped out. "Get in," he said curtly. "I'll take you home."

Sabrina walked even faster. "I don't want to ride with you."

She heard a muttered curse, and a moment later he was keeping step with her. "Don't be a ninnyhammer,

Sabrina. It's the middle of the night and you'll soon be drenched. Get in the carriage."

"I'd rather walk."

Sinewy hands grabbed her around the waist.

"What . . . ? Let me down," she screamed in astonished outrage as Jareth threw her over his shoulder and strode toward the carriage. Before she could put up more than a token resistance he deposited her on the seat and got in beside her, slamming the door. He picked up his cane and knocked on the roof to set the carriage in motion.

Chapter Thirteen

The carriage hadn't come to a complete stop at the juncture of the lane with the Latimer House driveway when Sabrina jerked the door open and leaped into the roadway. She began walking rapidly up the drive, only to be brought up short when Jareth grabbed her from behind. "I'm going with you to the house, Sabrina."

She tried to wrest her arm from his grip. "I don't want you to go with me. I walked here without an escort earlier in the evening. I can walk back again by myself."

"It's the middle of the night now. I'm going with you."

Sabrina ceased struggling. What did it matter? She'd soon be rid of him. Side by side they trudged up the driveway, barely able to see where they were going in the moisture-drenched darkness. They didn't speak. They'd driven the five miles from Newhaven in this same icy silence, carefully avoiding touching each other as they huddled on opposite sides of the carriage.

When they reached the end of the driveway, Sabrina spoke for the first time. Glancing at the darkened house, where the only light showing came from a rear window on the second floor, she said, "Please go now. Someone might see you."

Jareth cleared his throat. He swung her around, placing his hands on her shoulders. In the darkness she couldn't see his expression, but his voice sounded husky as he said, "I don't want to leave you this way. Can't we talk?"

"Talk about what?" Sabrina's heart started pounding as Jareth lowered his head, brushing her lips in a kiss that began tentatively and then deepened and clung when her mouth, despite herself, opened slightly beneath his.

"Sabrina—oh, Sabrina," he breathed, and his arms slid around her, drawing her closer.

Oh God, what am I doing? thought Sabrina, wrenching herself away from him. *Why do I still want to feel his arms around me, his lips against mine, after everything he's done to me?* She stepped back, pulling her hood down over her face, though it was so dark that he couldn't have seen the tears dampening her cheeks. She steadied her voice, saying, "Please don't touch me like that. You said you wished to talk?"

He cleared his throat again. "Yes, I—I wanted you to know that I've changed my mind about the immediate repayment of the money. Tell your brother he can have an extension on the debt."

Sabrina ignored the note of pleading in his voice. "I didn't ask you for any favors," she muttered.

His voice hardened. "I'm not doing you a favor. I'm doing one for myself," he replied tersely. "When I tried to force you to sleep with me tonight, I was coming down to your own level of duplicity and deceit. I don't feel comfortable there. I'll give your brother a reasonable period—say six months—in which to pay me back. That should allow him enough time to sell his estate, or to raise the money elsewhere. Then you and I will be quits. We can forget we ever had anything to do with each other."

His sudden open contempt stung, but Sabrina, forcing back the hurtful lump in her throat, merely replied quietly, "That suits me perfectly. Good night, Lord Jareth."

Turning on her heel, she left Jareth without a backward glance. She walked slowly around the side of the house, stumbling occasionally in the inky darkness, and slipped through the rear entrance and up the servants' stairs. She opened the door of her bedchamber and stopped short.

Her face torn between relief and distress, Daphne rose from a chair facing the doorway. "Sabrina! Where've you been? It's past three o'clock in the morning."

"How—? I told Lotte not to allow anyone in here," said Sabrina curtly, throwing off her damp cloak. "As long as you're here, help me out of this dress."

Obediently coming up behind her sister, Daphne began unbuttoning the long row of tiny buttons on the rear of Sabrina's bodice. "I came to your bedchamber late this evening. When you didn't come down to supper I thought you might be ill, and—and anyway, I wanted to talk about Gordon! Lotte did try to keep me out, but I paid her no mind. Sabrina, she was frantic about you. She'd no idea where you'd gone in the middle of the night, all dressed up in your lovely gown. I told her I'd wait up for you . . ." Daphne lifted her head, glancing at Sabrina's pale, set face reflected in the mirror in front of them. "Something's wrong. Something's happened. What is it, Sabrina dearest? Perhaps I can help."

"Nothing's wrong. Go to bed, Daphne." Sabrina let her gown slide to the floor, leaving it where it fell in a shimmering blue heap, and walked to the wardrobe, where she shrugged herself into a dressing gown.

"But . . . Sabrina, there must be *something*—"

"I'm tired, Daphne. I don't want to talk tonight. Please go."

After Daphne had reluctantly left the bedchamber, Sabrina sat down beside the fireplace, from which the banked coals still emitted a comforting faint warmth. She tried to force her mind to function, to begin coping with the problems that would soon drastically alter her family's circumstances, but she was too tired. Tomorrow she would deal with all of that, and with the hurt and terrible anger she knew was lurking just beneath the frozen surface of her consciousness. Tonight, though, she felt almost numb, and she was grateful for the respite.

Sabrina didn't emerge from her bedchamber until lunchtime the following day. When she entered the dining room she appeared composed, though her features were pale beneath the black cornet that concealed her bright hair. Daphne glanced searchingly at her without saying anything, but Fanny, usually so sharp-eyed, appeared not to notice anything amiss about her elder stepdaughter. Fanny had other things to occupy her mind.

"I received a note from Captain Ranger this morning," she announced with a purposeful stare at Sabrina. "He writes that he won't be able to come for dinner on Saturday, though, mind you, he'd accepted the invitation with the greatest of pleasure only the night before last at the Alfriston ball. He says he has business concerns that are taking him to London. He'll be gone indefinitely." She paused expectantly. "Well, Sabrina?"

Sabrina looked up from her plate. "Well, Mama?"

"Don't play the innocent with me, my girl! These sudden business concerns of Captain Ranger sound like sheer invention to me! Did you quarrel with him?"

"Of course not."

Lady Latimer peered suspiciously at her stepdaughter. "Did the captain make you an offer?" she asked abruptly.

Sabrina sighed. Ivo Ranger's sudden departure from Sussex didn't surprise her. He was an intelligent man, and a realistic one. He'd taken one long shrewd look at her and Jareth in the card room at the Star Inn on the night of the ball and had immediately grasped the truth that some fierce, raging emotion bound them together. It made no difference whether that emotion was love or hatred; it effectually barred Sabrina, at least for the time being, from a fulfilling relationship with anyone else.

For a fleeting moment she wondered if she shouldn't have accepted Ivo's proposal. But no, aside from the sheer crassness of asking a newly acquired fiancé for a large sum of money to pay her brother's gambling debts, she couldn't have brought herself to use Ivo Ranger as a way out of her difficulties. He was too nice a man. Fanny, however, would have to be put straight about the situation, because otherwise she certainly wouldn't abandon her campaign to find Sabrina a second husband.

"This mustn't go any farther than this room, Mamá, because I don't want Captain Ranger embarrassed, but yes, he did make me an offer on the night of the ball at Alfriston. I declined it for what I consider good and sufficient reasons, and I'd rather not discuss it."

But discussion seemed to be the last thing of which Fanny was capable. Turning a bright red, she sat opening and closing her mouth without making a sound.

"Hallo! Is there anything left to eat for a tired traveler?"

"Adrian!" shrieked Daphne. "What are you doing here?"

"Visiting my family, of course. How are you, Mama?" Adrian walked to the head of the table to kiss his stepmother.

"As well as can be expected, dear boy," Fanny replied,

recovering her composure with an effort. Keeping her eyes averted from Sabrina, she rang the bell for the maid and said, beaming at her favorite stepchild, "Do sit down, Adrian. I daresay Cook can find something for you. How is it you're able to visit us again so soon?"

"Well, the fact is, I need to consult Sabrina about a—about an estate matter."

Lady Latimer looked puzzled. "Really? I thought Sabrina was taking care of everything for you . . . I know what it is, you wicked boy. You've come down to wheedle another horse out of your sister. Admit it, now!"

"Oh, it's not anything as important as a horse, word of honor," Adrian replied with a forced good humor. "It's only a trifle. Sabrina and I will settle it in a trice!"

He looked anything but good-humored a little later, however, when he and Sabrina retreated to the library after lunch. He looked distinctly harried.

Sabrina sat down behind their father's desk, which had become hers. "What's this 'trifle' you wanted to see me about?"

"It's nothing to do with gaming, if that's what you're afraid of," Adrian replied hastily. He fidgeted with his watch fob and took several paces around the room.

For a few moments Sabrina waited patiently, reflecting, as she had so often, that she felt years older than her twin, and wondering what new development had complicated his life. Certainly the Latimer family didn't need any further problems at this time. Then, as he appeared unable to come up with the words for what he wanted to say, she took the initiative, saying, "I'm glad you came down. We need to talk about that ten thousand pounds you lost to Jareth Tremayne and—and other things."

Mention of Jareth's name seemed to galvanize Adrian out of his tongue-tied silence. "But that's why I'm here—Tremayne, I mean. You see, last night in the mess, my

244

friend Captain Carstairs happened to mention that Tremayne had dropped out of sight for several weeks. Well, he did, I gather, except for one mammoth gambling session at White's in the middle of that period, when he apparently surfaced temporarily. I hear he won a fortune that night. The man has the devil's own luck," Adrian added feelingly.

"But that's neither here nor there," he went on. "The thing is, Carstairs—who belongs to White's and always knows the latest *on dit*—says that Tremayne has gone to ground in Sussex, which none of his friends can understand. Again, according to Carstairs, it's well-known among the *ton* that Tremayne has avoided Sussex like the plague for years because of a quarrel with his brother. So I thought . . . I wondered—Sabrina, did Tremayne come down to Sussex to see you?"

Sabrina flashed him a straight, unsmiling look. "Yes, he did."

Throwing up his hands, Adrian collapsed into a chair opposite the desk. "I knew it. It's all to do with that silly masquerade, isn't it? I never had the courage to get to the bottom of that, but of course I knew in my heart that you were up to no good, posing as an Hungarian countess. It's all my fault," he said penitently. "I didn't quiz you more closely about the Countess Dohenyi because I was so anxious about my own selfish problems. I was so relieved to be able to repay the blunt I owed Tremayne, I didn't let myself speculate about what you might have done to obtain the money. Sabrina, I think you borrowed that ten thousand pounds from Lord Jareth, posing as an Hungarian countess so he wouldn't know I was your brother." Adrian paused, looking confused. "In that case, you must have intended to repay the money some time, but perhaps Tremayne became so angry when he found out who you really were that he raced down here to demand immediate payment?"

"I didn't borrow the money from Lord Jareth. I won it from him in a game of macao."

Adrian stared in astonishment. "But why has he come down here, then?"

"Because I used marked cards to cheat him out of the money, and he's found out about it. Now he wants his money back, of course."

"My God, Sabrina!" Adrian's face was twisted with horrified anger. "What kind of a woman are you? You're not the same person you were before you married Oliver and went off to live on the Continent. First I discover you're the secret owner of a smuggling vessel, and now it turns out you're a female Captain Sharp!"

"Adrian." The word cut the air like the sound of a pistol shot. Sabrina leaned forward, her hands resting on the desk, her body tense as a coiled spring from the accumulated strain of the past few days. "I think it's time you faced the reality of what gambling has done to this family. Father brought the estate to near ruin with his speculation on 'Change and his racing bets at Tattersall's. You nearly finished us off with a stupid game of macao. What did you expect me to do, let us all end up in Dun Territory?"

Adrian reddened. "I know I've been at fault, and Father, too, but cheating! How could you do it, Sabrina?"

"Easily. I lost my husband because of gambling, and my life fell apart. I wasn't going to let that happen to Daphne and Mama and you if I could help it." Leaning back in her chair, her eyes fixed on a mesmerized Adrian, Sabrina told him about Oliver in a flat, emotionless voice. She might have been talking about the weather or the price of corn.

After Sabrina had finished, Adrian sat in silence for an interval, staring at the floor. Finally he raised his head. "I'm sorry, twin," he said quietly. "Your menfolk haven't been a source of much happiness to you, have

246

they? Lord, when I think how you must have felt, listening to Daphne prattle on about your fairy tale romance with Oliver . . ." He braced his shoulders. "What's to be done, then? How soon does Tremayne want the money?"

"He says he'll give you six months to repay him. Time enough, as he put it, to sell the estate or raise the money elsewhere."

"Sell Latimer House?" Adrian's face crumpled.

"Can you think of an alternative?" Sabrina asked with a flash of irritation. "You were willing enough to consider selling the estate a few weeks ago when you came down here to tell me about your loss of ten thousand pounds to Lord Jareth."

"Yes, but then you saved the day by producing the money, and I didn't have to think about losing the estate. Until now. It takes getting used to the idea again." Adrian paused, furrowing his brow. At last he said, "You became so friendly with Tremayne in London, Sabrina. Oh, I know he must be angry with you for deceiving him, of course, but have you considered asking him for an even longer extension? Two or three years, perhaps? In that time we might be able to economize enough to recoup the ten thousand pounds. I could sell out of the regiment, and then there's your smuggling profits—" He broke off, turning a bright red.

"I wouldn't ask Jareth Tremayne for a sip of water if I were dying of thirst," Sabrina snapped. Before she could stop herself she added, "He's already offered me a way out of our difficulties. His price was too high. I refused to meet his terms."

His body turning rigid, Adrian stared at her out of narrowed eyes. "I think you'll have to be a little more explicit, Sabrina."

Mentally cursing her unguarded tongue, Sabrina said matter-of-factly, "It's not worth talking about, I assure you. We'll have to start making plans, Adrian. It's not going to be easy, selling the estate in a depressed market. We may have to accept less than the property is worth, but even so there should be enough money after you've paid your debt to provide for Mama's jointure and Daphne's dowry—"

Adrian cut her off. "Did Tremayne offer to forgive my gambling debt if you agreed to go to bed with him?"

"That's an insulting question, and one that's none of your affair."

"You're wrong, little sister. Your concerns are my concerns. I'd like an answer. I can always find out from Tremayne himself, you know."

Sabrina glared at Adrian. "Very well, if you must have it. Yes, Jareth did make a proposition. I said no, and that was the end of it."

Lunging to his feet, Adrian headed for the door of the library. Sabrina reached it moments before he did and stood barring the way. "Adrian, don't be foolish," she said urgently, grasping his arm. "This has nothing to do with you. It's between me and Jareth Tremayne. Let it be."

His eyes blazing, Adrian shook off her hand. "What do you take me for, a lily-livered country bumpkin who can't protect his own sister from a rake like Jareth Tremayne?" he demanded, wrenching open the door. He strode off down the corridor, turning his head to utter one last shot: "You needn't worry about any more trouble with his noble lordship. When I get through with Tremayne he'll think twice before trying to seduce another lady of quality!"

"Adrian, you idiot!" Picking up her skirts, Sabrina raced after him, catching at his arm in an ineffectual attempt to impede his rapid progress out the rear door of the house and into the stableyard. She came up behind him as he was directing his tiger to harness one of the estate horses to the dogcart.

"My team isn't rested enough to be driven yet," he said curtly to Sabrina. "I pushed the horses hard on the last stage. I'll take the dogcart, with your permission."

"Adrian, once and for all, will you stop this? I don't know exactly what you're planning to do, but let me remind you, Jareth Tremayne is one of the best amateur pugilists in England."

"He's also a crack shot, but what has that to say to anything? I'll do what I have to do, or lose every shred of my self-respect. You can't stop me, Sabrina." Adrian climbed into the dogcart and drove rapidly out of the stableyard.

Sabrina walked slowly back to the house. Should she have had the horses put to the carriage and chased after Adrian? What good would that have done, especially if he were heading for Fairlea, the most likely place for Jareth to be staying? She could easily imagine the flurry of village gossip if both the Latimer twins descended on him like avenging angels. On the other hand, Jareth might be out, or he might be staying elsewhere, in Newhaven, or Alfriston. Perhaps Adrian would wear out his urge for revenge if he were forced to drive fruit- lessly around the countryside for an afternoon. And even if he should confront Jareth, Sabrina doubted if the contest would last very long. Jareth would pop her brother a facer and that would be the end of it. Unless . . . She shivered. Would Jareth accept a challenge to a duel? No, she wouldn't let it come to that, even if Adrian never spoke to her again as a result of it.

As she walked past the morning room, Fanny called out to her. "Where did you and Adrian disappear to?"

"He took the dogcart to Fairlea. He had an errand."

"But why didn't he take care of his errand when he passed through the village earlier? Will he be back for dinner?"

"I think so." I hope so, thought Sabrina. She felt too restless to join her stepmother and Daphne in the morning room. "I'm going up to my bedchamber for a shawl, Mama. I believe I'll go for a stroll."

The landlord of the Fairlea Arms looked startled when Adrian burst through the door of the inn, hatless and disheveled. "Sir Adrian—good day ter ye. What kin I do fer ye?"

"Is Lord Jareth Tremayne staying here?"

"Indeed 'e is that. Is second visit in a matter o' weeks—"

"Is he here now?" Adrian interrupted.

"In me best parlor, 'aving a spot o' nuncheon," the landlord said, motioning to a door on the left. "If ye'd care fer a bite, I've got a nice bit of ham an' a tasty meat pie—" He broke off, open-mouthed, as Adrian swept past him and pushed open the door of the private parlor, slamming it behind him.

Inside the room, Jareth put down the glass of claret he'd just lifted to his lips and said politely, "Good afternoon, Latimer. Would you care to join me?"

Staring at Jareth's aloof dark face, which expressed only a rather languid interest in his unexpected visitor, Adrian felt his temper flare out of control. "Damn you, Tremayne, stop your playacting. You know why I'm here," he rasped. Grabbing Jareth by the collar, he hoisted him out of his chair and swung a wild blow at his face. Moving his head slightly to the right, Jareth easily evaded the blow and countered with an precisely aimed punch to the jaw that felled his opponent in an unconscious heap on the floor.

A few moments later Adrian opened dazed eyes to find he was sitting in a chair at the table with a wine glass at his lips. "Have some of this," came Jareth's calm voice. "You'll feel more the thing."

Blinking to restore his groggy sight, Adrian glowered at Jareth. "I'm not finished, Tremayne."

"Happy to oblige you at any time." Jareth sat down opposite Adrian. "For the moment, though, let's settle the business that brought you here. The ten thousand pounds you owe me . . ."

"I didn't come here to talk about money," Adrian interrupted. "I came to settle accounts with you. You tried to seduce my sister. You were going to force her to sleep with you as the price for saving my reputation and my estate. Fortunately, she realized that nothing was worth paying that kind of a price, but that doesn't absolve you from paying the reckoning."

Jareth's face changed. "I'm sorry Sabrina felt she had to tell you about that," he said abruptly. He'd lost some of the lounging assurance that had so infuriated Adrian. "It's—this is a private matter between your sister and me."

"Not any more, it isn't. You don't think I'll stand by like one of your London pimps while you proposition my sister, do you?" Adrian put his hand to his chin and grimaced as his fingers touched a sore spot. "You've just proved I'm no match for you with a bunch of fives, but I can cup a wafer with the best of them. Name the time and place where you'll meet me."

"Oh, for God's sake, must you be such a cloth-head? I'm not going to fight a duel with you," Jareth exploded. "Look, Latimer, I have something to tell you—"

"Save your words. I'm not interested. You'll fight me or the *ton* will find out you have a white feather. You'll hear from my second shortly. Before I leave this room, though, I'm going to tell you why Sabrina did what she did. I hope it makes you realize what a poor excuse for a gentleman you really are, in spite of your Bond Street clothes and your expensive clubs and your elegant bits of blood."

Jareth stiffened. "Your opinion of me is immaterial, but I prefer not to discuss Sabrina's affairs in her absence."

"Lombard Street to a China orange, Sabrina would say the same thing," Adrian shot back, "but I'd rather not have her misjudged even by a loose screw like you." He plunged into a description of Oliver Neville's gambling obsession.

". . . and when they brought his body home and Sabrina saw the hole that Austrian count had blown in Oliver's head, she realized that one thing, and one thing only, had killed her husband and ruined her life. From that moment on, she told me, she loathed gambling so much that even the sight of a pack of playing cards made her feel ill. Then she came home to England and discovered our father had nearly bankrupted the family estate with his gambling, and only recently I had to tell her I'd lost ten thousand pounds to you at macao." Adrian paused, appearing somewhat uncertain for the first time. Groping for words, he added, "You see, because of her hatred of gambling, Sabrina didn't regard that money as a morally just debt. What's more, she thought you'd taken advantage of me in some way, so — "

"So, she saw nothing wrong in bilking me out of ten thousand pounds because you would be returning it to me immediately," Jareth said, nodding. "According to her reasoning, I hadn't really lost anything."

At Adrian's gape of astonishment, Jareth smiled wryly. "Before you arrived today, and without knowing about Sabrina's husband, I'd already decided there wasn't a larcenous bone in her body and that she must have had some compelling reason for doing what she did. I see now what that reason was. Her own personal world had already crashed around her because of Neville's gambling. She wasn't going to let that happen to you and your sister and your stepmother. If you'd have allowed me to get a word in earlier, I was about to tell you I was cancelling your debt. Your sister is right. I should never have allowed a green youngster like you to play macao with me."

"Now see here, Tremayne, I don't need any cosseting from you," Adrian began hotly. "You'll get your blunt back, if it takes me until I'm a graybeard."

"That seems fair to me. How old are you now? Twenty-one, twenty-two? You have fifty years to repay me." Jareth stood up, eyeing Adrian with a measuring glance. "Am I correct in assuming you've changed your mind about calling me out?"

"I—no. I don't know." Adrian glared at Jareth. "You shouldn't have tried to force Sabrina into your bed."

"No, I shouldn't have. Will you let me put that right with your sister without any interference from you? If you force me to put a bullet through you on the dueling ground it will only add to her problems, you know."

"Well . . ."

"Latimer, can we have an end to this Cheltenham tragedy? Go on back to London with your worries behind you. And before you go, give Sabrina a message from me. Tell her I'm sorry for everything that happened. Tell her she has nothing to fear from me, now or in the future."

Chapter Fourteen

"Will ye have another sip o' the cowslip wine, Mrs. Neville?"

Sabrina smiled up into her hostess's solicitous face. "I think not, Mrs. Cavitt. It tastes wonderful, but I'll need all my wits about me if I'm to arrive home in one piece."

Ezra chuckled. "There, Mother, what 'ave I allus told ye? Yer wine is almost too powerful ter offer it ter females."

"Oh, you, Ezra Cavitt," sniffed his wife. "Well, if I can't git anything else fer ye, Mrs. Neville, I'll leave ye to yer business."

"Not that there's a deal of business ter discuss about the home farm," Ezra sighed after the door closed behind his spouse. "If the rains don't stop, we'll have trouble jist feeding the animals from this year's harvest. There'll be nothing ter send ter market."

"We're not the only farmers in trouble, Mr. Cavitt. We're all in the same boat. The weather's bad all over England."

"Oh, I know the good Lord hasn't singled us out," Ezra said with another sigh. "We're blessed, in one way. We've other means o' support, if I makes meself clear."

"What? Oh, yes, the *Mary Anne*." Sabrina intercepted another of Ezra's puzzled glances. She'd been alternately absent-minded and inattentive since her arrival at the farmhouse. Moreover, she'd last visited the Cavitts only three days ago and there was really nothing of any moment that required discussing about the farm or the smuggling boat. "When do you expect the *Mary Anne* to return to port?" she asked with a quick show of interest.

"Well, now, they'll be dropping anchor a bit later than usual — say in four days. Y'see, Nate was sailing first fer Danzig ter take on some tubs o' pitch, an' then ter Brest fer the usual cargo o' brandy an' Geneva, an' after that" — Ezra began to laugh — "after that he was going ter Guernsey fer pertaters."

"What's so amusing about potatoes, may I ask?"

"Nothing, Mrs. Neville, 'cepting these pertaters ain't pertaters. They're terbacco," Ezra grinned. "Remember what Nate was telling us about all the new-fangled ways o' hiding cargo? Them folk in Guernsey, they makes up rolls o' terbacco the size o' big pertaters, covers 'em with some kind o' thin skin and douses 'em with dirt. Nate says they'd fool anybody." His grin faded. "Ye seem a mite troubled, Mrs. Neville. Ye don't really like this smuggling, do ye? 'Course, I kin understand that, ye being gentry an' all . . ."

Sabrina forced a smile. "I won't deny I'll be happy to be finished with it. I hope the *Mary Anne* will soon be just a fishing boat again, as she was when I bought her. It's not that I feel I'm too grand to engage in the trade. If I'm ready to accept the profits I ought to be ready to keep my hand on the tiller, so to speak! What haunts me is the possibility that someone will get hurt, either a member of our crew or a revenue seaman. I'm afraid Nate Peggoty would turn violent if he were cornered."

"Nate's not been caught out yet, Mrs. Neville."

"No. Let's hope he never will be," Sabrina replied, rising to take leave of Ezra.

Poor man, he must be wondering why I came, she reflected as she stepped out of the courtyard and began the short walk back to Latimer House. She'd been wasting the hard-working farmer's time, repeating her fears about Nate Peggoty that Ezra had heard so many times. The truth was, she'd fled the house to avoid being alone with her own thoughts.

She ought to be feeling happy, giddy with relief, her mind free of anxiety for the first time since Adrian had broken the news that he'd lost ten thousand pounds in a macao game. Instead, she could think only of Jareth. His dramatic about-face, his apparent generosity to Adrian, had intensified rather than lessened her feelings of bitter resentment toward him. In a way it was like having an aching tooth removed. The dentist's forceps merely exchanged one pain for another.

Her thoughts reverted to the scene yesterday with her twin. After he returned from Fairlea, Adrian had tracked her down to her favorite solitary place on the cliffside path, where she'd retreated to wait tensely for the outcome of his confrontation with Jareth Tremayne.

Adrian ran toward her, shouting jubilantly, "It's all right, Sabrina. We're not going to lose Latimer House after all."

Whirling at the sound of his voice, Sabrina forgot her worries temporarily as she stared apprehensively at the ugly purple bruise on his chin. "Adrian, what have you done? Is Jareth Tremayne hurt?"

"Good Lord, no," Adrian exclaimed in surprise. He grinned reminiscently. "Oh, but he's a proper man with his fists. He planted me a facer before I could lay a finger on him. Then, after he'd milled me down, he informed me, cool as cucumbers, that he was canceling my debt to him."

Sabrina shot him a quick, confused glance. "He canceled the debt? Why?"

256

"Because he said you were right, he shouldn't have let me gamble with him. Of course, I can't accept Tremayne's generosity. That ten thousand pounds is a debt of honor. I told him I'd insist on repaying him. And *he* said—would you believe this?—he said I could have fifty years!"

"How generous."

"Isn't it?" Absorbed in his own concerns, Adrian missed the note of cold sarcasm in Sabrina's voice. "I tell you, Tremayne is a decent fellow, once you get to know him. Well, it stands to reason. The moment he learned about Oliver and why you'd masqueraded as a countess and all the rest of it, he admitted he'd been wrong about you and he wanted to make amends. He gave me a message for you. He said"—Adrian screwed up his face in an effort to remember—"he said to tell you he was sorry and not to worry about him in the future. Now, I call that a handsome apology." He gazed uneasily at Sabrina's set, unsmiling face. "What is it? There's nothing more to be concerned about. Latimer House is safe."

"Oh, yes, I'm happy about the estate." Sabrina drew her shawl more closely around her shoulders and began walking rapidly toward the house. "It's getting late. We'll have an early supper so you can make sure of a good night's sleep. I expect you'll want to start back to London at the crack of dawn tomorrow morning."

Adrian hurried after her. "Sabrina? You haven't said anything about Tremayne. Aren't you glad to find out you've misjudged him?"

Sabrina turned her head as Adrian drew abreast of her. "I haven't misjudged him. I know exactly what he is."

Sabrina gave herself a mental shake as she neared the end of the driveway to Latimer House. She had to stop thinking about Jareth. Adrian had left for London early this morning to resume his military duties, and now it

257

was time for her to pick up the threads of her life again.

Walking up the steps of the house, she paused at the door as Robin, the footman-cum-handy-man, appeared around the corner from the direction of the stables. "Oh, you're back from Fairlea already, Robin. Was there a parcel for me at the receiving office?"

"No'm. Not a parcel. There was this letter fer Miss Daphne. I wuz jist bringing it ter her."

"I'll take it, Robin. Thank you."

Sabrina found her sister with Fanny in the morning room. There was an atmosphere of strain in the room. Daphne's face was flushed and her lips were pressed tightly together as she bent over her embroidery frame. She looked up with an air of relief as Sabrina entered the room. "A letter for me? Thank you, Sabrina. Oh, it's from Betsy."

Fanny, too, appeared ruffled. Since Daphne's outburst of defiance several days previously, when she had threatened to marry Gordon Stanhope without her stepmother's permission, Fanny had made no mention of the incident, but both sisters knew she would never let the matter rest.

Composing her face in a sugary smile, she beckoned Sabrina to sit down beside her, saying, "I've been having a little chat with Daphne. What would you say if she went to Tunbridge Wells for a short visit? As I'm sure you remember, my sister Georgiana lives there, and I know she'd be delighted to see Daphne. The expense would be nothing, merely the post charges. Of course, the Wells isn't as fashionable as London, or even Bath, but still, there'd be no dearth of respectable society—"

Daphne lifted her eyes from her letter, biting her lip. "It's no use trying to enlist Sabrina in your scheme, Mama," she said in a trembling voice. "I've already told you I don't wish to go to Tunbridge Wells. When you say 'respectable society,' you mean 'eligible males,' and I've no desire to meet any of *them!*"

"I'm going to overlook that remark, my dear. I realize you're a little upset." Fanny's face assumed its familiar martyred look. "However, I trust you'll remember that I have only your best interests at heart—"

Goaded, Daphne burst out, "Then please let me judge what's best for me! I don't want to go to Tunbridge Wells because"—she paused, gulping at her own boldness—"because Betsy has just written to me, urging me to attend her wedding, and I've decided to do so!"

"What?" Fanny gave a gasp of outrage. "Never! I won't permit you to go into such common company. Farmers. Tradesmen, no doubt—"

"Then I'll go without your permission," said Daphne mutinously.

"That's easier said than done, my dear," Fanny exclaimed angrily. "I won't allow you to use the carriage; I won't allow any of the maids to accompany you—"

"Then I'll go by stagecoach. Alone."

Fanny dabbed a wisp of a handkerchief to the corner of her eye. "I can't think what's come over you, to talk to me in that fashion. When I think of all I've tried to do for you . . . Sabrina, do tell the child that I've never, ever, wanted anything but good for her."

"Daphne knows that," said Sabrina soothingly. She shot her sister a warning glance. What was the point of roiling the waters before it was necessary? There would be a battle royal with Fanny soon enough when she discovered Daphne was determined to marry Gordon Stanhope no matter what the opposition.

"I'm sorry, Mama. I didn't mean to be rude," Daphne said after a long, grudging moment.

Fanny accepted the apology graciously. "I knew I couldn't be mistaken in you, my dear. Yes, Rosie, what is it?" she asked the housemaid who had just entered the room.

"A gentleman ter see Miss Sabrina, my lady."

With a hollow feeling in the pit of her stomach, Sabrina took the card from the tray the housemaid was extending toward her. Leaning forward from her chair, Fanny peered inquisitively at the card. "Lord Jareth Tremayne!" she exclaimed, her eyes sparkling. "Were you expecting him to call, Sabrina?" Without giving her stepdaughter an opportunity to reply, she told Rosie, "Take his lordship into the drawing room. Tell him Miss Sabrina will be with him shortly."

As the housemaid turned to leave, Fanny chided Sabrina playfully. "You sly thing, you never said a word about Lord Jareth! Oh, I know you danced with him at the Alfriston ball, but still . . ." She looked critically at Sabrina's plain gray gown and black cornet. "You'll want to wear something more appropriate, of course. The green sprigged muslin, perhaps? Daphne and I will entertain Lord Jareth until you come down."

"I—" Sabrina opened her mouth and closed it again. She'd been on the verge of refusing to see Jareth, but she knew if she did so it would cause a domestic upheaval. Fanny had the matchmaking glint in her eye again, and she would be unable to comprehend why Sabrina would be averse to a visit from a member of the county's leading family, a man, moreover, who was prominent in the highest ranks of London society. Sabrina squared her shoulders. She could play out a charade one last time. Somehow she would make sure she didn't have to see Jareth again. "Very well, Mama," she said. "Perhaps I should change my gown."

In her bedchamber she found Lotte waiting for her, agog with curiosity. "*Meine Frau,* wasn't that the Herr I saw coming up the driveway?"

"Yes, it was. Lotte, please help me into the green sprigged muslin. I'm rather in a hurry."

"*Ja,* you'll want to look your best," Lotte nodded

wisely. "The Herr always liked that dress, too." Later, as she was arranging Sabrina's hair, crowning the tawny coils with a giddy cap of delicate lace, she observed, "The Herr looked *schön,* as always. Such fine clothes he wears." Unexpectedly she added, "So everything is all right now between the two of you, *nicht wahr?*"

"Lord Jareth is just paying a courtesy call," Sabrina replied impatiently. "I don't doubt he'll be going back to London soon." The expectant look died in Lotte's face.

In the drawing room Sabrina found Jareth talking to Fanny and Daphne as if he were in the company of old friends. He rose as she entered, bowing with his usual inimitable grace. From the masterpiece of a beaver hat he held in his hand, to his exquisitely cut coat and snowy cravat and his gleaming Hessians, he was the epitome of the elegant man about town, and her heart turned over.

"Good afternoon, Mrs. Neville. I trust you won't consider this an intrusion. I hoped I might venture to call after we met at the Alfriston Waterloo ball."

At least he had the grace to keep up the pretense in front of her stepmother and Daphne, thought Sabrina savagely. Aloud she said, "Indeed, it's a pleasure to see you again, sir."

Jareth bowed again. "The pleasure is mutual, I assure you," he replied solemnly. His dark eyes glinted with a familiar mocking amusement. As she settled into a chair next to Daphne, he sat down opposite her, saying, "I've taken the liberty of introducing myself to Lady Latimer and Miss Latimer."

"Yes, and would you believe it, Sabrina, Lord Jareth remembered meeting me years ago in London?" said Fanny archly. "I'd quite forgotten it myself, it was so long ago, years before I was married to your father. Why, Lord Jareth even remembered the occasion, a reception at Carlton House, and what I was wearing, a gown of silver tissue!"

"But dear Lady Latimer, it was no great feat of memory," protested Jareth. "Here I was, a very unimportant and undistinguished newcomer to London society. Why wouldn't I remember meeting a gracious and beautiful lady?"

He's got Mama eating right out of his hand, thought Sabrina, even more savagely. What does he want? Beside her, Daphne took advantage of another exchange of conversation between Fanny and Jareth to murmur under her breath, "Sabrina, I know that's the man I saw you talking to in Fairlea, the day we went to Newhaven with Captain Ranger to see Gordon. You didn't meet him at the Alfriston ball!"

Shooting Daphne a quelling glance, Sabrina turned her attention to Fanny. "I'm sorry, Mama. What did you say?"

"I asked you to ring the bell for tea, my dear. Lord Jareth, you'll stay?"

"With the greatest of pleasure."

Jareth continued to captivate Fanny, accepting three cups of tea, praising the iced cakes and cucumber sandwiches, expressing the hope he would have the pleasure of seeing her in London soon.

"Have you by any chance met my stepson in London, Lord Jareth? He's a lieutenant in the Life Guards."

"As a matter of fact, I have. A fine young officer."

"He left here only this morning. What a shame you didn't see each other while he was here."

"I'm sorry I missed Sir Adrian," lied Jareth.

"And how long are we to have the pleasure of your company in Sussex?" inquired Fanny. "Long enough, perhaps, to take dinner with us? I know, of course, that the Season is in full swing in London, and you must have many obligations."

"I plan to stay in Sussex indefinitely. I have important matters to settle here," Jareth replied, with a straight look at Sabrina. "I'm quite at your disposal. Only name the day."

"Friday, then? No, Saturday?" Fanny's brow wrinkled as she calculated the amount of time and ingredients Cook would need to produce a dinner fine enough for the Marquess of Winwood's brother.

"Saturday it is." Jareth rose. "Now I mustn't outwear my welcome. Mrs. Neville, I hear the gardens of Latimer House are very fine. Could I ask you to show them to me?"

"Sabrina would be delighted to do so, wouldn't you, my dear?" Fanny beamed.

"Oh, I fear the roses aren't at their best. We've had so much rain," Sabrina said with an air of innocence. Without creating a scene, she couldn't avoid this tête-à-tête that Fanny was conniving with Jareth to arrange, but she didn't have to make it any easier for them, either.

"I'm sure I'll enjoy seeing the gardens regardless of the state of the roses," Jareth replied. "It's very kind of you, Mrs. Neville."

The windows of the morning room faced out on the rose garden, and, although neither Fanny nor Daphne was actually visible at a window, Sabrina had no doubt as she and Jareth walked into the garden, that they were the object of an interested surveillance by her stepmother and her sister. The thought had apparently occurred to Jareth also. After a few perfunctory remarks about the roses, which were even more bedraggled than Sabrina had indicated, he motioned to the fruit trees behind the walled kitchen garden. "That looks like a very fine orchard. What do you grow there?"

"Apples, mostly. Some damsons and cherries."

"I'd like to see it."

"Of course." As they started walking toward the orchard Sabrina couldn't resist saying, "I had no idea you were so interested in horticulture."

"There's a great deal you don't know about me, Sabrina," Jareth said curtly. After they rounded the wall of the kitchen garden and were no longer in sight of the house, he stopped abruptly. The usual confident note was missing from his voice as he said, "I expected—I hoped I'd hear from you today."

"Why would you think that?" Sabrina asked with a chilly lack of interest.

"But . . . didn't your brother tell you about our conversation yesterday?"

"Oh, yes. Adrian is very grateful to you. It was generous of you to forgive his gambling debt."

"Oh, that." Jareth dismissed the topic impatiently. "The money wasn't important."

"Really?" Sabrina's blue eyes flashed like blazing sapphires. "You surprise me, Jareth. Two days ago you apparently thought the money was so important you were willing to ruin my brother and his family along with him!"

"Damn it, Sabrina! It was never the money, you *know* it wasn't the money—" He broke off, almost as if mesmerized, reaching out his hand to run a gentle finger along her cheek. "God, you're so beautiful. Your skin's like satin. I used to dream of how lovely you were," he breathed. He touched her frothy lace cap. "Why are you wearing that silly thing? It hides your glorious hair."

Jerking away as though the caressing fingers were burning coals, Sabrina snapped, "Don't touch me."

Jareth recoiled. "Sabrina, what is it? Didn't your brother give you my message?"

"That you were sorry? Oh, yes. I suppose you meant something like this"—Sabrina deepened her voice— " 'I'm sorry, Mrs. Neville, for calling you a cheat and a whore. I'll be a good boy from now on. No more forcing you into my bed like a common slut for value received. Now I just want to be friends.' That was your message, wasn't it, Jareth? Did you expect me to be grateful?"

"Hold on, Sabrina," said Jareth desperately. "Won't you give me a chance to explain? When I found that marked card on the floor of my room, I didn't mind so much that you'd cheated me out of the money. It was the thought you'd enjoyed doing it, making a fool of me, taking advantage of the fact I'd fallen madly in love with you . . . I felt flayed. Nothing that has happened to me has ever hurt so much. I wanted to strangle you with my bare hands. But I swear that, even before Adrian came to me yesterday to tell me about your husband and the way he died, I'd already realized you weren't the mercenary adventuress I'd accused you of being. I knew you must have had a reason for doing what you did. Sabrina, can't we forget what's happened these last few weeks? I love you. I want you to marry me."

His dark eyes looked so tender, so pleading. She moved away from him slightly. She couldn't think clearly when he was so close to her, and she knew she had to resist being swept along the remembered path of exquisite sensual delight, for the sake of her mangled and bleeding self-esteem. Looking away from him, she said, almost inaudibly, "I — I don't want your kind of love."

She turned to leave, but before she had taken more than a step or two his long arm had shot out to grab her shoulder. Spinning her around, he crushed her against his hard body, plundering her mouth with lips that grew steadily more voracious and demanding. A familiar wave of desire swept over Sabrina, and for a few shuddering moments she was aware only of Jareth's lips and hands that caressed and clung and claimed her for his own.

"I knew I couldn't be mistaken," he murmured huskily, lifting his head for a moment to look at her with eyes aflame with longing. "You want me as much as I want you. Tell me you love me, Sabrina."

"No," Sabrina exclaimed, pushing against him so suddenly and so violently that she was able to break away from the embracing circle of his arms. "I told you. I don't want your kind of love." But as she ran wildly away from him, acrid tears were stinging her eyelids, and she was fighting desperately against the impulse to return to him and throw her arms around his neck and admit she'd been lying.

Chapter Fifteen

Sabrina added the columns of figures for the third time and arrived at the same dispiriting total. If the weather didn't improve, and if Ezra Cavitt's crop predictions were correct, the estate expenses would far exceed the income for this year. Pushing aside the estate records, she unlocked the pillared door on the left side of the Gothic writing table, which her father had used only to scrawl an occasional hasty note or to sign an IOU. The massive desk now served as Sabrina's office. She took out the secret ledger in which she had recorded her share of the profits of the *Mary Anne*. The figures were impressive and comforting. A few days ago she would have estimated that within five years she could leave the smuggling trade with the estate out of debt and a respectable nest egg in hand. But now, if Adrian persisted in his Quixotic determination to repay Jareth Tremayne's ten thousand pounds . . . Sabrina shook her head, sighing resentfully. She'd been trying not to think about Jareth, and yet she couldn't even do her accounts without being reminded of him.

The soft knock at the library door and the sound of her sister's voice created a welcome diversion. Hastily replacing the smuggling records in the left-hand cubicle of the desk and turning the key in the lock, Sabrina called out, "Come in, Daphne."

As she entered the room, Daphne's expression was almost evenly divided between curiosity and concern. Without saying a word she handed Sabrina a letter. Sabrina glanced at the inscription written in a familiar hand. Then, her lips pressed together, she tore the envelope in half and then in half again.

Daphne drew up a chair beside the desk, sitting in thoughtful silence for a moment as she studied her sister's stony face. "I don't want to interfere," she ventured, "but don't you think you should at least read Lord Jareth's letters?"

"No. They don't contain anything I wish to know."

"How can you be so sure of that? He's been sending you a letter every day now for almost a week. He's trying to tell you *something*."

"I know what he's trying to tell me. I'm not interested."

"Oh, Sabrina!" Daphne threw up her hands. "You can't go on like this, surely you must see that. You'll have Mama on the road to Bedlam. I can still see her face when Lord Jareth arrived for dinner the other night and she was forced to tell him you wouldn't be down because you were seriously indisposed. I thought she'd have a fit of the vapors right in front of him, especially when he told her, in that mocking superior way he has, that he trusted your indisposition wasn't mortal and that he'd call the next day to check on your health. And *then* Mama almost choked on her words when she had to say that perhaps he shouldn't call because she was positive you'd be ill for at least a week."

"Mama will survive," said Sabrina, shrugging.

"Yes, I daresay, and I know this is very much your private affair, but the house is like an armed camp! Only this morning Mama cornered me to bewail the way you were throwing away opportunity after opportunity to establish yourself and to beg me to make you see reason.

Sabrina, I won't do that—harangue you, I mean—but do you think it might help to talk about it? Why are you so angry at Lord Jareth, for example? You can't tell me he's merely a passing acquaintance who's contrived to annoy you. I saw your faces when you were talking together that day in Fairlea. Only people who know each other very well, and who've meant a great deal to each other, get *that* angry. Sabrina, are you in love with that man?" Breaking off, Daphne looked aghast. "I'm sorry. Only a minute ago I told you I had no intention of interfering . . ."

Every nerve in Sabrina's body seemed to constrict into a painful knot. She couldn't talk to Daphne about Jareth. She couldn't reveal to anyone the anguished blow to her pride, the emotional devastation she'd felt when the man she loved had stripped her of her self-respect, treated her like an object, a thing. At last she said, "I'm not angry with you, but I can't—I don't want to talk about Lord Jareth. Let's just say there's no possibility we can ever be friends. It won't be a problem much longer, anyway. Jareth will grow weary of bombarding me with letters that never get answered, and then he'll go away, back to London where he belongs."

"And so, I trust, will be the case, for that poor man's sake," said Lady Latimer in trembling tones as she swept into the room, dressed in a pelisse and bonnet and carrying her reticule and parasol. She stared with distaste at the torn fragments of the letter on the desk. "As I know to my sorrow, there's a limit to patience and forbearance when one is exposed to repeated doses of incivility and lack of consideration, especially from those in whom one might expect to find those qualities!"

"Mama, I've told you before, I've no wish to be uncivil to you."

Fanny raised a commanding hand. "Enough, Sabrina. We'll talk no more about it. You've made it quite clear that my opinion means nothing to you. I merely came to inform you that I was leaving the house to call on Mrs. Arkwright and Lady Sloan. Doubtless my whereabouts are of no concern to you, but *I* at least can never be accused of lack of consideration for others!"

The sisters looked at each other as Lady Latimer swept out of the room. "That's not the end of it, you know. Despite what Mama said, she hasn't given up," Daphne observed. Her face clouded. "The situation in this house is bad enough now, but what will it be like when Mama is forced to accept the fact that she can't prevent my marriage to Gordon?"

Sabrina said tartly, "Perhaps Adrian will elope with a barmaid, and then Mama can wash her hands of all three of us!"

After a startled moment Daphne began to laugh. "Oh, dear, that was unkind," she said at last, wiping her eyes, "but it would serve Mama right if Adrian walked in with a barmaid on his arm." Her eyes widened as the housemaid, Rosie, entered the room bringing a letter on a tray. "Lord Jareth hasn't given up. He's written you another letter!"

"Nay, Miss Daphne. This letter's fer ye," said Rosie.

After the housemaid had left the room, Daphne examined the letter with a puzzled expression, saying, "It's from Betsy, but she just wrote the other day . . ." She broke the seal and opened the note. "Oh, my God—" Her face turned white, and the letter slipped from her hand to the floor.

"Daphne, what's wrong? Is there illness in Betsy's family? Her father—?"

"No. No. It's Gordon. He may die. Oh, Sabrina, perhaps he's dead already!"

Bending to pick up the letter, Sabrina scanned the few agitated lines. Betsy was in Newhaven, summoned from her farm home in the Weald by a message from the first

270

mate of Captain Stanhope's revenue cruiser. Gordon had been seriously injured. The surgeon considered his condition grave. Betsy and her father were urged to come immediately.

Daphne leaped from her chair. "I must go to him. Sabrina, you'll come with me?"

"Of course." Crossing to the bell, Sabrina rang for the housemaid. "I'll order the carriage. It will be waiting for us by the time we've dressed. No, I forgot. Mama has the carriage. The Lord knows when she'll be back. We can't wait. We'll take the dogcart."

Daphne's white-faced distress communicated itself to Rosie and from her, apparently, to the stables. By the time Sabrina and Daphne stepped out of the front door in their bonnets and pelisses, the groom was driving the dogcart around the corner from the stables. Coming from the other direction up the driveway was Jareth Tremayne's curricle. He halted his team, throwing the reins to his tiger, and ran toward the two girls, reaching them just as the dogcart stopped in front of the door.

"Sabrina, I've got to talk to you," he said curtly, his dark eyes flicking over Daphne as if she didn't exist. "I've been trying to reach you for God knows how many days now, but you won't answer my letters, you won't see me. If you'll only listen I know we can straighten out what's wrong between us."

"I thought I'd made it clear I don't want to talk to you," Sabrina said icily. "Nothing can change what's wrong between us. Please excuse me. I'm in a great hurry."

"Sabrina, for God's sake, why are you being so unreasonable? I only want ten minutes of your time. Is that too much to ask?"

"Yes." Evading the hand he put out to stop her, she darted around him, climbing into the dogcart. "Daphne, are you coming?"

"Sabrina, wait," he exclaimed angrily. "You're acting

like a resentful child instead of a grown woman."

Flashing him a scornful glance, she ignored him. Daphne hopped into the dogcart and Sabrina put the horse into a brisk trot down the driveway. Within seconds she heard the sound of wheels and horses' hooves, and Daphne, looking behind them, exclaimed apprehensively, "He's coming after us!"

The farm horse was no match for Jareth's superb bays. Soon the curricle was directly behind the dogcart, so close that the horses' heads were virtually touching the footboard. Turning her head, Sabrina shouted, "You idiot, are you trying to run me off the road? Move back!"

"Not until you agree to talk to me," Jareth flashed. "I'm making sure you won't get away from me this time."

"Sabrina, don't concern yourself about him," Daphne implored her. "Just hurry, get us to Newhaven as soon as possible."

Gritting her teeth, Sabrina tried to concentrate on her driving, flicking the whip to her patient horse for a little more speed. In the back of her mind was the nagging thought that as soon as she exited the Latimer House driveway and the narrow lane leading out of it, she would be on a wider road where Jareth could easily come abreast of the dogcart. But she'd deal with that when the time came. Rounding a curve, she swerved instinctively to avoid a rabbit crossing in front of her and ended up with a jolting collision against a tree beside the road. After a dazed moment she sensed that neither she nor Daphne was seriously hurt and jumped out of the dogcart. She was staring helplessly at the shattered right wheel of the vehicle when her sister joined her.

"Sabrina!" Daphne wailed. "What will we do now? I *must* get to Gordon."

"You won't be going anywhere in that dogcart, that's certain," said Jareth, stepping down from his curricle to

272

approach them.

"No thanks to you," Sabrina snapped. "I *told* you not to follow us so closely. Daphne and I could have been killed."

Jareth lifted an eyebrow. "My dear Sabrina, *I* wasn't driving this vehicle, and I certainly had no control over the rabbit that dashed across the drive."

"Oh, we both know you're never at fault," Sabrina exclaimed bitterly before she could stop herself. She bit her lip. No wonder Jareth had dropped the pretense that they were only formal acquaintances. Daphne wouldn't have been deceived, in any event, but after this exchange a mere child couldn't have failed to detect the powerful current of emotion flowing between them.

"I've been very wrong, as I've tried to tell you," Jareth muttered. Turning to Daphne, he said, "There's no reason to be upset, Miss Latimer. My curricle is at your disposal. Where do you wish to go?"

Daphne's woebegone face brightened with relief. "Oh, thank you, Lord Jareth. Could you take us to Newhaven?"

"With the greatest of pleasure. Sabrina?" He shot her a challenging look.

Gazing into Daphne's pleading eyes, Sabrina choked back an automatic refusal. "Thank you," she said reluctantly. "It's very kind of you."

Jareth glanced at Sabrina's horse, standing quietly in his harness as he munched the grass at the side of the driveway. "We can't leave him here." He beckoned to his tiger, directing him to unhitch the horse and take him back to the Latimer House stables. "I can manage without a tiger," Jareth said with a faint smile. "Tom's mostly for decoration, in any event."

Sabrina forced herself to thank him again, although the words nearly stuck in her throat.

"Not at all. It's my pleasure," he said with a formal

273

bow. "Shall we go?"

By trailing slightly behind Daphne as they walked to the curricle, Sabrina contrived to have her sister seated between herself and Jareth when he helped them into the carriage. From his cool straight stare she knew he was fully aware of her maneuver, but he didn't comment on it. As they got under way he made no attempt to talk to her. Instead he chatted pleasantly with Daphne. "You seem distressed, Miss Latimer. Is there some problem in Newhaven?" He listened with sympathy to Daphne's worries about Gordon and remarked, "You'll want to get there as quickly as possible, then. Let's see what speed we can get out of this team of mine."

It was uncomfortably crowded for three people in a seat intended for two passengers, but not as crowded, Sabrina reflected, as this same curricle had been the first time she'd ridden in it. That was the afternoon in Hyde Park when she'd feigned an injured ankle and Jareth had driven her and Lotte back to their hotel. She'd been sitting between him and Lotte's plump form on that occasion, at such close quarters that her thigh and shoulder had pressed closely against his body. She felt the warmth flushing her cheeks at the memory, and despite herself her thoughts reverted to those magical few weeks when she and Jareth had driven in this vehicle all over London and into the countryside, immersed in the tremulous joy of being together.

She roused herself as the curricle was passing over the drawbridge near the Bridge Hotel in Newhaven to find that Daphne was giving Jareth directions to Gordon's lodgings, which they reached after a drive of several minutes. After Jareth had helped the sisters down from the carriage he said to Daphne, "Your friends won't want a stranger here at a time like this. Supposing I wait for you at the Bridge Hotel." Looking at Sabrina, he said carelessly, "Would you care to accompany me? We could have tea, or a glass of Madeira, while we talked."

"No, thank you. I think I should stay with Daphne."

"As you wish. We'll talk later, then." His face was perfectly composed, but Sabrina could hear the note of implacability in his voice. Before he delivered her and Daphne back to Latimer House he meant to have that talk. To Daphne he said, "Stay as long as you like. When you're ready to return home, send a servant with a message for me at the Bridge Hotel."

"I will. Thank you, Lord Jareth."

As he stepped into the curricle and drove off, with one last intent, meaningful look at Sabrina, Betsy Stanhope came flying out of the house. "Thank God you're here," she exclaimed tearfully, throwing her arms around Daphne. "It's been so awful, trying to cope by myself."

Disengaging Betsy's clinging arms, Daphne asked anxiously, "How is he? Your note said Gordon was badly injured."

Betsy's face crumpled. "He hasn't recovered consciousness yet. He lies there like a stone. You can see him breathing, ever so faintly, but otherwise he might as well be dead. The surgeon was here a few minutes ago on his afternoon rounds, and he just shook his head when I asked him how soon Gordon might regain his senses. Oh, Daphne, I'm so afraid."

Sabrina took charge. "Shall we go in the house, Miss Stanhope?" She led the unnerved Betsy up the steps and into the parlor. "Now, then, tell us what happened," she said, settling Betsy into a chair. "First, though, is Captain Stanhope alone? Shouldn't someone be with him?"

"The landlady is with him. She's been so kind . . . Father couldn't come to Newhaven, you see. He's suffering from an attack of the gout and he was in such agony he couldn't put his foot to the ground. Daphne, Mrs. Neville, I'm so glad you've come. I've been feeling so alone, so helpless."

"We'll stay as long as you need us," Daphne assured her. "But what *happened*, Betsy? How did Gordon get hurt?"

"He was trying to apprehend a smuggling vessel. I really don't know all the details, but apparently the smugglers fired on Gordon's cutter and succeeded in getting away. One of the revenue crew was killed and another injured, and Gordon was hit in the shoulder. It was a clean wound, the surgeon said, though Gordon lost a great deal of blood before the crew could bring him ashore. But apparently as he fell to the deck after being shot his head struck against one of the ship's guns. The surgeon's very worried about the head injury. He says the longer Gordon remains unconscious, the greater the possibility of complications, like brain fever, or paralysis."

"But can't the surgeon *do* anything?" Daphne cried.

Betsy shook her head. "Just wait, like the rest of us." She jumped up, her eyes widening apprehensively, as a middle-aged woman dashed into the parlor. "Mrs. Dorrance, what is it? Is Gordon—?"

"Oh, Miss Stanhope, the captain's opened his eyes," the landlady exclaimed joyfully. "He was trying to say something, too. A name, I think. I couldn't make it out. Dorothy? No, that wasn't it."

"Daphne?" said Betsy, her eyes shining.

"Why, yes, I believe it was."

Betsy tore out of the room and up the stairs, with Daphne hot on her heels. Sabrina followed more sedately. She stepped inside the bedchamber to find Daphne in a chair beside Gordon's bed, clutching one of his hands in both of hers. His eyes blinking, Gordon was saying weakly, "Daphne? Why are you . . . Where am I?"

"It's all right, Gordon," Daphne murmured soothingly. "You're in your lodgings in Newhaven."

"Newhaven? What am I doing in Newhaven? My ship . . ."

Standing next to Sabrina at the door, Betsy murmured, "Dr. Conover said Gordon might have a temporary memory loss when he regained consciousness." She raised her voice. "Your ship is docked here too, Gordon. You fought an engagement with a smuggling boat. You were shot, but you're going to be fine. Your first mate, Mr. Killian, took command and brought the ship in."

"I fought an engagement?" Gordon sounded dazed. "I don't remember. Was there any damage? Was anyone else hurt? I should go down to the dock right away —" He made a move to sit up.

Daphne put her arms around him, holding him down. "Gordon, darling, please try to lie still. You'll hurt yourself. I promise you, everything is being taken care of. You trust this Mr. Killian, don't you?"

At Daphne's touch, Gordon visibly relaxed. "Yes. Yes, I do." Groping for Daphne's hand, he brushed his lips against it and closed his eyes, murmuring, "You'll stay with me, love?"

"Of course I will. I wouldn't think of leaving you."

"Perhaps we should leave them together, Miss Stanhope," Sabrina said in a low voice. "Daphne seems able to quiet him. I think what the captain needs now is a natural sleep."

"Yes, I think you're right. I'll send for the surgeon, too, to see what he thinks. Can I offer you tea, Mrs. Neville? I'd certainly be the better for a cup!"

In the parlor a few minutes later, Betsy settled back in her chair with her second cup of tea, the tired lines in her face smoothing out. "I feel as if a tremendous load had been lifted from me," she sighed. "From the moment the message about Gordon's injury arrived at the farm, I had the most horrible conviction he was going to die."

"It's a dangerous profession, the revenue service."

"Yes, but until now I didn't worry all that much. Gordon always seemed to lead a charmed life." Hesitating, Betsy added shyly, "Do you think I might call you Sabrina? It looks very much as if we're about to become related!"

"By all means," Sabrina smiled. "After that scene we just witnessed in your brother's bedchamber, he'll be obliged to make an honest woman of Daphne!"

"I was so happy to receive Daphne's letter telling me you'd given your approval for the marriage. It meant so much to her, to all of us," Betsy exclaimed, glowing. Glancing toward the doorway, she hailed the tall man who stood on the threshold. "Come in, Mr. Killian. The news is much better this afternoon. Gordon's recovered consciousness! Sit down and have a cup of tea with us. Oh—Sabrina, do you remember John Killian, Gordon's first mate? I believe you met that day we visited the boatyard with your friend Captain Ranger."

"Pleased to see you again, ma'am," said the mate, his bronzed weather-beaten face wreathed in a broad smile. He sat down, accepting a cup of tea from Betsy. "I'll sleep easier tonight, knowing the captain is recovering." He shook his head, drawing a deep breath. "Lord, when he was wounded like that and we couldn't stop the bleeding, I wasn't sure he'd still be alive when we got him back to port."

"What exactly happened, Mr. Killian?" Betsy inquired. "Now that I'm not worried to death about Gordon's condition, I'd like to know more of the details."

"It happened so fast, I'm not sure I remember everything," replied the mate ruefully. "We were cruising off the Seven Sisters, toward the end of the third watch, a dark windy night with no moon. We spotted a flash of blue light from the cliff and shortly afterwards we made out a vessel heading for shore. So we hoisted the King's colors—not that anyone could see it on a night like

278

that!—and hailed the boat, ordering her to heave to. When we got no reply, we fired a warning shot across her bow, and she immediately started firing back. We had a regular duel going there for a while, and we were giving as good as we got. But then our topmast was shot through in two places, and our main boom was put out of service. By that time the captain was hit and several of the crew. One dead. So I ordered the action broken off and we limped back to Newhaven."

Sabrina leaned forward, her eyes intent on the first mate. "When did this encounter take place, Mr. Killian?"

"The night before last, shortly before midnight."

"And you say there were dead and injured among your crew?"

"Yes, ma'am. John Arnold, our second mate, was killed instantly."

"John Arnold? Oh, what a shame," Betsy exclaimed with quick sympathy. "He had a large family of young children, I recall."

"Six young ones. Twins, last month. The other injuries, thank the good Lord, were minor, except for Brad Stoke. The surgeon says Brad may lose his leg."

"Do you think you'll be able to apprehend the smugglers, Mr. Killian?" Sabrina inquired quietly. "Did you recognize the ship?"

The first mate shook his head. "She was an ordinary cutter, like scores, hundreds, of other ships in the trade. Round about a hundred tons, I'd say. Six, eight, maybe ten guns. Of course, she must have taken some damage from our carronades—her sails riddled with shot, at the very least—but by the time we caught up with her the damage would already have been taken care of in some friendly boatyard. The locals won't inform on their friends and neighbors in the trade, you know."

Setting down his cup, the mate pulled out his watch,

saying, "I must be getting back to the ship. Miss Stanhope, do you think I might see the captain? Only for a minute or two. Just so I can tell the crew I've seen him and he's coming along all right. I won't say a word about ship's business."

When Betsy and the first mate left the parlor to visit Gordon, Sabrina left her chair to pace the floor restlessly, trying to reason away the dark fears that were taking control of her mind. Why, after hearing the account of the attack on Gordon's cutter by a smuggling boat, had she jumped to the conclusion that the *Mary Anne* might have been involved? As the first mate had said, there were numerous smuggling ships similar to the *Mary Anne* operating out of local ports. Any one of them might have been Gordon's opponent. And yet . . . The sea fight had taken place off the Seven Sisters, which was the area where the *Mary Anne* normally landed her cargoes, and it had occurred on approximately the date when she had been expected to return from her latest voyage. And then there was the captain of the *Mary Anne*. Despite all Sabrina's warnings against violence, Nate Peggoty's first instincts would have been to fight if he were cornered rather than attempt to escape a revenue cutter by outsailing her.

Her brooding thoughts were interrupted when the first mate returned to the parlor, Daphne was with him. "You'll see, Miss Latimer," he was telling her, "the captain will be getting on like a house on fire. In no time at all he'll be back to his command."

After Killian, looking much relieved, had left the house, Daphne burst out, "That man seems to think he's being comforting when he tells me Gordon will soon resume his command! Apparently it hasn't occurred to Mr. Killian that my heart will be in my mouth every moment of every day Gordon is at sea in the future!"

"I know it's hard for you, but at least you know Gordon is well on the way to recovery. Don't you think we should send a message to Lord Jareth that we're ready to leave? It's getting late, and you'll recall that Mama doesn't know where we are."

Giving her head a defiant toss, Daphne said abruptly, "I've just persuaded Gordon that we should be married as soon as he's well enough to walk down the aisle, by special license if necessary. Then, if he should ever be injured again, I'd be notified first as his wife and I could go to him immediately. And I could stay with him until he gets well, instead of being obliged to go home to Mama and leave him to his sister!"

Swallowing hard, Daphne gazed at Sabrina with the air of one summoning courage to confront a pride of lions in the arena. "Well?" she demanded. "What do you think?"

Suddenly Sabrina felt beaten down from the pressure of problems, her own and those of her family. "Daphne, for heaven's sake, do your own thinking," she said with an angry impatience. "I'm hardly in a position to give you advice, in any event. I can't even seem to manage my own life."

Jolted out of her own preoccupation, Daphne gave Sabrina a look of surprise. After a moment she said quietly, "You're right, of course, we should start home. I'll find the housemaid and send her off to the Bridge Hotel with a message for Lord Jareth."

When Jareth arrived to pick them up, he was clothed in his usual man-about-town mantle of imperturbability. He didn't so much as try to catch Sabrina's eye, but she knew he was only biding his time. Nemesis in a coat by Weston and a perfectly tied cravat, she thought, almost too weary in spirit to be concerned. During the drive from Newhaven to Latimer House he kept up a cheerful chatter with Daphne, inquiring about Gordon's condition, expressing a polite interest when she revealed with a shy new-found independence that she planned to marry Gordon.

"But you're not to tell anyone yet, Lord Jareth," Daphne exclaimed in sudden confusion. "Especially not Mama!"

"My mouth is sealed," he assured her.

At Latimer House, handing the sisters from the curricle, Jareth retained an unobtrusive but iron grasp on Sabrina's arm as he turned to accept Daphne's thanks. "I was happy to oblige, Miss Latimer," he said graciously. "If you should need transportation to Newhaven tomorrow to visit Captain Stanhope, please call on me."

"Why, thank you, that would be—" Daphne looked at Sabrina's unresponsive expression. "I'm sure Mama will allow me to use the carriage," she said hastily. "Good-bye, Lord Jareth."

"Good-bye, Miss Latimer." He stood waiting with a smiling politeness for her to walk up the steps to the house.

Daphne hesitated. "Sabrina?"

"Sabrina will be with you shortly. She and I have matters to discuss."

"I'll be along in a moment," said Sabrina evenly.

After the door had closed behind Daphne, Jareth swung around to Sabrina, saying, "Well, thank goodness you've come to your senses—" He recoiled at the blue flash from Sabrina's eyes.

Suddenly the accumulated stresses of the past few days, added to by a torturing new load of apprehension about the *Mary Anne,* were too much for Sabrina. She couldn't cope with Jareth too, and his arrogant attempts to explain away conduct that was unforgivable. "What did you expect me to do, struggle with you in front of my own house?" she exclaimed scathingly. "I don't doubt Mama is peering at us out of the drawing-room window at this very minute. Please release my arm and go away.

282

Even if I wanted to talk to you — which I don't — I haven't the time. I must see the manager of my home farm immediately."

Jareth stepped back, releasing her arm. "I can see you're upset. We'll talk another time, then. Where is this home farm? Is it far? I'll be happy to take you."

Sabrina's eyes glittered dangerously. "Would you just leave? I don't need transportation. I'll take the dog-cart — Oh, damn!"

"For God's sake, Sabrina, stop cutting off your nose to spite your face," said Jareth angrily. "Get in the curricle. I'll go collect my tiger and then I'll drive you to this farm. No obligation."

As Jareth disappeared around the corner of the house on his way to the stables, Sabrina hesitated briefly, glancing at the curricle, and then set off down the driveway at a rapid pace. She had to see Ezra Cavitt as soon as possible. It was probably foolish not to accept Jareth's offer to drive her to the farm. He certainly couldn't talk about anything more serious than the weather with his tiger standing directly behind them. But the thought of being further beholden to him, or of having any more contact with him today, made her want to scream. In her present state of distress and uncertainty about Peggoty and the *Mary Anne*, she knew it would take very little contact with Jareth to make her break down in front of him and the tiger and confess the horrible morass into which she'd fallen. And accept Jareth's help she wouldn't and couldn't do.

When Jareth drove up beside her in his curricle several minutes later, she said, not meeting his eyes, "Thank you for offering to drive me, but I'd really rather walk. Just drive on, please."

"Damnation, Sabrina—" The leaping anger in Jareth's voice softened to a note of tenderness that brought a catch to Sabrina's throat. "All right, love.

Whatever it is, I don't want to make it harder for you."

Ezra Cavitt entered the parlor of the farmhouse, followed by his son Tom. Both men wore such hangdog looks that Sabrina's worst suspicions were confirmed before they opened their mouths.

"Ezra, was it the *Mary Anne* that was in that fight with Captain Stanhope's revenue cutter?"

"I'm sorry, ma'am. I'm afeared it was." Ezra sat down heavily. "My Tom, 'e jist got 'ere a while back, all the way from 'Astings, ter give me the terrible news."

"Oh, God." Sabrina turned a pasty white. "I was afraid of this."

"The cutter an' crew, we're all right, Mrs. Neville," Tom hastened to say. "Nary a scratch on any o' us, an' nothing wrong wi' the cutter, neither, that a new sail an' a bit o' fresh paint won't cure. Nate, 'e took the ship ter a small yard in 'Astings fer repairs. Them revenooers will never track us down. We'll be landing the cargo a mite later than we planned, that's all."

Sabrina shuddered. "I don't care a whit about the ship or the cargo either," she said passionately. "Do you realize that one of the excisemen is dead, leaving a large family of children, and another may be a cripple for life?"

Tom lowered his eyes. "We 'eard rumors, ma'am. I knew as 'ow ye'd be upset."

"Upset?" Sabrina flung up her arms in sick anger. "Tom, how did we come to this? You know I've told my crew over and over again that I'd rather lose the *Mary Anne* than one human life. Could this tragedy possibly have been avoided?"

Tom hesitated. "I ain't never been one ter tell tales, but . . . Mrs. Neville, there's nothing faster'n the *Mary Anne* in these waters, an' I thought we could 'ave outsailed that revenue cutter, an' so I told Nate. But 'e said something like, 'Wot's the use o' guns if ye don't use 'em?' An' so . . ." Tom shrugged. "Nate's yer captain."

"Not any more, he isn't. Tom, I'm appointing you the captain of the *Mary Anne,* as of this moment. You're not to fire a shot at a revenue ship, is that clear? If worse comes to worst and you can't outrun an exciseman, you're to get the crew off safely and abandon ship. Will you accept the command under those conditions?"

"I will, ma'am, an' I'll do me best fer ye. But Nate, 'e won't like this."

"That 'e won't, Mrs. Neville," chimed in Ezra, his forehead furrowed with concern.

"Let me worry about Nate Peggoty," Sabrina snapped. "He doesn't own the *Mary Anne,* and he doesn't own me."

Chapter Sixteen

Sabrina pulled the hood of her voluminous old-fashioned cloak closer around her face. She should have brought an umbrella. Few people in England in this terrible summer of 1816 ventured out without one. Her feet were protected by her thick-soled wooden pattens, but the fine rain was now falling faster and had begun to penetrate the heavy woolen fabric of the cloak. Well, she was almost home, and a little wetness never hurt anyone.

After a sleepless night Sabrina had stolen out of the house at sunrise, hoping that a long solitary walk would help her to sort out her jumbled thoughts. Several hours later she was a little clearer in her mind about her problems, if not closer to a solution. At least now she could see how wrong she'd been in her blithe assumption that she could enable herself and her family to live happily forever after by investing in a smuggling boat.

It had all seemed so simple. After a few profitable voyages, Adrian could enjoy an estate on a sound footing, Daphne would have an ample dowry and make a good marriage, Fanny would have her jointure and with luck might elect to have her own establishment, and Sabrina would have a nest egg that would allow her to live as an independent woman free of all ties.

Sabrina marveled that she hadn't seen the great flaw in the underpinning of this line of thinking. Sooner or later the *Mary Anne* was certain to encounter a revenue cutter, and then she'd be forced to use those guns she carried and someone would get hurt. Now it had happened, and Sabrina knew she couldn't live with the prospect that it might happen again. Which meant, logically, that she had to dispose of the *Mary Anne* and leave the smuggling game. Yesterday she'd tried to evade making that decision. She'd ordered Tom Cavitt to avoid a gun fight at all costs, and he'd promised to do his best. Realistically, though, if Tom were faced either with certain capture or the loss of the boat, wouldn't he be tempted to use his guns? Could she blame him?

Supposing she did sell the boat? Could she make the mortgage payments and maintain the estate? It was doubtful. Her moral qualms might cause the loss of a property that had been in the Latimer family for generations and condemn all of them to lives of genteel poverty. Moreover, she'd be depriving the Cavitts and the crew members of the *Mary Anne* of their livelihoods. Didn't she have an obligation to these people? And wasn't there a possibility that Tom Cavitt could outsail and outrun any challenge from a revenue cutter, avoiding further bloodshed and making it unnecessary to sell the boat?

Sabrina sighed. After so much hard thought she hadn't been able to make up her mind what to do about the *Mary Anne*. Her brain must be filled with mush. What had happened to the independent, incisive woman who a year ago had vowed to repair the family fortunes and live a life of her own choosing, unfettered by convention and certainly free of domination by any male? That woman had the backbone of an eel, she thought contemptuously. That woman had fallen into the arms of the first attractive gambling man who came along. What's more, even after he'd treated her like a fancy piece and ground her pride in the dust she'd been hard put to fight down the physical yearning she still felt for him. Now he'd changed his arrogant mind and apparently thought he could whistle her back with a facile apology and a liberal dose of sensual male magnetism. Sabrina drew a deep breath. Perhaps she couldn't wave a magic wand and make it possible for Adrian and Daphne and Fanny to live happily ever after, but she could at least preserve her own self-respect. She'd show Jareth how wrong he was.

"Sabrina, where have you been? I've been looking all over for you."

Shaking herself out of her thoughts, Sabrina looked up to find Daphne running down the driveway from the house. "I went out for an early morning walk. Is something wrong?"

"It's Mama, what else?" Daphne retorted. "I sent Rosie to the stables a bit ago to order the horses put to the carriage, and she came back with the news that Mama had already sent word that I wasn't to have the carriage today. When I spoke to Mama, she said I couldn't have the carriage because you needed it for a meeting with the Vicar's wife."

"Oh, Lord, I'd forgotten. I volunteered to help with the plans for the summer festival."

"You know Mama doesn't care a ha' penny for the summer festival," Daphne said bitterly. "If we had a dozen carriages, she'd find some excuse to deny me the use of every one. She doesn't want me to go to Newhaven to see Gordon, that's what it is."

"Well, in all fairness, you should recall that she was very upset when we disappeared yesterday for hours and she didn't know where we were. Let me go upstairs and change my clothes and have a cup of tea and then we'll beard Mama in her den."

A little later, cornered by both her stepdaughters in

her inner sanctum, the morning room, Lady Latimer fought a losing battle to have her own way. "I'm sure you'll agree it would hardly do for you to disappoint the Vicar's wife, Sabrina," she began with a sweet smile. "Mrs. Varrick was telling me only the other day how much she was depending on your help in planning for the summer festival. Now, ordinarily, you might offer to drive the dogcart into Fairlea, so that dear Daphne could have the use of the carriage. However, I'm told the dogcart had some kind of mysterious accident yesterday."

With an air of triumph, Fanny turned her attention to Daphne. "So you see, my dear, that it will be quite impossible for you to visit Captain Stanhope today. And really, it's much better this way. Think about it. It doesn't look well for an unmarried young woman of good family to visit a bachelor at his lodgings. That's bound to make you the subject of unpleasant gossip. Another day, perhaps, Sabrina might accompany you to Newhaven — after all, it's our duty to visit the sick! — but I don't care to have you go there alone."

Angry color tinted Daphne's cheeks. "I can hardly be considered unchaperoned with Betsy and the landlady and several servants in the house. Very well, Mama. I won't argue. God gave me two good legs. I'll walk to Newhaven. And if some kind soul stops to offer me a ride, I'll accept with thanks and explain that I'm reduced to walking because my stepmother won't allow me the use of her carriage!"

"Well! Anyone hearing you speak, my dear Daphne, might very well conclude I was justified in being concerned about the proprieties!"

"I'm sure Daphne realizes she was overly hasty," Sabrina soothed her stepmother. "It's just that she's concerned about Captain Stanhope. Look, I have an idea. Fairlea is on the way to Newhaven. I could drive with

Daphne to Newhaven, leave her with Betsy Stanhope, and return to Fairlea for my appointment with Mrs. Varrick."

Lady Latimer eyed the calmly determined face of her elder stepdaughter and wisely gave up the struggle. "Do that, Sabrina," she said graciously. "After all, Betsy Stanhope is Daphne's good friend. One wouldn't wish to be remiss in her hour of need."

Later that morning, after she had dropped Daphne in Newhaven — mercifully, Gordon's condition continued to improve — and was driving back to Fairlea, Sabrina reflected that coping with her sister's affairs of the heart was beginning to be very wearing. These confrontations with Fanny would continue as long as their stepmother believed she could succeed in discouraging Daphne's feelings for Gordon Stanhope. Perhaps it would be better to break the bad news to Fanny immediately that Daphne intended to marry the revenue captain and that Sabrina supported her decision. There would be one grand burst of fireworks, after which Fanny might bow to the inevitable.

When they arrived in Fairlea, her driver remarked as he was letting down the steps of the carriage in front of the vicarage, "Old Dickie's got a loose front shoe, Miss Sabrina. I'd best go along ter the smithy."

"Fine, Robin. I'll join you there when I've finished with my meeting. I won't be long."

About to unlatch the gate of the vicarage, which was situated at the end of Fairlea's single street next to the church, Sabrina paused to watch another carriage drive up and stop in front of the house. She recognized the crest on the door of the vehicle. She'd seen the crest reproduced on several objects in Jareth's rooms at the Albany in London. The Marquess of Winwood got out of the carriage and turned to help his wife down the steps.

"Mrs. Neville, I thought I recognized you. How nice

to see you again," exclaimed Christabel, hurrying over to greet Sabrina, followed leisurely by her husband.

"Lady Winwood. Lord Winwood." Sabrina bowed formally. Seen in the glare of daylight, Christabel's fragile silver-gilt beauty was as flawless as it had appeared in Lady Marston's softly lit drawing room. Standing beside the tiny black-clad figure, Sabrina felt awkward and outsized.

"How do, m'dear," drawled Lionel. "I caught a glimpse of you at the Alfriston ball but I never managed to catch up with you for a dance." He favored her with a knowing sidelong leer that made Sabrina long to scratch his eyes out. It wasn't yet afternoon, but already she could smell liquor on his breath. "I've brought my wife to Fairlea to allow her to play Lady Bountiful," he continued, smirking. "Christabel has so much talent for good works, and the worthy vicar's wife appears to think she can't organize a village fete without advice from the Lord Lieutenant's wife."

Christabel seemed not to notice the undertone of hurtful derision in her husband's voice. The sweet smile remained pasted on her lips. "And what brings you to the vicarage, Mrs. Neville? Has Mrs. Varrick enlisted your help for the festival too?"

"Indeed, yes. Perhaps if we put our heads together, we can come up with some fresh ideas."

"I'm afraid I can't guarantee anything original," Christabel said, laughing. "I'll be happy to offer moral support, however . . ." She broke off, her eyes widening at the sight of the tall figure striding rapidly toward the group in front of the vicarage from the direction of the village green.

"Sabrina, wait," Jareth called, as she made a quick instinctive movement toward the gate. "I was coming out to Latimer House this afternoon, but now that you're here—" He cut himself off, slowing his steps as he recognized the identity of the two people standing with Sabrina. "Hullo, Christabel, Lionel," he said as he came up to them.

Sabrina sensed the tension in Christabel's slight figure as she said, "Good afternoon, Jareth. You're paying Fairlea a very long visit this time, are you not? You've been away so much we were beginning to think of you almost as a stranger."

"Yes, I marvel you find anything in this quiet backwater of Sussex to occupy your time," Lionel gibed. "Tell me, how are the fleshpots of London getting along without the leader of the *ton?*"

"I don't worry about other people's dissipations, Lionel," Jareth replied coolly. "I have enough trouble coping with my own."

Sabrina caught her breath as she looked at the brothers standing side by side. They were so much alike they might have been twins, but where Jareth was all lean elegance and controlled grace, Lionel was now only a coarse and blurred copy of the man he had been.

Jareth turned to Sabrina. "Could I have a private word with you?"

She shook her head. "I'm afraid you must excuse me. Lady Winwood and I have an appointment with the vicar's wife."

"I'd be happy to wait."

"Oh, I couldn't ask you to do that. I have no idea how long I'll be. Shall we go inside, Lady Winwood?"

"Lionel?" Christabel glanced uneasily from her husband to his brother. "Aren't you coming with us? I believe you wanted to discuss the repairs to the church roof with Mr. Varrick."

"In a moment, my dear. You go along. I so seldom have the opportunity to talk to my brother."

Watching Christabel walk up the path to the vicarage with Sabrina, Lionel flashed a taunting grin at Jareth.

"Mrs. Neville doesn't seem impressed with your charms, brother mine. That must be quite a blow for a man so accomplished in the petticoat line. Perhaps it's because you don't have much experience with widows? Of course, a widow like Mrs. Neville—beautiful, young, well-traveled—must have higher standards in men than the lightskirts with which you usually sleep."

Jareth's jaw clenched, and Lionel laughed. "A bit thin-skinned, are we? See here, how would it be if I had a go with the beauteous Mrs. Neville? If I find out anything interesting about her preferences, I could pass them along to you."

"Damn you, Lionel!" His hands balled into fists, Jareth took a quick impulsive step toward his brother, then froze in his tracks, inhaling a long difficult breath.

"Go ahead, hit me," Lionel snarled, all trace of his previous heavy-handed good humor disappearing from his face. "And then I'll have you up before the beak for disturbing the peace. I've told you before, Jareth. I want you out of here. There's not enough room in this part of Sussex for both of us."

"And as I told *you* before, I'll leave when I'm good and ready." Jareth swung on his heel and walked down the street in the direction of the Fairlea Arms. Lionel stood in the roadway, his shoulders hunched, staring malignantly at his brother's departing form, until he was roused by the vicar's voice.

"My dear Lord Winwood, pray do come in," called Mr. Varrick, hurrying down the path from the house. "The ladies are already hard at work on festival matters! Lady Winwood tells me you wish to discuss the repairs to the roof, but first, let me offer you a glass of very decent claret, if I do say so myself."

In the parlor of the vicarage, closeted with Christabel and the plump, motherly Mrs. Varrick, Sabrina found her attention wandering from talk of fancy work booths and children's games and how much to charge for chances on the French silk shawl that Lady Winwood was donating as one of the prizes in the annual raffle. It could never have occurred to Jareth, Sabrina thought wryly, not in the wildest stretch of his imagination, that one day his first love and his last love would be sitting quietly together making plans for a village fete. She hoped maliciously that it was making him uncomfortable.

She became aware she had lost the thread of the conversation when Mrs. Varrick raised her voice, apparently repeating a question.

"What? I'm so sorry, Mrs. Varrick, I must have been woolgathering."

"I was wondering if your servant might be willing to provide some of those wonderful Viennese pastries we've all heard so much about for the tea tent," said the vicar's wife. A housemaid appeared in the doorway and Mrs. Varrick rose, excusing herself. She was back in a moment, saying, "Would you excuse me for a little? One of our perennially troubled parishioners is in difficulties again, and nothing will do but she must see me."

After Mrs. Varrick had left the room, Christabel remarked with a smile, "I'm so glad to have the opportunity to see you again today, Mrs. Neville. I have so few friends in the area my own age. Since the evening we met at Lady Marston's dinner I've been meaning to drop you a note, inviting you to take tea at Winwood Park." She paused, shrugging. "To tell the truth, my husband doesn't care very much about seeing guests these days. Oh, he takes part in affairs like the Waterloo ball at Alfriston, because he feels it's expected of him, as Lord Lieutenant of the county, but his heart's not in it."

"That's natural, isn't it? Your loss is so recent."

"Oh, of course, you of all people would understand. Personally, I'm convinced that seeing people and going out in society help to keep one's mind off personal problems. However, Lionel doesn't feel that way, so . . ." She shrugged again.

Up this close, Christabel's beauty still was incredible, but now Sabrina could detect the faint shadows marring the porcelain skin beneath the violet eyes. She was still suffering from the loss of her child, of course, but was something else troubling her? She spoke and behaved like a dutiful, concerned wife. Could she really be in love with Lionel? Or had she simply made up her mind to ignore his boorish digs at her, his roving eye, his drunkenness, for the sake of her position as Marchioness of Winwood?

Christabel's next remark took Sabrina by surprise. "I hadn't realized you and Jareth were such old friends."

"You're quite mistaken," Sabrina said hastily. "I don't know Lord Jareth well. I've been acquainted with him for a matter of weeks only." As soon as the words were out of her mouth she realized her mistake. Christabel seized on the slip immediately.

"Weeks? Really?" Christabel's face expressed only a friendly interest, but there was a determined undertone in her voice. It was obvious she meant to satisfy her curiosity. "Jareth's been visiting in Sussex just since the Alfriston ball, I believe, so you must have met elsewhere. London, I suppose? But no, that couldn't be. You told me at Lady Marston's dinner that you've been living at Latimer House since you returned from the Continent. Did you meet Jareth abroad, then? No, how silly of me. Jareth hasn't been traveling on the Continent, as far as I know. Well, he couldn't have, of course. Because of the war with Napoleon, I mean."

"No, Lord Jareth and I didn't meet abroad."

The clipped, uncommunicative reply didn't put Christabel off. She flashed Sabrina an ingenuous smile, saying, "I daresay you think I'm a dreadful busybody!

295

Surely you can't have forgotten how everyone knows everyone else's affairs in a small village like this. Yes," she nodded, as she saw Sabrina's eyes widen, "the tongues have been clacking. It's common knowledge that Jareth, who hasn't visited Fairlea in many years, has been extending his stay in the area, paying frequent calls at Latimer House and bombarding the widowed Mrs. Neville with letters. You can't blame me now, can you, for being a little curious? After all, Jareth is my brother-in-law!"

Servants, thought Sabrina with loathing. The Latimer houseman, Robin, came to Fairlea frequently, and the mother of Rosie, the housemaid, lived in the village. A word or two from either Robin or Rosie had obviously started a trail of gossip among the servants in the great houses of the vicinity. Probably Fanny had done her share also. She had a circle of cronies in the neighborhood. She probably hadn't been able to resist titillating her friends with accounts of her stepdaughter's pursuit by the Lord Lieutenant's brother.

"Are you going to marry Jareth, Mrs. Neville?"

The unexpected question rocked Sabrina's composure. "No!" she exploded angrily. She glared at Christabel. "I don't even like the man!"

"I beg your pardon, I had no earthly right to ask you a question like that," Christabel said, overcome with confusion. "I don't know what came over me. Please believe I don't usually pry into other people's affairs or say things that embarrass my acquaintances. It's — you see, I'm quite fond of my brother-in-law." A wave of color suffused her delicate features. "We were — we were very good friends, years ago before I married Lionel. I'd like him to be happy."

She's still in love with Jareth, thought Sabrina in a burst of insight. Does her husband suspect she's never stopped loving his brother? It would certainly explain why Lionel's dislike for Jareth had grown stronger and more virulent over the years. Suddenly Sabrina was no longer angry. She even felt oddly sorry for Christabel. "I'm sure I wish Lord Jareth every happiness, Lady Winwood, but it won't be with me," she said quietly.

"Thank you for putting the situation straight. Again, pray accept my apology for my inquisitiveness." Christabel looked as relieved as Sabrina felt when Mrs. Varrick returned to the room, putting an end to the conversation.

A little later, when the arrangements for the summer festival had been settled to everyone's satisfaction, Christabel said to Sabrina, "Your carriage isn't here? Will someone be coming for you? I know Lionel would be very happy to drive you home when he finishes his talk with the vicar."

"That won't be necessary, thank you. My carriage is at the smithy. One of my horses had a loose shoe."

Sabrina walked quickly away from the vicarage toward the center of the village. She was glad to be out of Christabel's presence. The woman's deep-boned unhappiness was so unmistakable that it made Sabrina feel uncomfortable, even vaguely guilty. Which was ridiculous. Why should she feel any guilt in connection with the Marchioness of Winwood?

As she neared the lily pond on the green, a familiar voice hailed her. "Wait now, Mrs. Neville, I want a word wi' ye."

Fighting down an instinctive impulse to turn and run, Sabrina paused, standing her ground as Nate Peggoty lurched toward her from the door of the Fairlea Arms. Before he reached her, it was obvious from his unsteady gait that the ex-captain of her cutter had been drinking, and when he came up to her the fumes of liquor on his breath were overpowering. His face beneath several days' growth of beard was distorted in a malignant scowl

297

and his clothing was dirty and disheveled.

"What is it, Mr. Peggoty? I thought it was understood we were to keep our distance in public."

"That was afore ye took away my command, Missy. The rules o' the game are different now. I don't 'ave ter do what ye say, not any more." Peggoty's voice was so slurred that Sabrina had to strain to understand what he was saying.

"Lower your voice, please," she said with more calm than she felt. "What is it you want from me?"

"I wants what's coming ter me. I wants my command back. It ain't fair, what ye did, making a young 'un like Tom Cavitt the cap'n o' the *Mary Anne*. I'm the best seaman in these parts, an' well ye know it."

"Yes, I do know it, but you're also a violent man who won't follow orders and ends up killing people. No, I'll not change my mind. Tom Cavitt stays captain of the *Mary Anne*."

"An' what am I ter do, tell me that? I got a missis, kids. 'Ow am I supposed ter feed 'em?"

"You've got a legitimate grievance there. I was going to send you word I'm allowing you a crewman's share of the profits from each voyage for the next six months, unless I terminate my ownership of the cutter before that. I must warn you, I'm thinking seriously of getting out of the trade."

"No ye don't, not whilst I got breath in my body," snarled Peggoty. He grabbed Sabrina's arm, thrusting his livid face close to hers and sickening her with his foul breath. "Ye ain't selling the *Mary Anne,* an' ye ain't keeping Tom Cavitt on as cap'n. I'll see ye an' Tom an' old Ezra too in perdition afore I lets ye take away me rights, and ye can lay ter that!" As she tried to pull away from him, his raging expression changed into a leer. He wrapped both arms around her, snickering, "What's the hurry, Mrs. Neville? I've fancied ye fer a long time, y'know. Ye're a good-looking piece, an' no green girl, neither, what with being a widow an' all."

"Let go of me," she exclaimed in a burst of revulsion, struggling frantically to free herself, momentarily uncaring that this confrontation was bringing her hitherto secret relationship with Peggoty out into the open. Suddenly he released his grip with a howl of pain as an iron-hard arm encased in a sleeve of blue superfine circled his neck from behind and crushed his windpipe.

Jareth stepped back from Peggoty, giving the sailor a shove that sent him reeling backwards. "I'll give you two minutes to get out of the village, you scum, or you'll find yourself even the worse for wear," Jareth said contemptuously.

Recovering from the initial surprise of Jareth's attack, Peggoty sneered, "Why, if it ain't 'is 'igh and mighty lordship, poking 'is nose inter some'un else's affairs agin. I let ye get away scot-free a few weeks back, me lord, when this lady 'ere insisted on saving yer 'ide, but I ain't going ter make that mistake twice."

"What are you talking about?" Jareth demanded. "I've never seen you before in my life. Not that it's important. I want you out of here. Now."

"Not until I've taught ye a lesson yer lordship won't fergit." Peggoty launched himself at Jareth, flailing wildly with his powerful arms. Sidestepping neatly, Jareth jarred Peggoty with a blow to the jaw that would have felled an ox. The sailor grunted, shook his head groggily, and renewed his attack with a bellow of rage. Jareth had the advantage of superior boxing ability and a clear head, but Peggoty, fueled by a drunken rage, made the contest almost equal at first with his great strength and bearlike rushes and his chin that seemed impervious to any blow.

Sabrina watched the two men tearing into each other, her heart in her mouth as she saw Jareth pummeling and being pummeled, seeming to absorb as much punishment as he was meting out. In a few minutes the fight became a public spectacle, with what looked like the entire population of the village ringing the green in breathless suspense. It took Jareth ten minutes of savage battling before one last epic punch battered Peggoty into insensibility. Then, using the last of his strength, Jareth heaved the sailor into the duck pond and lurched back on stumbling legs in Sabrina's direction. She caught her breath at the sight of his swollen, blackened eye and the blood splattering his waistcoat of pristine white marcella.

"Jareth, you're hurt," came a wailing cry behind her. Startled, Sabrina looked around to see Christabel tumbling out of the Winwood carriage, halted on the edge of the green. Rushing to Jareth, Christabel put her arm around his shoulders, crooning soothingly, "Let me help you. We'll get you to a doctor—"

"Oh, for God's sake, Christabel, I'm not dying," said Jareth wearily, edging away from her supporting arm. "That damned sot, whoever he was, popped a good one on my nose, that was all. I always bleed like a pig. I'm fine. Don't bother about me."

"An excellent suggestion," said Lionel, striding up to his wife's side. There was an ugly edge to his voice as he added, "I need hardly remind you, I hope, that you aren't my brother's keeper." He glanced sourly at the duck pond, from which Peggoty, coughing and cursing incoherently, was being extricated by several of the villagers. "If a member of my family wishes to make a public spectacle of himself by engaging in a common brawl with the dregs of the lower classes, that's his problem. Come along, Christabel. I'm sure Mrs. Neville will excuse you."

"Oh . . . Yes." Christabel seemed a trifle dazed, and then, glancing quickly around her, somewhat embarrassed. "I'm glad you're not injured, Jareth. Good-bye, Mrs. Neville."

As the Winwoods walked away, Sabrina turned to Jareth. "Are you really all right?" The eye was beginning to close, but aside from the bloodied nose, his face seemed unmarked.

"Yes. Oh, I may be a trifle sore for a while. Although my opponent wasn't very handy with his fives, he did land several good wallops in my ribs. But I'll survive."

"I'm glad." Sabrina cleared her throat. "Thank you for helping me." Nodding good-bye, she turned to go.

"Sabrina, wait." When she didn't stop, Jareth caught up to her, keeping pace with her as she walked across the green, past the inn in the direction of the smithy. "Who was that fellow I was fighting with?"

"I don't know who he was." Sabrina hurried her steps. "A passing stranger, a vagrant—it doesn't matter."

"Of course it matters! He threatened you, attacked you. You ought to have him charged."

"And call more unpleasant attention to myself? The whole village was watching us. I'd rather just forget about it."

Jareth stopped, placing himself squarely across her path. "There's something strange about all this. I think you know more about that ruffian than you're saying. He seemed to know both of us. What did he mean by saying—how did he put it?—oh yes, that he once let me off scot-free when you insisted on saving my hide?"

A chill swept over Sabrina. She'd hoped he hadn't noticed Peggoty's drunken reference to the night when she'd prevented the smuggler captain from doing away with the unconscious Jareth. "I have no idea what he meant. Jareth, I can't stop to talk now. I'm on my way to Newhaven to fetch my sister."

"Now, look, I'm not going to let you put me off again," Jareth expostulated. "I insist—"

"Insist? What right do you have to insist on anything? Must I say it again? Leave me alone, Jareth. *Leave me alone!*" Sabrina swept past him to cross the road to the smithy, where Robin was harnessing her newly shod horse to the carriage.

"We're all ready fer ye, ma'am," Robin said. His eyes were alight with excitement. "Say, now, that was a proper fistfight between those two fellers. Ain't seen a real mill like that in ages. That gentleman you was speaking to jist now, 'e was a pretty fighter. One o' the villagers was tellin' me he's the Marquess of Winwood's brother."

Chapter Seventeen

Daphne poked her head around the door of her sister's bedchamber. "Oh, you're not ready to go?"

Sabrina looked up from her dressing table. "I'll be with you as soon as Lotte finishes with my hair."

"Humph! *That* won't take long!" Lotte sniffed, as her deft fingers wound Sabrina's heavy mass of hair into a simple coil on the crown of her head.

Daphne grinned. It was an old grievance. Lotte didn't feel that Sabrina's present quiet country existence gave her talents enough scope. The abigail had been in her element in Vienna, arranging Sabrina's hair in elaborate coiffures and dressing her in the latest fashions for diplomatic dinners and gala balls. "Shall we say five minutes, then?" Daphne asked. "I'll go order the carriage."

Lotte settled the little lace cornet on Sabrina's hair and went to the wardrobe for a pelisse and bonnet. "You'd best take an umbrella, *meine Frau*. It rains not yet, but I'm sure it will. *Gott in Himmel,* will we ever have an end to this dreadful weather? We should have stayed in Vienna."

"You wouldn't have been any happier in Austria," said Sabrina matter-of-factly, easing her bonnet over her lace cap. "It's been raining all over Europe this year."

Looking skeptical, Lotte changed the subject. "So you're going along with *Fräulein* Daphne to visit her sick friend? I expect that will please the Lady Latimer, *hein?*"

"Oh, yes. You know Mama is a firm believer in chaperons." Sabrina's composure wasn't ruffled by Lotte's comment. Given the abigail's lively curiosity about family members, there was probably little concerning Daphne's romance that Lotte hadn't guessed. She was certainly correct in assuming that Sabrina was accompanying Daphne to Newhaven today in order to mollify Fanny about her younger stepdaughter's continuing visits to Gordon Stanhope's sickbed.

Without changing her tone, Lotte inquired, "Was the Herr Tremayne hurt fighting in the village yesterday? That Robin, he could talk of nothing else at supper last night. He says the Herr saved your life, or as near as makes no difference."

Sabrina hunched her shoulders resignedly. She'd told Fanny and Daphne about the incident in Fairlea, because there seemed no way of keeping it from them. After all, it had taken place in front of the whole village! And it was probably asking too much of human nature to expect Robin not to gossip about it to the other servants. It must have been the first time the footman had seen a titled gentleman engaged in a public brawl.

"My life was never in danger, Lotte. Lord Jareth simply prevented a drunken lout from pressing his attentions on me."

"And so, you and the Herr have mended your quarrel, *nicht wahr?*" Lotte's mouth curved in a reminiscent smile. "The Herr was such a fine gentleman. Always a kind word for me, never failed to ask how I was feeling. It will be a pleasure to see him again."

"There was never any quarrel to mend," Sabrina said coldly. "Lord Jareth and I are acquaintances, nothing more."

Lotte's expression was frankly disbelieving, but all she said was, *"Ja, meine Frau.* Just as you say." She helped Sabrina into her pelisse. "Will there be anything else? Then I'm off to show Cook how to make a proper *Gebäck."*

Buttoning her pelisse, Sabrina's fingers slowed as she felt a wave of cold fear sweeping through her. Talking with Lotte about yesterday's confrontation with Nate Peggoty had suddenly made her realize that she hadn't been thinking straight about the incident. She'd assumed the gossip would soon die down and there'd be no aftereffects. Peggoty wasn't known in the village, and the mere fact that Jareth had leaped to her defense wouldn't result in their past relationship becoming known. Presumably he would have rushed to rescue any damsel in distress.

What she'd failed to remember was the character of Nate Peggoty. It was no accident he'd been in Fairlea yesterday, no bit of bad luck. He'd gone there searching for her, in a blind rage at being dismissed from his command of the *Mary Anne,* and he'd threatened her when she refused to reinstate him. Knowing his capacity for violence, especially after his humiliating thrashing at Jareth's hands, Sabrina didn't doubt that Peggoty would find some way to get back at her. She could only wonder why the danger hadn't occurred to her before now. Perhaps she hadn't wanted to think about any added complications in her life, when her problems were already so heavy.

Shaking her head to dispel the cloud of foreboding that hung over her, she finished buttoning her pelisse and picked up her reticule. As she walked to the door to join Daphne, Lotte bustled into the room, gingerly grasping a rather grimy bit of paper between two fastidious fingers. "A dirty-looking man just came to the kitchen door with this, *meine Frau.* Said to give it to you right away."

Sabrina unfolded the paper, which contained a short message in an awkwardly executed scrawl. "Go to the spinney on the cliff path, Mrs. Neville," it read. "Ye'll see I means what I says."

It was Peggoty's undisciplined handwriting. Sabrina recognized it from the brief lists of smuggled items and projected profits that he'd been supplying her after every voyage of the *Mary Anne*.

Seized by a chilling panic, she pushed past Lotte, ignoring her quick exclamation of concern, and raced out of the room, down the stairs to the ground-floor vestibule and out the front door of the house. Still running at breakneck speed, she reached the cliff path. Then, nearing the spinney, she slowed her steps. Her feet dragging, she reluctantly entered the little copse of trees, stopping abruptly as she stepped on something soft and yielding. Her heart was pounding as she forced herself to look down at the object, a crudely fashioned cloth dummy, not quite life-sized, which had been splashed with a dark red liquid. Around its neck was a placard inscribed with the name "Tom Cavitt." A knife skewered the placard to the dummy's chest.

Sick with horror, Sabrina stood paralyzed, unable to tear her eyes away from the grisly object. Finally her mind began to clear and the strength started to flow back into her limbs. She stumbled blindly out of the spinney, uttering a strangled scream of fear when strong arms wrapped themselves around her.

"My God, Sabrina, what's the matter?"

At the sound of Jareth's voice Sabrina went limp, collapsing like a rag doll against his chest.

"Sabrina, what *is* it?"

For a moment longer Sabrina lingered in the haven of Jareth's embrace. Then, drawing a deep shuddering breath, she lifted her head, drawing away from him. "I can't think how I came to be such a noddy," she said, attempting a smile. "I got frightened by some kind of child's prank, that was all."

Jareth stared at her, his dark eyes boring into hers. After a moment, turning on his heel in a sudden quick movement, he strode into the spinney. He was back in a few seconds. "When are you going to stop lying, Sabrina?" he asked grimly. He reached out to grab her shoulders, giving her a little shake. "That thing in the spinney was no part of a child's prank. It was pure evil. You were right to feel frightened."

"Whatever it was, it's no concern of yours," Sabrina retorted, attempting to twist away from him.

For an instant Jareth glared down at her, his face registering the angry frustration he felt. Then, pulling her hard against him, he bent his head, swooping down on her mouth with eager lips in a kiss that deepened and clung and sent the familiar quicksilver magic throbbing through her entire body. When at last he released her mouth, he looked down at her with his heart in his eyes, saying shakily, "I love you, Sabrina, I adore you with my whole being. I'll never love anyone else for as long as I live. And don't bother to deny it, I know you love me. I'm sorry I tried to force you to sleep with me, and I'm sorrier still I misjudged your character, but it will never happen again and we've got to put it behind us. It's time to put an end to this stupid estrangement and get back to loving." He gave her another gentle shake. "Is that understood?"

Swallowing hard, Sabrina fought one last time to balance her stiffnecked pride against the pull of passion and remembered joys, and failed. "Yes," she murmured. "You're a rogue, and I ought to avoid you like the plague, but I can't help myself." With a gentle finger she touched his right eye, still an alarming shade of deep purple from one of Nate Peggoty's blows. "I love you,

Jareth."

Expelling his breath in a vast sigh of relief, he hugged her joyously. "Thank God," he exclaimed. "I thought this moment would never come." Taking her arm, he guided her to a convenient boulder beside the path and sat down with her, cradling her against his shoulder. "Now, before we settle down to arranging our wedding, I have to know what kind of rum go you've gotten yourself embroiled with."

She hesitated, opening her mouth and closing it again. She was so accustomed to coping with her own problems that she found it difficult to confide even in Jareth. Then the dam burst, and the story of how she'd attempted to save the Latimer fortunes by entering into the smuggling trade with the *Mary Anne* began tumbling out.

"You mean you owned the ship that fired on—what was the fellow's name? Oh, yes, Stanhope—on Captain Stanhope's revenue cutter? And now this fellow Peggoty is threatening to kill you because you won't give him back command of your ship?" Jareth asked incredulously. "I can't believe . . . Look, Sabrina, my mind is in some kind of a fog. Start from the beginning and tell me everything."

Once started, Sabrina didn't find it strange that she was spilling out secrets she'd been guarding closely for over a year. As a matter of fact, she felt a sense of release, as if she were transferring some of the burden that had been wearing her down to Jareth's strong shoulders.

When she'd finished, he sat dumfounded for a moment before erupting into a bout of uncontrollable laughing.

"What's so funny?" Sabrina demanded resentfully. It certainly wasn't the kind of response she'd expected.

"Oh my love, you are," he gasped when he could finally speak. "I've never met a woman like you. You're

308

not just one woman. You're two or three females occupying the same body. You're an adventuress and actress who managed to fool me completely. You're an estate manager the equal of any experienced bailiff. You're a gambler with a flair for winning that would make you a fortune if White's and Brooke's and the other clubs admitted women. And now I find out you're a successful smuggler. I'm almost afraid to marry you. I'd never know in what new guise you might pop into my bed!"

The laughter died out of his eyes. "First, though, we've got to get you out of this fix you're in. Do you really think the Peggoty fellow will try to make good on his threats? Couldn't he simply be trying to frighten you into giving him back his command?"

Sabrina shivered. "No, he's past that, half-crazed with resentment and rage at losing so much face. He's a violent man, and a vicious one. I think the *Mary Anne* is less important to him now than his urge to take some kind of revenge on Tom Cavitt, Ezra, and me. You, too, Jareth," she added in sudden alarm. "He'll never forgive that beating you gave him yesterday."

"Don't worry about me, love. I'd take great pleasure in milling him down again." Jareth's forehead furrowed in a thoughtful frown. "I wonder what Peggoty has in mind? He certainly can't be planning to inform on you and your crew to the revenue authorities. He'd only be incriminating himself."

"You saw that dummy in the spinney. He means to kill us!"

"He can't do that without marching himself straight to the gallows, after the trail of threats he's left behind him," said Jareth reasonably. "No, I'm convinced he's just trying to scare the wits out of you. Your idea of paying him off was a good one. Leave it to me. I'll track him down and offer him a goodly sum to shake off the dust of Sussex from his feet forever."

Apprehension shadowing her eyes, Sabrina shook her head. "I'm not sure Nate will settle for money. He wants blood."

"I think you'll find that Peggoty is more avaricious than you think," Jareth said firmly. He eyed Sabrina with a quizzical smile. "Now to the next order of business. I think you'll have to sever your connections with the smuggling trade, my love. You have too many moral scruples against killing innocent revenue men to stay in the game."

She nodded, the worry lines returning to her face. "I'd already half-decided that. It means Adrian will probably lose Latimer House, and my crewmen will have to find some other way to earn their living."

"Why should it mean that?"

"Because I haven't any money, that's why!" Sabrina retorted.

"You can solve your crewmen's problems by making them a gift of the *Mary Anne*," said Jareth calmly. "If they clash with the excisemen it won't be your responsibility. And you won't need the income from the boat to save Adrian's inheritance for him, because as soon as I get back to London I intend to pay off the mortgages on Latimer House."

"Adrian and I couldn't possibly let you do that," said Sabrina stiffly. "We've never asked for charity, and we won't begin now."

"Charity? My darling pea goose, I'm talking about a marriage settlement. Adrian won't object to your using that money as you see fit, will he?"

"No, but . . . Jareth, do you have any idea how much my family owes? I know you don't have any money to spare. You're a younger son, and you've told me yourself, time and again, that you earn your living from gambling."

He tightened his arm around her, leaning down to

310

nuzzle her ear. I wasn't being entirely truthful, I'm afraid. I could live, and live well, on my gambling income if I had to, but fortunately I don't. Last year my Great-uncle Augustus Pennyfeather, full of juice from his years with the East India Company, died in the odor of sanctity and left me his fortune. So you see you needn't worry about the ready. I've got enough blunt for both of us, and Adrian and Daphne and Lady Latimer, too."

For a fleeting moment, Sabrina's face registered the bliss of being worry-free about money for the first time in many years. Then her expression subtly changed. "King Cophetua and the beggar girl," she murmured, half to herself.

"Oh, no, you don't," Jareth exclaimed. Jumping up from the boulder, he pulled Sabrina to her feet, crushing her against him and kissing her into mindless, breathless ecstasy. Tearing his mouth away at last, he said huskily, "That was to make it perfectly clear that I'm not going to risk losing you again. I know how fiercely independent you are, I know you'd rather not accept a shilling from me, but you'll just have to learn to accept me and Great-uncle Augustus Pennyfeather's fortune."

"Yes, Sire," Sabrina replied with a slow, mischievous grin. "It shall be as you decree, O King."

Jareth broke into a chuckle. "Oh, how I've missed you. Those weeks we shared in London had a magical quality about them. I'd never met anyone with your enchanting sense of fun. I'd wake up every morning giddy with eagerness to see you again." He kissed her again, hard but briefly. "We'd best be getting back before Lotte suspects I've abducted you."

"Lotte! What on earth . . . ?" Sabrina paused, looking perplexed. "How did you know I was up here on the cliff path? What made you decide to come after me?"

"It was Lotte," Jareth replied, grinning. "You

wouldn't talk to me, so I decided to try to reach you through Lotte. I knew how close you are, more like mother and daughter than mistress and servant, and I always thought she liked me . . ."

"What an understatement! You had her sitting in your pocket!"

"Come now, you exaggerate my powers," said Jareth, laughing. He put his arm loosely around her waist as they began walking slowly along the path toward the house. "However, as I was saying, I always thought Lotte liked me, so this morning, when I arrived at Latimer House, I asked for her instead of you. Your little housemaid seemed a bit surprised at my request, but she produced Lotte, who gratified me no end by declaring she'd never been so happy to see anyone in her entire life. She was beside herself with worry. You'd discarded the note that sent you rushing out of the house looking as if the Furies were after you, and Lotte had read it. She was convinced you were in great danger. Before I came on the scene, she was debating whether to go after you herself, or to notify Lady Latimer and your sister."

"And now she'll think you're more wonderful than ever." They were within sight of the house now, and Sabrina wriggled out of his hold, her face suddenly stricken. "Jareth! I can't possibly marry you!"

"What the devil—?" Jareth's expression was a ludicrous mixture of hurt dismay and searing rage. "Now, see here, Sabrina, I won't let you put me through any more of your shilly-shallying. You love me and you're dashed well going to marry me!"

"Not if our marriage would ruin you in the eyes of society. We've forgotten something, Jareth. You introduced me to your friends at Melbourne House. How will you explain away the Countess Dohenyi when you marry Sabrina Neville?"

Jareth looked startled. "Lord, I *had* forgotten." A slow

smile curved his lips. "If *that's* all that keeps you from accepting my hand . . ."

"All! My masquerade as an Hungarian countess could cause a crashing scandal, and well you know it!"

He chuckled, dropping a kiss on her nose. "My dear goose, you've overlooked the fact that I'm the arbiter of society since Brummell left. I can do as I like."

"Don't be an idiot," said Sabrina crossly. "This is a serious matter."

"Not as serious as you think," Jareth replied, sobering. "Look, the only two people who matter among my friends are Lady Melbourne and Alvanley. If I tell her the truth, Lady M. will laugh heartily and admire you for your independence and courage, I promise you. Lord Alvanley will just laugh. He has an eye for the ridiculous. And if any malicious rumors start spreading, Alvanley will scotch them by dropping a confidential hint or two that you and I wagered him that you could pose successfully as a Viennese adventuress. Society will conclude that I've acquired a refreshingly dashing young woman as my wife." Kissing her lingeringly, he murmured against her lips, "Trust me, love. *Nothing* can keep me from marrying you."

The worry fading from her eyes, Sabrina disengaged herself, casting a laughing look at the house. "My reputation will be in ruins if I'm seen cuddling with a man in public," she protested to Jareth with a mock gravity.

"That's no problem," he said promptly, catching her to him in a quick embrace. "I've already told you I'm prepared to make an honest woman of you."

The door of the house opened suddenly and Daphne stood looking at them in open-mouthed surprise. "Oh. I didn't know . . . I was looking for you, Sabrina. You said you'd go with me to Newhaven . . ." She broke off, her fair skin reddening with embarrassment.

Coming to her rescue, Jareth walked up to her and

kissed her on the cheek. "Wish me happy, sister-to-be. Sabrina has just agreed to marry me."

"Really? How wonderful!" Daphne looked blissful. "Lord Jareth, I never could bring myself to believe that Sabrina disliked you!" Rushing to hug her sister, she exclaimed, "Lord, what will Mama say to all this?"

As it happened, Lady Latimer's reaction to the news was enthusiastic, voluble, and predictable. When Jareth entered the morning room, she looked at him with considerable surprise, casting an apprehensive glance at Sabrina, standing beside him. "Lord Jareth. How nice to see you again." Taking a closer look at his battered eye, she exclaimed, "I was so sorry to hear you were injured."

"It was in an excellent cause, I assure you. Lady Latimer, I've come to ask a very special favor. Will you do me the honor of bestowing upon me Sabrina's hand in marriage?"

Sabrina smothered a smile. She was her own mistress, and Fanny no longer had any authority over her, but, for all that, Jareth was going through the motions of asking for her hand with just the proper air of deference and respect.

After a single startled moment, Fanny beamed. "With all my heart, Lord Jareth. Sabrina, my love, my heart is fairly fluttering with joy for you! Daphne, do please ring for Rosie. We must have a glass of wine to celebrate such a wonderful occasion."

After the housemaid had brought the tray with the wine decanter and glasses, Fanny proposed a toast to the newly happy couple, and then, leaning forward with an anticipatory smile, she asked, "Well, now, have you thought about a date for your marriage? I hope you'll allow me enough time to plan a proper wedding!"

Her frame of mind still mildly incoherent after the changes that had taken place in her life during the past few minutes, Sabrina replied vaguely, "We haven't thought that far ahead, Mama."

"Oh, but *I* have," Jareth said calmly. "The wedding will take place in the village church in Fairlea as soon as the banns have been published."

"But — that will only give us three weeks," Fanny spluttered. "Surely this is being overly hasty?" She appealed to Sabrina. "You and Lord Jareth have known each other for so short a time. You met at the Alfriston ball, and that was mere days ago."

Sabrina met Jareth's eyes, brimming with laughter, and knew without words that he, too, was thinking of their enchanted, rapturous interlude in London.

"I don't think time is very important, Lady Latimer," interjected Jareth. "Sabrina and I fell in love the moment we first saw each other. I think we've waited long enough to be together."

"Oh. Well, of course . . ." Plainly flustered at this open and unconventional display of feeling on the part of her prospective son-in-law, Fanny tacitly agreed to the suggested wedding date by plunging into a discussion of wedding apparel and guest lists, a discussion that proved so engrossing to her that it lasted through luncheon and well into the afternoon.

Later, when Sabrina was saying good-bye to Jareth in the front hallway, she teased him, saying, "Now you've got Mama in your pocket, too. She agreed to everything you said. She didn't even turn a hair when you refused to ask your brother to be your best man."

"Oh, Lionel. Let's hope he'll have the decency not to come to our wedding. In any case," Jareth added firmly, "you must get it into your head that I'm not going to let anyone or anything interfere with our getting married as soon as possible." He kissed her good-bye, his mouth roughening and becoming more demanding with each passing second, until he released her with a smothered groan. *"That's* why I won't wait," he muttered. "I'd better go, lest I be tempted to drag you away to the nearest vacant room! Until tomorrow, love."

When Sabrina returned to the morning room, Lady Latimer was still bubbling with joy at the realization of her fondest hopes. "You're a deep one, my dear Sabrina. All the while you were refusing to see Lord Jareth or to answer his letters, you were fully determined to have him! Was it a lover's quarrel of some kind?" Without waiting for a reply, she went on, sighing pleasurably, "Lady Jareth Tremayne. It has a nice ring. And what a pleasant surprise to learn about Lord Jareth's legacy from his great-uncle. You'll have your own town house in London *and* a small estate in Surrey. And perhaps much more," she added, her eyes widening. "Had you thought that Lady Winwood may not have another child? She only had the one, the poor little boy who died. Even if she had another child, it might be a girl. Or girls. Sabrina! There's an excellent chance that some day you'll be Marchioness of Winwood!"

Leaving Latimer House, Jareth drove his curricle back to Fairlea in such a state of blissful, unreasoning happiness that his driving was purely automatic. His thoughts were full of Sabrina and the miracle of their reconciliation and the glorious promise of their future life together. The miles slipped by unnoticed, and he found himself entering the village without any clear idea of how he'd gotten there. Stopping in front of the Fairlea Arms, he flipped the reins to his tiger and strode into the inn and up the stairs to his rooms, where his valet pounced upon his caped driving coat and began immediately to brush away the dust of the Sussex roads.

"I'll have a glass of the landlord's excellent claret, Harris," said Jareth, tossing his beaver hat on a table and throwing himself into a comfortable chair. "Pour yourself a glass, too. Congratulations are in order. I'm about to become a married man."

The faintest ripple of emotion crossed Harris's imperturbable face. "Indeed, my lord. What splendid news. I take it you'll be increasing the size of your establishment? At the very least, I daresay you'll require a housekeeper, a cook, a butler."

"By Jove, yes. I hadn't thought about that. I'll need a much larger domestic staff." Jareth cocked his head at his valet. "Not to worry, Harris. You'll still be in complete charge of my wardrobe. Nobody will lay a finger on one of my Hessians without your consent."

"Yes, my lord. Might I inquire the name of her prospective ladyship?"

"You may. You're already acquainted with the lady. She's Mrs. . . ." Jareth paused, wondering if he and Sabrina would ever cease to be reminded of her madcap masquerade in London. He plunged on. "She's Mrs. Neville, but you know her as the Countess Dohenyi."

The valet's eyes lighted up. "Ah. So that's why—" He choked back his words, looking distinctly ruffled.

"Yes, that's why I've been calling so often at Latimer House, visits that seem to have engaged your curiosity," said Jareth, draining his glass. "I may have a reputation as a Casanova, but I tend to confine my attentions to one lady at a time. Mrs. Neville and the Countess Dohenyi are one and the same." He smiled at his discomfited valet. "Cheer up, Harris. I'm not in the least annoyed with you for your interest in my affairs. I've long known that a man can't keep secrets from his valet!"

That evening, sitting in his rooms over the remains of his solitary dinner, Jareth raised a glass of port in a silent toast to Sabrina and their coming happiness, smiling to himself about the number of congratulatory glasses he'd drunk that day, the latest round having taken place at the vicarage that afternoon, where he'd gone to request Mr. Varrick to post the banns on the following Sunday.

Sipping his wine, Jareth paid no attention to a soft knock at the door, or the low-voiced conversation that ensued when Harris answered the knock.

"A lady to see you, my lord. She wouldn't give her name."

Glancing past Harris to the opened door and the black-cloaked figure in the corridor, Jareth rose abruptly from his chair. "I'll see her. You may go, Harris. See that I'm not disturbed."

As soon as the door had closed behind the valet, Jareth exclaimed, "In heaven's name, Christabel, are you dicked in the nob? Don't you realize that your coming here is a scandal in the making? What if someone should recognize the wife of the Lord Lieutenant of the county as she keeps a secret assignation with her husband's brother? That's what people would think, you know. That's what Lionel would think!"

Christabel pushed back the heavy hood that had concealed her face. "I had to take the chance I might be recognized," she said in a trembling voice. "I had to see you, and there wasn't time to try to arrange a meeting elsewhere. It wouldn't have done any good anyway. There's no place in the neighborhood where they don't know my face."

His exasperation fading as he observed the distress that had clearly brought her close to the breaking point, Jareth took her arm, guiding her to a settee near the fireplace, and sat down with her. "What's troubling you, Christabel?" he asked quietly. "And how can I help?"

Catching her breath, she said softly, "That's so like you. No reservations, no recriminations, just, 'How can I help?'" Her face crumpled and she reached for his hand, clutching it spasmodically. Tears filled her eyes as she murmured, "Oh, Jareth, how could I have been such

318

a fool all those years ago? I ruined my life; I ruined yours. I thought love wasn't important. I thought I'd get over you, stop dreaming about you, stop regretting I'd lost you, but I never have. I still love you so much it hurts even to think about you."

Gently freeing his hand, Jareth said quietly, "I'm sorry, Christabel. We're two different people now. It's useless to try to reclaim the past."

She nodded, swallowing hard against her tears and delving into her reticule for a handkerchief. Dabbing at her eyes, she said, "I know. Even if you still loved me . . . But you don't, do you? You're in love with that beautiful widow, Mrs. Neville."

"Yes." Jareth gave her a steady, direct look. "Sabrina and I will be married in three weeks."

"So soon?" Christabel bit her lip in chagrin after her startled question.

"I'd marry her tomorrow if I could, by special license or by eloping to Gretna Green, but that would only set the tongues to wagging. Sabrina's had enough of that."

"You love her so much." There was wistfulness in Christabel's voice, but no jealousy.

"More than I ever thought I could love anyone," replied Jareth simply. "Christabel, why did you come here? Won't Lionel wonder where you are?"

At the mention of her husband the fear returned to her eyes and she said urgently, "He's too drunk to miss me tonight, that's why I risked sneaking out. But tomorrow—Jareth, you must leave Fairlea immediately. Go back to London and stay there. If you don't, Lionel will kill you."

"That's what you came to tell me?" Jareth moved his shoulders impatiently. "We went through all this at the Alfriston ball. Lionel hates me, he'd probably be happy to see me dead, but he's not mad, and he's certainly not going to risk his own neck by trying to kill me. Even a peer of the realm couldn't escape the gallows if he were convicted of murder!"

"Jareth, listen to me. I think Lionel *is* mad, at least when he's drinking. And he's been drinking almost continuously since yesterday, when we returned from Fairlea. He was—the only word I can think of is obsessed—he was obsessed with you and that fight you had with the man on the green. He kept saying you'd disgraced the family, brawling like that in public, and it would have been better if you'd never been born. Late last night he collapsed into a stupor and the servants put him to bed, but he started drinking again this morning, and now—now he's begun to make threats." Christabel shivered. "It's so dreadful. Lionel sits there in the library, hour after hour, a bottle in one hand, a horse whip in the other, repeating over and over that he's going to teach you a lesson, make sure you never have another opportunity to 'soil' the Winwood name. I'm so afraid, Jareth. Please promise me you'll leave Fairlea, tonight if possible."

Jareth shook his head, saying, "I'm not leaving Fairlea until after my wedding." He rose, extending a hand to help Christabel to her feet, and stood looking down at her. "You're making too much of this," he said gently. "I've seen Lionel castaway times without number, and he's all bluster, no performance. He'll collapse again tonight without making any attempt on my hide! What's important right now is for you to return home before anyone sees you here and before anyone at Winwood Park realizes you're gone. How did you get to Fairlea?"

Christabel dismissed the subject impatiently. "What does it matter? I rode. I saddled my mare myself and left her tied to a tree at the edge of the village. No one saw me." She stared up at Jareth with a desperate intensity. "Why won't you believe me? You're wrong about Lionel. This time he won't collapse into a drunken stupor —"

The door crashed open, slamming into the wall beside it. Lionel stood in the doorway, swaying noticeably, his eyes bloodshot in his ravaged face. A riding whip trailed from one hand. "I thought I'd find you here, my lady wife," he sneered, his slurred words barely comprehensible. "It's just as well. I want you to see what's going to happen to this fellow you can't seem to keep out of your mind or your heart — or, it seems, your bed! That darkened daylight he's sporting from his brawl yesterday is nothing to what he'll look like when I get through with him."

Jareth took a quick step forward. "Lionel, for God's sake, it's not what you think. Christabel came here because —"

"I know why she came here. She's a slut, always has been." Raising his hand with the heavy whip, Lionel flailed at Jareth, narrowly missing his eyes, but sending him reeling back from a vicious slash to his shoulders. He fell heavily, striking his head a glancing blow on one of the fireplace andirons.

"Lionel! Stop it!" Christabel launched herself at the arm holding the whip. Scarcely glancing at her, Lionel shoved her brutally aside. She crumpled to the floor, lying in shocked stillness for a moment. Then, as she saw Lionel raise his arm and lurch purposefully after Jareth, who was dazedly trying to stagger to his feet, she leaped up, screaming, "I hate you, Lionel."

Pausing in mid-stride, he said contemptuously, "I don't care any more, m'dear. As soon as you give me an heir, you can go your own way. I don't want you."

A slow, vindictive smile distorted Christabel's beautiful mouth. "You'll wait forever for an heir, then. The truth is, you're no better than a eunuch, Lionel. You couldn't father a child if you had a hundred wives." The cruel smile became even wider. "Don't call up my little

Daniel's memory to reassure yourself of your virility. Daniel wasn't your son. He was Jareth's. I knew I was pregnant with Jareth's child when I agreed to marry you."

"Christabel!" Jareth's voice arced through the air in a cry of pain.

Lionel's massive frame seemed to shrink. "I don't believe it. You're saying it to get back at me," he mumbled.

"Am I? Didn't you ever wonder why Daniel was our only child? Or why, despite your best efforts, I haven't conceived since my little boy died? No, Lionel. Think twice before you harm Jareth. He's the only heir you'll ever have."

Lionel staggered backwards, his mouth open, his eyes blank in his ravaged face. For several moments he looked fixedly at Christabel, opening his lips to speak and closing them again without uttering a word. Then, walking like a man suddenly aged, he lurched out of the room.

Getting slowly to his feet, Jareth gazed after his brother's departing figure, and then, stumbling over to Christabel, he took her by the shoulders, staring down at her with dark eyes filled with anguish. "If this is true, Christabel, why in God's name didn't you tell me? I had a right to know I had a son."

She stared back at him, white-lipped, without replying.

He dropped his hands. He knew the answer. Christabel had wanted to wear a coronet, whatever the cost to her lover or her own happiness. She'd given him a son, but he could never acknowledge Daniel, even in death. Not even to the woman he now loved with all the passion of his being. He couldn't risk losing Sabrina's love for the sake of a small boy he'd seen only once in his life, at the child's christening.

Chapter Eighteen

As Daphne came out of the house with Sabrina and Jareth she said shyly, "Are you sure I'm not imposing on your good nature, Lord Jareth? It's very kind of you to offer to drive me to Newhaven, but you and Sabrina just became engaged yesterday, and I'm sure you'd rather spend some time by yourselves."

"Actually, I'm being quite selfish," Jareth replied, smiling. "If Sabrina and I were to stay here today we'd be constantly under the eye of your stepmother. I'd much rather have you for a chaperon!"

"It's a matter of simple justice on our part," Sabrina interjected. "Yesterday you had to cancel your visit to Gordon because of all the excitement of our engagement!"

"Very well, I won't argue against my own best interests," Daphne said with a laugh. Jareth helped her and Sabrina into the curricle. As they turned out of the Latimer House driveway into the narrow country lane they encountered a horseman, who, as he cantered up to them, called out, "Mrs. Neville, could I speak wi' ye?"

"Jareth, will you excuse me for a moment?" said Sabrina as he reined in his team. "It's estate business. Tom Cavitt is the son of the tenant of our home farm."

"Cavitt? Isn't he — ?" Jareth coughed, covering his

323

slip, and jumped out of the curricle to help Sabrina down the steps. He said in a low voice, "This man Cavitt is the new captain of your boat? Good. I want a word with him."

"You want to talk to Tom? Why?"

"Because I need to contact Nate Peggoty as soon as possible and make sure we've spiked his guns." Jareth took Sabrina's arm and walked over with her to Tom, who had dismounted and stood watching their approach.

"Mrs. Neville." Tom touched his cap, darting a wary sideways look at Jareth. Probably, Sabrina conjectured, Tom had recognized Jareth from their first encounter on the night that Jareth had blundered into the smuggling operations of the *Mary Anne*. "Ma'am, I'd like to speak ter ye privately, won't take but a minute or two o' yer time."

Sabrina interrupted him. "Tom, this is Lord Jareth Tremayne. He'd like to talk to you. It's all right. He's a—a good friend. He knows all about my ownership of the *Mary Anne*."

Disregarding the carefully blank expression that had settled over Tom's face, Jareth said bluntly, "I'm looking for Nate Peggoty. Can you tell me where I can find him?"

"Ah." Tom studied Jareth. "I 'ear as 'ow ye throwed Nate inter the duck pond," he ventured.

"Yes, I did, but that's not why I want to locate him," Jareth replied with an impatient wave of his hand. "Do you know where he is?"

"Sorry, m'lord. Ain't seen nor 'eard from 'im since—since our last voyage tergether."

"I see. Thank you. Sabrina, there's no hurry. Take as long as you like to discuss your business."

As Jareth walked away, Sabrina asked, "Is that true, Tom? You don't know Nate's whereabouts?"

324

Tom shook his head. "Nay, I ain't seen Nate." Hesitating for a moment, shifting uneasily from foot to foot, he finally muttered, "Mrs. Neville, I don't understand. Why did ye tell this 'ere lord about the *Mary Anne?* Ye've always been so careful ter 'ide yer connection with the boat."

"Lord Jareth won't give us away, Tom. We're to be married. He wants to make sure Nate Peggoty doesn't cause any trouble for us, for you and me and your father and the crew."

"Oh? Wot makes 'is lordship think Nate's out fer trouble?" For the first time, Sabrina noticed the newly etched lines of worry around the young sailor's eyes.

"Because I told him how violent Nate can be. Because Nate's threatened me. Tom! Has he threatened you and Ezra too?"

"Nay, that 'e 'asn't, ma'am. Not yet, leastways. Not but wot me an' Father ain't been a mite anxious . . . Well, we've told ye all along that Nate wouldn't take kindly ter losing the *Mary Anne.*" Tom hunched his shoulders. "But that's neither 'ere nor there. I came ter tell ye the boatyard in 'Astings 'as finished the repairs on the *Mary Anne.* I'm on my way ter 'Astings now ter take command an' sail the ship back ter New'aven. We'll take on a full crew and be on our way ter Jersey in two days' time."

"Fine. Thank you for coming, Tom. Have a fair voyage and a prosperous one."

Perhaps I should have mentioned to Tom the possibility of owning the Mary Anne, Sabrina reflected as she walked slowly back to the curricle. No, better to wait until she and Jareth had made all the arrangements to transfer the boat to the crew. Her thoughts shifted to Nate Peggoty. The fact that Tom so obviously felt uneasy about the ex-captain revived her own fears. Yesterday Jareth had persuaded her that a large sum of money was all that was needed to get Peggoty out of their lives. Now she wasn't so sure. She was convinced that Nate's smuggling profits had always been less important to him than his feelings of power as the commander of the *Mary Anne,* or his compulsive need to strike back at any fancied insult.

Her apprehensions about Peggoty continued to occupy her mind during the drive to Newhaven, so much so that the journey was nearly over before she realized that Jareth was unusually quiet. He answered questions when spoken to, he even offered an occasional comment, but his mind was clearly somewhere else. For that matter, his manner had been somewhat subdued since his arrival at Latimer House that morning. She hadn't expected him to enfold her in a passionate embrace, of course, not in front of Fanny and Daphne, but neither had his dark eyes interlocked with hers in a silent declaration of love, telling her she was at the very center of his being. Something was troubling him. What could it be?

After their arrival at Gordon Stanhope's lodgings in Newhaven, Jareth seemed to make a conscious effort to rouse himself from his preoccupation.

"Betsy, the most wonderful news!" announced Daphne as soon as they were inside the door. "Sabrina and Lord Jareth are engaged!"

Jareth accepted Betsy's shy congratulations, and then, flashing his familiar quirky grin in Sabrina's direction, he remarked, "I must confess that I'm having a little difficulty thinking of myself as an engaged man, Miss Stanhope. I fought so hard for so many years to remain a bachelor, you know."

"Indeed, yes," Sabrina retorted. "I daresay hope kept springing eternal in the hearts of your female acquaintances, however. I shouldn't be surprised if half the ladies in London go into mourning when our betrothal is announced!"

Betsy appeared mildly shocked at this exchange until Sabrina and Jareth looked into each other's eyes and began to laugh.

"They're just funning, Betsy," said Daphne placidly. "Let's go up to see Gordon."

The revenue captain, though still confined to the upper floor, was sitting in a chair when his visitors entered, and appeared to Sabrina, who hadn't seen him for several days, to be well on the road to recovery.

"Daphne's talked so much about you I feel I already know you very well," Jareth remarked to Gordon after the two men had been introduced. "What's more, I understand we'll soon be brothers! Sabrina has promised to marry me in three weeks time." He added as an afterthought, his eyes twinkling, "Actually, if Sabrina and I weren't getting married in such haste, I presume Lady Latimer would insist on a double wedding!"

Daphne looked stricken, and the smile died out of Gordon's face. He said heavily, "You'd be dead wrong, Lord Jareth. Lady Latimer doesn't know yet that Daphne and I definitely plan to marry. She only suspects and fears the possibility. When she does find out, she won't be happy. She's already hinted she'd move heaven and earth to prevent such a catastrophe. That's why we're getting married by special license, as soon as I can drag myself out of this cursed room."

Jareth looked around him at the circle of faces. "I seem to have missed something."

"It's a matter of ancestors, Lord Jareth," said Gordon. "You have 'em, I don't. My father is a yeoman farmer in the Weald."

"Ah." Jareth seemed somewhat taken aback. "Perhaps time will soften Lady Latimer's prejudices," he said politely. Sabrina felt vaguely disappointed at the noncommittal response, but what comfort, after all, could Jareth have given? Gordon's ancestry, and Fanny's disapproval of it, were facts that could not be changed.

After a few minutes of desultory conversation, Jareth

suggested to Sabrina that they drive to the Bridge Hotel for luncheon, leaving Gordon and Daphne to have a private visit. Sabrina accepted eagerly, welcoming the opportunity to be alone with Jareth and, incidentally, to discover what was at the bottom of his earlier preoccupation.

In the private parlor of the hotel, however, over a simple meal of cold meats and pastries, Jareth lapsed into the same absent-minded silence that had marked his behavior during the drive from Latimer House to Newhaven. He made no move to kiss her, or hold her in his arms, or to discuss the wedding or their plans for the future, and he seemed unaware of what he was eating. When, for the third time, he failed to respond to a question, Sabrina reached across the table to take his hand, saying abruptly, "Jareth, what's the matter?" She added, with what was meant to be a playful smile, "Have you had second thoughts about getting married?"

He erupted in startled astonishment. "Good God, no! How could you think such a thing?"

"You haven't been yourself since you arrived at Latimer House this morning. Have you had bad news, then? Jareth! Has Nate Peggoty threatened you? Is that why you were so eager to talk to Tom Cavitt about him?"

"No. No. Don't worry about Peggoty. I told you I'd take care of him."

"Then what is it?"

His face darkening, he stared down at their clasped hands while the seconds ticked by. At last, still keeping his head lowered, he said reluctantly, "I didn't want to burden you with it. I didn't know how you'd react to it. . . ." He lifted his eyes suddenly. "Sabrina, last night I discovered I had a son."

Once started, Jareth's story didn't emerge smoothly. He stopped frequently in his account, obviously drifting back into memories that were very painful to him. At the end he said in a shaking voice, "It was horrible, watching Lionel's face when Christabel screamed at him that little Daniel was my son, not his. You've seen my brother, Sabrina. You know what a big man he is. Before my very eyes he seemed to collapse inwardly, to shrink to half his real size. In moments he became a shell, a mere husk of a man. Without saying a word, he shambled out of the room. Suddenly he looked old and sick and feeble."

Jareth's face twisted. "I almost felt sorry for him. He's hated me all his life, he's always been fiercely glad that I was excluded from any share in the Winwood estates and title, and now he's found out he can't have another son and there's nothing he can do to prevent me from succeeding him."

"Not unless you die first." The words slipped out before Sabrina could prevent them. She felt cold and sick as she looked at Jareth's drawn face. For the first time since she'd known him, all his thoughts and his emotions were fixed, not on her, but on someone, or something else.

He wasn't listening. "I feel so guilty," he muttered. "I had a son and I never knew him. I let my anger and resentment keep me away from Sussex all those years. If I'd tried to mend the rift with Lionel and Christabel I might have been able to see little Daniel occasionally, perhaps establish some kind of a bond between us."

"Jareth, listen to me," Sabrina said urgently. She put her hand to his face, forcing him to look at her. "You're not making sense. Christabel never told you Daniel was your son. Lionel never welcomed you to Winwood Park. There was nothing you could have done that would have changed what happened. Above all, you weren't responsible for Daniel's death. Nobody was."

Jareth drew a long, difficult breath. "I know. I've told myself that, but . . ."

"But you feel some kind of responsibility for what happened."

"Yes." Jareth nodded slowly. "I *am* responsible in some sense," he added suddenly, "not just for what happened in the past, but for what will happen in the future. What am I to do about Christabel? I'm afraid for her. Even before last night Lionel was becoming dangerous. He is drunk all the time and is beginning to mistreat her physically. Now that he knows she never loved him, that she married him knowing she was carrying my child, that he'll never father a son of his own—there's no telling what he might do. I don't think she's safe at Winwood Park with him. She should leave him, go to her parents' house, before he injures her, or worse." He beat his fist on the table in frustration. "I know her too well. She'd be too afraid of public disgrace to separate from Lionel. All her life she's been afraid of what people will think."

"Jareth, I think there *is* a possibility that Lionel might become violent, but all you can do is advise Christabel to leave him," said Sabrina with an edge to her voice. "You've neither the right nor the obligation to do any more than that."

"No obligation?" Jareth stared at Sabrina angrily. "I loved Christabel once. She's the mother of my child. How can I stand back and do nothing?"

A knife twisted in Sabrina's heart. She bit back the words forming in her throat, but she couldn't repress her rebellious thoughts. *Perhaps you still love Christabel more than you think, Jareth. Perhaps you made yourself believe you'd stopped loving her because she was unattainable. But now, in the back of your mind, are you wondering what would happen if Lionel divorced Christabel?*

After a moment Jareth said contritely, "I'm sorry, Sabrina, I shouldn't have snapped at you like that. What you said was true. I don't have the right to interfere in Christabel's marriage. At the same time, I can't bring myself to turn my back on her completely, or to refuse her my help if she wants it." He added anxiously, "You understand, don't you? You know it hasn't anything to do with how I feel about you."

Sabrina looked into Jareth's pleading eyes and tried to swallow her misgivings. "Of course I understand." She hoped her reply sounded convincing. She hoped it was only some kind of wild imagining that made her feel the presence of a small seven-year-old ghost.

Jareth jumped up from his chair, pulling her into his arms. Holding her close, he whispered against her hair, "I'm so glad I could talk to you about this, my love. Now that I've shared it with you, I feel as if a weight has rolled off my shoulders."

During the drive back to Latimer House from Newhaven, it did appear that Jareth had shed some kind of burden. He accepted with every indication of pleasure Lady Latimer's invitation to stay for tea and for dinner afterwards. It was while they were having their after-dinner coffee in the drawing room that he made the remark that destroyed Fanny's peace of mind.

"Dear Lady Latimer, it must be an exciting experience indeed to have two weddings in your family in so short a space of time," Jareth said blandly, ignoring Daphne's gasp of alarm.

"Two weddings?" said Fanny frostily. "I fear you've been misinformed."

"Really? From what Captain Stanhope said . . . But there, I must have misunderstood. Please excuse me."

Fanny surveyed her younger stepdaughter with an icy stare. "I must ask you to set Lord Jareth straight. Pray tell him you are not contemplating a mésalliance with Captain Stanhope."

Before Daphne could answer, Jareth said with an air of innocent surprise, "Mésalliance? Surely I couldn't have heard you correctly? I understand that Captain

Stanhope comes from one of the oldest families in Sussex."

"If he told you that, he was lying," Fanny snapped. "The Stanhopes are yeoman farmers in the Weald."

"Of course they are. They've been occupying their lands from time immemorial. Since long before the Conquest. The Tremaynes and the Latimers are rank newcomers compared to native Saxon aristocrats like the Stanhopes."

In a voice trembling with rage, Fanny said, "Saxon aristocrats, is it? Doubtless Daphne will be able to take great comfort from that thought when she's snubbed and ostracized by society for marrying outside her class."

Jareth raised an eyebrow. "What society are you talking about, Lady Latimer? I can assure you that *my* friends—Lady Melbourne, Lady Cowper, Lord Alvanley, 'Ball' Hughes, the Countess Lieven—will be happy to greet Mr. and Mrs. Gordon Stanhope when they visit Sabrina and me in London."

Fanny's face looked curiously like a child's kaleidoscope, as her expression gradually changed from angry disbelief to pleasurable acceptance. "Countess Lieven," she murmured.

"I hear her receptions at Ashburnham House are quite magnificent."

A little later, as Sabrina walked into the hallway with Jareth to say good-night, she murmured in a voice choking with laughter, "Poor Mama. She's a puppet in your hands. I'm sure you could convince her that black was white. First you transformed Gordon into a Saxon aristocrat, and then you had him hobnobbing with the most exclusive society in London. Is Stanhope really a Saxon name?"

"I have no idea," said Jareth, grinning. "Results are what count. If Daphne and Gordon press their advantage they'll be at the altar before Lady Latimer can catch her breath." He kissed Sabrina thoroughly and satisfyingly. "I won't see you tomorrow until dinnertime, love. I'm going to spend the day making inquiries of Nate Peggoty, and also"—he hesitated, looking faintly uncomfortable—"also I think I should call at Winwood House. Christabel may not think it wise to see me, of course, but at least she'd have some indication that I was standing by in case she needed help."

"A good idea," said Sabrina instantly. "I know how concerned you are for her." A look of gratitude, another kiss, and Jareth was gone.

As the door closed behind him, Daphne rushed into the hallway to hug her sister. "Mama just agreed that Gordon and I could go see the vicar about the banns as soon as Gordon is well enough to walk," she said with a blissful sigh. "Lord Jareth is such a wonderful man."

"Yes," Sabrina murmured. "He is." But she couldn't banish from the back of her mind the twin wraiths of the living Christabel and the dead little boy who never knew his real father. She wasn't jealous. That was the wrong word for what she felt. She was afraid. Afraid of Christabel's fragile beauty and the pull of Jareth's bittersweet memories of his early love for his sister-in-law.

Fanny walked into the drawing room, every ribbon on her cap quivering with indignation. "Where can Lord Jareth be?" she demanded of her stepdaughters. "Cook says if she has to hold the duckling and the roast of venison for more than a few minutes longer they won't be edible."

"Doubtless Lord Jareth has some good reason for being delayed, Mama," said Daphne quickly.

"Yes, I'm sure Jareth will be here soon, or he'll send a message," said Sabrina edgily. Giving vent to her own growing impatience, she got up from her chair and walked to the window, looking out over the shrubbery, where the first shadows of twilight were beginning to fall. It was past nine o'clock, and Jareth was well over an hour late for dinner at Latimer House. Daphne was right, there must be some perfectly adequate reason for his tardiness, she told herself. Perhaps he'd been drawn far afield in his search for Nate Peggoty. Or one of his horses might have gone lame. Or . . .

Still standing at the window, Sabrina hunched her shoulders in an effort to shake off the apprehensions that had been chilling her spirits since late afternoon, when Ezra Cavitt had arrived at the house. He'd glanced uneasily around the library, asking, "Be ye sure no'un kin over' ear us?"

"Yes, very sure. Is something wrong?"

"I dunno. I 'opes not, but . . ." Ezra shook his head, his weatherbeaten face drawn with anxiety. "I'm fair out o' my mind with worry. As ye know, Tom was supposed ter sail the *Mary Anne* from 'Astings ter New'aven yesterday."

"Yes, he was going to take on the full crew and sail for Jersey tomorrow." Sabrina's attention sharpened. "Are you telling me the *Mary Anne* didn't arrive in Newhaven?"

"Nay, ma'am. They dropped anchor in New'aven afore sundown yesterday. An' then, according ter the first mate, Tom got some kind o' message an' walked off the ship an' didn't come back, nor 'e ain't been seen since. Mrs. Neville, it ain't like my Tom ter neglect 'is duties like this, the very day afore 'e takes out the *Mary Anne* fer the first time under 'is own command. I'm afeared fer 'im. Fer all we know, 'e may be layin' dead somewheres."

Sabrina didn't waste her breath trying to reassure Ezra. It was all too possible that Tom had met with foul play and been left for dead or dying. "Nate Peggoty," she muttered.

"I fear so, ma'am. I've told ye, time an' again, that Nate is a dangerous man."

"What's to do, then? Have you reported Tom's disappearance to the magistrates?"

"Nay. Wot could I tell 'em? That I suspect Nate Peggoty of injuring my son because of a falling-out over smuggling? Wouldn't 'elp Tom none, and like as not we'd all be forced from the frying pan into the fire. Nay," said Ezra heavily as he rose and prepared to leave, "I came because I thought ye should know about Tom, but there ain't nothing we kin do 'cept wait an' pray my boy's all right."

So Ezra Cavitt had left Latimer House, leaving Sabrina a prey to worries that grew sharper with each passing hour. If anything happened to Tom, part of the responsibility would be hers. She should have taken into account the danger she might be inflicting on the young Cavitt before she gave him Peggoty's command. And where was Jareth? She didn't want to give in to morbid fancies, but was there a possibility that Jareth had fallen a victim to Peggoty along with Tom?

"Sabrina."

She turned away from the window. "Yes, Mama?"

"Daphne and I are growing very concerned about Lord Jareth, my dear. Surely he'd have sent word by now if he'd been delayed. Could he have had a carriage accident? Or been waylaid by footpads?" Fanny's mouth relaxed in a smile as the maid Rosie entered the room with a note on a tray. "Ah. A message from Lord Jareth. Thank goodness. What does he say?"

Opening the note eagerly, Sabrina drew a quick, surprised breath as she scanned the letter, and then, more slowly, read it again. Lifting her head, she carefully folded the paper. "Jareth sends his regrets, Mama," she said calmly. "He was detained near Hastings until early this evening, and when he got back to the Fairlea Arms he received a message from his brother asking him to go to Winwood Park on urgent family business."

"Oh, dear, I hope neither Lord nor Lady Winwood is ill."

"I don't know. Jareth doesn't say."

"We'll hope for the best. Well, then, shall we have our dinner? Or what's left of it? What a pity about the duckling. Cook says it was the finest, fattest specimen she's seen since Christmas."

"I'm not hungry, Mama. I have the headache. I believe I'll ask Lotte to bring me some tea and buttered toast in my bedchamber."

Hurrying her steps as soon as she was beyond sight of Fanny and Daphne in the drawing room, Sabrina flew up the stairs and into her bedroom, where Lotte had left a lamp burning against the rapidly encroaching twilight. With trembling fingers Sabrina unfolded the note and read it again. The small, graceful handwriting didn't resemble Jareth's slashing hand.

"Dear Mrs. Neville," it read. "I must see you. I've discovered that Jareth is in deadly danger, and I must get a warning to him as soon as possible. You are the only person I can turn to. Please meet me tonight at the home of my old nurse. Her house is situated to the east of the Seven Sisters on the cliff at Birling Gap. You can't miss it as it's the only house on that stretch of the cliff, and I've asked Nanny to leave a lighted lantern at the door. Come alone and don't tell anyone where you're going, if you value Jareth's life. Christabel Winwood."

Drawing a deep breath, Sabrina crumpled the note, allowing it to drop to the floor. Almost immediately, remembering Christabel's warning about secrecy, she bent to pick up the note and tucked it into a drawer of her writing table. As she walked hastily to the wardrobe and pulled around her the folds of her heavy black

336

hooded cloak, frightening questions for which she had no answers raced through her mind. What was the nature of Jareth's danger? How had Christabel managed to learn about it? Could she, Sabrina, get word to Jareth in time? She couldn't allow herself to think about these things now. She had to concentrate on getting out of the house undetected and then on finding the house where she was to meet Christabel.

Leaving her bedchamber, she slipped down the back stairs, into the passage leading past the kitchens, and out to the stables. She paused, listening, just inside the entrance. The only sound was the faint movement of the horses in their stalls. The long northern twilight was ending, leaving the stable in almost complete darkness. Groping her way to her favorite mare, she led the animal out of the stall and saddled her, adjusting the straps and buckles more by instinct than by sight.

Walking the mare on the grassy verge to avoid noise until she reached the end of the driveway, she put the horse to a trot when she debouched into the lane. The last faint glow of the sunset had faded now from the horizon, and since it was the time of the new moon there was little visibility as she rode cautiously along the narrow uneven country roads, heading east toward Birling Gap.

She was vaguely familiar with the place of rendezvous. During her drives to Eastbourne she'd often seen in the distance the lonely house on the cliff, and had heard since childhood the rumors that the owners were connected with the smuggling trade. Christabel's old nurse must be a member of the family.

There it was now, its outline barely visible on the cliff against the dim vault of the sky. A lantern beside the door cast a faint illumination. Her nerves beginning to tighten at the thought of what she might discover here, Sabrina dismounted. She tied her reins around a low bush and started walking with slow, reluctant steps up the steep rough path to the house. At the door she hesitated, a prickling sensation at the back of her neck. She had the feeling that eyes were watching her from the surrounding darkness, but there was no sound except the murmur of the waves below and the plaintive cry of a night bird.

She tapped lightly on the door. Seconds later it opened a crack, allowing her a glimpse of an aged face bordered by wisps of untidy gray hair. Suspicious, unfriendly old eyes stared at her. "I'm to meet Lady Winwood here," said Sabrina, swallowing against the lump of nervousness in her throat.

Nodding, but not saying a word, the ancient woman grudgingly opened the door wide enough to permit Sabrina to edge through it. The small room—it was the kitchen of the house—was illuminated only by a single candle and the light from the banked fire in the fireplace. Sabrina stepped into the center of the room, saying, "You must be Lady Winwood's nurse. Is her ladyship here yet?"

Wordlessly the crone pointed in the direction of the adjoining room. Feeling chilled, Sabrina pushed the door open and stepped over the threshold into darkness. Rough hands seized her upper arms from behind, and at the same time the darkness lifted from the room when Nate Peggoty removed the covering from the lantern on the crude table next to him. An ugly parody of a smile twisted his lips. "A good evening ter ye, Mrs. Neville."

"Sabrina!"

At the anguished cry Sabrina turned her head sharply, her eyes widening with horror as she saw Jareth on the floor with his back braced against the wall. His hands were fastened behind his back, his feet were tied together, and the streaks of dried blood on his face made a grisly contrast with the rumpled folds of his once-immaculate cravat.

"Jareth! Oh, Jareth, what have they done to you?" Sabrina struggled frantically to free herself from the iron grasp of the man behind her.

Peggoty snickered. "Let 'er go, Amos. Wot 'arm can it do, now, ter let the lady speak ter the gent?"

The man Amos relaxed his hold, and without a glance at him, Sabrina rushed to Jareth, throwing herself on her knees beside him. He stared at her with haunted eyes. "Oh, God, Sabrina, how did they trick you into coming here?"

"I got a note from Christabel asking me to meet her here," replied Sabrina impatiently. "Jareth, are you hurt? Here, let me untie these ropes. . . ." She recoiled with a stifled scream at the prick of sharp metal on her neck. Looking up, she saw Peggoty looming over with a knife in his hand.

"It's see and not touch, Mrs. Neville."

Biting her lip, Sabrina said, "Yes. All right." Peggoty backed away.

Sabrina clenched her hands together in front of her. "Jareth, what happened? Why are you here?"

"I got a note from Christabel too," Jareth said dully. "I'd gone to Winwood Park this morning, but the butler said she couldn't see me. Later, back in Fairlea after my fruitless search to find Peggoty, I was dressing to go to dinner at Latimer House when I received a note from Christabel asking me to meet her in a copse of trees at the end of the village. As soon as I entered the wood I was hit from behind. When I came to my senses I was here in this room."

As he finished speaking, Sabrina heard a groan of pain and peered fearfully into a darkened corner of the room.

"It's Tom Cavitt," Jareth muttered. "I think he's hurt."

Sabrina raced over to the prone form in the corner.

Sensing her presence, Tom opened his eyes, groaning again as he made an instinctive effort to move his bound arms. "Mrs. Neville," he said weakly. "They got ye too?"

"Tom, Jareth says you're hurt."

A spasm of pain crossed his face. "It's my collarbone. I think it's broken."

Jumping to her feet, Sabrina confronted Peggoty, saying fiercely, "I demand that you release Jareth and Tom and send for a doctor immediately."

Peggoty laughed. "It'd be a waste o' time, Mrs. Neville. Before this night ends, ye three will be at the bottom o' the sea. Me'n Amos, we'll carry yer bodies down ter the water by those steps cut in the rock o' the cliff, the same steps our smuggling brethren have used lo these many years ter land their cargo. A longboat will be waiting fer us, manned by friends o' mine. We'll row ye out from shore and throw ye in, properly weighted down, o' course, an' that'll be the end o' yer meddling in my affairs. An' ye can jist say a word o' thanks that I'm a merciful man. Ye'll not die by drowning. Ye'll be dead before ye land in the water."

Too astounded to feel fear, Sabrina exclaimed, "You must be mad, Peggoty. You can't hope to get away with such a scheme. We're all well known here. We'll be missed."

"Can't I though? Nobody knows ye came here, I've seen ter that. The people in this 'ouse won't talk. Amos an' 'is mates won't talk. Ye three will simply vanish off the face o' the earth."

"Peggoty, listen to me," Sabrina cried desperately. "Why risk going to the gallows for murder? Lord Jareth stands ready to give you any amount within reason to compensate you for the loss of the *Mary Anne*."

"Save yer breath. 'Is lordship's already offered me a tidy sum. I ain't interested." He paused, lifting his head to listen intently. Soon there came the faint sound of the outer door of the house being opened, and in a moment a tall figure stepped into the room from the kitchen.

"Lord Winwood!" Sabrina gasped. "Oh, thank God you're here!"

Her heart turned to stone when Peggoty said, chuckling, "I'm right glad ye're 'ere, yer lordship. It's growing late, an' I'd like ter get this over an' done with well before dawn."

Leisurely removing his gloves, Lionel smiled at Sabrina. There was a strong odor of liquor about him and his speech was considerably slurred as he said, "I'm sorry to disappoint you, my dear. There'll be no rescuing tonight. Oh, I don't care about you and that young sailor over there in the corner. You could go free with my blessings. However, what Captain Peggoty chooses to do by way of private revenge is nothing to me. By the way, it was a fortunate thing that I was a witness to that brawl in the village. I realized that Captain Peggoty was a man who hated my brother almost as much as I did. When I decided to rid the earth of Jareth, I tracked down the captain, who was more than willing to help me with my plans. For a price, of course."

"A goodly price, m'lord," grinned Peggoty. "Enough guineas ter buy my own boat. An' the chance ter get even with the widow an' young Tom."

Placing his gloves in his pocket, Lionel drew out a large pistol and walked over to Jareth, staring down at him malevolently. "You couldn't have thought I'd allow you to succeed me after I found out you'd cuckolded me."

Jareth said in a strained voice, "For God's sake, Lionel, do whatever you want with me, but don't let Peggoty kill Sabrina and Tom Cavitt. They've never done anything to harm you."

"What kind of an idiot do you take me for, little brother? Let Mrs. Neville and the sailor go free to inform the authorities about what happened here to-night?"

"Yes, I do think you're an idiot," said Jareth contemptuously. "You've proved that by coming here tonight. Now at least two people besides Peggoty know that you're involved in kidnapping and murder: that ruffian over there—Amos, is that his name?—and the old woman in the other room. What if they should talk?"

Even in her state of near paralysis from fear and shock, Sabrina felt a quiver of surprise. Why was Jareth provoking Lionel like this?

"Peggoty will see to it they don't talk," Lionel said shortly.

"I wouldn't be so sure of that." Jareth cocked his head. "Why did you come here tonight, Lionel? To give yourself the pleasure of observing my reaction when I found out you were responsible for sending me to my death?"

Sabrina caught her breath. Jareth had sharply jerked one of his bound arms forward, but Lionel was clearly too drunk to notice the sudden motion.

Lionel raised the pistol and cocked it. "Yes, I wanted you to know I was responsible. I also wanted the added pleasure of killing you myself." As he aimed the pistol toward his brother's head, Jareth pushed back against the wall with his newly freed hands and thrust himself upward, grabbing at the gun. The pistol flew out of Lionel's hand, landing at Sabrina's feet. In a purely instinctive reaction, she dove for the pistol and picked it up. Making eye contact with each of the three men—Lionel, Peggoty, and the man Amos—she motioned them back with the gun. "Get back, all of you," she commanded. Hesitating momentarily, they began edging slowly away from her to the opposite corner as she called out, "I know how to use this. In fact, I'm a very good shot. Peggoty, throw me your knife."

Peggoty stalled until Sabrina waved the gun at him

peremptorily, prompting him to toss the knife in her direction. Behind her, she could hear Jareth, his ankles still bound, propelling himself along the floor to seize the knife. In a moment he was standing beside her, the severed ropes falling away from his ankles. "I'll take the pistol, Sabrina."

In the split second when the pistol was changing hands and Sabrina's and Jareth's attention was diverted, Nate Peggoty launched himself at Jareth's knees and Lionel rushed toward Sabrina. The roar of an explosion filled the room. Peggoty collapsed, and Lionel, clutching at his chest, toppled to the floor beside the seaman. Instantly Jareth hurled himself against Amos, standing open-mouthed and petrified at the speed of what was happening. An expert blow to the jaw sent Amos to his knees, and before he could recover Jareth had twisted his arms behind his back and bound his hands and feet.

In a daze, Sabrina stared down at the prostrate forms of Lionel and Peggoty. She shuddered at the blood that was rapidly drenching Peggoty's waistcoat. She whispered, "Is he . . . ?"

Turning away from Amos, Jareth knelt down beside the other seaman. After a moment's examination, he said curtly, "Yes, Peggoty's dead." He looked at his brother's still form. "Lionel . . ."

"What's wrong with him?" Sabrina's eyes were bewildered. "You had only the one shot . . ."

Bending over Lionel, Jareth said after a moment's hesitation, "I think he's had a heart attack." He strode quickly into the adjoining kitchen, coming back a few seconds later to report, "Lionel's curricle is out there on the road. He needs a doctor. We'll take him to Newhaven. It's only two miles or so from here."

Jareth's instant decision to get medical help for his brother didn't surprise Sabrina. It was—it was just Jareth. "What about Tom?" she asked, moving to the dark corner where the young man lay huddled.

Jareth joined her. "We can't take both of them." Sinking to one knee, he began freeing the young sailor's limbs. "Tom, will you be all right for a short spell? I'll tie up the old lady before we go."

"I'll be fine, m'lord," Tom whispered.

Sabrina said suddenly, "Jareth, what about later? There's a dead man over there. How do we account for him?"

Jareth shook his head. "We don't. Once we get Tom safely out of here, we'll forget we ever saw the place. The smuggling brethren who use this house as their headquarters will dispose of the body. They're no more anxious than we are to call attention to themselves from the authorities."

Later, Sabrina could remember very little of the wild drive. After Jareth had carried Lionel over his shoulder up the path and deposited him in the curricle, Sabrina supported the inert body while Jareth whipped up the team and the carriage careened over the narrow roads to Newhaven. They left her mare behind to be retrieved later.

"Drink this, Jareth." In one of the private parlors of the Bridge Hotel, Sabrina handed a shaken Jareth a glass of wine. The doctor had just come in to inform them that Lionel was dead.

"Lord Winwood had a shock, I gather," said the doctor. "It was too much for his heart. There was an accident?" he added, looking keenly at Jareth's disheveled garments and bloodstained face.

"Yes," Sabrina said quickly. "Lord Winwood and Lord Jareth overturned in their curricle." Now there would be no scandal, no suggestion that Jareth was in any way connected with Lionel's death.

"A tragedy," nodded the doctor. "My condolences to you, Lord Winwood."

After the doctor had left, Sabrina stared wonderingly at Jareth. "Did you hear what the doctor called you? Now you're the Eighth Marquess of Winwood. After everything that Lionel tried to do to prevent it, you've succeeded him." She drew a quick breath. "Christabel. We should go to her immediately to tell her Lionel's dead."

"Yes, let's do that. And then I never want to see her face again," said Jareth savagely. At Sabrina's look of shocked surprise, he added, "Those notes, luring us a to a rendezvous . . ."

"But I thought—I assumed they were forgeries. She wouldn't hurt you, Jareth. She loves you."

"They weren't forgeries. Christabel's not like you, Sabrina. You'd die before you'd let anyone force you to harm the people you love. She's weak inside. She'll always love Christabel best."

Sabrina felt a quiver of happiness. Christabel's ghost would never come between her and Jareth again.

He jumped up, clasping her in a hard embrace that glorified as it hurt. "My darling, I never knew happiness, I never knew love, until I met you. You fill my life and my heart and I'll never let you go again."

Epilogue

At the sound of the door opening, Sabrina called out in relief from her chair in front of her dressing table. "Lotte, I need you. I can't manage this clasp." Not looking up, her head bent, she continued to wrestle with the recalcitrant clasp of the famous Winwood diamond necklace.

In a moment, caressing fingers brushed her neck. Startled, she looked into the mirror at Jareth's laughing face behind her. "You don't really need an abigail, you know," he observed, fastening the clasp. "I'd love to do for you in *everything*." His hands glided provocatively over her shoulders and edged beneath the bodice of her gown. Bending, he buried his face in the corn gold mass of her hair, his fingers continuing their slow, sweet exploration of her breasts.

"Jareth, now isn't the right time," she protested breathlessly.

"It's always the right time, love." With a sudden lithe movement he pulled her out of the chair and into his arms. Ruthlessly his mouth fastened on hers, forcing her lips apart so that he could taste the beguiling delights within. Feeling her will power evaporating, drowning in a swelling wave of ecstasy, Sabrina pushed desperately at Jareth's chest to free herself.

His arms relaxed their hold and he lifted his head, saying in mock hurt, "You won't even let me kiss you? Are you tired of me already after only six months of marriage?"

"Your kisses always lead to a great deal more," Sabrina retorted. She reached up to give him a quick hard kiss and moved away again, evading his clinging hands. "And normally I'm more than happy to be led down the primrose path, but *not* just before a formal dinner party." She glanced into the mirror and groaned. "Look what you've done to my hair. Lotte will have my hide, and yours, too."

Jareth grinned, rolling his eyes. "Then I'd best get out of the line of fire and leave you to cope with Lotte." He turned to leave, then paused, cocking his head, "About that primrose path . . ."

"Tonight. After our guests go home. I'm looking forward to it. Now, will you please go, my lord?"

Laughing, he strolled to the door, which opened as he reached it. Lotte stood on the threshold, casting a disapproving glare at Sabrina's disheveled hair.

"I'm going, Lotte," Jareth said hastily.

"And a good thing, too, *mein Herr*," sniffed Lotte. When the door closed behind him, she marched over to the dressing table and without a word began to repair the damage to Sabrina's coiffure. Her expert fingers quickly rearranged the rope of pearls threaded through the reddish gold curls. "The pearls are pretty, *meine Frau*, but you would look so *schön* in this toque." She picked up the white satin evening hat with its nodding plumes and held it up, admiring it.

"Yes, it's beautiful, but you know Jareth doesn't like me to cover my hair," said Sabrina serenely.

"And *natürlich*, you always do as the Herr wishes," said Lotte, her eyes twinkling.

"Naturally. Most of the time." Sabrina laughed, adding, "Thank you, Lotte. I won't need you any more this evening."

After Lotte left, Sabrina rose from her chair, shaking out the skirts of her sarsnet gown, its hem edged with a deep flounce of lace trimmed with pearls and white roses. It required a definite stretch of the imagination to describe the deep violet color of the gown as lavender, which convention decreed she should be wearing in the second stage of her year of mourning for Lionel. Sabrina didn't care. This gown was very like the beautiful dress Jareth had once purchased for her in London, and she would rather please her husband than any carping Mrs. Grundy.

Her thoughts wandered back to the fatal evening when Lionel died, eight months ago. She still found it hard to believe that the tragic incident had faded into memory without any unpleasant consequences. As Jareth had foretold, there'd been no firestorm of malicious rumor to connect her and Jareth to the death of Peggoty, whose body had been spirited away by the smugglers who owned the hut in which he'd been killed. Ostensibly, Peggoty had simply disappeared. Lionel's death, too, remained untainted by scandal. The world accepted that he had been killed in a driving accident. The *Mary Anne* was still flourishing as a smuggling boat, even more prosperous now that young Tom Cavitt, his father, and his crew were the joint owners, and, to date at least, there'd been no run-ins with revenue cutters.

Nor had there been any gossip surrounding Sabrina's marriage to Jareth, which had taken place by special license two months after Lionel's death. Not unexpectedly, Lady Latimer had put up a fight. She wanted them to wait out the full year of official mourning for the Seventh Marquess of Winwood and then to have a lavish society wedding at St. George's, Hanover Square, in London. "I need Sabrina by my side in these tragi-

348

times," Jareth had told Fanny earnestly, "and of course, since I *am* in mourning for Lionel, we must keep the ceremony modest."

Not all Jareth's charm, however, had entirely reconciled Fanny to a small wedding in the parish church of Fairlea until her bedazzled eyes glimpsed the portly figure of the Prince Regent being escorted to a front pew. "My dear Lady Latimer," his Royal Highness had assured Fanny solemnly, "not even the most pressing affairs of state could have prevented me from attending the marriage of my old friend Tremayne — I mean Winwood, of course. Keep forgetting Jareth is a marquess now."

A smile lingering on her lips at the thought of the Regent's swift conquest of her stepmother, Sabrina glanced at the clock on the mantel. She must join Jareth in the drawing room. Their guests would be arriving at any moment. But before she could make a move toward the door Jareth walked into the bedchamber, followed by a wraithlike figure draped in deepest mourning. "Christabel wanted to have a brief word with us," he said quietly.

It was a shock to see Christabel again after so many months. Sabrina had almost forgotten her existence. After Lionel's funeral, his widow had left Winwood Park to stay with her parents in Yorkshire.

"I'm so sorry to intrude," Christabel began, throwing back her heavy veil. Sabrina noted that the exquisite face now had tiny lines that hadn't been there a few months before. "Jareth tells me you're hosting a party in honor of your sister's coming marriage," she went on. "I won't keep you long, I promise. I was on my way to Brighton to leave for the Continent, and I decided to detour a few miles to see you. I'll be living for a time in Italy. I have a cousin in Florence."

"I hope you'll be happy in Italy," said Sabrina politely.

"Thank you. What's more to the point is your happiness, yours and Jareth's." Christabel hesitated, lowering her eyes, and fidgeting with the strings of her black reticule. She shot a quick sideways glance at Jareth, standing quietly beside her.

She's still in love with him, thought Sabrina, with a touch of sympathy rather than jealousy.

"I came here tonight because, before I left England, I wanted to clear up anything unpleasant which may have been between us," Christabel continued with an obvious effort. She lifted her head, looking directly at Sabrina. "For one thing, I never sent you my felicitations on the occasion of your marriage. I'd like to wish you happy now. For another, you should know that I have no intention of taking up residence at the Dower House, or of attempting in any way to interfere with your life at Winwood Park. And lastly, I promise you that I will never breathe to a living soul that my darling Daniel wasn't Lionel's son."

Christabel lowered her veil around her face. "That's all I have to say. There's no need to answer. Good-bye to both of you. Pray give my best wishes to Miss Latimer." Before either Jareth or Sabrina could think of a reply, Christabel slipped quietly from the room.

Jareth broke the silence. "That must have been hard for her."

"Yes. I'm sorry for her."

"I suppose I am, too," said Jareth after a pause. "I never thought I'd say that." He cleared his throat. "Your guests have begun to arrive, Lady Winwood. The vicar is already here. I left him in the tender care of Alvanley."

Sabrina began to laugh. "*That* should be an interesting conversation. Lord Alvanley, one of the greatest dandies in London, and poor Mr. Varrick. What on earth will they find to talk about?" She took Jareth's arm, and as they walked companionably down the corridor, she said, "Do you know, I really believe that Lord

350

Alvanley's offer to be Gordon's best man was the final straw that convinced Mama she should allow Daphne to marry Gordon."

"That, and the news that Lady Melbourne was to be a guest," grinned Jareth.

As they entered the cavernous foyer, the party from Latimer House was just coming through the door. Captain Stanhope, tanned and fit in his blue uniform, shook hands with Jareth, saying, "I was afraid that a squall last night would keep me at sea, but we managed to make port."

Daphne, glowing in pink silk, said happily, "Oh, I knew you couldn't miss our party, Gordon."

Lady Latimer tapped Sabrina on the shoulder with her fan. "My dear girl, are you blind? Look at Adrian!"

"Mama!" exclaimed Adrian with a slight blush, but he couldn't resist looking down at his shoulders. He was now wearing two epaulets instead of one, with a gold star blazing from each of them.

"You look even more impressive as a major than you did as a lieutenant, Adrian," Sabrina said with a quick hug. It had taken considerable persuasion to make Adrian consent to the purchase of his majority by his new brother-in-law. If Jareth had his way, Sabrina smiled to herself, Adrian would have a regiment one day.

The other guests were pouring in now. Hours later, when the evening was over, it would be generally agreed in the county by those fortunate enough to have been invited that Lord and Lady Winwood's party to celebrate the nuptials of Miss Daphne Latimer and Captain Gordon Stanhope was the social event of the year. Sabrina and Jareth realized how successful the evening had been when they overheard part of a conversation between Lady Latimer and Lord Alvanley.

"I don't think most people realize that we in Sussex have a native aristocracy," Fanny was saying impressively. "Are you aware, Lord Alvanley, that Captain Stanhope's line of decent predates the Conquest?"

Lord and Lady Winwood looked at each other and heroically refrained from laughing.